Praise for *Concord: A Novel*

Don Zancanella's gloriously vivid novel is time-travel of the most evocative sort—viscerally palpable, and far less dangerous than a nuclear-powered DeLorean! In these pages, a reader lives among well-known writers and thinkers as they go about their days, sharing in their quotidian satisfactions and trials as well as their public triumphs and disappointments, their greatest personal losses and most intimate pleasures. Not since Colm Tóibín's *The Master*, or Rachel Cohen's *A Chance Meeting*, have I felt so wholly immersed in the literary world of another time. *Concord* is a fascinating look at how these thinkers influenced and spurred one another to the works for which they're known, but it's also a book of interwoven love stories. These are the very real, embodied people behind the classic texts—the human beings who longed and lusted, desired and lost, who yearned for things and people they couldn't have— and some they could! and did! Their lives were shaped by ideals and dreams, yes, but also by ordinary circumstance, practical necessity, and by daily interactions with the intimates we don't so often read about. We struggle alongside Thoreau over the wording of a love letter, worry with Margaret Fuller about the seating arrangements at one of her Conversations, and watch out the window beside Sophia Peabody to see if her strange but intriguing neighbor, Nathaniel Hawthorne, might pass by. Beautifully rendered and wholly engrossing, Zancanella's *Concord* gives us the characters behind the classics, and is very much a classic in its own right.

    —Thisbe Nissen, author of *Our Lady of the Prairie* and
        How Other People Make Love

Don Zancanella's delightful novel *Concord* follows a "coterie of eccentrics" as they fall in and out of love with one other, and with ideas about what their lives and societies might become. That some of those eccentric ideas have since become famous is one of the pleasures, but not the point, of this vivid, intimate novel that channels both the bold and the hidden voices of history.

—Caitlin Horrocks, author of *The Vexations* and *Life Among the Terranauts*

This enthralling novel depicts Thoreau and his contemporaries not as the cultural luminaries they became but as young adults whose futures were being shaped by their passions and choices, by their triumphs and losses. Zancanella animates this moment of possibility through rich characterization and new insight. His portrait of 1840s New England reveals it to be both wonderfully ordinary and the most interesting place in the world."

—Elise Blackwell, author of *Hunger* and *The Lower Quarter*

Zancanella brings his characters—who happen to be among the foundational characters of American culture—to vivid and altogether human life. By the end, we feel that we've gotten to know their hearts as deeply as we already knew their minds."

—Jon Clinch, author of *Finn* and *Marley*

Concord

a novel

Don Zancanella

SERVING
HOUSE
BOOKS

Concord

Copyright © Don Zancanella

Published by Serving House Books

Copenhagen, Denmark, and South Orange, NJ

www.servinghousebooks.com

ISBN: 978-1-947175-46-4

Library of Congress Control Number: 2020951609

Member of The Independent Book Publishers Association

First Serving House Books Edition 2021

Cover Design: Peter Selgin

Cover Image: Houghton Library, Harvard University

Serving House Books Logo: Barry Lereng Wilmont

Concord

a novel

Don Zancanella

SERVING
HOUSE
BOOKS

Concord

Published by Serving House Books

Copenhagen, Denmark, and South Orange, NJ

www.servinghousebooks.com

ISBN: 978-1-947175-46-4

Library of Congress Control Number: 2020951609

Member of The Independent Book Publishers Association

First Serving House Books Edition 2021

Cover Design: Peter Selgin

Cover Image: Houghton Library, Harvard University

Serving House Books Logo: Barry Lereng Wilmont

For Tony and Jean-Louise

PART ONE

Are the stars too distant, pick up the pebble that lies at thy feet, and from it learn the all.

Margaret Fuller

HENRY

The room is packed with boys, six rows across, ten boys deep, two to a desk. Sixty if they're all present, which they never are. Some are taller than Henry and some barely reach his waist. The walls of the room are made of bare planks, unpapered, unpainted. The only color is that which can be seen through the windows—the yellow-green of trees beginning to get their leaves, and lilacs coming into bloom.

Henry is still learning his students' names. He has about half of them memorized but which Robert is Robert Bunson and which is Robert Diehl escapes him, and there are five Jacobs and four Jacks, a bushel basket of Js he may never get straight. He's been reading aloud to them from Virgil's *Georgics*, translating as he goes. Given that much of the poem is about farming, they ought to be fascinated but there's scant evidence they are. The older ones drowse, the younger ones fidget, and those by the windows gaze out at a wagon filled with barrels of lamp oil as it rumbles past. He can't blame them—although it's early May, the air in the room is so warm it might as well be July.

Upon reaching the end of the page, he closes the book.

"That's enough for now. I say we go down to the river for lunch."

Suddenly all eyes are on him. They know it's too early to end their morning lessons but they're not about to argue. The river! With any luck they won't return until the middle of the afternoon. Just as he's about to give them permission to leave their desks, the door to the classroom bursts open. The boys' heads swivel around and Henry swallows his words. Standing there in his black suit and wide-brimmed hat is Deacon

9

Nehemiah Ball, the school inspector. For a moment no one moves. Then Deacon Ball speaks: "Please do continue. I'm here only to observe."

Henry looks at the boys. Never before have they appeared so crushed. Not even when he handed back their first set of themes which he had marked with a severity he didn't know he possessed. Reluctantly, he reopens the *Georgics* and begins to read from where he left off.

"*The olive thrives almost by neglect, needing no encounter with hooked hoe or sickle blade once it's found its feet in the fields and faced the winds . . .*"

He lowers the book. "Of course, there are no olive trees in—Adam Hightower, fold your hands." It would have to happen now, wouldn't it? He never should have said "river." "Joseph, still your tongue." After each admonishment, he glances in the direction of Deacon Ball who stands at the back of the classroom like an undertaker waiting to start his work.

He resumes reading but his mind wanders. This is the school Henry himself attended. On his first morning as a teacher, he came early and stood alone in the room, amazed to find himself there again. He swept the floor and dusted the desks and windowsills. He straightened the benches and made sure his books and pencils were neatly arranged. And he wondered if, upon hearing Henry Thoreau was the new schoolmaster, any boys would bother showing up.

Then, from somewhere in the middle of the room comes a cry: "Ow! Oscar pinched me!" Henry thinks he knows which one is Oscar but he's not entirely sure.

"Oscar, come to my desk," he commands. No one moves. But it's not him they're afraid of, it's Deacon Ball. With Ball present, they're willing to risk anything to keep from being singled out.

"Oscar Winkle. Arise and come forward," he says again.

Still no movement.

10

Now, in a voice like the creaking of a dead pine in the wind, Ball speaks: "Mr. Thoreau. I should like to speak with you."

Henry doesn't know what to say. For a moment he stands and gapes. Then he follows Ball outside. In the instant before the door is fully shut, he can hear the boys begin to whisper. Fortunately, there are no windows on the front of the schoolhouse so they are unable to look out.

"Quite disturbing," Ball says. "You have no control."

"Oscar, he's . . .they're . . . What do you suggest?"

"I've been given to understand you seldom use the ferrule."

Henry's face falls. "No sir. I prefer not to."

"You prefer not to? Whatever do you mean? It's not a matter of preference; it's a matter of necessity. You *must*. Now march in there and show me. Do it with vigor. I can hear them plotting as we speak."

Henry nods solemnly and re-enters the classroom with Ball right behind. At the sound of the latch, the boys try to still themselves, but there is a good deal of shuffling and whispering before they quiet down. From the front left corner of the room, Henry fetches the ferrule. It's a stiff one, made of alder with a brass handle, a full two and a half feet long. Looking not at the boys but at the back wall, he speaks:

"Robert Yates, Jacob Hart, Oscar Winkle . . ." He stops at seven. They are not the ones who are badly behaved, they're the ones whose names he knows.

He needn't explain what they've been selected for. It can be only one thing. He looks at their faces as they line up across the front of the room. Half of them are expressionless, just wanting to get it over with; the others are already in tears. Each boy holds out his left hand.

Before he can lose his nerve, he begins:

Thwack. "Return to your seat."

Thwack. "Return to your seat."

Thwack. "Return to your seat."

11

Thwack. "Return to your seat."

One hard stroke on each palm. The air whistles and when the rod makes contact, they yelp or whimper or gasp. Jacob Hutchins has the thick calluses of a farm worker, which seems unfair, so for him, a little more speed.

By the time he's done, he's forgotten Deacon Ball is even present. It was simply a task he had to complete. And now he must finish it. He walks down the center aisle and whips the ferrule toward Ball. He has no intention of striking the man but he's pleased to see him flinch.

"*Relinquo,*" Henry says and hands over the rod.

Ball looks bewildered.

"Sir, I resign." Then he walks out of the classroom, not bothering to shut the door.

When he's almost to the corner, he pauses to look back. The little schoolhouse is smack in the middle of Concord, facing the village square. From where he stands, he can see Millicent Croft washing the windows of her shop, Dolly Sidley going somewhere in a hurry, Ig Nottick talking to his mule, and Lewis Perkins angling across the square carrying a table on his back—a small table, or Henry would offer to help. Instead he goes in the opposite direction, out of town. He passes the Henderson house, the Gilmore house, the blacksmith shop, the long narrow field that holds Mr. McBride's oxen and goats, and the empty, falling down house where old Mrs. Eccles once lived. Then, Concord behind him, he crosses an open meadow and enters the woods beyond. As he walks, he thinks, I did exactly the right thing. Deacon Ball is a tyrant. He can teach them himself. Hah, I'd like to see that! But before long his thoughts begin to change. Soon, he's wondering why he quit. Teaching positions aren't easy to come by. He'd been happy to find a job right here in Concord and now look what he's done.

What will his parents think? They let him go off to college, encouraged it even, but with the understanding it would prepare him either to preach or teach. Some of his former classmates are having so much difficulty finding work they plan to migrate West, into the Ohio Valley, to Kentucky or beyond. Will he have to do that now? It wasn't really Deacon Ball's fault. If Oscar Winkle hadn't felt the need to pinch the boy next to him, he'd still be back there teaching. After lunch they were going to start solid geometry. He'd been looking forward to that.

But it's a lovely spring morning. If you must lose your job, you couldn't pick a better day. He passes through the Tibbetts' orchard where every tree is in blossom. He had taught for only twenty-three days.

He walks all through the afternoon, well past the time when school lets out. Old Ball probably just sent them home. And that's what they'll remember: "It was the day Henry Thoreau got fired. We were let out early and went fishing. Caught quite a number of perch." He goes almost to Framingham, then turns around and comes back.

By the time he gets home it's after dark. His mother is alone in the kitchen, which is seldom the case. Their house is large, but between his parents, his siblings, and the boarders they take in to help make ends meet, it's rare to have a room to oneself.

"My goodness, you're late," she says. "I hope you didn't keep the boys this long."

"I did not. Because I'm done with them."

"What on earth do you mean?"

His sister Helen comes in from the parlor looking curious— she must have overhead.

"Deacon Ball came to watch me teach," he continues. "He didn't like what he saw so I quit."

His mother's face falls. She'd been looking forward to having Henry earning money instead of spending it in Cambridge at school. "Then you must find other work," she says.

13

His eyes go to Helen. He'd like to explain, to tell the whole story, just not right now.

"Don't worry, I will," he says. "I can always chop wood."

Upstairs in his room, he lights a lamp, sits down, and removes his boots. He wishes his brother was here. John would say something calming or amusing, or start a different line of thought. But he's teaching as well, in the town of Taunton, some fifty miles away.

He stands at the window and unbuttons his shirt. His room is under the eaves at the rear of the house, hot in summer, cold in winter but with a view across the fields. At present the moon is rising, large and silver-white. Suddenly he realizes he left his book, the Virgil, back at school. How shall he retrieve it? He can't ask Deacon Ball for it—not after what happened today. The only remedy is to return right now. He re-buttons his shirt and puts on his boots. His family is used to him taking walks at all hours. With a moon like this one, he might stay out all night.

MARGARET

In Providence, at the Green Street School, another teacher stands before her students, all girls. Every one of them adores her. "Oh, Miss Fuller," they say, "how did you come to know so much?"

She is flattered but not fooled.

"I only appear to know a great deal because you know so little," she replies. But her students don't take offense because she says it with a smile.

She teaches about spiders, worms, Greek mythology, notable women, and the movement of the stars.

"Today I shall tell you about Boadicea, who lived a very long time ago in England. How many of you have heard of her?"

Not one hand goes up.

"Well isn't that a fine state of affairs? Everyone learns about William the Conqueror, but Boadicea, his equal in every respect, is virtually unknown. I intend to remedy that."

If one were to speak only of Miss Fuller's face, she might be considered plain, but her bearing, her speech, her intellect, render any such judgment invalid. She also likes fine clothing. She can't always afford it, not on a teacher's salary, but no matter what she wears, heads turn in her direction even before she speaks.

Prior to coming to Providence she worked in a school in Boston. It was a peculiar place, run by a man named Bronson Alcott, who had peculiar ideas. He thought children were unspoiled beings who should be allowed to run free. Margaret doesn't share his theories about education. If she were to let the young women seated before her do as they please, the only subject they'd study is young men.

15

As she continues, the girls' eyes follow her every move. "Now, when she had determined it was time to attack the Romans, how did she know where to find them? According to Tacitus . . ." She raises her lorgnette to her eyes and reads: "*Boadicea removed a rabbit from the folds of her cloak and set it free. It dashed off across the heath and from its bearing, she determined which way to go.*"

"You mean the rabbit led her to the Romans?" asks Clara Whitmore.

Margaret looks up from the text. "No, it was more magical than that. Have you ever heard of someone reading tea leaves? Well Boadicea understood how to read the tracks of a rabbit. It was a form of divination."

Next, she describes the battles Boadicea fought, the magnificence of her chariot, and how the England of today would not be the England of today had it not been for this ancient warrior queen.

Later, in midafternoon, she reads aloud the most recent installment of *Nicholas Nickleby* and the girls are on the edges of their seats:

Nicholas stammered out an awkward apology, and was precipitately retiring, when the young lady, turning her head a little, presented to his view the features of the lovely girl whom he had seen at the register-office on his first visit long before. Glancing from her to the attendant, he recognised the same clumsy servant who had accompanied her then; and between his admiration of the young lady's beauty, and the confusion and surprise of this unexpected recognition, he stood stock-still . . .

She lowers her spectacles and looks at the girls. "Oh my, is this what I think it is?"

"Nicholas, he's . . . he's falling in love," says Mollie Hughes.

Margaret nods thoughtfully, dramatically. "So it appears," she says. "So it appears."

Margaret also requires her students to write in their journals each and every day. "There should be no limits to your expression," she tells them. "If you are not willing to communicate all that is in your mind, you do not belong in my class." The girls bend over their notebooks with great earnestness and she worries they believe in her too much. Certainly more than she believes in herself.

If she has a weakness as a teacher it is her tendency to be facetious. When they read a poem by the currently popular Miss Landon she says, "The correct response is to sigh and weep. You must also affect to have the neck of swan because only ladies with swanlike necks can fully appreciate such verse." A student asks if Miss Landon's heart has been broken.

"Apparently so, but I'm sure it can be fixed. Most likely with putty," she says.

Mr. Hiram, who owns the school, can't believe how lucky he is to have found someone of Margaret's talents. Girls now flock to the Green Street School so he's making more money than ever before. Of course that doesn't mean he'll raise her pay. She struggles to get by. Margaret is the eldest of seven siblings and, since her father's death three years ago, the support of her mother and two youngest brothers has fallen to her. Not that she's put off by hard work. To keep up with her own self-assigned studies, she rises at 4:30 every morning and reads and writes until it's time to leave for school.

Despite her success as a teacher, she's not sure it will be her life's work. Ever since she was a girl, she's had a habit of asking questions such as *Who am I? What is my purpose?* and *How should I spend my days?* There was a time when she thought she would eventually arrive at the correct answers, and that when she did, her future would open before her like an unlocked door. But now she knows better. She can see the same hope for easy answers in her girls. She tries to help them see that the truth is often complicated, but do it in a way that doesn't crush their dreams.

She's a bit lonely here in Providence, away from her family, away from Boston and her circle of friends. Her students provide companionship of a sort, but it's not fulfilling enough. She worries about her mother, who is now alone with her younger brothers. If she lived closer, she could provide more than just monetary support.

The cholera killed her father. If there is such a thing as a peaceful death, his was not one. He could be demanding and narrow-minded, and when it appeared his time had come, he refused to yield. It was that same strict nature that led him to insist she learn Latin at age six, as well as mathematics and Greek. One of her earliest memories is standing before his desk and conjugating Latin verbs. He gave her his full attention and tolerated no errors.

One weekend she goes up to Boston to see two friends off at the wharf. Anna Barker and Sam Ward have been invited by a Harvard professor and his wife to accompany them on a European tour. Margaret was invited as well but then realized she couldn't afford it. After she told them she couldn't go, she went home and cried. She has always wanted to go to Europe, and to do so with Anna and Sam would have been wonderful, the fulfillment of a dream. They both are a few years younger than Margaret so she feels a bit like an older sister or perhaps a very young aunt. They will be gone for at least a year. Maybe they'll never return.

She gets there just in time to give them each a kiss on the cheek. It's been raining all day, so they stand beneath umbrellas and watch as their trunks get loaded on board.

"We'll bring you something special," Sam says, but she can sense that their minds are already on the journey and not on her.

"Write letters, that's all I ask," she says. "Tell me everything you do and see."

By the time the ship has departed, it's almost dark and the rain has stopped. She's just finished closing her umbrella when, from out of the shadows, comes a boy on a runaway horse. It's galloping straight at her. With no time to think, she aims her umbrella and thrusts. Her motion is so direct and confident it brings the horse up short. The boy rolls off its back, tears of relief in his eyes, as a man runs up and grabs the reins.

"Thank you, thank you," he cries. "He'd a been killed if not for you." Then, holding the horse with one hand, he rummages in his pocket with the other. "Let me reward you for your trouble," he says.

Margaret shakes her head, partly in bewilderment, partly in denial. "I hardly know what I did. I gave it no conscious thought. I can't accept payment for that."

"Well, you are not only a fearless young woman, you are a selfless one," he says, "I've never seen the like." Then the three of them, man, boy, and horse, collect themselves and continue on their way.

She lets out a breath. While it was happening she was terrified but now she feels rather odd. He called her *fearless*— is she really? Did she do it from instinct or did she analyze the situation first? A line from Coriolanus comes to her: *action is eloquence*. A line from Goethe comes to her: *thinking is easy, acting is difficult*. And yet she tells her girls to value contemplation, avoid rash behavior, and always, always, think before you act.

She straightens her hat and jacket and looks out across the water. Whether or not she was heroic, it was an alarming experience, and now her thoughts are in a whirl. When they come together again, the usual questions appear: *Who am I? What is my purpose? How should I spend my days?*

SOPHIA

Sophia Peabody's sister Elizabeth has managed to borrow a painting by the estimable Washington Allston. She brings it to the suite of rooms they share on Beacon Hill, sets it on an easel and says, "There. For you to study."

"Elizabeth! Where did it come from?"

"It's on loan from Mr. Hoyt. I told him I'd take good care of it. You should paint a copy. What better way to learn Allston's technique?"

"Oh I couldn't. I haven't the skill."

"Nonsense. Of course you do."

They stand side-by-side before the painting, Elizabeth looking over the tops of her spectacles, Sophia's face in a scrutinizing frown. They see craggy gray cliffs, blighted yet majestic pines, a sky filled with swirling clouds, and two crows harassing a man in prayer.

"It gives one a good deal to think on," Elizabeth says.

Sophia nods.

"It's the moment before a thunderstorm," Elizabeth says.

Sophia shakes her head. "It's the moment before the end of time."

In the days that follow, Sophia spends hours gazing at it. She feels small in its presence but likes to disappear into it and forget her surroundings. The crows are threatening, also beautiful. The cliffs are stark, also beautiful. It hadn't occurred to her that such opposites could be combined. Thus, she begins to understand Allston's craft. Looking at the painting even relieves her headaches. When she's in it, she's a different person, a spirit without a body and, therefore, without pain. Then one day she cleans her brushes, gets out her paints, and begins to do just as Elizabeth suggested: copy Allston's work. She doesn't expect to faithfully reproduce every brushstroke, but maybe she can use it as a scaffold to reach her higher self.

For an entire week she works without respite, stopping for only a single meal a day and short periods of sleep. Elizabeth looks in on her from time to time. At first she's pleased: "I can't wait to see it." Then, somewhat alarmed: "Your face is flushed. You look spent. Perhaps you should stop and rest."

Sophia has painted since she was child. Living in the shadow of her sister Elizabeth, who knows everyone and can do anything, and of her sister Mary, who is by far the most beautiful of the three, painting is the one thing that is hers alone. Her parents have always supported her, paying for materials and lessons, and now allowing her to share an apartment with Elizabeth instead of living in the family home. Even with their help, Sophia struggles with the idea of being an artist. Shouldn't she be doing something useful, teaching perhaps, or at least working in a shop? Men can be artists of course, but what woman has painted anything of genuine merit, anything the wider world couldn't do without?

Although she has copied a number of other works, this is the first time she has found the process so fulfilling. It's as if Allston's painting is a score and she is playing it. When a pianist plays Beethoven, is the music merely a copy or its own work of art?

She shows it to her sister when she's done. "Oh, Sophia," says Elizabeth. "It's beautiful. I do believe your colors are even more vibrant than his. You've outdone yourself. Or should I say you've outdone him."

"That's not true. It's only a copy. A study. A way for me to learn."

The next day, Elizabeth goes out. But she comes back sooner than expected, flying through the door. "Sophia, I ran into Mr. Allston on the street. I explained what you've been doing and now he wants to meet you. He'll be here within the hour."

"You didn't! Please say you're teasing."

Elizabeth shakes her head. "This room's a mess. We need to tidy up before he arrives."

They scurry about but Sophia's not much help. She keeps going to the window and looking up the street. She's terrified. He'll be furious. Some call him "the Tiger," although whether it's because of his regal bearing or the hot temper he's reputed to have, she's not sure. She's seen him only once, from a distance, his mane of white hair making him clearly visible as he moved through a crowd.

Suddenly there's a knock at the door.

"Oh my, he's here," Sophia says. She goes to the window and strikes a pose, one she hopes will look nonchalant.

Elizabeth opens the door and there he is. Tall, ruddy faced, smartly dressed, his hair as white as Sophia remembers, his eyes surveying what now seems like the shabbiest of rooms.

Allston steps inside—Sophia has long ago stopped wondering how her sister manages to meet everyone of importance—and Elizabeth introduces them.

"So, my dear," he says, "I understand you've taken an interest in my work."

"It's nothing. A poor attempt. I did it as a parrot copies human speech." She's feeling faint and places a hand on the back of a chair to keep from collapsing onto the floor.

"You're being too modest, I'm sure. Let me see what you've done."

Sophia has both paintings covered so she removes the cloth from hers. He reaches out and lifts it from the easel, turning the canvas to catch the light.

"Mr. Hoyt gave his permission," says Elizabeth. "I hope you don't mind." Sophia can tell Elizabeth is nervous too.

Maybe inviting him here was a mistake.

"Not at all," he says, returning Sophia's copy to its easel. Then, with a bit of a flourish, he whips the cloth off his own painting so he can inspect them side by side. He leans in. He steps back. And when Sophia thinks she can tolerate the suspense no longer, he speaks:

"It does you great credit. I find no fault in your work. In fact, I am quite surprised. When your sister told me the task you'd undertaken I was dubious. But it is superior to what I expected. Superior by far."

At last Sophia can breathe. "I'm so very gratified," she says.

He invites them to visit his gallery anytime they are free and then lets himself out the door. As soon as he's gone, Elizabeth turns to Sophia and says, "You see, he liked it. There was no reason to be afraid."

Sophia puts a hand to her head. "I must sit down," she says. "That was all a bit much for me. I'm not feeling well."

For as long as Sophia can remember, she has suffered from headaches. Hours before one arrives she knows it's on the way. Prior to its arrival, she may actually feel better than usual—energetic, almost giddy, capable of tremendous bursts of work. But at last the darkness closes in and she falls into a well of pain.

"Would you like me to stay?" Elizabeth asks.

"No, I'll just go to bed. I'm to see a doctor on Wednesday anyway. Someone Mary knows."

Two days later, Sophia is with her other sister in the office of a Dr. Vardemann, whose specialty is applying leeches for the relief of pain. She has been treated with leeches before but according to Mary, Dr. Vardemann's are the best in Boston: skillful, well-trained leeches, if such can be imagined.

While they wait for the doctor in the examining room, Sophia tells Mary about her meeting with Washington Allston. "It was terrifying," she says. "I was afraid he'd take offense."

But then her mind turns to the leeches and she begins to fret. "I don't like it when they remove them. It hurts. And I dislike meeting new doctors. I feel they're judging me."

"What they're judging is how much money they can get from you," Mary says. Their father is a dentist, and although they have the utmost respect for him, growing up around practitioners of the medical arts has left them skeptical of the profession at large.

Sophia rubs her temples and studies her sister. Mary's best feature is her dark eyes. Elizabeth's is her intellect and her small feet. Sophia isn't sure what hers is, although her mother often comments on the smoothness of her skin and the pink glow of her cheeks. "What's taking him so long?" she says.

"I'm sure he'll be here soon," Mary replies, adding, "I do hope he's handsome," in a tone more fit for a garden party than for taking your sister to be bled.

Yet when he enters, they see he is old and fat with a yellow-gray mustache that makes him look like a walrus. Sophia raises an eyebrow at Mary and almost gets her to laugh. While the two of them are quite different in temperament, they became close several years ago when Mary was hired by a wealthy family to travel to Cuba to serve as a governess and Sophia accompanied her there. They lived on a coffee plantation for two years, depending on one another for companionship and support.

Dr. Vardemann introduces himself and directs Sophia to recline on a divan. He places a blue bib over her neck and shoulders so her dress won't be stained. Then he approaches and hovers over her, a white ceramic canister in hand.

"Imported from Sweden," he says proudly as he reaches into the canister, removes a leech, and dangles it in the air. It is olive-colored and worm-like, no different from other leeches she's seen; he proceeds to place it on her temple, beside her left eye. She can scarcely feel it—there is only a cool wetness, as if

24

it's a single drop of water. He doesn't show her the next one, which he applies at the same location, or the two after that, which go beside her other eye.

He inspects his work. "Now we wait," he says, pats her hand, and leaves the room.

As soon as he's gone, Mary says, "He comes highly recommended. Mrs. Thorndike says that under his care her swelling has been quite relieved."

Sophia can feel a slight tugging on her skin, nothing more. "Are they filling up?"

"Yes, they're like little plums. I'm surprised they come from Sweden. You'd think it would be too cold."

Sophia shuts her eyes. While Mary talks about some fabric she has seen in a shop on Newbury Street, she thinks about what she knows of Sweden. Houses in the woods with gingerbread trim? Reindeer pulling sleighs? Perhaps, but from this day forward it's leeches and only leeches that will spring to mind.

"I can't decide between the blue linen and the green silk," Mary says.

"You can't afford either."

"Be quiet. It disturbs the leeches when you talk."

At last the doctor returns. "You may find this uncomfortable," he says, but this time it's not so bad. As he plucks each one off there is only a pinprick of pain.

The procedure over, they leave Dr. Vardemann's office and walk up the street. Before they've gone very far, Mary asks her how she's feeling.

"Tired. More from the worry beforehand than from the experience itself."

"I'm rather hungry," Mary says.

HENRY

Henry returns to the school to fetch his book. The shops on Main Street are closed and no one is about. Just as he's getting ready to put his key in the lock, he hears the sound of wheels. He turns and peers into the darkness. It's Isaac Tharp, coming up the road in his oxcart. Henry pretends he has dropped something and waits for the old man to pass. Then he opens the door and slips inside.

His book is on the front desk exactly where he left it. He also collects a Greek grammar and a half-used notebook, one he used for jotting small descriptions of the boys, as if they were animals in the woods: *Edwin Butcher. Very white teeth. Voice musical but nasal. Demented laugh. John Neill. Sandy hair and blue eyes. Prefers to keep out of sight.*

The moonlight streams in the window and the room is a ghostly blue. Already he feels like an interloper on foreign ground. He shouldn't have hit them; he should have just walked out. Why make the boys suffer for what was properly between himself and Ball? But at the moment it happened he was unable to think. He walks around the perimeter of the room, making sure he's left nothing else.

Then through the window he sees someone coming up the street—a tall man, all in black. It looks like Ball although he seems to have lost his hat. Henry drops to the floor so he won't be seen. Why would he be coming here now? He did his best to stand up to him this morning, but he hasn't the courage tonight.

There's only the one way out and he'll be spotted if he tries to escape. He peeks over the sill—yes, he's still coming, straight toward the school. Better to just stand up, tell the truth about why he's there, and make a hasty retreat. He gets to

26

his feet, throws open the door, and steps outside. But instead of Nehemiah Ball, he finds himself face to face with Waldo Emerson, who looks partly bewildered and partly amused. Like Ball he's tall and thin and wears a black frock coat so Henry can see how he made the mistake.

"Mr. Emerson," he says. "You startled me."

"Mr. Thoreau. You startled me as well. It appears you keep late hours."

"I forgot my books." He holds them up as evidence. News travels fast in Concord, so if Emerson's heard what happened this morning, he might question why he's here.

"Ah," he says. "'Trust not too much to appearances.'"

"Yes—Virgil," Henry replies, acknowledging the quote, but he can think of nothing else to say. After an uncomfortable moment of silence, Emerson speaks again:

"Do your students take to him?"

"Some do, some don't. They're a varied lot." He shouldn't have resigned. He was just getting to know them. Another week or two and he'd even have gotten the Jacobs and Jacks sorted out.

"Well then, good evening," Emerson says, and continues on his walk. His head is tilted back as if he's looking at the stars.

Emerson moved to Concord while Henry was away at school, so he doesn't know the man well. But he's read some of his writing, and when Henry graduated from Harvard College several months ago, Emerson gave a speech. It made him feel proud to know that someone from his small hometown was important enough to be asked to appear on such an occasion— even if he hasn't lived here long. Henry thumps the side of his head with his hand. That's what he should have said just now: "I enjoyed your talk in Cambridge." Because he had—it gave him food for thought:

Man, said Emerson, can live in one of two states. He can be

set off from society or be part of the whole. He said you should think for yourself and not copy other men's thinking. He said we should walk on our own feet, work with our own hands, and speak our own minds. He also said something about making a soup out of grass and boiled shoes, which made Henry laugh, although the point of that passage escaped him.

The evening is so beautiful he can't bring himself to go home. He walks out of town, past Colonel Buttrick's smokehouse and the Hildreth farm, and on into the woods, the moon lighting his way. There's a weasel he's been keeping his eye on lately, and he decides to pay it a visit. It lives in a hollow tree on the far side of Bateman's Pond. Henry is curious about its habits. He's always been under the impression weasels are nocturnal, though on more than one occasion he's seen this one at midday.

He keeps changing his mind about quitting his job—was it the right thing to do or not? He's afraid he'll have to leave Concord to find a new position. When he went away to college, he pretended to his mother and father and friends that he was going off to make his way in the world, but in his heart he knew he'd come back.

He finds the tree with no difficulty. And there's the hole into which he's seen the weasel disappear. A few yards away stands a great white oak with its roots spread wide so as to form a backrest with an armrest on either side. He makes himself comfortable and watches, waiting for the weasel to arrive—or if he's wrong about its habits, maybe he'll see it depart. The weasel is a fascinating creature. So small but so very fierce. Most people consider them vicious, owing to the damage they do to chickens, but isn't one creature's viciousness another's industry? If a weasel murders a chicken, is the fault in the weasel's nature or in the shoddy construction of your coop?

Henry has great endurance when it comes to observing.

It's surprising how much one's eyes can take in once they've adjusted to the dark. For a long time there is just the tree and the hole and, in his mind, a feeling of tranquility, wherein he is awake and watchful while having no active thoughts.

It gets colder but still he sits. It rains a little but still he sits. Then, suddenly, there it is—the weasel, returning home from hunting, carrying a bird, a fat bobolink, nearly half its own size.

Now the weasel goes to work pulling the bird into its hole, even though the hole is no more than two fingers in width. He almost expects to hear a "pop" when the bobolink finally disappears. Then just when he thinks there's nothing more to see, the weasel pokes its head out and meets his gaze—as if to make sure he's properly impressed.

Once he's certain the weasel is gone, he stands, shakes out his stiff joints, and heads toward home. He may sleep for a while in the shed instead of going into the house, so as not to disturb the other members of his family who keep more regular hours. As he crosses the fields, he recalls something else Emerson said in his speech, "Life is our dictionary." True enough. So what words did he learn today?

In the weeks that follow he discovers some residents of Concord resent the fact that he quit. Who does he think he is, throwing away a perfectly good job? Millicent Croft intimates to his sister Helen that he must think he's above them. He went off to college and now can't be bothered with teaching the children of Concord.

"I don't think that at all," he says. He and Helen are outside in the garden planting potatoes. They put some in last week but now they've dug a second plot so they'll be sure to have enough.

"I know. I'm just telling you what I heard."

"It's not the children, it's Nehemiah Ball. I won't take orders from a man like him."

His mother, working nearby, overhears him and says, "If you think you get to choose who you work for, then you'd better think again. I suggest you shoulder your knapsack and go out on the road. Ask at every town you come to if they need a schoolmaster. When you find a job, write us so we'll know where you've landed."

She's not usually this harsh. Maybe she's been stung by comments of the kind Helen has heard. He knows that strong young men in their twenties (not to mention those who have a college education) are supposed to be happy to explore the world, but he likes it fine right here. At the moment he quit his job he was filled with self-righteous pride, but now he's sorry he did it. Helen looks in his eyes and notices the dismay.

"You don't have to go," she says. "Stay here and live with us."

That afternoon he finds a job chopping wood for the Welshman Barris Lloyd. It pays one-quarter of what he would have earned teaching school. Henry's father has a small pencil-making concern and he could go to work for him, but he's afraid that if he starts, he'll never stop. That might be another reason for his mother's strong words. She has the same fear. He'd ask Jonas Buttrick if he needs help at his smokehouse or Steph Woods at his tan yard, yet those too would involve commitments he's unprepared to make.

He actually doesn't mind chopping wood. It's hard work but requires little thought so he can let his mind escape. When he has finished considering and reconsidering the events of his final day at school, he thinks about fishing, about woodpeckers (there's one over there in a sycamore) and about Plutarch's ideas regarding reincarnation. According to Plutarch, the soul is like a bird and when a person dies, it flies away in search of a new body in which to take up residence. He likes the part about the soul in flight but feels sad that it must return so quickly to the sorrows of the world. Why can't it simply remain aloft?

He also thinks about money and decides to give his mother everything he earns this week. That might make her less angry with him for losing his job.

And then, as he's swinging the ax, an idea comes to him. His given name is David Henry but he has always been called Henry. He prefers Henry and has no use for David. From this moment on he will be Henry David. He will sign his name thus and not answer to the old one. Although it's a small change, it makes him feel better. On the page, the H looks sturdy, two uprights and a cross-brace, while a light wind could blow the D over onto its fat belly. Why hasn't he thought of this before? Henry David he is and shall be. It's as if a knot in his chest, one that's been there for years, has suddenly been untied.

MARGARET

Margaret too has the pleasure of hearing Emerson speak. In her case it's in Providence, at the end of an unseasonably cold day in May. She first learned about him from Elizabeth Peabody, and if Elizabeth Peabody says someone is worth your attention, then of course you must take note.

She arrives at the lecture a little late and is sorry to find there are no empty chairs up front. She'd been hoping to get a good look at his face. Apparently his appearance is distinctive. Tall, angular, a hawkish nose and sand-colored hair, with eyes like pale blue flames. Or so Elizabeth says. Margaret's shoes are hurting her and she wishes she could take them off and wiggle her aching toes.

She enjoys going to lectures and these days Providence is awash in them, Boston even more so. You can take in two per evening if you so desire. Everyone has an opinion, whether about politics or religion or the raising of children or the relationship between the sexes, and if one has an opinion, then why not tell it to the world? A good number of the lectures she has attended have been a waste of time, but on occasion she has felt herself entering into a kind of mental conversation with the speaker, responding to each assertion and being unsurprised when the speaker answers back—as if he (it's nearly always a he) can actually hear her thoughts. After such an event she walks out into the night air, her face flushed, her heart beating more rapidly, her mind roiling with ideas.

As Elizabeth predicted, Emerson's speech is the kind Margaret most enjoys. He challenges his audience to follow him through labyrinths of thought. The argument he makes is that Americans should no longer remain in thrall to the ideas and arts of other places and times long past, but should instead construct their *own* edifices of their *own* materials, on their native soil. At least that's how she understands it, how she'll describe it to her girls.

When Emerson's speech is over, she approaches him, thinking she'll introduce herself and perhaps even share a few thoughts. Lately she's been reading Goethe and there are some questions she'd like to ask. But at the last instant, when he's looking directly at her, she panics, turns, and scurries out of the hall. This has happened before. She aspires to know interesting people, important people, people of intellect and value, yet just as she is about to meet them she thinks, "Why would they care to know *me?*"

Outside, it's gotten colder—is it really May?—and by the time she gets to her room she has a chill. She brings the fire back to life, takes off her shoes at last, and puts on the teakettle, while pondering Mr. Emerson's remarks. Then, finally getting warm, she does as she often does when she's overflowing with thoughts and writes a letter to her friend James. She can tell him everything, even the embarrassing part about how she almost spoke to Ralph Waldo Emerson but lost her courage and fled.

She first met James Clarke when they were both nineteen. She was living in Cambridge and he was at Harvard when they happened to attend the same party. During a brief conversation she mentioned that she wanted to read Sheridan's play, *The Rivals*. The next morning he was at her door, a copy in his hands. Pushing it toward her, he said, "You may borrow this if you promise to discuss it with me after you've read it. I offer it as an assignment, not as a gift." Never before had a young man given her an assignment. It was so much better than a gift.

Thereafter, they met in person only occasionally but exchanged letters at least twice a week. He told her what he thought of Coleridge and she told him he was wrong. She asked him which German authors she should read and he sent an annotated list. He described how in one of his classes they were slogging through the *Iliad* at a dismal pace and she—having been required by her father to read it at age eight—told him which parts he could safely skip. When he replied with outrage—*Skip even one word of Homer?* She wrote back, "My dear James, life is short and there are more books in the world than you will ever be able to read. If taking my advice makes you feel wicked, it has had its intended effect."

But their correspondence wasn't only about books. He told her about a girl named Amelia, how when he tried to court her she took no interest in him. Did Margaret have any thoughts regarding what he should have done? She replied that she preferred not to discuss such matters. That wasn't entirely true. In fact, she was quite interested in how men related to women but felt he was treating her like one of his Harvard classmates, as if her name wasn't Margaret but Martin. When she saw him in person she said, "I hope you don't think of me as a cousin. Because you're more to me than that." He was embarrassed and pretended not to understand her meaning. Their subsequent letters returned to books.

There had been one moment when she thought he came close to expressing his true feelings. They were walking along the Charles River on a golden autumn day.

"Every time I receive one of your letters, I feel stronger and more daring," he said.

"Is it only my letters that accomplish such magic?"

"You and your letters are inseparable. No matter how many miles are between us, I will always cherish your words."

But then he spoiled it by saying, "You really should be a writer. The reading public would pay good money for your thoughts. It could be a career." She had wanted to talk about their friendship, not about her career. Besides, she has always pictured herself living a life of action; writing seems so passive, so unadventurous. Not to mention that from what she's heard, writers are paid even less than teachers, if they are paid at all. Although she's published a couple of brief essays, the paper and ink she used to produce them cost as much as she earned.

After James graduated from divinity school, she thought they might spend some time together. Letters are nice but without his studies to keep him busy they could go to lectures together or simply sit and talk. But before any of those things could happen, he told her he was moving to Kentucky, to accept the pastorship of a church.

"Already?" she said. "Is there nothing closer to home?"

He shook his head. "Unfortunately, no. Still, it may be a blessing. In such a remote place, I can set my own direction instead of following an existing path."

"Won't you miss me?"

"Of course I will. I'll miss many things. Being away will put me to the test."

She was as angry as she was sad. Angry with him for being so self-centered. Angry with herself for being sad. He didn't know about the hope she had invested in him and she couldn't tell him now.

They still correspond regularly—in fact their letters are longer than ever before—but there remains between them a mixture of passion and distance. If he were to show up on her doorstep and confess his undying love, she doesn't know what she'd do.

When she's finished her letter to James about Emerson's speech (her initial excitement having cooled, she becomes a bit critical, explaining that Emerson seems to think his abstractions need no material support), she throws open the window and looks down at the street below. A butcher's wagon and an open carriage have gotten crosswise with one another and neither wants to back up. She wonders what it's like in Kentucky. James has written to her about the rolling hills and about the Ohio River which, according to him, puts the rivers of Massachusetts to shame. But he doesn't seem happy there. Some ladies walked out on one of his sermons because they considered it too original. His country church needs a new roof. Yet it's difficult to offer real sympathy by way of a letter—she's good at making arguments on paper but prefers to convey her emotions face to face.

SOPHIA

Sophia's sister Elizabeth has opened a shop at 13 West Street, half a block from Boston Common, across from Beacon Hill. The name on the door says "The Foreign Library," but it's much more than that.

In selecting the merchandise and in making the place inviting, she enlists the help of her sisters and parents. The front parlor features homeopathic medicines, herbal tinctures, and even surgical instruments, on the recommendation of their dentist father. Also art supplies, and, on the walls, some of Sophia's drawings—for decoration as well as for sale. She and Elizabeth discuss an appropriate price.

"I feel I should just give them away," Sophia says. "Exchanging them for money violates the spirit in which they were done."

Elizabeth looks at her and shakes her head. "Go ask Mr. Allston what he thinks. He'll tell you that the spirit in which his paintings were done is the spirit of the dollar. Sometimes, dear sister, you are remarkably naïve."

A larger room at the back is home to Elizabeth's "Foreign Circulating Library and Bookstore." Literature from the Continent is all the rage, at least among a certain group, and patrons can either buy or rent. From Voltaire to Schlegel to Mme. De Stael. Even Swedenborg and the Bhagavad-Gita. Those who wish to subscribe are allowed two books at a time for five dollars a year. But the shop is more than a shop and the library is more than a library. On one table sits an ornate brass astrolabe, a stuffed pelican, the skeleton of a monkey, a stack of abolitionist pamphlets, and a ceramic flask that looks like something from the Arabian nights. In a sconce burns a scented candle, filling the air with spice.

Sophia watches the patrons come and go. They are some of Boston's most prominent citizens, or at least they are prominent within the literary and philosophical sphere—writers and artists and clergymen and teachers, and if there's one thing they can do, it's talk. Which means Elizabeth is in her element. Ask her about Buddhist scripture. Ask her about the Chartists. Ask her about the plight of the various Indian tribes and how President Jackson has contributed to their misery. Ask her even about the best way to preserve peaches. Her curiosity is insatiable. It seems the more she knows, the more she wants to know. Sophia sometimes thinks people come to the shop not for books or medicines but simply to be treated with Elizabeth's words. "She is our encyclopedia," Mary often says.

Today, however, it's raining and only Sophia is in the shop, caring for it while Elizabeth is out. On dismal days like this, she wishes she could return to the island of Cuba, where she and Mary spent two years. The Morrell family estate was on a coffee plantation in the San Salvador Mountains, a day's ride from Havana. Before then, neither she nor her sister had traveled outside the boundaries of New England, and from the moment of their arrival, Sophia was overwhelmed by the beauty of the place. The lime hedges surrounding the estate were the greenest of greens, the rows of cocoa trees met overhead to form Gothic arches, and the coffee shrubs were covered in blossoms, turning entire hillsides white. Here and there, in small alcoves and at the end of blind alleys, marble statues stood surrounded by mango, almond, and orange trees. And the sun, well, she had no words—how could she describe it when all she'd grown up with was the pallid New England sun.

The letters Sophia wrote home were so filled with extravagance, Elizabeth, who remained in Boston, accused her of making things up:

"Thank you for providing such a thorough description of your surroundings. But can the sky there really be so different

38

from the sky above Boston? I think you let your artistic sensibility get the better of you sometime."

In response, Sophia wrote, "Combine all your ideas of glory and softness and freshness and music and fragrance and you'll have some idea of this place. Yesterday, I took a ride after sunset and the blue-green sky looked as if a spirit had flown across it with a brush dipped in purest gold. Surrounded by such beauty, I sleep more soundly and my health is greatly improved." Before she sent it, she showed it to Mary.

"You delight in tormenting her, don't you?" Mary said.

"I'm not trying to torment her. I just don't like my veracity to be questioned. When I say avocados are food for the gods I'm only being truthful. What words would you have me use?"

Since the shop is currently empty, Sophia sits down with her sketchbook. In a vase on the table is a single peacock feather, but feathers and hair are always difficult to draw with their range of darks and lights. A teacher once told her not to focus on the thing itself but an image of the thing. At first it seemed like a silly remark; now she understands. It's a way of saying you should trust your mind as well as your eye.

She begins with tentative marks and then some that are more assured. When she finally pauses, the rain has stopped, the clouds have parted, and the brown buildings outside have turned gold. Drawn to the window to observe the change, she notices that as people emerge from the houses and shops to go about their business, every one, without exception, takes a moment to look up at the sky.

Just then, a red-faced boy comes in and asks if he can place a handbill in the window.

"For what purpose?" Sophia asks.

"Mrs. Connie Park is going to be speaking about animal magnetism on Thursday" he says, reciting what is obviously a memorized speech. "She is renowned on the subject and will be at Water Street Hall for only one night."

She gives her approval and watches as he takes a glue pot from his satchel and affixes the paper to the glass. Sophia has no idea what animal magnetism is but it sounds like the sort of thing Elizabeth would approve of. It wouldn't surprise her if she already knows a good deal about it, quite possibly more than Mrs. Park.

One thing she didn't put in her letters home was *waltzing*. When she was in Cuba she attended a dance where a young man named Fernando taught her to waltz. The next day she went horseback riding with him and a week later they waltzed again. In Boston waltzing is frowned upon. Girls are expected to dance only the quadrille and if they go horseback riding, must be chaperoned. In Cuba she waltzed and went horseback riding on tropical mornings and even went alone with Fernando into the jungle after dark to see the night-blooming cereus. The night-blooming cereus wraps its vine-like stem around a tree as if the tree is its prey. It looks like an old piece of rope unless you see it at midnight when its flowers open, each one a spray of white petals with a fountain of gold inside.

"What do you think of it," Fernando asked.

"It's breathtaking. I'd like to paint it. If I simply describe it to people back in Boston, they won't believe it's real."

"There must be flowers in Boston."

She shook her head. "I've never seen one like this."

But these days, if she talks about Fernando, even Mary scoffs: "He wasn't as attractive as you say. You've made him out to be some kind dashing hero. And I don't think that dance you did was an actual waltz."

They've always done this to her. It's because of her headaches. They treat her like an invalid and even sometimes like she's not in her right mind. Fernando was an excellent pianist. He looked like Apollo. She played chess with him. They went riding together in the moonlight. He showed her the night-blooming cereus. When they waltzed—so many times she lost count—she scarcely touched the floor. Perhaps it was animal magnetism. Perhaps it was just a dream. But whatever it was, it was thrilling, and she fears she'll never feel that way again.

HENRY

Chopping wood is fine for a few days but it would be a hard life's work. He knew that before he started, yet doing it for a full week, from sunup to sundown, helps drive the fact home. So he goes to his father and offers to assist him in the family business. His father is delighted. A small, quiet man, John Thoreau inherited his pencil-making shop from his uncle Charles. To make a pencil, cedar from the Esterbrook Woods outside town is milled into thin sticks. Then a groove is cut in each stick and a hot paste of glue, bayberry wax, spermaceti, and plumbago— the soft black ore that makes marks on paper—is poured into the groove. Finally the two sticks are pressed together to make a single pencil. It's a painstaking process with many steps and his father can always use another pair of hands.

His father doesn't say much while they work. Although Henry wonders what's going on inside his mind, he doesn't like to intrude. They've lived together for over twenty years, and if he wanted to share his private thoughts he'd have done so by now. He seems to express himself best in music. He plays the flute and is always ready to sing. Of course Henry's not loquacious either, at least not in his father's presence. The two of them can be shoulder to shoulder for hours without exchanging a word.

Fortunately, Helen and his younger sister Sarah often assist, stirring the plumbago mixture while it heats and tying the finished pencils into bundles of ten. They *do* talk, especially about gossip they've heard in town.

"Ann Macrorie and Burt Kirby are going to be married," Sarah says. She is nine years old and intensely interested in romance in all its forms.

"Henry, if you wanted to take a bride, what sort of girl would you choose?" Helen asks. "Ann Macrorie for example? What do you think of her?"

"I'm not considering marriage at the present time. I don't know much about Ann Macrorie. Are there certain attributes you'd like me to discuss? I'd find it easier if you'd list them out."

"All right then, her hair," Helen continues.

"I can't picture it."

"Don't be stubborn. You know what she looks like. You went to school with her."

"Her hair is satisfactory," Henry says.

"Her hair is satisfactory," Sarah sings and then she and Helen laugh.

"He pretends he doesn't care," Helen tells Sarah. "But someday we shall see the spectacle of Henry in love."

In the evenings, Henry writes letters to schools near and far, inquiring about positions. Even though he would much prefer to remain in Concord, he must be realistic about his future. His older brother John is teaching in Taunton and seems to be doing fine. In his letters of inquiry, he tries to make himself stand out: *I would strive to make education an uplifting thing, by which I mean nourishing to the mind and soul. The master should earn the respect of his students rather than demand it. He should keep the schoolroom tidy and be honorable in all his affairs. He must also be punctual. Nothing opens the door to anarchy like a schoolmaster who is late to school.* Yet thus far, they've all said no. He hears about a job in Alexandria, Virginia, for which he seems well qualified—they want someone with a knowledge of Latin and Greek and are willing to pay six hundred a year plus washing and board—but his letter gets no response. He even hears of a vacancy at another school in Concord; however, when he learns Nehemiah Ball will be on the hiring committee, he tears up his letter of application and throws it on the fire.

Why is he so attached to Concord? Is it that he doesn't want to leave his family? Yes, but it's more than that. The size of the village appeals to him, two thousand and seventeen residents at last count. Yet there are plenty of other villages of a similar size so why not one of those? It's partly because he's so familiar with the place, but many people are born and raised in a town or city and upon reaching their majority, can't wait to escape. Several of the youngsters he grew up with are already gone. No, it's more than family and more than familiarity, it's something he can't quite figure out.

Then one evening when he is out walking, he passes the big white house on the Cambridge Turnpike where Mr. Emerson lives. He's almost past it when he hears a voice:

"How goes the Virgil?"

Henry stops and glances back. It's Emerson himself, out digging in his garden. He thrusts his shovel into the earth and ambles over to talk.

"I was reading it to my students," Henry says as he approaches, "but I'm no longer in the school's employ."

"So I heard. What caused you to resign?"

Outside of his family, he's told no one the details. At the time he felt virtuous, but according to Helen, not everyone in town agrees. Now for some reason he tells Emerson the whole story, as accurately as he can. He concludes by saying, "If I had it to do over again, I don't know that I'd quit."

Emerson frowns. "I've never favored the caning of children. Although I'm aware there are some who deserve it. I may have been one myself."

"It wasn't so much the caning I objected to. It was his meddling."

"Have you found another position?"

"In my father's shop. But it makes no use of my education."

Emerson looks at him intently. It's as if he's conducting

44

some sort of appraisal. At last he blinks, owl-like, and says, "Come inside."

Henry follows him up the garden path and through the front door. Then they enter a room on the right.

When the lamp is lit, Henry's eyes go wide. It's a library with book-filled shelves covering every wall, shelves all the way to the ceiling, far higher than even a tall fellow like Emerson could possibly reach. In the middle of the room is a large desk, and across from the desk, a straight-backed chair toward which Emerson now directs him. Henry owns fewer than twenty-five books. When he graduated from Harvard, the thing he hated most was leaving the college library behind.

"Where'd they all come from?" he asks. He's not simply making conversation—he'd genuinely like to know. It looks like the accumulation of a lifetime, but Emerson, now seated at his desk, couldn't be much more than ten years older than he—thirty-five at most.

"I follow the advice of Erasmus—when I have a little money I buy books. And if there's any leftover I buy food and clothing."

"So I see," Henry replies. He motions to the desk. "Are you working on a lecture? I was fortunate enough to hear you speak in Cambridge. On my graduation day."

"And what did you think?"

"I was well pleased. Although I don't agree with everything you said. You told us to ignore all those who came before us. You don't really mean that, do you? Take Virgil for instance."

"Not at all. But neither should we be slaves to their views. They were men like us."

"Oh, I'm no Virgil. Nor will I ever be."

"Perhaps not. I wasn't referring to individuals. I only meant that relying on the traditions of the past can be an excuse for not relying on ourselves."

Henry nods, yet he's not convinced. "I'll have to think on it," he says.

"Would you like a cup of tea?" Emerson asks. "I can have Lidian make some for us."

He likes everything about the room—the books, the view out the window to the trees, and especially the smell. Still, he's not sure why he was invited in. "I should be going. I . . ." he says, but Emerson interrupts.

"Do you keep a journal? You should try putting your thoughts on paper. You needn't pen an entire lecture. Simply write your observations in a notebook as they come."

He thinks of the notebook in which he wrote about his students. He could use the remaining pages of that. "I suppose I should. Thank you for suggesting it. I've enjoyed speaking with you. I ought to be on my way."

"Of course," Emerson says, motioning toward the door. But as Henry rises he asks him if he'd like to borrow some books.

It's an offer Henry can't refuse. He takes a few moments to scan the shelves, settling at last on a volume of Scottish poetry and the selected orations of Cicero, which he studied in college and would like to read again. He says thank you and departs.

As he walks up the road in the twilight, he calculates the number of books in Mr. Emerson's library. Assume an average of fifty books per shelf, with three sets of shelves on each wall and ten shelves from floor to ceiling. How many days of wood chopping would it take for him earn enough to fill a single shelf? Before he can arrive at an answer, he is distracted by an enormous owl gliding down out of an oak, wings moving soundlessly, eyes great yellow orbs, and so low to the ground he feels the need to duck.

A few days later an idea strikes him. He and John should start their own school. They are both teachers. Why work for someone else? He writes a letter to John and awaits his reply. It doesn't take long. He says he will return to Concord at the end of his current school term, which is only weeks away. This time

Henry doesn't want sixty students. Twenty would be about right. And no Nehemiah Ball to tell him what to do. The more he thinks about it, the better the idea seems. John is only two years older and they've always gotten along. As boys, Henry was bookish and a better student, while John was outgoing and had more friends. When Henry couldn't bring himself to speak up in class, John would start talking and he'd join in.

He tells his parents and they seem moderately pleased. "It's what you studied for," his father says, while his mother, a bit more cautiously, adds, "Do you think you can make a go of it? You won't just be teaching, you'll be overseeing the whole school." But Helen is delighted: "Oh, I was so afraid you were going to leave and not come back."

While he's awaiting John's return to Concord, he begins to plan. It gives him great pleasure to think about the course of study, what to include and what to leave out. John will want to be in charge of geography (most likely from Smith's book) and grammar (Parker and Fox, both parts). Henry will do algebra, Latin, composition, and perhaps a little Greek. On a piece of tallow-colored paper he draws a plan of the school room. If each student has his own desk, there'll be less poking and pinching and if they use pencils for their compositions (available from his father at cost), they could do away with the infernal inkpots that are forever getting spilled.

By the time John arrives, Henry is certain their school can't be anything but a success. They might even run Nehemiah Ball out of business. That would put the old vulture in his place. The first evening John is home the family has a feast, with all the Thoreaus as well as old Mrs. Sewell and her daughter Prudence Ward, who have been boarders in the house for years. Prudence is a bit proper for Henry's taste and Mrs. Sewell has become more and more silent as she's become more and more deaf, yet they all get along quite well. The meal consists of ham, pulled chicken with cream, and potatoes roasted to a delightful crispness straight out of the fire. After supper, their father plays his flute.

"No one else gets such a welcome," Henry tells John. "Apparently you've been missed."

The next morning they go to look at a possible location for the school. Wallace Long has an empty building on Main Street which Henry thinks might do. It's little more than a wooden box with no glass in the windows and an uneven floor, but they could fix it up. What they can't fix is the price. Long wants double what they can afford. He's a morose fellow, known for his frugality. They couldn't have picked a man less likely to offer them charitable terms.

As they walk dispiritedly toward home, John says, "You can't blame him. He knows we're not going to get rich from keeping school. He's afraid we won't pay the rent."

"Do you want to be rich?"

"I don't *not* want to be rich."

"How is that different?"

Instead of replying, John changes the subject. "I think we'll have to start our school at home. Mother will let us use the big bedroom at the back. I expect it will hold a dozen boys."

One of the things Henry likes about his brother (but would never admit) is that John resists being drawn into debates. No doubt it's a skill he developed from being around Henry, who will debate any subject at any time.

That night Henry sits down at his desk and lights a candle. The house is silent, everyone else asleep. He reads for a time, then opens his notebook and tries taking Emerson's suggestion. To begin, he simply records the conversation they had in his library: *"What are you doing now," he asked. "Do you keep a journal?"* So I make my first entry today.

MARGARET

Although she's as busy with school as usual, she can't get Emerson's lecture out of her mind. She keeps returning to his ideas, the words he used to express those ideas, and the way his voice filled the room. If only she'd spoken to him when she had the chance.

At last she decides to write him a letter. Composing it takes all day. She tells him how interesting she found his argument and describes her own work, especially a translation of Goethe's conversations with Eckermann which she has recently begun. She writes to him partly to express her authentic admiration and partly because she has a vague sense that she needs to build up a circle of acquaintances who share her interests. She hungers for intellectual companionship and the sort of person who might care about Eckermann's conversations with Goethe is rare. There was a time when her father provided all the talk about books and ideas she needed, but now he is gone. Of course thinking a man like Emerson would be interested in her company is presumptuous in the extreme.

She posts the letter and puts it out of her mind. To her amazement, he responds:

I thank you heartily for your thoughts. I regret we did not meet in Providence. I am slow in writing because I enjoyed your message so much I wanted to compose an adequate reply.

She likes his tone. He manages to be both measured and direct, both formal and familiar. Though now she has to write back. She finds that intimidating. It's one thing to send an admiring letter to someone you haven't been introduced to, but she now realizes it's quite another to have them reply. It takes her a week to work up the courage to begin:

Dear Mr. Emerson. Thank you for your recent letter. Are you certain writing to a schoolmistress who happened to attend one of your excellent lectures is not a poor use of your time? I think you are being polite when you praise the letter I sent you. But if you found it valuable in even the smallest amount, I am pleased.

This time she tells him a little about her teaching—"I endeavor to convince my girls that timidity of thought is no virtue"—as well as more about translating Goethe. It's how she spends her mornings and evenings so there's not much else to discuss.

Again he replies. And this time his letter ends with a sentence that causes her to smile: *Would you tell me of your reading? I can't seem to get enough of the thoughts others have about books.* "Of course I would," she whispers. "I'm delighted you asked."

So begins a conversation-by-post. It develops rapidly, more rapidly than Margaret has any right to expect. Its progress is reflected in her closings. Her first two letters she signs, "Devoutly if not worthily yours, S. M. Fuller." Yet that makes her sound too much the supplicant so she changes it to "Always yours, S.M.F." And then finally, on the fourth letter, she drops the "S" (for Sarah, which she never uses anyway) and simply signs it "Affectionately yours, Margaret F."

The content changes as well. Where once she made blandly cautious remarks such as, *The weather in Providence is unseasonably cool,* she now writes about issues of genuine interest: *In my view, Goethe's ideas about youth apply only to the German culture. Whereas the youth of our country do not dwell on the past.*

Emerson replies in kind: *Carlyle's interpretation of that passage is rather different from yours. Consider the following words . . .*

Then, the ice shattered, she pushes back: *What fault do you*

CONCORD

find in Goethe's lyrics? Each one gives a mood of the mind with marked expression and intense language. If you want sympathy, read Schiller.

But there are dangers in such frankness. Perhaps she's been too intense. In his next letter he retreats: *It seems you've read a good deal more Goethe than I have, so I must defer. Presently my knowledge extends only a little beyond* Faust. He also begins to include some remarks about life around his Concord home—his pigs, his forty-four newly planted pine trees, his tomatoes and the insects that eat them, his rhubarb, and his potatoes, so abundant this year he has shipped a barrel full to a cousin in New York. She feels a bit chastened. It's as if he's saying, "Books are of value but there is a life beyond them we ought not to neglect."

Margaret has no rhubarb or tomatoes about which to tell, but as time passes she writes not only of Goethe and Schiller but of herself:

I wish to study ten-thousand things this winter—Every day I become more sensible to the defects in my education—I feel ignorant and superficial. Every day new questions occur to me to which I have no answer and don't know what books to consult.

As soon as she sends those words, she wants to call them back—she has been too forthcoming. But in his reply he says, *I understand. There is so much to do and the clock never stops.*

She has numerous correspondents, yet soon she looks forward to his letters more than any except the ones from James Clarke. However, James is in far-off Kentucky, while Mr. Emerson is only a few miles away.

Then one day she hears he has given a particularly provocative address—incendiary even—at the Harvard Divinity School. Apparently he argued that the moral judgment of the individual is superior to the morality of the church.

Hearing about the speech gives her the courage to invite

51

herself for a visit. She's more curious than ever to meet him in person and explore his thoughts.

I find my mind turns incessantly toward you. I wish we could pass an afternoon together. When the school term ends I am free to travel, and Concord is not far.

Of course, he replies, (she has left him little choice): *The Concord stage runs three days a week and arrives here at 6 o'clock.*

But once she has the invitation in hand, she begins having second thoughts. Are her letters really that interesting? Will they have enough to talk about? And for a week with a philosopher in the country, what exactly should one wear?

However, before she can go to Concord, there is the whirlwind that is the end of school. Some of the girls will be back next year, but others are leaving for good. There are parties and ceremonies and tearful goodbyes. Abigail Freeh gives her a set of ivory hair combs, Rebecca Barkley, a volume of Horace's epodes, and Millicent Fox, one of her favorites, writes a satiric poem about the books they have read together, managing to rhyme Austen and Boston in a way that makes her laugh.

At last the students are gone, the school is locked up, and it's time for her to leave. Although she hasn't told Mr. Hiram yet, she doubts she'll come back the next term. Instead she might go live with her mother and younger brothers in Jamaica Plain. It's close to Boston and she could spend more time on her own studies there. But how will she make a living? What other paths are open to women like herself? Perhaps her visit with Mr. Emerson will give her time to think about her future. He might even have an opinion on the matter. After all, he is considered by some to be an oracle—although it's difficult to imagine an oracle in a village in Massachusetts, amidst the rustic plowmen, boorish shopkeepers, and unconfined chickens and pigs.

CONCORD

To get to Concord she takes the train from Providence to Boston and then a two-horse coach on to Concord that stops at the center of the village, in front of the Middlesex Hotel. As Margaret steps down from the coach, she asks a boy standing nearby for directions to Mr. Emerson's house. He gives her a funny look and shakes his head, and for an instant she thinks he might be deaf. But then he says, "Turn around ma'am, he's standin' right there." And indeed he is. But he has yet to notice her so she takes a moment to study him. He is taller than she remembers and thinner too. A scarecrow of a man, albeit a stately scarecrow. An instant later their eyes meet and he grins.

"Welcome to Concord," he says. "Was your journey pleasant? Let me carry your valise."

"So nice of you to invite me. The trip was easier than I expected. No difficulties or delays."

"We live a short walk from here. Lidian has supper prepared."

As they proceed up the street, he tells her a bit about Concord, pointing out the line of trees that mark the river and sharing an anecdote about an escaped bull that chased everyone off the streets yesterday afternoon. She expected him to be stern and forbidding in manner but he talks easily and walks with a relaxed, loose-limbed gait.

When they arrive at the house, which is larger than she expected, his wife Lidian meets them at the door. Almost as tall as Emerson himself, she has a rather severe countenance, yet Margaret thinks she detects a certain drollness in her eyes. She serves a meal of cold beef, beans, and a sweet cornmeal cake.

"I've been thinking about what you said regarding Goethe's aesthetics," Emerson says but Lidian cuts him off.

"She only just arrived. Let her eat. Perhaps she has interests other than Goethe. Tell me, Miss Fuller, do you find Providence a pleasant place to live?"

Before Margaret left Providence, she made some inquiries

about Emerson. She learned he was married once before, his first wife having died very young, and that he resigned as pastor from his church in Boston over doctrinal disputes. It wasn't difficult to obtain information, as his lectures are making him well known.

"It's quite tolerable. There is a good deal of commerce springing up there, new factories and mills."

When lunch is over she is shown to her room and they leave her to rest. She unpacks, placing her things in the walnut wardrobe. She wishes she'd brought more to wear, if only for variety's sake. Out the window, there are no passing carriages and no nearby buildings, only grass and trees. If she didn't know better, she'd think they were deep in the woods.

Margaret is still a little agog at having been invited to visit, but should she be? She's read his book *Nature* and heard him speak, and in what she's written to him, she feels she's held her own. Most of his reputation comes from being a contrarian— from resigning his pulpit and disagreeing with the conventional dogma of the Boston clerical elite. As a rule she admires those who go against the grain yet sometimes they have little else to offer. She's not entirely sure of her role here. Have the two of them become friends through the post? She's uncertain. Is she his student? If so, she can't afford to pay. Perhaps they are colleagues, but toward what end? Well, she is to be here for a week. She will find out soon enough.

SOPHIA

Sophia's father announces he is moving his dental practice back to Salem. There's too much competition in Boston and rents are too steep. Her mother thinks she and her sisters should come too.

"But I can't," Elizabeth tells Sophia. "I'd have to close the shop. And Mary would be loath to leave her friends, especially that widower she's befriended, Mr. Mann."

"I don't think I'd mind Salem," Sophia replies. "Mother says the house they've found is quite large so we'll have plenty of room."

In the end Sophia and Mary make the move, while Elizabeth remains behind. However, she hires a girl to help at the shop so she can visit them now and then.

Although the Peabody sisters grew up in Salem and have fond memories of those early years, they find the town has become a shadow of its once-grand self. The wharves are dilapidated; arriving ships discharge cargos not of riches from China as they previously did, but of cotton and molasses and hides that carry with them the smell of putrefaction; and fully half of the once thriving warehouses stand empty, their rafters home to birds and their subfloors home to rats. The town began its decline with Jefferson's wartime embargo and has now been eclipsed as a port by Boston and New York. When the members of the Peabody family take stock of their situation, they feel they too have fallen somewhat. Yet it's always been their nature to make the best of what's at hand.

In this case what's at hand is a big, ramshackle place on Charter Street, with six drafty bedrooms, peeling wallpaper, and sloping floors. Sophia turns the largest bedroom into a studio, with a plaster bust of Apollo and a vase of dried flowers on a side table, an array of her drawings on the wall, and two easels positioned to take full advantage of the light. She rather likes the fact that their house sits adjacent to the oldest cemetery in Salem, what's known as the Burying Point. Although she sometimes goes for days without leaving her room, when she can't stand being indoors any longer, she steps outside and walks among the headstones beneath the sweeping elms. The last row of graves stops only feet from their house. She's quite familiar with Salem's dark history and finds it intriguing that any headstone she passes might mark the grave of a witch. Right now the leaves are falling and the skies so often gray it all seems appropriately melancholy. And if the sexton is supposed to scythe the grass he's doing a poor job of it, which adds to the grotesque effect.

Sophia is still uncertain of her skill as a painter. She wonders if she's being urged to copy by men like Allston because no one expects a woman to produce original work. He was very helpful to her so she bears him no ill will, but if it was a man he was advising, she thinks he might have said, "It's time to stop mimicking what others have done and get on with your career." On the other hand, she's become a good copyist and there is money in that. Although right now she has nothing in her possession she wishes to reproduce.

Then early one evening, she is at work in her studio when she hears someone at the door downstairs. They must have a visitor. Perhaps Horace Mann from Cambridge to see Mary, perhaps someone to see her father after hours with a sore tooth that won't wait. But before long, she hears footsteps coming up the stairs. She can tell by the light, quick step it's Elizabeth, who already seems to be spending as much time in Salem as Boston. A few seconds later, she enters the room.

"Mr. Hawthorne has arrived, with his mother and sisters. Come down and say hello."

Sophia glances up, her mind still on her work. "Mr. Hawthorne?"

"Don't you remember? You never listen. I told you yesterday he might be stopping by." She lowers her voice. "He's quite splendid. Handsomer than Lord Byron. You should at least say hello. No, you *must* say hello."

Elizabeth is always wanting her to meet someone or other. Yes, maybe she does recall being told he might visit. The boy from the house behind them when they lived in Salem before. But she remembers almost nothing about him. He was shy. He walked with a limp. They were both merely children. So why is Elizabeth so excited? It's enough to pique Sophia's curiosity, but not enough to make her leave her room.

"I'm busy," Sophia says. "Tell him I'm indisposed."

"Oh, Sophia, please don't be like that. You'll thank me when you see how he looks."

Still, she doesn't budge. "If he has come once, he will come again," she says. Before the door is even latched, she is back at her easel, brush in hand.

After a while she hears them leaving. They didn't stay very long.

Later that evening she goes out. It rained earlier so instead of walking through the wet grass of the cemetery, she goes toward the waterfront. As often happens when her mind is free to wander, she begins to think of Cuba: of Fernando and dancing the waltz and the tiny blue-green hummingbirds called *zunzuncitos*, no bigger than her thumb. What if she had stayed? Although it was only three years ago, back then she let Mary make all the decisions so she never considered doing anything but coming home. In addition to hummingbirds, there were crimson snakes and yellow-headed lizards and once she heard a terrifying noise in the forest that sounded exactly like the scream of a child. But Fernando said it was only a bird. Then he kissed her. Mary couldn't wait to leave. Mary said the way they treated the Negroes was shameful but Sophia didn't want to challenge Fernando so she accepted his explanation: although it was necessary now, in time things would change.

When she reaches the wharf, she pulls her cloak tight around her but still shivers in the ocean breeze. The water laps the pilings, the ships are dark, and their anchor chains clank with the motion of the waves. If she were a real artist she'd go to Paris to study. Instead she has come to Salem, to a house next door to a graveyard—a graveyard she rather likes.

When she returns from her walk, her mother admonishes her for going out without telling anyone. "I sent your father to look for you," she says.

"This isn't Boston," Sophia replies. "Who or what do you fear on the streets of Salem?"

"Don't be impertinent," her mother says, treating her like a child. Maybe moving back here was a mistake.

A few days later Elizabeth knocks at her door again. Mr. Hawthorne has returned.

"All four of them?" Sophia asks. It's late. She's taken the combs from her hair and is just unbuttoning her dress.

Elizabeth nods. "They walk together in the evening."

"Why do you insist on my meeting them? For what purpose do they come?"

"He's here because I invited him. I read a book he wrote and then realized we knew the author as a child. Why should you meet him? I don't know, Sophia—simply to be neighborly. They live only a few streets away. Isn't that enough?"

But once again she refuses. She's not sure why—partly because her enthusiasm tends to shrink as Elizabeth's grows, and partly because she thinks Salem is provincial. Anyone who grew up here and never left must be rather dull.

Over the next several weeks, she leaves her room less frequently than usual. If she goes out at all, she goes after dark. It's as if the house holds two worlds—the solitary one she inhabits and the one where the rest of the family welcomes her father's patients and entertains guests, sometimes several a day. Occasionally she thinks she hears Mr. Hawthorne, but Elizabeth no longer comes up the stairs to tell her and she doesn't know his voice well enough to be sure it's him.

But then one day Elizabeth tries again. "He's curious about you. He knows you're up here. Do you want him to think you're mad?"

Sophia sighs. She could continue to resist, but Mary is off visiting a friend and their parents have gone to Boston, so leaving Elizabeth alone to entertain guests doesn't seem fair.

"I'll be down shortly," she says.

When Elizabeth is gone, she refastens her dress and fixes her hair. She tries to think of something to talk about. Her recent move to Salem. The unexpected windstorm that blew down some trees last week. The decline in shipping at the docks. She checks herself in the mirror. If he's a writer, why isn't he at home writing? She opens the door to her room and glides swiftly down the stairs.

There he stands. He is quite beautiful, just as Elizabeth said. Tall, with gray eyes, a full mouth, and luxurious hair. Behind him stand his mother and sisters, all dressed in black. If she's seen more dour-looking women, she can't remember when.

Elizabeth introduces them and they go to the parlor and sit. Elizabeth offers them tea and they decline.

"I'm so sorry to interrupt you," Mr. Hawthorne says. "Every time we come, your good sister tells me you are hard at work. She says you are an accomplished artist, which I do not doubt."

As if signaled to do so, Mrs. Hawthorne and his sisters, Ebe and Louise, solemnly nod.

"She *is* a good sister," Sophia says brightly. "That much is true."

"When—when we were children," he says, a slight stammer tripping him up, "you wore a red cape. If I saw you from my window I'd come outside and we'd talk through the fence."

"I'm sorry, I don't recall," replies Sophia, shaking her head. "Elizabeth, do *you* remember? We were all so very young."

"Of course. Mr. Hawthorne had a wagon. He pulled his sisters around the yard."

Sophia glances at the sisters, expecting some response, at least a smile. Yet they remain expression-less, as if they failed to hear.

"Have you found the weather to your liking lately?" Sophia says, hoping to draw Mrs. Hawthorne out.

"It's been tolerable," she whispers. Sophia nods and smiles, thankful for even that.

Now there is a painful silence. Sophia thinks they'll all be happy if this means they're done. Then Mr. Hawthorne speaks again. "Miss Peabody tells me you lived in—in Cuba for a time. What an adventure that must have been."

She glances at Elizabeth. Why has she been talking about her and how much has she said? "Yes, it was indescribable. Quite beyond words."

"That's not exactly true," Elizabeth says. "You wrote plenty of letters while you were there and brought back that immense journal. You can't claim it was beyond words."

"A journal? About your trip to Cuba?" He seems genuinely curious—even enthusiastic. "I would be most interested in reading it if you'd allow me. Perhaps it's too personal . . ." Their eyes meet but she can't hold his gaze.

"First, you should read Mr. Hawthorne's stories," Elizabeth says.

Maybe her sister thinks her journal isn't worthy of being read by someone outside the family. Still, Sophia is relieved to have the subject change.

"What sort of stories are they," she asks.

60

"Very fine ones," his mother interjects, speaking at full volume. It is so unexpected, Sophia jumps.

"I think not," he says firmly, giving his mother a disapproving look. "They are tales, merely tales. Stories I've heard through the years, put into my own words."

What an odd family, Sophia thinks. She's had enough of them. She should have stayed in her room.

"I really must return to my work," she says and stands to leave. Although she knows it's rude to be so abrupt, she doesn't care.

Mr. Hawthorne rises as well and says, "Thank you for your hospitality," but he's speaking to her back because she's on her way upstairs.

Later, she begins to recall a little more about what he was like when they were growing up. He stayed inside his house while other boys roamed Salem's streets and wharves. When he looked at you, he studied you, as if you were a specimen or a strange case. Or he averted his eyes. If she talked with him through the fence it was on rare occasions. She didn't go outside much because of her headaches. She does remember the red cape. It had black stitching on the collar and pockets to put things in. But he didn't come down because of what she was wearing. He came down because he saw her looking up, searching the windows for his face.

HENRY

A few days after John's return, Henry comes home from working with his father and finds visitors waiting in the parlor. It's Ellen Sewall and her brother Edmund, there to see their Aunt Prudence and Grandmother Sewell, boarders in the Thoreau house.

"I'm preparing refreshments," his mother says. "Helen, help me lay the table. Henry, show them where to put their things."

Henry leads them upstairs, Edmund to the little blue room, scarcely larger than a closet, and Ellen to his sister Sarah's room, which they'll share. Edmund asks him if they can go fishing and Henry says yes. But Ellen overhears him and says, "Don't let him inconvenience you, Henry. He has no manners and thinks only of himself."

"Mind your own business, sister," Edmund replies. "He can take me fishing if he likes."

Ellen and Edmund will be spending a week in Concord, having come over from Scituate, on the coast. The last time Henry saw them was five years ago, before he went off to college, so Edmund is twice as tall, and Ellen wears her hair up like a young woman instead of on her shoulders like a girl.

Back downstairs, Mrs. Thoreau and Helen serve gingerbread and tea. Although Helen, Henry, John, and Ellen are all adults or nearly so, on this occasion, Mrs. Thoreau treats all the young people the same, insisting each report on his or her recent activities. Edmund tells about finding an enormous squid on the beach near Scituate, Ellen describes a dog the Sewall family has acquired (Aunt Prudence looks disapproving), Henry and John say a few words about their plans to open their own school, and little Sarah is admonished for trying to talk while her mouth is full.

Next, Grandmother Sewell and Aunt Prudence open packages Ellen and Edmund's mother has sent. Aunt Prudence is delighted with writing paper and a pair of gloves and Grandmother receives some ribbon and a large piece of gray calico, which she holds up for all to admire.

When they're done eating, Mrs. Thoreau sends the young people on a walk. "Go find me some blueberries. There are still plenty left to pick. It'll do you good to be out."

Henry fetches tin pails and they take a shortcut across the open fields rather than following the road. Edmund insists on being next to Henry, while up ahead, Ellen is between John and Helen, speaking to one and then the other, a few tendrils of her light brown hair coming loose along the way. Sarah ranges far out, scampers back, and then goes out again. Over the years, the Thoreau children have come to see Ellen and Edmund as cousins, and it takes little time for them to be comfortable with each other again. They stop to pet a donkey who puts his gray nose over a fence. They startle a calf sleeping in tall grass and watch it bound off into the trees. The sun appears and disappears as clouds cross the sky.

Edmund says, "Maybe I could go to your school. I don't like mine."

Henry raises an eyebrow in the boy's direction. In his experience, nine-year-olds can be astute critics of schooling, so Edmund's opinion ought not to be ignored.

"What is it you don't like?" he asks.

"The headmaster is mean-spirited. He picks out one boy and one girl every morning and canes them first thing as a reminder of what will happen to anyone who misbehaves. When I knew my time was coming I stayed home sick but that didn't help. He was waiting for me the next day."

"Want my advice?"

Edmund nods and looks up at him expectantly.

"Get yourself a shovel and dig a ditch."

"But why?"

"So next time you'll have calluses on your hands."

"Haw, haw," Edmund says, eager to show he understands Henry's joke.

When they reach the river, they set to berrying. At first they make it a contest, girls against boys, but then Sarah gets into some nettles and needs Helen's attention. After that the most diligent berry-pickers are Ellen and Henry. They work their way upstream, standing on rocks to reach the high ones and then taking off their shoes and wading out into the current to pick the ones that can't be reached from dry land.

"I'm awfully glad you're here," Ellen says. "When we came last time you were away at school and John was in Taunton so it wasn't much fun."

"How did you spend your time?"

"Aunt Prudence sent Edmund and Sarah out to play and put me and Helen to work. Aunt Pru said, 'Since it's just the two of you, I'll teach you about keeping house.'"

Henry laughs. "This time John and I will protect you from Prudence."

"I would appreciate it," she says. "Pull down that branch and I'll get the ones up there."

Henry stretches to his full height and loses his footing on a slick patch of mud, toppling over backward into the river. He splashes and gasps, while managing to keep the bucket of berries over his head and safe the entire time. When he finally flails his way upright, everyone is laughing at him from the bank.

"Go ahead and laugh," he says, as he comes out dripping. "Laugh as much as you please."

John reaches out and pulls him up the bank to dry ground and Helen tries to relieve him of his berry pail but he won't let it go. "These are mine," he says with mock seriousness. "I have gone through too much to give them up now."

On their way back, Ellen asks Henry why they decided to start their own school instead of finding jobs at one that already exists.

"My brother and I have some ideas about education we'd like to try out," he explains. It's mostly a lie though. They're starting the school because he hasn't been able to find a position elsewhere and because he'd like to stay near Concord. And then it occurs to him he's not sure why John wants to do it. He proposed the idea and John said yes. It was as simple as that. But saying they have ideas they want to test makes them sound smart and ambitious and he'd like Ellen to consider him both.

This time they go through Concord so they can stop at Mr. Jewell's shop for sweets. Henry, still soaking wet, waits outside. A few minutes later they emerge with bags of lemon drops, peppermints, and rock.

"Have some, Henry," says Sarah.

He shakes his head. "I seldom eat sweets. I consider them an extravagance."

Helen sidles up to him and whispers, "Henry, what are you trying demonstrate?"

"I don't know what you're talking about," he says.

In the short time since Ellen and her brother have arrived, Henry has made an unexpected discovery. The last time he saw Ellen Sewall she was twelve and he was seventeen. Back then she talked too much and could beat him in a footrace because she ran like a deer. But now she's the one who's seventeen and is nothing like he remembers. Her smile is captivating, her manner is lighthearted and engaging, and when she looks at him with her brown eyes, he forgets what he meant to say.

MARGARET

She has now been in Concord for four days. She still finds it difficult to believe he invited her—although it would be more accurate to say she requested an invitation, and he was too kind to say no. The household consists of Waldo Emerson, his wife, their year-old child, and Emerson's mother. The child is called Waldo as well, which prompts Margaret to think *Waldo major and Waldo minor, the great and the small.*

Thus far Emerson has read several pages of her translation of Eckermann and written copious notes in the margins. In return, she has read two of the essays he is working on and written some notes of her own, although hers are more sparing. It's not that she mistrusts her ability to critique, but she's unsure what he expects of her. Each day is the same: they rise, work all morning, and then the three of them, Waldo, his wife Lidian, and Margaret have lunch while his mother watches the child. In the afternoon they go back to their papers and books. Margaret observes his relationship with Lidian with interest. Waldo is so consumed by his work that Lidian makes many household decisions without consulting him, even some that involve significant expense. On the other hand, when he enters a room, he commands it—not because he is intimidating but because he invites respect.

Shortly after arriving, Margaret said to Lidian, "I like your name very much. It's one I've never heard before."

"My given name is Lidia. But when Waldo and I were married, he asked me to change it. He said he thought the added consonant would make it more euphonious when placed before the name Emerson. So of course I did."

She didn't know how to respond. It seems rather an odd

reason to change one's name. If *she* were to marry and her new husband suggested she drop the "T" at the end of Margaret and replace it with an "X" or a "Z," would she comply? Or, an even more interesting question, would a husband change a letter in *his* name to suit his wife? She thinks the incident must say something about the Emersons' relationship, although she's not sure what. Perhaps names don't matter if you're truly in love.

At night, after supper, she reads in her room, but Waldo often goes on walks. She hears him leave, humming as he departs, and then, when she is lying in bed with her window open, hears him come humming back.

Little by little her uneasiness diminishes. Each day their interactions seem more natural and they talk for a longer time. When they discuss their manuscripts, Waldo gives her his full attention. He studies the words on the page and then looks at her with his hawk-like eyes.

"But is that what you really mean?" he asks.

"Which aspect of it are you questioning?"

"Not the words themselves but their implications. The meaning that lies beneath . . ."

Before long, their thoughts and words are spiraling away, circling, weaving, coming back and then flaring out again like swallows in flight. Sometimes, when the discussion gets especially fervid, they stand side-by-side, the pages of whatever they are working on spread across his desk. He points at something and she points at something else and then one of them reads a passage aloud. A page slides off the edge and flutters to the floor.

His nose is just the right nose for such a personage—dignified, skeptical, and direct. An uncommonly eloquent nose. When she came here, she thought being around him might be a bit like being around her father, a stern taskmaster. Maybe he would even insist she recite. But no, he doesn't treat her like an

67

apprentice or pupil, he treats her like an equal. It lifts her heart.

He reads *Nature* to her and then awaits her response. She read it some time ago, when it was first published, but hearing it in his voice doubles its power:

The tradesmen, the attorney comes out of the din and craft of the street, and sees the sky and the woods, and is a man again. In their eternal calm he finds himself. The health of the eye seems to demand a horizon. We are never tired as long as we can see far enough.

She likes the idea of the eye demanding a horizon. And when his voice moves from *din* and *craft* to the *eternal calm*, she can feel the shift in her body as well as her mind.

"I wish I could do that," she says when he stops. "You speak even better than you write."

"Oh," he says. She can tell he's taken aback. "If that's true then I'm sorry to hear it. Speaking before an audience from a prepared text requires no great talent. It's almost a kind of trick."

"I intended to take nothing away from your writing." She pauses and tries to figure out how to explain what she meant. "Your voice—if it's a trick, it's a very effective trick."

"But you are a remarkable *conversationalist*," he says, turning the tables. "And you do it without a script or preparation. To my mind, *that* is an art."

From time to time they are interrupted—the Emerson house is not without visitors. A Mrs. Gillicutt comes to see Lidian and her voice is so loud it penetrates every room in the house. The butcher makes a delivery and Waldo has a long conversation with him about the cutting of meat. Waldo takes a great interest in the sorts of work done by blacksmiths, butchers, coopers, and millers. Margaret does not. Why spend time talking about such matters when there are questions of morality and meaning and existence that haven't been answered. Haven't even been properly *asked*. But his openness to the world is part of his charm. A man with a cloudy eye brings a letter to the house and asks Waldo to read it to him. It's from his brother in Poland. As far as Margaret knows, Waldo does not speak Polish but somehow he manages to decipher it. One of Waldo's pigs develops a skin rash, so he makes a study of pig ailments, applying himself to the project with as much intensity as he does to reading Montaigne. He dotes on his pigs.

He also dotes on his child. Although Lidian and his mother care for him most of the day, it's not uncommon for Waldo to scoop the boy up and carry him about the garden, nonchalantly, as if holding a melon or a loaf of bread. Her father was quite the opposite—forbidding, demanding, distant, though he taught her most of what she knows.

One day Waldo tells her at some length about the two brothers he's lost to illness over the past three years. She has the feeling it's not something he talks about often. But, along with the death of his first wife, it helps explain the melancholy she sometimes senses behind his often-abstract words.

"The loss of a sibling is especially painful," he says. "They knew my truest self."

"Does such a thing exist?" she asks. "For any of us?"

He looks surprised. "A fair question. So let me say it this way. They knew my *earliest* self."

Near the end of the week, a young man stops by to borrow some books. She and Waldo are in the library and when they look up, standing in the doorway is a rustic young fellow, short, broad-shouldered, with deep-set eyes beneath heavy brows. Although Margaret is seated in the middle of the room, he speaks only to Waldo and, even after they are introduced, looks right through her, as if she's not there.

"I've heard about your plan for a school. I trust it's going well," Waldo says.

"John has come back from Taunton to help. We intend to open in one month. We've just begun advertising for students."

Margaret could tell him a thing or two about schools and teaching but doesn't like his manner and holds her tongue. However, Waldo does not:

"Miss Fuller is a teacher at a school in Providence. She's quite well regarded. The two of you should talk."

For a strange and startling moment, Margaret thinks Waldo is playing matchmaker. Her eyes go wide and she looks at him, trying to express her horror at the thought without using words. Yet the visitor is no more interested in her than she in him.

"I'm on an errand for my father," he says, rotating his straw hat in his hands. "Perhaps some other time."

Thank goodness. For a moment she was afraid Waldo was going to send them off on a stroll.

The young man pulls down an armload of books from Emerson's shelves—she tries to get a look at the titles, but he keeps them concealed—and then he's gone. She didn't particularly like him. He wasn't shy, he was aloof. At least that's how he seemed.

Two days later, she gets up early, packs, and prepares to leave. Now that she understands what a visit with Waldo entails, she'd like to stay longer, but she's not brave enough to ask. She also feels she's spent too little time visiting with Lidian—even though her purpose was to study with Waldo, it wouldn't have hurt to pass an afternoon or two with the lady of the house.

"I had a lovely time," Margaret tells her. "You have a delightful child."

Lidian thanks her and then, after a moment's thought, says, "When we moved here, Waldo said his dream was to bring to Concord people with whom he could share his thoughts. Then he wouldn't have to go to Boston or New York. He could remain at home and converse and write. But not everyone finds it convenient to come. He is thankful for your visit. More than he's able to say."

Margaret is flattered—she thought he was granting her the favor and not vice versa. It never occurred to her that *she* might have something *he* would need. Yet she also senses in Lidian a coolness. Perhaps she thinks Waldo's need for others somehow diminishes her.

SOPHIA

After the Hawthornes leave, Sophia goes to the battered
trunk where she keeps the journal she wrote while in Cuba,
takes it out, and turns it over in her hands. It has a red cloth
cover, the corners are reinforced with blue leather, and, as she
opens it, she fancies she can smell the tropics, a musky floral
scent rising from the pages. Or maybe that's from an old sachet
buried somewhere in the depths of the trunk.

She wishes Elizabeth hadn't told Mr. Hawthorne about the
journal. To Elizabeth it's simply an account of a girl's visit to an
exotic land. A naïve travelogue. But to Sophia, it's much deeper
and more important than that. In Cuba, she felt for the first
time as if her life was her own and not of a piece with the life
of her family. Even though she was there with Mary, she spent
a great deal of time alone. In the morning, she would leave her
room and walk across the Morrell compound on paths of hard
red earth, along the pine hedges, and then into the tropical
forest to a warm spring where she could bathe. Dismissing the
servant who was assigned to accompany her, she would slip
into the water and lie back. Above her, trees formed a ring of
green around a pool of sky that mirrored the pool in which she
swam. In her journal she wrote, *The degree to which things
grow here is frightful. There are flowers shaped like stars and
goblets and swords. One day I went out and let the warm rain
fall upon my bare skin. I myself was as a flower blossoming. It
was a pleasure unlike any I have felt before.*

She's not about to allow Mr. Hawthorne to read such
passages. Even picturing her sisters reading them makes her
blush.

As forthcoming as she was in the journal, it does not tell

the whole story of her time in Cuba. Yes, there are passages about going on rides with Fernando Zayas, but not about what they spoke of as they rode. And, yes, there are passages about the glamorous balls she attended, although not about what happened after those balls, when Fernando took her strolling under the long row of palms whose white trunks looked like marble columns in the moonlight. And most definitely not about what happened beneath the archway where the moonlight was obscured.

The dress I wore had a blue satin bodice laced in front over a white chemisette.

A few days later, Elizabeth brings her another painting by Washington Allston to copy. This one she borrowed from Harriet Gordon, who is said to be the wealthiest woman in Boston—yet another of the many people of importance Elizabeth knows.

Sophia places it on an easel in her room and stares at it nightly. It is only a small painting, but according to Elizabeth, Mrs. Gordon paid $500. It depicts Jessica and Lorenzo, the two lovers from "The Merchant of Venice." They sit beside one another in a posture that is both tentative and intimate. She wonders if she could capture herself and Fernando in a painting. It would have to be from memory because she will never see him again.

After she and Mary left Cuba and returned to Boston, Elizabeth and her mother asked about "this Fernando" whom she had mentioned in her letters home. Before she could even speak, Mary interrupted and said, "Don't believe everything Sophia tells you about Señor Zayas. I think she was a bit overwhelmed by him." She said it in a joking manner, but her meaning was clear: Poor, infirm Sophia with her headaches and neurasthenia and artistic temperament likes to imagine lovers where only friends and acquaintances exist. Obviously only someone as beautiful as Mary could attract a man like him.

Then again, she does wonder about some of what transpired. Perhaps for someone like Señor Zayas a kiss under the palms was of little importance. He seemed passionate but when you yourself are under the influence of passion your perceptions can be flawed. *The dress I wore had a blue satin bodice laced in front over a white chemisette.*

The next morning, Sophia goes looking for Elizabeth. She finds her in the parlor, sitting beside the window doing needlework. Pulling a chair up beside her, she says, "Tell me again about Mr. Hawthorne. What prompted you to contact him?"

"What does it matter? You didn't like him, I could tell."

"He did seem strange. Standoffish and overly familiar at the same time. But it was his mother and sisters I found disagreeable. Did they really live right behind us? If I'd known what they were like, I think I'd have been scared to death."

Elizabeth considers the remark and then nods as if she understands. "When his stories began to be published anonymously, I tried to find out who had written them. I was told it was his sister Ebe and thought, 'Oh, they used to live on Herbert Street. I should stop in and give her my regards.' But then I discovered they were written by Nathaniel. After I spoke with him, I thought you might enjoy seeing him again. Apparently, I was wrong."

"What are they about?"

"His stories?—you'll have to read them for yourself. Did you know one of his ancestors was a judge when the witches were tried? Well, you can see it in his words. It's as if he feels he has blood on his hands."

"Now you're being dramatic."

Elizabeth shrugs. "I don't believe I am. Since he's come back from college, he's been up in his little room writing and writing every day. His sisters bring his meals to him so he can remain at his desk."

"I haven't forgiven you for telling him about my journal," Sophia chides. "It wasn't intended for strangers."

"Don't be foolish. It makes you seem adventurous and exotic. Who wouldn't want to be perceived as such?"

"I call you my good sister, but in fact you are a meddlesome sister. I shall be in my room."

Upstairs, she closes the door and looks again at the Allston painting. Is it "Jessica and Lorenzo" or "Lorenzo and Jessica"? She can't recall. Jessica looks upon Lorenzo admiringly while he gazes off across the Italian countryside. It's twilight. In the background is a stately villa and beyond that, the city of Venice, its towers and cupolas visible against the darkening sky. Jessica's hand reaches out to him. It's a small painting, not more than twelve inches on a side. Sophia thinks she has studied it enough. It's time to start making her copy. Copying is really rather mindless work and yet people seem so pleased when you do it well. "It's almost as good as the original," they say. She's not sure she can stand hearing that again. It makes her want to take the canvas and slice it with a knife.

In Cuba, her headaches disappeared entirely. Even after she came back, it was a while before they returned. But now, she feels one coming on. There's a blurring at the edges of her field of vision. And a metallic taste on her tongue. The leeches helped, but she can't be going to the doctor every week. Sometimes she feels as if going to the doctor has been the primary activity of her life.

She begins painting, first the outline of Jessica and Lorenzo, and then the buildings behind them. It comes easily and before long she can see how to proceed. But the headache won't abate. She has a variety of pills and tinctures at her disposal. Although most of them make her sleep, when she wakes up the headaches are rarely gone. Nonetheless she takes a pill now, a yellow one, and then puts herself to bed. She dreams about her sisters, about Fernando, about Lorenzo and Jessica, but mostly about the neighbors' goat who is always jumping the fence and coming into the cemetery to graze. In the dream the goat becomes threatening, no longer a farm animal but a malevolent, golden-eyed beast.

She awakes with a start. Her heart is pounding, and she gasps for breath. She lies there for a moment waiting for the nightmare to recede. The house is utterly silent and there are no sounds coming from without. It must be after midnight. She's a little surprised to have slept the entire day away, but it's happened before. The yellow pills in particular have that effect. She stands and goes to the window. It's raining, a light mist. Her head does feel a bit better. She likes the sensation of the cold wooden floor against the bottoms of her feet. Then out the window she sees something moving. A man with a limp walking up the street.

PART TWO

I never intend to have a husband. Or rather I should say I never intend anyone should have me for a wife.

Sophia Peabody

HENRY

When he arrives home with his borrowed books, he sits in the kitchen and reads. Perhaps if Ellen Sewall finds him thus, she'll be impressed. But then Helen comes down the stairs followed by Ellen and they tell him they're going to see a shadow play at a traveling theater on Sudbury Road.

"Come with us," Helen says.

"I'd prefer to read," he replies, shaking his head. But as soon as they're gone, he regrets it. Ellen didn't even glance at the books.

By the time they return he is asleep with his head resting on an open volume of Pliny's letters. Hearing the door, he comes awake and rubs his eyes.

"Henry, you should have gone," Helen says.

Their faces are fresh and alive from being out in the night air. "What was it?" he asks.

"A shadow play, silly," Helen teases. "A funny little man made wooden silhouettes dance in the firelight."

"You know what I mean. What was it *about?*"

"Beauty and the Beast," says Ellen. "But done in a humorous manner. We laughed so hard."

"He was a *beast of a fellow*," Helen says, and they shriek with laughter but quickly clap their hands over their mouths upon remembering the rest of the household is asleep. Henry doesn't know what's funny because he didn't attend the play, yet he enjoys seeing them filled with mirth.

Then Helen looks at him, lifts her eyebrows, and says, "Cider, Henry. We need cider."

"You and I must be related," he says. "We seem to think alike."

He leads them outside and around to the back of the house and then disappears into the spring house. When he returns, he's holding a brown jug. They sit in the grass beneath a beech tree and begin passing the jug, each of them tilting it up for a swig when their turn comes. Helen and Ellen do it two-handed but Henry loops his finger through the handle and rests the jug on his forearm like a plowman. He's showing off a bit.

"I'll bet you don't do this in Scituate," Henry says.

"You'd be surprised at what we do in Scituate," Ellen replies.

For some reason her comment seems like the funniest thing they've heard all night, even funnier than the joke about the beast. This time Henry joins in and their laughter rolls out across the field and into the woods, almost enough laughter to shake the leaves on the trees.

The next day Henry, his head pounding from last night's drink, takes Ellen's brother Edmund fishing. They leave before dawn, hook enough pan fish to make a hearty breakfast cooked over an open fire, catch sight of a skunk with five kits, and are back before lunch. He likes Edmund. When the boy is around Henry, he says little, doesn't complain, and concentrates at the task at hand. All of which Henry finds admirable, especially in a child.

In the afternoon, Henry and John set about building some benches for their new school. As they work, Henry says, "Ellen has changed, don't you think?"

"She's gotten older."

"Well obviously. But she's also quite pretty."

"She is."

"So you've noticed too."

John looks at him as if he's an imbecile. "How could I possibly not?"

For a moment now they must attend to their work. John holds the planks in place while Henry drives the nails. They are using yellow pine and the smell of the cut wood and the look of it in the sun is pleasing. They've always done joinery together and can turn out a bench or a table in short order. Their plan is to make most of the furniture they'll need for their school and even build the school itself if they can't find a place to rent.

Henry continues: "I should have gone out to the shadow play with them."

"Why didn't you?"

John was away last night, visiting a friend in Assabet Village. If he'd been at home he'd definitely have gone.

"I assumed they didn't want me."

"Don't be foolish. You didn't go because being around Ellen makes you nervous. You shouldn't be so shy."

Henry makes a harrumphing sound to indicate his displeasure. He knows he's shy but doesn't like to be reminded of the fact. He prefers to think he can remedy any shortcoming in his personality simply by force of will. Now, as they begin to clean up, his mind wanders back to other times he has been reticent or made himself unapproachable, usually with a girl. He's recalling one particularly painful incident during his college years when John interrupts.

"Before we open our school, we ought to take a little trip together and see some country," he says.

"We have work to do here," Henry replies. "Besides, where would we go?"

"I'd favor a boat trip. Just get in the river and head north." With the hammer, he indicates the direction he has in mind.

"We'd have to build a new boat. The one I made last year leaks something awful. But we ought not to leave until Ellen is gone."

"Of course," says John. "Not 'til Ellen is gone."

Henry hopes John isn't losing interest in the school. But he likes the idea of a trip. They could come back fresh and ready to start.

That evening all the young people sit outside—Henry,

John, Helen, and Sarah Thoreau, and Ellen and Edmund Sewall—and attempt to practice the currently popular art of phrenology. They designate a particular chair as "The Chair" and then each one takes a turn. Since Sarah is the youngest, she goes first.

"It won't hurt, will it?" she asks.

"*Sit*," Helen says.

John stands behind Sarah and plunges his fingertips into her hair. "How interesting. There's a prominent one here in the back and on this side, one shaped like a . . . well, like a parsnip."

Helen reads from a pamphlet by a man named Spurzheim. It tells how to interpret what they find. "The bump in the back means she likes to be praised," Helen says. "I see nothing here about parsnips, but apparently something in that location means she's quick tempered. And has the appetite of a bear."

"That tickles," Sarah says.

"It does?" says John. "What about here? And here?"

Soon she's giggling so hard she tumbles off the chair.

Helen is next, with Henry examining her and Ellen reading the pamphlet. If he is correct about what his fingers are feeling, Helen's bumps mean perseverance, self-control, and love of home.

"It makes me sound dull as dust," Helen says.

"It makes you sound perfect," Henry says. "Which we all know is far from the truth."

They try to get Edmund in the chair, but he refuses. "Knead my brain like a ball of dough? No sir," he says and then runs out into the field and watches from afar.

When it's Henry's turn to sit, Ellen steps up behind him. He shuts his eyes as she begins. Her fingertips move in slow circles across his skull. He feels himself blushing and when he opens his eyes, both John and Helen are studying him. They may have suspected he has feelings for Ellen but now they know for sure.

"Well, this is strange," Ellen says. "Henry's head is perfectly smooth. I can feel no ridges, no swellings, no bumps. Nothing at all. Does the book say anything about that?"

They all wait expectantly while Helen reads. "It says an absence of irregularities indicates the subject is either a genius or a cretin. But which one, it's impossible to tell."

Everyone laughs, including Henry, although in his case it's more from relief than delight. He couldn't have tolerated the feeling of Ellen's fingers moving through his hair for much longer. He's taken an interest in girls on occasion but he's not like some of the boys he knew at school who could think of nothing else. Yet now he is smitten. When she was touching him, he feared he might pass out. He wanted to stand up and take her in his arms.

That night in his journal he writes just one line: *There is no remedy for love but to love more.*

Over the next few days, Henry screws up his courage and arranges to be in Ellen's company every chance he gets. They go walking to Fairhaven Bay and to Walden Pond and then for a buggy ride with her grandmother and Aunt Prudence. Aunt Prudence uses the opportunity to tell Ellen how she went to hear a speech by William Lloyd Garrison at the Boston Women's Anti-Slavery Society:

"Would you believe that when he was done, a mob came after him and dragged him through the streets at the end of a rope. We watched it happen and could do nothing to prevent it. They released him but the poor man nearly died."

Henry knows why she's doing this. Ellen's father is a rather conservative minister and Aunt Prudence hopes Ellen will carry some abolitionist thoughts back to him. Both her grandmother and Aunt Prudence are great believers in the cause.

"Was his talk informative?" Ellen asks.

"Indeed it was. I have some of his newspaper writings in

my room. You may read them if you'd like."

Henry doesn't want to get between Aunt Prudence and Ellen's father, so he restricts his remarks to comments about the landscape. "When we get over this hill I'll show you a tree that was struck by lightning," he says.

The next day, he manages to take a walk with Ellen alone. According to a handbill he saw nailed to a fence, a camelopard will be on exhibit at a certain place by the river the following day. Ordinarily he'd have invited everyone in the house but right now all he cares about is her.

"There's something we should go take a look at. An animal I'll wager you've never seen."

She studies him, clearly considering his motives. She's not dim.

"You have to tell me what animal. Perhaps I have seen one. For all *you* know."

"Well, it's a camelopard. They look like—"

"I know what they look like."

He's afraid she's about to turn him down. But no, she grabs her shawl and says, "Come on then, let's go."

They step out into the cool June morning and Henry feels wonderful. Although there's a bit of fog, it's burning off fast. He keeps glancing over at Ellen, so pretty and right beside him. At one point their hands touch. Even after the amount of time he's spent with her this week he becomes tongue-tied in her presence. Still, he has resolved to be confident, so confident he is:

"John and I are thinking about taking a trip on the river . . ."

"He told me all about it. I wish I could come along."

If that's not flirting, he doesn't know what is. "I don't expect your father would approve."

"He'd fall over dead is what he'd do. But I still wish I could go."

As they walk, Henry takes the opportunity to show off his

knowledge of local flora and fauna. He alerts her to the song of the oriole, the smell of the huckleberry, a sparrow's nest with three eggs hidden in the tall grass, and the almost invisible tracks of a fox. She acts as if this is all news to her, yet she might be feigning ignorance. His hands hang at his side and feel too large, like pork chops or blocks of wood. He wishes he could simply ask what she thinks of him but suppose the answer is one he'd rather not hear?

And then they see it, from a long way off. It glides out from between two trees, its head atop a long, long, impossibly long neck, its body covered in a brown and gold mosaic, its legs carrying it with stately grace. They lurch to a stop as if they've reached the end of a rope, while in unison they gasp.

"I had no idea," Ellen says.

Henry shakes his head and whispers, "How wondrous it is."

The camelopard pauses to take a bite from the highest limb of a birch.

When they reach the river, they find a garishly painted wagon and crowd of perhaps twenty spectators, every head tilted back. As Henry and Ellen approach, a man with a cinnamon-colored mustache and a green top hat comes over and says if they want to stay and look, they need to pay two bits. Henry gives him the money and they find a place to stand.

Ordinarily one describes an animal in terms of another—a fox is like dog with a pointed nose and bushy tale; an osprey is like a hawk but larger. How then, to describe this? Like a goat with brown spots, the legs of a horse, and the neck . . . the neck of no other animal on earth. It gazes down on them with large sad eyes.

"My goodness," Ellen says. "The poor thing must get exhausted from holding its head up there all day."

Henry stares at it. He doesn't know what to say. On the way over, he'd been holding forth about the forest and fields and the creatures living there. He's always felt there is a sense and a symmetry to nature. All its various parts fit together and belong. Never before has he encountered a creature that appears not to be of this world. It makes him uneasy. He would say it's not natural, yet clearly it is part of nature. There it stands, there it breathes, it has legs and a body and a head. It has eyes with which to see.

"Do you suppose it can be ridden?" Ellen asks, but he fails to respond. She looks over at him, as if to make sure he's still there. "I think I should like to visit Africa if this is the sort of thing one finds there. Are you all right, Henry? You don't look well."

Henry continues to gape. The problem is the animal has been wrenched from its natural surroundings. A weasel pulling a bobolink into the tree is a fascinating sight, but weasels have been doing just that in the woods near Concord for a thousand thousand years. Whereas no camelopard has walked upon this meadow until today. If he had the money, he'd buy it a ticket on a sailing ship and send it back from whence it came.

"We ought to go home," he says.

"So soon? Are you afraid they'll talk about us?"

But Henry is so lost in thought he scarcely hears her words.

SOPHIA

"Elizabeth," Sophia says, "I've been thinking. Perhaps I'd like to see Mr. Hawthorne again. Would you invite him?"

"What? Even after you were rude?"

"I was unprepared for that visit. And I intend to apologize. As I told you, it was the rest of the family I disliked. If he wishes to read my journal, I'll allow it."

Sophia isn't sure why she's doing this. The idea just came to her. It has as much to do with the journal as with Mr. Hawthorne. She wants someone outside her family to read it, someone who will look upon it as a record of her experiences and observations rather than as a record of her symptoms. Someone who will judge it fairly. He is, after all, a writer.

"He may no longer be interested," Elizabeth says.

"Use your powers of persuasion. I've never seen them fail."

That same day, Mary comes to her room with news. "I expect Horace to propose to me very soon." Sophia has never seen her like this. Mary knows men find her attractive and therefore she has learned to be skeptical of their advances. But now her eyes glow and her skepticism is gone.

"Oh, Mary, that's wonderful. Are you certain?"

"I think so. Yes, I'm sure. All that remains is the asking. We have spoken of our future together."

Sophia always assumed Mary would be the first. And Horace Mann will be a good husband. He is accomplished, ambitious, and, having been all but destroyed by the death of his first wife, needs Mary as much as she needs him. He comes to Salem to see her often, almost every week. Mary is much more likely to be happy in marriage than either she or Elizabeth. Finding a husband who could keep pace with Elizabeth will be close to impossible, and as for herself, she considers art her true passion, one she's not willing to relinquish.

She's especially pleased Mary has achieved a good match because there have been times when Mary has accused her of making it difficult for her to do so. When Sophia was just thirteen, she went walking in the woods with Frank Dana and the next day in school everyone was talking. Although they'd done nothing wrong, Mary was mortified.

"People will think badly of us," she cried. "Don't you know that any gossip about you reflects on *me?*"

Even worse was what happened with the Alcott school. Back in Boston, Elizabeth helped Bronson Alcott set up his school and assisted him in teaching there. But they had a falling out, so Sophia took over her duties. Shortly thereafter, Alcott published a book about his methods which revealed the nature of the dialogues he had with children—dialogues which, in print at least, sounded highly inappropriate, focusing as they did on the physicality of male-female relationships and even the act of conception itself. When it was published, Boston society erupted, and Alcott found himself accused of blasphemy, obscenity, even outright insanity. Sophia had nothing whatsoever to do with the book but once again, Mary blamed her for damaging her reputation. This time Sophia argued back.

"Your good name is your own," she said. "If you tend to it properly, nothing I do will damage it." She wanted to add, *A girl with your looks doesn't need a good reputation. She has other ways of getting what she wants.*

"Alcott is such a strange fellow," Mary replied. "Perhaps he's the genius people say he is, but you and Elizabeth put too much stock in men's intellects. I don't know why you let yourself be associated with him."

"I was never *associated* with him. I worked at his school for a short time. And now his school is closed, so it's no longer a problem."

Looking back, it already seems like a small, rather forgettable episode. The voices of outrage diminished over time and Alcott landed on his feet. In any event, she's relieved Mary can now turn her attentions to Horace Mann and stop worrying about what she has to gain or lose by being a member of the Peabody clan.

As for Mr. Hawthorne, Elizabeth has invited him to come to tea. Sophia decides to make it a literary affair. She will inquire about his work. She will give him her Cuba journal to read and request advice about her style. In truth her literary ambitions don't run very deep, but it will give them something to discuss while they drink their tea.

"You're sure he won't be bringing the weird sisters with him . . . ?" Sophia says.

"You are a terrible person, but yes, I'm sure. I said I hoped *the three of us* could renew our old friendship, as we share an interest in the arts."

On the day of the event, Sophia, Elizabeth, and their mother scurry about making preparations. Though Sophia wants it to be informal, her mother takes over and turns it into something more. She cuts flowers from the garden, makes teacakes, and arranges the parlor as if they were expecting some well-known minister from Boston instead of a rather unsociable writer who lives only a few streets away. But at least this time Sophia is prepared.

When Hawthorne arrives, their mother answers the door and invites him in. He is wearing a dark brown coat, a wine-colored vest, and a cravat of gold and cream. Sophia looks to see if he's as handsome as she thought the first time and yes, indeed he is. His best feature is his thick, lustrous hair, and not far behind are his gray eyes. His brow is wide, giving him a look of dignity, not unlike Mr. Allston. Yet where Allston is imposing, Hawthorne appears reserved, as if his decorous manner functions as a shield.

"I brought this for you," he says. It's a book, the book he wrote, and he seems unsure who to give it to. At last, he hands it to their mother who thanks him, hands it off to Elizabeth and then, flustered, disappears. The idea of a book being given by the self-same author of the book as an arrival gift is too much for Mrs. Peabody to bear. Elizabeth deftly takes over and guides him to a chair by the fire.

He sits, back straight, his eyes focused on the wall.

"So good of you to come, Mr. Hawthorne," Elizabeth says. "Sophia and I have been looking forward to your visit."

"Thank you for inviting me. Since we met last I have been recalling my childhood. When you lived next door, one of you often helped your mother tend her flowers . . ."

"Oh, that was me," Elizabeth says, a little too eagerly. "I was quite a gardener. The hollyhocks were my favorite. The morning glories too."

"And do you garden now?"

"I'm afraid I've given it up," Elizabeth says and then proceeds to tell him all the things she does instead, from writing to teaching to raising money for the poor, such a list of good works that when she's finished, Hawthorne, overwhelmed, says only "How admirable" in reply.

After an awkward pause, Sophia takes her turn. "I understand you went to college in Maine." It's a sentence she'd worked out in advance.

"Indeed I did."

At that moment their mother appears with the tea. As she pours, she says, "Can I interest you in a slice of cake?" and then, "If you need anything else please tell me. I shall be in the next room."

As soon as she's gone, Sophia continues with her prepared inquiries: "How did you like Maine? Was it very cold?"

"It was cold on occasion. There was a good deal of snow."

Elizabeth is glaring at her. It's probably because Elizabeth thinks her social skills are lacking. Which they no doubt are.

90

"I saw you out walking last night," Sophia says. This is an unplanned sentence. She simply blurts it out.

Hawthorne looks taken aback. His lips twitch. His cup and saucer quake. When people go for solitary walks late at night, they usually don't want to be seen.

"I myself like walking in Salem," she adds, trying to undo her error. "Preferably by the sea."

There is a long pause. *Elizabeth, save me*, she thinks. But it's Hawthorne who speaks next: "Salem suits me. Its streets and alleyways are inscribed upon my brain."

Fortunately, their mother now returns, fusses about the cakes, which she insists aren't up to her standards, and says, "I overheard you talking about Salem. Sophia has settled in nicely. She stays upstairs all day and paints. Elizabeth insists on going back and forth between here and Boston. She has responsibilities there she cannot forsake."

After their mother is gone again, they exchange a few more pleasantries and Sophia decides to try to move the conversation toward an end. She can see how uncomfortable this is for him. While having tea it's not customary to reveal what's inscribed upon your brain. She wonders why he bothered to accept the invitation. Maybe he's taken an interest in Elizabeth. Maybe he has no other friends.

"The last time you visited, you said you might like to read the journal I kept in Cuba," she says. "When I wrote it I wasn't intending to share it with others, but you may read it if you wish."

His eyebrows go up. He glances at Elizabeth to see if she'll be offering an opinion about the matter, yet she remains silent.

"Yes, I would like that," he says.

Sophia excuses herself and goes up the stairs to fetch it. She's still not sure why she's doing this. It's not a simple travel journal of the kind young women often keep. Something came over her when she was in Cuba. She wrote about things she'd never imagined putting into words.

When she comes back down the stairs, Mr. Hawthorne is standing by the door.

"I would welcome any comments," she says, holding it out.

"I'm sure I shall have only praise."

Once the door is shut behind him, Elizabeth says, "Well. I wonder if you'll get it back."

"What do you mean?"

"I don't know. There's something almost spectral about him. I can imagine him disappearing and taking your journal with him." She smiles wryly.

"Oh, you're teasing."

"I do find him interesting, don't you?"

"If by interesting you mean peculiar, then yes," Sophia says. "Yes I do."

MARGARET

From Concord Margaret travels to see her mother and younger brothers, Richard and James, in Jamaica Plain, outside Boston. On her way, she thinks about Waldo's praise of her skills as a conversationalist. And then it comes to her that she ought to put into action the idea she had the night she heard Emerson speak. That is, rather than giving lectures as Waldo does, she should send out a notice inviting people to a series of *conversations*. She will not stand in a pulpit or upon a dais. She will sit amongst the attendees and engage them in artful talk.

Or perhaps not. She is confident in her knowledge, in her mastery of literature and philosophy, but she is not so confident in her ability to interact with others. Schoolgirls are a special case. They are, in a sense, in captivity. They are in the classroom involuntarily. While that presents its own set of problems, she never has to worry they'll simply walk out. Convincing people to attend lectures (or rather conversations) is like selling shoes. No one is required to buy a pair and if your customers decide the ones you're selling are badly made, they'll find another shop.

These days, Margaret is the primary support of her mother and siblings, so when she arrives in Jamaica Plain, she finds herself looking at the house with a proprietary eye. As the roof needs to be repaired or it will soon begin to leak, she arranges for a man to do the job. As the well needs to be repaired because the lining is collapsing, she arranges for a man to do the job. It wouldn't be this way if her father's estate hadn't gotten entangled and diluted. He had debts she and her mother didn't know about and his will was poorly made. If his passion for learning had included more interest in financial matters they'd be better off today.

In addition to making sure the members of the Fuller family are clothed and housed, she tries to play the parent when she can, especially for her youngest brother Joseph. During this stay he seems to be at loose ends, so she recruits him to serve as copyist for her translation of Eckermann. His work is error-ridden yet she doesn't feel she can be as harsh a taskmaster as her father was. Instead, by being gentle but firm, she helps him to improve. By the end of the month Joseph has begun to consider himself something of an expert on Goethe, and the manuscript is complete. She sends it off to Emerson and then begins worrying about what he'll think.

While waiting for him to respond, she goes to visit her friend Elizabeth Peabody and shares her idea: she would like to invite the women of Boston to meet with her at the Peabody bookshop on West Street. The purpose will be to discuss questions of great significance. They will sit and talk of morality and free will and reason and faith. They will read Plato and Horace, and when they get to Goethe, she will ask them to discuss one of her favorite lines: "Every creature has its own reason to be."

"I don't believe I've ever seen you so enthusiastic," Elizabeth says. "How much do you intend to charge?"

Margaret looks at her, astonished. "Charge? Do you think I should make them pay?"

"By all means. Why not? Your knowledge didn't come to you at birth. It came through long hours of study. You ought not to provide it for free. If you're successful, perhaps you could spare a little to support the shop. Book sales alone do not pay my bills."

They sit down and begin to scratch out figures: how many conversations, how many ladies can be accommodated at each one, should they offer refreshments, and how might the proceeds be divided?

"Tell me again what the purpose is," Elizabeth says, still sounding less than fully convinced. It's as if she admires Margaret's passion but isn't sure she'll follow through.

"If done well, the events I have in mind will provide a point of union for well-educated and thinking women in a city which, despite great pretension to mental refinement, offers nothing of the kind."

"A 'point of union,'" Elizabeth muses. "Now I understand."

Afterward, Margaret is full of energy. She walks up the street thinking about everything she'll have to do to make such conversations a success. As she turns the corner, she runs into Edna Dorset, another friend.

"I thought you had left Boston," Edna says.

"I was in Providence teaching but now I'm back. I'm living with my mother in Jamaica Plain."

"I was pleased to hear about James Clarke," Edna says. "I hear she's from Pennsylvania. Do you know when the wedding will take place?"

Margaret looks at Edna and blinks. She feels a cold bubble rising in her chest and numbly shakes her head. "He hasn't . . . I'm not sure . . . I don't believe they've set a date."

"He will be a fine husband. Of course, you're aware of that—you've known him for so long."

When they part, Margaret's eyes fill with tears. She turns down an empty side street so no one can see. Why didn't he tell her? A girl from Pennsylvania. He never mentioned Pennsylvania. They exchange letters about Goethe. They exchange letters about Coleridge. But not about this. Maybe he doesn't even think she cares. If so, then it's she who is to blame. She has no right to feel bereft. She should be happy for him. She hopes he takes his new bride to Kentucky and never returns.

Back at her mother's house there's a letter waiting for her. Perhaps it's from James. It will all turn out to be a misunderstanding. Edna Dorset must have heard wrong. But no, it's from her young friends Anna and Sam, the ones on the European tour. Margaret is thankful for the diversion. She heard from them a few times early on, then no more. They've probably gotten so involved with meeting new people and seeing new places that it's difficult to find time to write. She opens the letter and reads. Since their last one, from Paris, they have gone on to Florence. Sam, who is a fine artist, has included not just a description of the sights but some small sketches as well. Florence. The Duomo. The Palazzo Vecchio. Yet as she recalls that she was originally supposed to go with them, her delight changes to sadness. It's almost too painful to read. She wonders if she'll ever go to Europe. Certainly not on a teacher's salary. Certainly not when she has a house and relatives to maintain. One dismal morning she'll get out of bed and find she's gotten too old.

HENRY

On Ellen's last Saturday in Concord they all attend a dance. It's at the schoolhouse and everyone makes jokes about Henry returning to the place of his triumph—or ignominy depending on your point of view.

"I hope Henry doesn't cane us," Helen says.

"Maybe Nehemiah Ball will be there to judge how well we dance," adds John.

"You're all highly amusing," says Henry. He doesn't mind being teased. He's going to be spending the evening with Ellen and cares about nothing else.

All the desks and benches have been carried outside to clear the floor, and a pair of fiddlers from the nearby village of Acton are supplying the tunes. There is pie and cider on long tables and through the window can be seen an almost full moon, the color of freshest cream.

Henry is determined to steal a kiss, or better yet, have one offered to him. Over the last several days, he has spent as much time as possible with the lovely Ellen Sewall, and when she leaves on Monday he intends for her to be thinking of him all the way home. His focus on Ellen has been so consuming he and John have barely talked about the school they're starting or their boat trip. In fact, he's not even sure what John has been doing these past few days.

Henry doesn't consider himself much of a dancer, but the room is so packed with people it makes no difference. Everyone is shoulder-to-shoulder, everyone stomps and claps, they dance reels and jigs and hornpipes as the lamplight casts great swaying shadows on the walls, and when it gets too hot and crowded, the dancing spills outside. Each time he and Ellen touch, he's thrilled.

At last the musicians stop to rest and the dancers mingle and chat. Ellen stands next to him with John on her other side. Helen is off talking to some girls she knows and Sarah and Edmund are out chasing fireflies with other children their age.

"When do you think you'll come back to Concord?" John asks.

"Maybe instead you and Henry should come to Scituate," she replies. "We could go sailing. It's lots more fun than paddling around some pond."

"I would like that," says Henry. "I've sometimes thought of signing on with a ship and going off to see the world." That's not true but at the moment it seems like a good response.

"Then I shall expect it. I'll take you to see our lighthouse, which was once defended by two young girls during a British raid. As you have learned, the girls of Scituate are a rare breed."

After the dance, Henry has difficulty shaking free of his siblings, but as they walk home he and Ellen hang back. When the others have rounded the last corner and are no longer in sight, he gets his kiss, "Only because you were such a good host," she whispers.

That night he lies in bed and thinks about the strangeness, the unexpectedness of life. He thinks about the camelopard and how it looked unnatural while, upon closer examination, it was as natural as any beast. He thinks about the remarkable way the tortoise hides her eggs. He thinks about the language of birds. And he thinks about the past. A thousand years ago some young fellow his age was trying to get to sleep on the other side of the world, in India or China, and having thoughts not unlike the ones he's having now, thoughts that seem simultaneously prosaic and profound.

The next morning, everyone is getting ready to go to church when Ellen realizes Henry is staying home.

"You aren't going with us?" she asks. "Why ever not?"

He shakes his head. "You all enjoy yourselves. I'll see you

afterward." He'd like to explain why but it's difficult. Although he's no atheist, he gave up some time ago on preachers and the churches they inhabit.

"He won't change his mind," Helen explains. "I've tried."

Most weeks John doesn't go either; yet rather than stand on principle like Henry, he claims to be busy with some chore. Today, however, he combs his hair, puts on a clean shirt, and stands waiting by the door.

Henry can tell Ellen is concerned, even annoyed—"Oh, Henry, do come," she says—but he shakes his head. Back when he first started refusing to attend, his mother would get furious. Now she accepts it. "Don't be stubborn," John says, to no avail.

While they're gone he works on the boat he and John are building for their river trip. He takes a full half hour to sharpen the draw knife and then uses it to shape one of the long slats that will form the craft's sides. Soon big golden curls of wood litter the ground. Suddenly Sarah's laughter comes ringing through the trees. Is the service over already? How time passes when you're working with your hands.

Then, to his dismay, the day of Ellen's departure arrives. The whole Thoreau family, even their father, walks her and Edmund to the town center where the coach will stop. She thanks them all and says she'll give their regards to her parents and that she is already looking forward to coming back. She also reminds Henry and John of their promise to visit Scituate.

"This is the first I've heard of such plans," Helen says. "I expect an invitation as well."

"You should all come," Edmund says.

In anticipation of this moment, Henry has prepared some words to tell Ellen about how much he has come to care for her yet can't bring himself to say them now—not while the horses are prancing impatiently, and not in front of everyone else. He realizes he should have written them in a letter to slip into her bag. As the driver snaps the reins and the wheels begin to turn, Ellen looks back and Henry fancies her smile is meant only for him.

In the days that follow, Henry and John throw themselves into the twin tasks of getting their school ready and finishing their boat. Henry wonders if it's a mistake to take a trip so close to the opening of their school, but John's description of what the river will be like at this time of year is impossible to resist. Besides, they'll be back in two weeks.

The day before they are to leave, Henry finds John wrapping a package to mail. It hasn't been sealed up yet, so he can see what's inside: some Indian artifacts—arrowheads, a stone knife, a clay pot that's in pieces but can still be reassembled— and a large blue butterfly mounted on square of oak.

"Who's that for?" he asks, yet even before John can answer, he knows. They were walking in the woods with Ellen when they found the artifacts. She must have forgotten to take them with her when she left.

"They were on the back stairs," John says. He glances up at Henry. "And I happen to know she likes butterflies so I'm sending this too."

"I see. How good of you," Henry says. He watches as John inserts a letter into the package and ties it up with string. When he's done, Henry goes up to his room.

He sits on his bed, his mind blank. He doesn't know what to think. Slowly, he begins reviewing Ellen's time with them. It simply never occurred to him. As far as Henry can recall, John wasn't with Ellen except when they were all together in a group. He didn't take her to see the camelopard, and at the dance he was her partner only once or twice. He and John are close, but they seldom talk about girls. If John had a sweetheart when he was teaching in Taunton, he hasn't mentioned her. Surely, John is aware of Henry's feelings for Ellen, so maybe the package is merely a package. He'd like very much to read the letter John wrote. Right now he's rather confused.

CONCORD

The next morning is filled with preparations for their trip. For food they take potatoes, melons, a little bacon, some flour, and a couple of loaves of bread. It's not much but they can always pull out of the river and walk to a town for more. They're proud of the boat they've built. It's a fifteen-foot dory, painted blue and green, with two masts and sails, and two sets of oars. The hull they tarred with a mixture of tallow and resin, in a ratio of one to four. They even made a set of wheels so they can take it out of the water and roll it rather than carry it on their backs. When they stop at night, one of the masts can be removed and used as the center-pole of their tent. They christen it the *Musketaquid*, which is the Indian name for the Concord River. Every so often Henry thinks about the package John sent to Ellen. John should have asked if he wanted to include a letter or some small souvenir. If he hadn't walked in on him, he'd never have known the package existed—which may have been John's intent all along.

Their friends and family come to see them off. It's a gray, drizzly morning and for a time they stand under the trees wondering if they should postpone for a day. Their father is more talkative than usual: "Stow your money in the flour can or, better yet, hollow out a melon and stick it inside. If any rough-looking characters hale you from the bank, keep on paddling. Even if they wave and smile."

At last, the sun breaks through, and they say good-bye and push off. In less than a minute they round the bend and are out of sight. Their plan is to travel down the Concord River to the Merrimack and then continue on the Merrimack as far as they please. Maybe they'll do some hiking up in the north country. They've been telling everyone they'll be back in two weeks, but who knows? On either bank, beneath the willows, the rose-colored polygonum and the pure white arrowhead are in bloom. They startle a bittern; it shrieks and glides away on sluggish wings. At Ball's Hill they stop to pick berries. Then on they go until dusk when they pull out and pitch their tent. For supper they have bacon on bread with hot cocoa to drink.

While they were on the river, Henry chose not to say anything about Ellen. It wouldn't do to have an argument while confined to a boat. Now as they sit staring into their small campfire, their backs to the gathering darkness, he speaks:

"I'm going to miss Ellen," he says. "I suppose you will too."

"Yes indeed."

"If she lived in Concord, I would be quite pleased."

"Scituate isn't too far away."

A breeze blows through their camp and the flames bow down and then rise up as the breeze abates. "John, are you fond of her?" Henry asks. "I didn't think you paid her much attention. I have to ask because I saw that package and noticed the letter inside."

"I don't know what you mean. I was with her a great deal. One night we stayed up and talked until dawn."

Henry feels as if he's been punched. And yet he knows he has no more right to her affections than John has. He simply wasn't aware. "So I guess we're both fond of her."

"Yes," John pauses. "I guess we are."

At that moment they hear something moving nearby. They turn and see a large raccoon, its face illuminated by the fire. Neither of them moves as the raccoon inspects their campsite, offering a little half bark that could be either greeting or threat. John says, "Git now," but the animal ignores him. It sniffs and follows its nose toward their stash of food, its bushy tail flopping left and right. Henry gets to his feet and picks up a stick, which he starts waving in the raccoon's direction. Still, it stands its ground. "You there, begone," he says, but the raccoon refuses to depart. Not only that, it snarls. At last Henry draws himself up and shouts, "*Sed convivatoris, uti ducis, ingenium res Adversae nudare solent, celare secundae.*" That does it. The raccoon turns, throws a Henry backward glance, and ambles off into the woods.

"What was that?" asks John. "I didn't recognize it."

"Horace. It was all I could think of: 'Adversity discloses talents that prosperity conceals.'"

"Ah. Very fitting," he says.

They don't return to their discussion about Ellen Sewall. Instead, they sit looking into the fire, each lost in his own thoughts. After a while, John says good night and goes into the tent, but Henry remains outside until only glowing coals remain.

SOPHIA

Sophia has found the book Hawthorne gave to her mother and takes it up to her room. She's curious about what someone like him would write. He said they were old stories but that doesn't tell her much—old stories about what? She lights a lamp and lies down on the bed to read. The title isn't very intriguing—*Twice-Told Tales*. If she saw it in a shop, she wouldn't pick it up.

The first story opens with a festival of some kind—no, not a festival, a wedding celebration. They're dancing around a maypole. The people seem happy and innocent, almost like forest nymphs. Yet she has the feeling something darker is coming. And yes, before she's read many more pages it arrives—in the form of the Puritan John Endicott, who, she knows from growing up in Salem, liked to cut off people's ears for religious offenses. Or bore holes in their tongues with red-hot wires. She reads on. In this story the offenders get off easy. They're whipped and have their hair cut, but it's alarming nonetheless.

She looks up from the page. This is not what she was expecting. She's never read anything quite like it. But picturing Mr. Hawthorne now, his aloof, forbidding gaze, perhaps she shouldn't be surprised.

The next one is even stranger. A traveler in search of a place to stay the night knocks on the door of a house on a mountainside and is invited in. He is talking about his plans and ambitions when, without warning, an avalanche comes cascading down and all inside the house die, crushed beneath tons of stone. *Down came the whole side of the mountain, in a cataract of ruin . . . Their bodies were never found.* My goodness, Sophia thinks, what kind of man would write such a thing? She's not one to ponder death, at least she tries not to. Although she and her sisters lost their brother George to illness, it wasn't sudden. He was bedridden for months and in the end it seemed a blessing for him to be released from pain. But to be healthy and looking toward the future, only to have your life obliterated—if Mr. Hawthorne's goal is to shock, he's accomplished that.

The third story she reads is the most peculiar of all. A minister, a Mr. Hooper, one day dons a black veil and thereafter wears it morning and night. No one knows why. He won't even tell his betrothed. Did he commit some terrible sin and does he fear his face will make the sin's nature evident? Of course, they can't marry now, not if he insists on living his life behind a black veil. He appears to be an otherwise good man, but even on his deathbed he refuses to take it off.

Sophia has no idea what the meaning of the story is. There's something horrifying about a man who obscures his face, whether behind a mask or a veil, especially when he will remove it for no one and for no reason. The final sentences make her shiver, but she feels compelled to read them a second time and then once more:

Still veiled, they laid him in his coffin, and a veiled corpse they bore him to the grave. The grass of many years has sprung up and withered on that grave, the burial-stone is moss-grown, and good Mr. Hooper's face is dust; but awful is still the thought, that it mouldered beneath the Black Veil!

She sets the book aside, partly alarmed, partly annoyed. But also intrigued. She cannot think of a time when something she's read has so troubled her. "Awful is still the thought" indeed. She's afraid she'll be unable to sleep.

The next morning, she goes in search of Elizabeth. "His stories—you didn't warn me—they're very . . . singular," she says.

"Quite so. Like visions. I told you I went looking for the author of the book because I was so taken by it."

"Now I see why. I'm not sure I understood them."

"I'm not sure they're meant to be understood—at least not every aspect and not on a single reading."

"Do you think they are a true reflection of him? Are his beliefs as morbid as his stories?"

"Perhaps not. Think of the painting of Allston's you copied—the one with the crows. I do not think Allston's character or ideals are on view in that painting. A work of art need not mirror its maker."

Of course Elizabeth is right. Still, the stories are exceedingly strange. Each new one she reads offers fresh possibilities for nightmares. Yet they are told as if they actually occurred.

The next day Elizabeth returns to Boston. And Mr. Mann seems to have all but relocated to Salem, so Mary is occupied as well. With no one to talk to, Sophia remains in her room, working on her paintings, continuing to read Hawthorne's tales, and looking out at the treetops and the sky. She wonders if he's reading her journal and what he thinks about it. Maybe she shouldn't have given it to him. It could make her look shameless, possibly even indecent—but only if he's looking for such things. Isn't that what they say—that readers find in books what they *want* to find, whether the author has put it there or not?

That evening before supper her mother hands her a note. "This was left for you," she says. Sophia opens it and reads: "I am finished with your journal. It would give me great pleasure to discuss it with you. Please inform me of how this might be accomplished. I do not wish to intrude. Respectfully yours, Nathaniel Hawthorne."

She looks up from the note, thinking, "I'll let Elizabeth manage the arrangements, she'll do it better than I." But before the thought is complete, she remembers that Elizabeth has returned to Boston and won't be back for at least two weeks. That means she alone will have to figure out what to do. A feeling of dread comes over her. It's one thing to have Elizabeth bring her peculiar friends around and insist Sophia and Mary meet them; it's quite another to have to deal with them on her own.

MARGARET

She advertises her conversations by placing a sign in the window of Elizabeth Peabody's shop. Margaret knows all three of the Peabody sisters—busy, dynamic Elizabeth, lovely, self-centered Mary, and artistic but reclusive Sophia who drew some of the pictures that adorn the walls of the shop. Lately, she has heard that Mary is being courted by Horace Mann, whom everyone expects to do great things one day. Margaret sometimes wishes she were the fourth sister. How comforting it would be to have such talented siblings to support you and take an interest in you and perhaps correct you when you set off down a path all except you can see is a mistake.

Yet one can find comradeship outside one's family. Since her visit to Concord, she and Emerson have corresponded on a regular basis. Waldo says he wants her to come back and stay longer and give him lessons in German, especially proper pronunciation. They exchange manuscripts and she tells him bits of Boston news.

It's good she has Waldo to write to because she has ceased corresponding with James Clarke. Sending letters to a man who is soon to be married seems inadvisable, even if your relationship with him has never been less than chaste. It's a tragedy, because she used to be able to ask him anything. Last year, just after he moved to Kentucky, she discovered that Goethe, her intellectual idol, a man whose works she has spent countless hours translating, cohabited with his mistress for years and had several children with her while they were living in sin. Margaret was stunned. In her eyes Goethe was not only brilliant but morally pure, and now she had discovered otherwise. It's true that in his writings he values love over convention, but she had no idea he was *acting* on that belief. The only person with whom she felt comfortable discussing the matter was James.

As soon as she informed him he wrote back saying he'd suspected as much but hadn't wanted to upset her. Her reply? *What then should I do?* Should she stop reading Goethe? Should she abandon her thoughts of someday writing a biography of him? James wrote back:

We know very little about the ancients. Some may have been less than admirable or even downright villains, and yet we still admire their contributions to our culture. The same may be said of Goethe. We have learned about his actions but not their cause. We can never see into the hearts of others. Only into our own.

She replied: *Does this mean there are no absolutes?*

Again he wrote back, *For yourself, for your own life, your understandings and beliefs are absolute. That must be enough.*

Now she ponders that exchange. Was it about more than Goethe? Was he saying each person is a law unto themselves and that everything else is impermanent and malleable? At that time, had he already met the girl from Pennsylvania? Margaret wonders if James and his new wife will share the kind of intellectual intimacy she had with him. Is such intimacy common in marriage? She doesn't see much of it between Waldo and Lidian. She certainly does not think they discuss Goethe's moral failings at their supper table. But perhaps she is wrong. Just then she pictures Waldo and Lidian together in a manner most inappropriate for her to consider. She blushes. There must be physical intimacy, otherwise how did Waldo Minor come to be? The problem is that the intellectual and the physical ought not to be at odds with one another, though they often are. If James Clarke had come back to Massachusetts and by some strange twist had ended up with her instead of the girl in Pennsylvania, could their minds and bodies have become one?

From Elizabeth Peabody, Margaret hears that a well-known scholar from Germany, Dr. Francis Leiber, will be visiting Boston. She writes him a letter, hoping it will reach him before he leaves Heidelberg. Fortunately, it does. He replies and agrees to meet with her. He knew Goethe personally. She can't afford a trip to Europe but perhaps she can gain some insights into the great man by talking with someone who was a colleague before his death.

They meet at Elizabeth's shop. Dr. Leiber is very much as she expects him to be. Graying, a bit corpulent, with a monocle and a cane. But when Elizabeth introduces her to him, he says, "I thought you were a . . . a gentleman. However, I see you are not."

Margaret gets flustered. It's her fault. She signed her letter "S. M. Fuller" so there's no way he would know. She tries to make light of it. "How amusing. I suppose it's my handwriting—a clumsy, masculine scrawl."

He shakes his head and looks at Elizabeth. "I thought I was meeting a gentleman," he says again, and suddenly Margaret can see he has no intention of speaking with her now. She looks helplessly at Elizabeth. He must smoke a different sort of tobacco from that found in America—there's a bitter smell in the air.

"Let me leave you two alone to converse," Elizabeth says. Margaret's not sure if she thinks that will help or just wants to escape. She hopes it's not the latter. To be honest, she doesn't want to be left by herself.

But Leiber won't allow it. "I am extremely busy," he says. "I must go." Then, at the door, he turns. "I give lecture tonight. Please attend." And then he's gone.

"Oh Margaret, I'm so sorry," Elizabeth says. "I don't know how he could have misunderstood. Germans can be rather abrupt."

Margaret goes to the door, almost as if she intends to

follow him and then comes back across the room, feeling ready to erupt. She says, "He didn't even give me a chance." If anyone should know what it's like to be overlooked like this, it's Elizabeth, though even to one another they don't know what to say. Margaret is embarrassed and hurt and outraged. She has confidence in her intellectual abilities but what good are they if her attempts to use them are thwarted. She fears she will die and leave no trace.

As if she has heard her thoughts, Elizabeth says, "You have a great deal to offer. There is no one else I expect to go further in life."

Margaret just shakes her head.

A few days later, when she is back in Jamaica Plain, redemption arrives, in the form of a letter from Waldo. He is done reading her manuscript. It is *intelligent*. It is *clear* and *expressive*. It presents Goethe's thought *as it is* rather than as some wish it to be. The preface alone is *brilliant*. When it is published, it will *surely be noticed*. She reads it again and again. She goes walking in the forest, but it feels like more than walking. She is gliding, dancing (her preface alone is *brilliant*), exhilarated and breathless with joy.

HENRY

Their second morning on the river they awaken to fog. The trees drip and they can't see the opposite bank. After a cold breakfast they shove off and are instantly enveloped. But before they have rowed many rods, the August sun rises, the fog disperses, and the day turns bright and hot. They pass a man on the shore, fishing with a long birch pole, a dog at his side. They pass Billerica Falls and, a little further on, turn into the Middlesex Canal. There's a well-trodden towpath, so they get out of the boat and pull it along with a rope, making better time than if they rowed.

They encounter a family dressed for church and Henry greets them, but the father only frowns and hurries his children past them. "In that fellow's eyes, we're going in the wrong direction," John says.

"That fellow is envious," Henry replies.

Just before noon they reach the locks that can lower them to the Merrimack. According to the rules of the locks, a small boat like theirs isn't allowed, but the lock keeper shrugs and lets them proceed. They have a lunch of bread and cheese and melon, then continue to float downstream.

Although it's turned into a fine day, Henry is having difficultly enjoying it. He can't get last night's conversation out of his head. John said he'd been with Ellen "a great deal." It sounded almost like a boast. Henry is beginning to wish he hadn't invited him back to Concord to start the school. Yet what has happened with Ellen isn't something he could have predicted. They've both known her for years, for as long as her grandmother and aunt have been boarders. Yet this time she was so different. Part of him wants to talk more about the matter but part of him fears what John will say.

CONCORD

In the afternoon they pass Wicasuck Island and then stop
near Tyngsborough for the night. They finish erecting their tent
just as it begins to rain. John is asleep in minutes, his breathing
deep and even. This infuriates Henry because he knows he
won't get to sleep for hours. He will think and worry and
wonder what Ellen is doing tonight and analyze everything he
said or did during the past few weeks.

The next day they continue on. They see dozens of
waterfowl and watch an eagle pluck a fish from the river only
a few boat lengths ahead. Occasionally one of them gets out
and walks along the bank and when they pass canal boats, they
chat with the men on board.

"Where're ya headed?" asks one fellow with a beard that
nearly reaches his waist. His boat must be twenty yards long.
It's laden with new sawn lumber and bundles of shingles from
a mill.

"Wherever the river takes us," Henry says.

He scratches his head. "For what purpose?"

"For no purpose. To leave purpose behind."

This infuriates the boatman. He begins to swear, picks up
a chunk of wood and throws it at Henry, but his missile falls
short.

Eventually, Henry begins to feel expansive. There's nothing
he can do about Ellen Sewall so why not enjoy the trip? This is
time out of time, just the two of them and the river, which takes
them further from Concord every hour. At one point they have
to go around a falls, so they try out the boat's wheels. Working
as intended, the wheels allow them to make what could have
been an arduous portage with relative ease.

Two days more and they are into New Hampshire. After
some uncertainty about what to do next, they leave their boat
with a farmer below the Hookset Falls. From there they take a
coach to Franconia and go walking into the White Mountains.
They follow along a rushing brook, bordered on one side by

113

a precipitous bank and on the other by a gentle slope. The further they go, the wilder the brook becomes. At last, they emerge from the trees onto a mountainside of bare and broken rock. Upon reaching the summit of Mount Washington, Henry says, "I'm glad we did this, John. When we're old, we'll look back and say, 'Remember that time we went up north to have a look around?'"

"Suppose we keep going? We could get a piece of land somewhere and farm it. We could even go into Canada and see what it's like up there."

"We could," Henry says, but he doesn't mean it. When he was a boy he found stories about those who picked up and went north or west disconcerting. As far as he could tell, they did so because they had no choice. They'd gone broke or fallen out with their family and needed to start somewhere new. But he is not destitute and he likes his parents and his siblings. He might not be happy with John at the present time, but he doesn't expect that to last. If their school isn't a success and he has to leave Concord for work, he'd prefer not to go too far.

"I'm serious," John says. "There's no rule says you have to spend your whole life where you were born."

Henry looks off across the landscape, the endless waves of hills. "But what about our school?"

"Well, all right. After we try the school. Maybe in two or three years."

The day they reclaim their boat, the weather changes. They go to bed in summer and awake in fall. A cold wind is blowing and they can feel the coming frost. From the farmer who kept their boat they buy a watermelon, having concluded that having some ballast helps. "We should change its name to *The Melon Hauler*," says John.

On the return trip, John is all for getting home as rapidly as possible, but Henry insists they make a few stops. At one point they pull out and go into Chelmsford where they purchase an

114

apple pie. As they sit on a bench in the town square and eat, Henry says, "When we get back, we'll need to see if we can locate a few more students. Sixteen would be ideal. Although if we could get twenty, we could pay ourselves more."

John looks at his half of the pie. Henry's is already gone but his has scarcely been touched. "As soon as we get back, I need to make a short trip," he says.

"A trip? Where to?"

"I promised Ellen I'd go up to Scituate. Just for a few days. Then I'll come back and be ready to help."

Henry is without words. He lowers his eyes and studies the remaining scraps of crust. He takes a deep breath and blows it out with force. "For what purpose," he asks at last. He realizes he's just repeated the question the boatman asked him and now feels sorry for having given the old fellow an impertinent response.

"For a friendly visit, nothing more."

"She invited us both . . ."

"I didn't know you cared for her so much. I didn't know about you and you didn't know about me."

For the first time Henry can remember, he'd like to punch his brother in the nose. They tussled when they were boys, but he always looked up to John and they've never had a serious fight. If he'd had the same conversation with Ellen—and why didn't he?—he'd be planning a trip there as well. For a moment he considers inviting himself along but he's sure John doesn't want that and he's not about to beg.

"We ought to get going," he says.

Maybe it's because the wind is behind them or maybe it's because now all Henry wants to do is row; in any event, they cover close to fifty miles each of the last two days—while speaking hardly at all.

SOPHIA

After receiving Mr. Hawthorne's note requesting a meeting, Sophia secured Mary's assurance that she would be there to help, and then penned a reply, inviting him for tea two days hence. She felt she had to, if for no other reason than to get her journal back. What will they discuss? He may have things he wants to tell her about her journal, but she's not sure what she can say about his tales that won't be offensive. The word that seems most accurate is *disturbing*. She gives his book to Mary; she reads just one story before tossing it aside.

"How unpleasant. Are they all like this? Much too dark and strange for me."

"Then can you think of something else we can talk about?"

"Of course. He lives with his mother and sisters. I'll inquire about them."

"Have you seen his mother and sisters recently? They too might be described as dark and strange."

Mary shrugs. "All the better. One's peculiar relatives are an excellent topic for conversation. Surely you know that by now."

She resolves to let Mary do most of the talking. She's quicker on her feet. But when the time comes for his visit, Mary and her mother are out with Horace and late getting home. They were supposed to be back at two and now they're half an hour late, with Mr. Hawthorne set to arrive at three. She knows what happened. Their mother is very taken with Mr. Mann, so when he's around, she becomes almost giddy. And he indulges Mary, purchasing things for her and even for their mother they couldn't otherwise afford. No doubt the three of them are in a shop somewhere, thinking of nothing but picking out hats.

She paces and checks the teakettle and smoothes the cushions on the chairs. She looks out the window, hoping to see Mary coming up the street. The street is empty. And it remains so until she sees Mr. Hawthorne round the corner and stride purposefully toward the house, his brow furrowed, as if he's having the deepest of thoughts.

When his knock comes, she takes a moment to collect herself. Then, no other options left, she opens the door.

"Miss Peabody," he says, and she invites him in.

For the next several minutes she calms herself by attending to his cape (black and dashing), showing him to a chair, and escaping into the kitchen to check the kettle. When she returns, he has her journal sitting squarely, almost ceremonially, on his knees.

"I don't intend to take much of your time," he says. "But since you allowed me to read it—or rather since you were forced into doing so by your sister—I didn't want to simply leave it on your doorstep or send it through the post."

So he's aware of Elizabeth's meddling. "That's good of you," she says.

"It's a very . . ." He looks up. "I'm sorry, should I begin?"

She thought they'd have tea first, but she nods. Better to get it over with. If he found her journal detestable, she can skip the tea and send him home.

"It's a remarkable account. Your perceptions are quite fine. I'm not surprised you're a painter."

"My purpose in writing it was to preserve my thoughts and experiences for the future. So I could go back and be reminded of how things were. It's now been ten years since I was there. I was just a girl."

"I found it to be an excellent chronicle—vivid and engrossing. I have traveled only as far as Maine but now I feel as if I have visited Cuba, or at least the wonderful parts you describe."

"I'm so glad. I was afraid you'd think it childish . . ."

"It is true that there is a child-like charm to your enthusiasm. But child-like is different from child-*ish*. I take the first to mean a point-of-view that is innocent but not simpleminded. I take the second to mean foolish."

She feels herself blushing—she didn't expect him to have so much to say. "The tea," she says and goes to the kitchen. While she's there, she steps out the side door for a moment to get some air. Still no Mary and Mother. Back inside, she sets the tray and then carries it into the parlor. He looks as uneasy as ever. She has yet to see him smile.

As Sophia pours, it occurs to her she needn't go any further. They could exchange half an hour of small talk and say good-bye. But she really is curious about his stories. Especially the one about the avalanche. The poor traveler did nothing to deserve his tragic fate. And the one about the minister. Actually, all of them.

She takes her own seat, sips her tea, and says, "I read your book as well."

"Did you?"

"Yes. I don't know quite what to say. Would you be offended if I called it . . . strange?"

"I would not. I would be offended if you called it ordinary."

"Oh, it is by no means ordinary. You said they're tales you heard in your travels. I know a number of well-traveled people and they do not seem to have heard such stories. Perhaps you have an ear for the uncanny."

She didn't mean it in a humorous way but for the first time she thinks the corner of his mouth wants to go up. Of course, he puts a stop to it.

"It seems to me the world is full of the uncanny. Yet most prefer not to be made aware of it. They avert their eyes. They shut their ears. Suppose you are alone in an old house and you hear a noise in another room. Do you say to yourself, 'That was only the wind?' Or do you—"

Suddenly there's a commotion at the door. It's Mary and Horace and Mother arriving at last, just in time to prevent the conversation from becoming excessively intimate. She thought she wanted to know where his stories came from but perhaps it's better to let him keep his secrets. And, as Elizabeth pointed out, what he writes may not be a reflection of who he is.

It turns out Hawthorne and Horace have met before, and they chat for a moment while Mary and Mother put their parcels aside. It's just as Sophia suspected—they were looking at hats and yard goods and lost track of the time.

"I'm *so sorry*," Mary whispers. "Are you surviving? I kept telling them we needed to hurry but you know how Mother is. I should have left them behind."

"It hasn't been as bad as I feared," Sophia says.

Mr. Hawthorne takes advantage of their arrival to make his escape. There is clearly a limit to how sociable he can be. Yet Sophia didn't find their meeting as uncomfortable as she expected and doesn't think he did either. The next day she receives a note of thanks from him—more than a note, in fact. In it, he tells her how much he enjoyed their conversation, how flattered he was by her comments about his book and asks if she would consider going walking with him some afternoon.

MARGARET

Margaret schedules her first Conversation for Wednesday morning so those from out of town can stay on for an evening lecture Mr. Emerson will be giving at the Masonic Hall. Her subscribers include former students, the wife of the mayor, the wife of the president of Harvard College, George Bancroft's wife Elizabeth, bright young Cary Sturgis, Horace Greeley's wife Mary (up from New York), and Sarah Clarke, the sister of her friend (if she can still call him that) James—twenty-five in all.

She arrives early to help Elizabeth prepare the shop for the event. They carry as many things as they can into the back room to make space for all the borrowed chairs.

"Thank you for the use of your shop," Margaret says. "I can think of no better place."

Elizabeth looks out toward where the audience will soon be. "I don't believe I'd be brave enough to speak before such a group. But I'm sure you'll do quite well."

"I appreciate your confidence. Whether it is well-placed or not, we shall see."

When the guests begin to arrive, Elizabeth, in her role as proprietress, stands at the door and greets them, while Margaret remains off to the side gathering her wits. She hopes her voice doesn't tremble. She wishes there was a mirror handy so she could inspect her hair.

Once everyone is seated, Margaret thanks them for coming, takes a calming breath, and speaks:

"Our purpose today is to begin a conversation about questions of great importance. Not a conversation about daily life but a conversation about eternity. With the understanding that daily life and eternity are not as separate as they seem."

After a few more sentences, she pauses to survey her audience. To her surprise, the women are looking at her as if she is a seer. "Tell us, Margaret," their eyes say. Is it the setting? Is it her tone? It makes her a bit uneasy, so she smiles gently to soften the effect. "To reach our ends, we must work together," she continues. "Therefore, I will be expecting each of you to join in our discussion, to contribute and not sit mute. Only through a genuine exchange of thoughts can we reach our goal."

Now they look stricken, even terrified. They had come expecting her to hold forth. When she sat down in a chair instead of standing at a lectern, they may have begun to sense this was going to be something different, but now she has made it clear. They are to *participate*. And worse yet, it is too late to escape.

The topic this morning is Greek Mythology. Not just as an historic relic, but as a means of guiding one's life in the present day. They know the names Apollo and Hera and Pysche but perhaps they think they are merely characters in some ancient tales. No, according to Margaret, they can serve as models, to emulate and critique.

At first the ladies remain stubbornly reticent. Then, after she tells the story of Cupid and Psyche, a few brave ones begin to speak:

"Venus is the goddess of beauty. How can she be jealous of Psyche?" asks Jane Tuckerman. Although her voice quakes a bit, Margaret's expression is so approving Cary Sturgis joins in:

"Why does Psyche trust Cupid when he comes to her at night? Can you imagine? I most certainly would not." Cary is a friend of Margaret's so she's not afraid to be bold. Her comment elicits some laughter, which Margaret is thankful for.

"You say we should not view them as characters in a story. Does that mean we should view them instead as aspects of human nature?" ventures Hannah Shaw.

Margaret nods with enthusiasm. "Please say more about that, Hannah. What aspects of human nature does this tale represent?"

As a rule, good wives say little in public, at least not about matters of substance, and unmarried women say even less. In Margaret's view it is not because they cannot or do not wish to; rather it's that they haven't been given the opportunity. It appears she is correct.

A little later Eliza Fitch wonders aloud if it's appropriate for Christians to look to a heathen literature and culture for inspiration. Margaret explains that they are not setting one against the other—they are simply considering how the Greeks can inform their Christianity (which is self-evidently superior). Everyone breathes a sigh of relief. Even the prudish Mrs. Quincy seems satisfied—although that's partly because she can't tell when Margaret is being sarcastic. It is among Margaret's gifts—those who are ready to think more adventurously can follow along and those who are not can remain behind without feeling left out.

"I'd like us to discuss Psyche and Cupid a little more," says Cary. "The feminine, the masculine, and most especially, love."

Margaret raises an eyebrow. "I think Cary is guiding us toward our next discussion. I hope you're as curious as I am about where we shall end up."

When Margaret says it's time to stop, they're surprised. When, in any of their lives, has two hours gone by so fast? Even after she leaves her seat some of them continue talking with one another. In the end Elizabeth has to all but shoo them toward the door.

"My goodness," Margaret hears one of them say, "that was

quite satisfying," and another, "I can't wait until next week."

"You have such a talent for talk," says Elizabeth when it's just the two of them again. "They all came here thinking they were going to have a glass of cold tea and hear a few diverting remarks. But by the time they departed, they'd been positively transformed."

"You're embarrassing me. I treated them like my students—who I don't allow to be self-effacing. They must stand on their own feet—and express their own ideas. I only hope I didn't frighten them. Some looked overwhelmed."

"I think they *liked* feeling overwhelmed," Elizabeth says. "Indeed, this may be the first time some of them have had such a feeling. In matters of the intellect, they lead rather cosseted lives."

That night at Mr. Emerson's speech, Margaret sees a good number of the women who attended her Conversation. To her surprise she seems already to be something of a celebrity. She notices herself being pointed out and remarked upon. Some of the less timid women approach and tell her how much they enjoyed the morning. They even ask if, when they come to the next one, they can bring a friend. She's glad she took care with what she's wearing. Then again, she always does. She tries hard to look her best without spending too much on clothes. She's taught herself the art of making a plain dress look striking with the addition of a bit of brightly colored ribbon or an inexpensive brooch.

Mr. Emerson is speaking on "The Present Age," a misleading title because Margaret knows from her correspondence with him that he'll be talking mostly about literature. He has come to believe that there are three kinds of literature, the moral, the imaginative, and the scientific, and that their significance and value should be ranked in that order. More importantly, he says that each individual may make his or her own judgment on history and literature and not bow down before the beliefs of others, even if those others are powerful or wealthy or in positions of authority. When he says this, a ripple of whispered concern courses through the audience. Should one really be allowed to make one's own sense of a book?

As she listens she decides she wants to go back to Concord in the spring, when her Conversations are over. In his letters, Waldo has encouraged her to do so but so far she has declined. His invitations have confirmed what Lidian told her about his vision of Concord as a sort of American Athens, a place where poets and philosophers and artists might gather and live and read and write and learn from one another. It's a lovely idea and she almost believes it's possible. But if it did happen, she's not certain she'd like it. She'd prefer to have Waldo to herself.

Nor does she think Concord, as lovely and congenial as it is, could hold her interest for long. She wants to travel. She may not have the money now, but she will someday. She intends to put a little of whatever she manages to make from her Conversations aside for that very purpose. Imagine visiting the places Goethe lived. She feels a brief pang of jealousy about her friends Anna and Sam, then puts it out of mind.

When the lecture is over and Emerson's admirers have dispersed, he finds her at the back of the hall.

"How did you like it?" he asks.

"Very well. I found myself agreeing with half of what you said and disputing the other half—precisely what I've come to expect."

"I'm relieved. In truth I'm relieved whenever the audience doesn't rise up and attack."

She laughs. He has such presence. She wants to make another comment about his speech, but before she can form the words, he says, "I've been told your meeting at the Peabody's shop was exceptional. If I hadn't had this lecture to prepare, I would have been there myself."

"That wouldn't have been possible. Men were not invited." She's partly serious and partly joking. If he'd asked, she might have let him attend, but part of what made this morning so successful was that the ladies in her audience weren't waiting for their husbands to hold forth.

"Not invited?" he says, as if he's somehow misheard.

"Just so. Excluded by design."

He nods, although she can't tell whether it's to show he approves or only comprehends. "If I'm not allowed to attend, then I guess you'll have to come to Concord again," he says. "There's no one I'd rather have visit. Stay as long as you like."

No one? Can he really mean it? She finds his attention thrilling. She feels her face getting hot.

"Perhaps I shall," she says, doing her best to remain calm.

By now the hall is nearly empty. "May I offer you a ride to your lodgings?" he asks. His voice is cool and direct as always, yet if she doesn't end this quickly she fears she might faint.

"No thank you. But I'll write soon." Then she turns and hurries out into a humid August night.

HENRY

Henry fumes. John has done it, gone off to visit Ellen Sewell in Scituate. She was delighted to hear he could come so soon. Or so he says. Now Henry doesn't know what to do with himself. He walks and walks and walks. He should be readying the schoolroom but he's too distracted. Maybe he should have heeded his mother's advice and found a job somewhere other than Concord. Then he wouldn't have invited John back and neither of them would have been present during Ellen's visit.

To take his mind off John and Ellen, he works extra hard at the pencil factory and, as he works, he begins to wonder why the pencils his father makes, in fact why all the pencils made in America, seem so inferior to the pencils from Germany. German pencils make a clean black line while those from America crumble and smear.

One morning he gets up before dawn and walks the eighteen miles to Cambridge. He goes to the Harvard Library where old white-whiskered Mr. Armitage looks up from his desk, peers at Henry for a moment over the top of his spectacles, and says, "You again?" even though it's been over a year. Henry starts to explain that although he's no longer enrolled, he wishes to be admitted to the stacks, but before he can speak two words, Armitage waves him through.

Once he's among the books, a feeling of tranquility washes over him. He is so at home here. He begins to search for any information about the manufacture of pencils, especially in Germany. He tries not to be distracted, although there is so, so very much to be distracted by. He quickly finds plenty of German books about philosophy and poetry and history but not one about the arts of industry. Yet he is undeterred. Henry

126

spends the entire morning pulling down volume after volume, carrying them to a table, and examining them one-by-one. How, he wonders, might he get a job like the one Armitage has? The sunlight streams in the window and the golden wood of the tabletop glows.

His first introduction to Emerson's writing happened at this exact spot. He'd heard about his book *Nature* and came here to read it. He did not think it a work of genius. But he did find it interesting, and now that he's had the opportunity to talk with its author, he would like to read it again. Although not this morning. If he started, he wouldn't finish until closing time and his questions about pencils would remain unanswered.

He continues his search until finally, in mid-afternoon, he comes upon an item in a Scottish Encyclopedia that tells him what he wants to know. He should have guessed—the Germans mix their plumbago not with wax and glue but with clay, which they then bake. Naturally they end up with a harder substance that does not crumble or smear. The article even names the type of Bavarian clay they use. It probably can't be gotten in America, but maybe there's something similar. No doubt baking is key.

He takes two pages of notes, thinking wryly of the fact that he's writing about his father's pencils with one of his father's pencils, then folds the paper, tucks it in his pocket, and bids Mr. Armitage good-bye. As he walks back toward Concord in the gathering dusk, he realizes he thought not once of John and Ellen during his time at the library—a welcome respite—but now they trouble him the entire way home. They are probably walking along the seacoast this very instant. Ellen said she would prefer Concord to Scituate if Concord was beside the ocean. She said watching waves gives her a feeling of peace. Perhaps the waves are giving John a feeling of peace right now too. By the time Henry is halfway home, he has again worked himself up into a rage. His hands are in fists, his feet pound the surface of the road making small dusty explosions, and his mouth is set in a scowl. He refuses even to consider what the outcome of John's visit might be.

When he arrives home, Helen is outside, shooing the last errant chicken into the coop for the night. "Did you find what you were looking for?" she asks.

He's been in such a choler he's forgotten all about the pencils. He stops and collects himself. Although he may be furious with John, he has no right to impose his anger on Helen.

"In fact I did. It may take some work, but it should help. Better pencils will increase sales, I suppose."

"You're a worker of wonders, Henry," she says, taking his hands in hers. "I expect father knows the pencils could be improved but it never would have occurred to him to find the answer in a library. You should insist on a raise in pay."

Two days later, John returns. Henry is in his room when he hears him climbing the stairs, so he sits down at his writing table and opens his journal. That way if John comes in he can pretend to be busy and not have to look him in the eye. But John goes to his own room without stopping.

Well, as long as his journal is open, he might as well write: *Experience is in the fingers and head. The heart is inexperienced.* And (looking out his window): *When I consider how, after sunset, the stars come out gradually in troops from behind the hills and woods, I confess that I could not have contrived a more curious and inspiring sight.* After filling the page, he sets down his pen and picks up a book.

Finally, around midnight, John taps on his door.

"I'm back," he says. "I know you didn't want me to go."

Henry looks up. "You can do what you want. But we can't start this school if you're going to be running off all the time."

"You're right," he says apologetically. "I won't be traveling anywhere for a while."

"Did you have a pleasant visit?"

"Her father has no sense of humor. He glowered at me the entire time."

"That's all you have to say?"

"You ought to write her a letter. She considers you a good friend."

"I suppose I should." They are both silent for a moment. Then Henry speaks again: "Tomorrow we need to tell the families who said they want their children to come to our school that we're ready to begin."

Starting a school is no small matter—there are so many things to do. They decide they'll need two rooms in the house, one upstairs and one down, so they can divide the group. Each of them will take one half in the morning and the other half in the afternoon. The elder Thoreaus are not enthusiastic—it means the house is about to become a beehive of activity, some of it disruptive, but if it will bring in money they won't say no.

"Just for a few months," Henry tells them. "We'll continue to look for another place."

"You be strict," his mother says. "Don't let those children run wild in my house." His father, who values his quiet, looks toward the heavens: "As long as they're gone when I get home."

The school hours will be from half-past eight to half-past twelve and then from two to four. Each morning they will have a thirty-minute recess and lunch will be a leisurely affair, good digestion being necessary for good learning. Weather permitting, there will be a walk at least once a week to some point of interest where matters of local history, agriculture, and natural philosophy may be explored. Cost of tuition: six dollars per quarter, or ten if two brothers enroll. Some schools are beginning to admit girls and they decide to do that as well.

"So," Henry says as he looks at his class of four on the first day, "every enterprise must have a beginning and this is ours. If one sets off on a journey with the intention of doing good, how much better are his prospects than one who sets off intending only to endure? We are like the crew of a seagoing vessel. Only if we work together can we reach the farthest shore."

The students, all boys so far, gaze at him. (There are four more downstairs with John). For now at least they seem fascinated. Who is this man and what does he plan to do with them? But before an hour has elapsed one boy calls another boy a goddamned son-of-a-bitch, a clear violation of the rule that oaths are not allowed. Henry thinks it would be bad to impose too severe a punishment on the first morning of the first day, so he suggests they all agree to substitute the word "bootjack" for the usual epithets when they feel inclined to swear.

"That fellow who wronged me was a genuine *bootjack*," he exclaims. The class erupts in laughter. "I'm going beat the *bootjack* out of him when I see him again."

An image of Nehemiah Ball appears in his mind's eye. What would the vile old school inspector think of him now?

That evening after dark Henry and John sit outside and review the day.

"I think you should teach geography," John says. "You've always been in love with maps."

"I'll trade you geography for Latin. I can't manage another language. Greek will be enough. I'm going to start them off with *Alcibiades in Nepos* and see how they fare."

Helen comes out and joins them. She always seems happy enough, but Henry worries that she has no beau. Surely there must be some young fellow in Concord who might court her. Why is it that those who are most deserving of love sometimes end up alone?

She says, "I was coming up the path this afternoon after you dismissed them and two of your boys were walking along calling each other 'bootjacks.' So I am forced to wonder: What exactly are you teaching these children and is it worth six dollars a term?"

SOPHIA

To go walking with Mr. Hawthorne, she will require a chaperone. Once again she turns to Mary who promises that this time she won't go shopping and come back late.

"It wasn't my fault," Mary says. "Though to be honest I'm not sorry I missed hearing him talk about his dreadful book."

To arrange the event, notes are exchanged. What day would be best and what time of day and would the waterfront be of interest? Thursday next, mid-afternoon, and yes, the waterfront would be perfect. Provided it does not rain.

"At first I didn't like him," Sophia muses. "I'm still not sure I do."

"That's the way it always starts," says Mary. "I didn't like Mr. Mann in the beginning. I thought he looked sickly. But it turned out that what I took to be sickness was actually emotional debilitation brought on by the death of his wife. So I changed my view of him. He is sensitive but not sickly. I would not have wanted a sickly man."

"Well, he's not sickly. In fact, he looks quite robust. Mr. Hawthorne, I mean."

They are in Mary's room, which looks like a proper young woman's bedchamber rather than like an artist's garret as Sophia's room does. Which is to say, it's uncluttered, prettily decorated, and lacks the intense odor of paint.

"What will you wear?" Mary asks.

"I haven't given it much thought."

"Oh, Sophia, you can't be serious. I'll help you. You can borrow one of my dresses." From the look in her eyes, Sophia can tell she is finally becoming the sister Mary has longed for, one who goes for walks with gentlemen callers instead of staying in her room to paint or going to the doctor to be bled by leeches.

She is trying not to think too much about Hawthorne in advance. She has spoken to him on two occasions and this will be a third. There's no need to make it more than it is. She's unsurprised Mary finds it exciting. Now that Mary is close to being engaged, all that matters to her is courtship and weddings, and the idea that a man and woman might take a walk together and not have everlasting love on their minds is simply beyond her comprehension. (Although Horace Mann does seem to be taking his time proposing—Mary told her it was imminent weeks ago but nothing has happened yet.)

"My gray and yellow taffeta will be perfect," Mary says, "though we'll need to give some thought to your hair."

Sophia is worried she'll come down with one of her headaches and have to cancel. Mr. Hawthorne probably wouldn't mind, but Mary would be crushed.

"I wish I was a bit younger," Sophia says.

"You're hardly old."

"I will be eventually. In a few years."

"Stop talking and sit still. I need to tie this bow."

The preparations with Mary are so involved that when the walk actually takes place, it's something of an anti-climax. Although it happens on a perfect September day, the kind that would seem to invite high spirits, Mr. Hawthorne is extremely reserved; each exchange of remarks is followed by an extended silence. And it doesn't seem like the time or place to continue their talk about his book (for one thing, Mary would disapprove). Sophia has never a met man who seems less interested in ordinary conversation. On several occasions she and Mary glance at one another and Sophia sees her sister go from anxiety to disappointment to dismay. Then she remembers Mary's directive to inquire about his family.

"Your mother and sisters are well?" Sophia asks.

"They are."

"Does your mother go out much?"

"No, she prefers not to," Hawthorne says. "Although she will if circumstances require it."

"And your sisters, do they like to go out? For instance to Boston and such?"

"No, they prefer to stay home as well."

Sophia wonders how Mary is now feeling about her strategy. She looks at her imploringly, hoping for some help.

"I find your sisters rather tall," Mary says. "Unusually so."

"It depends on your point of comparison," Hawthorne replies. "But I must agree, my sisters are rather tall."

Hawthorne had said something about the waterfront, but they follow no predetermined route and never actually get close to the wharf. Eventually they find themselves walking down a lane lined with graceful elms and Mary has the sisterly discretion to pause and pretend to examine a tangle of wild roses so Sophia and Hawthorne can be alone. He must have been waiting for such a moment, because as soon as Mary is out of earshot, he says, "I have been thinking about your time in Cuba."

"I was too young to fully understand what I was seeing and experiencing. It was all so new."

"What I have been thinking is that I may write a story about you. Or rather about a girl like you who goes on a journey to a place like Cuba—a distant and enigmatic land."

"Really? About me? I can't imagine that would make for an interesting story." Herself in a work of literature? She can feel herself begin to blush.

"As I say, not about you precisely."

"Of course, I understand."

Sophia looks back and realizes Mary is waiting for some kind of sign. Should she scurry up and rejoin them or remain several steps behind?

"If you do write something about me—or about someone

similar to me—I'd be very interested to read it," she says.

"I expect you would be. And I'd like that a great deal."

Now he too glances back at Mary. "Your sister is being helpful," he says.

Sophia laughs. She can't believe this morose fellow made a joke, or at least the semblance of one. "I gave her no instructions. She is improvising."

They wave at Mary and she waves back, apparently unaware they are signaling to her to come. Then she sees what they mean and quickly catches up. "I've never seen a rose quite like that one," she says. "So very pink—I had to stop and look."

Their route has taken them in a large circle and now they are almost home. The cemetery is on their left, overgrown and gloomy even in mid-afternoon.

"Your window looks down upon the graves," Hawthorne observes.

"Indeed it does," Sophia says, realizing as she speaks that he seems to know exactly which room is hers. Is he just guessing, or has he actually seen her standing there at night? She isn't prepared to interrogate him on the matter, but Mary is:

"How would you know which room is hers? To my knowledge you have never been to the top of the stairs."

His eyes get wide and he puts up his hands as if he expects to be attacked. He looks at Sophia and says, "When I came to talk about your journal and you served me tea, you said you see the sunrise from your room. Therefore, I deduced it was on this side. I knew only because you told me."

"Yes, yes, I remember, I did say that. Mary, you jump to conclusions. Poor Mr. Hawthorne is innocent."

"Well," Mary says, "Then it is your fault, Sophia. You should not be talking about what you see from your bedroom window. It's too personal to share."

It seems the walk is over. Hawthorne says his good-byes

and leaves them at their door.

"I am so sorry, Sophia," Mary says as they cross the threshold, shedding hats and gloves. "I had no idea he was such a bore. I blame Elizabeth for bringing him round." Then she shrugs dismissively. "If he can write, you'd think he'd be able to talk."

The next day, late in the afternoon, Sophia gets an idea. What if she were to illustrate one of Nathaniel's tales? She picks up his book and re-reads her favorite story, the one called "The Gentle Boy." As soon as she's done, she begins to sketch. In it, a boy, Ilbrahim, is crying as he sits beneath the tree from which his father was hung for heresy. The writing is so vivid she can picture the scene perfectly. She likes the idea of doing it without Nathaniel knowing. She also likes how thinking about the story in this way makes it less frightening to her, even though it's as macabre as the rest. Viewed thusly, it feels less like a nightmare and more like a work of art. He created the characters and now she is *re*-creating them, based on the images that come to her as she reads. It's a peculiarly intimate act, like reading his mind. Like putting on his shirt and shoes, feeling the soft fabric against her skin and her little feet inside his black boots. She works far into the night.

MARGARET

Margaret's second Conversation is as successful as the first. Elizabeth Peabody says all she's heard over the past several days is, "Will I see you at Margaret Fuller's next event?"

Once again the topic is the Greeks. But this time the ladies are prepared. They have been thinking about the first Conversation and have questions. For instance: why is Apollo so ruthless and how did the Greeks perceive the institution of marriage and, given that they've been using the term "character," shouldn't it be defined? Margaret is thrilled. This is precisely how she envisioned things happening. There would be a free exchange of ideas. She will share her knowledge but not dominate the discussion or make others feel small. On the way to the shop she passed a flower girl and bought a bouquet of blood red carnations which she has placed in a vase on the table beside her. She feels they are somehow emblematic of the moment—beautiful, vibrant, organic—and she resolves to bring flowers every week from now on.

Once again Cary Sturgis is her most spirited respondent. Although she is among the youngest in the group, she has a quick tongue and likes to tease.

"If I had to trust my parents to select my husband, as young ladies did in ancient times, I would go to a nunnery." She pauses for effect. "Because I happen to know who they'd choose."

Naturally, there are a few attendees who are not so fully engaged. Mrs. Hart asks Margaret about her necklace. Does so right in the middle of the discussion, as if the topic had suddenly changed from mythology to jewelry.

"May I ask where you bought that locket? I'd like to purchase one for my niece."

"I am reminded," Margaret says, lifting the necklace away from her breast and fixing her gaze on Mrs. Hart, "of the Necklace of Harmonia which brought misfortune to all of its wearers, most of whom were queens and princesses of the House of Thebes." She lets the necklace fall and continues, "It all began when Hephaestus discovered his wife Aphrodite was having an illicit liaison with Ares . . ." By the time Margaret is done, Mrs. Hart is blushing and sweating and any thoughts she was having about necklaces have been routed from her mind.

When it's over, many of the women remain to thank Margaret, to congratulate her, to ask her about the next meeting, and Margaret basks in the adulation. As a girl of twelve or thirteen, she wasn't well-liked at school—she read too much and had an answer for every question and didn't understand how to behave with other girls her age. Yet these women flock around her and seem to desire her friendship.

The only difficult part is that one of those who speaks to her after the meeting ends is Sarah Clarke, the younger sister of James.

"I went to Philadelphia to see him," she says. "He seems quite content and sends his warm regards."

"Will he be coming to Boston anytime soon?"

"Oh, I think not. He is very busy. I met his fiancé and found her quite nice. She has family north of Philadelphia. They are Quakers, which will be quite a challenge for my father. But I expect he'll adjust."

"When he left I assumed it was only temporary" Margaret says. "But now I suppose I shall have to depend on the post to sustain our friendship." And then she sighs inwardly because neither letters nor visits can make things as they were before.

Over the next several weeks, her Conversations continue to go well. So well in fact that she begins to consider having one that includes men. Can men sit together with women and think deeply about matters of true significance? Perhaps it's time to find out.

Elizabeth Peabody is skeptical: "I don't see the point in making changes when you're having such success. What makes you think any men will care to attend?"

"Mr. Emerson says he would."

"Ah, you've recruited him."

"No, he suggested it himself. But if he is interested, others might be as well."

"What will you discuss?"

"The same things we've been discussing. How to live one's life."

"And you expect the men to be as open and attentive as the ladies? You have a higher opinion of them than I."

As it happens, Margaret has little difficulty convincing men to attend. She quickly realizes it's simply because they're curious, but she doesn't care what motivates them as long as they come. Actually, her greatest fear is that the women will be bored. Some of the men will be better read—one of her reasons for holding these events is that authors such as Ovid are considered an essential part of schooling for boys but an extravagance for girls. And yet the men could be surprised. She and her female participants have reached such an elevated level of discourse they may have to return to earth to bring their male counterparts along.

Emerson writes to say he'll attend but will refrain from speaking. This annoys her. Is he putting himself above her and her guests? Lidian will be accompanying him even though she's expecting their second child. Will the wives speak in the presence of their husbands? Will the young, unmarried women and young unmarried men forget why they've come and spend the evening examining one another? The more she thinks about it the more interested she gets in the event as a social experiment. How will they all behave?

It takes place on the warmest evening of the year. By the time Margaret arrives, Elizabeth has opened all the windows and set out a box of paper fans.

"I'm nervous," Margaret says. "I don't know what to expect."

Elizabeth offers her a supportive smile. "I'll tolerate no bad behavior. Not in my shop."

In addition to Waldo, the men include Henry Yates, Bronson Alcott, Frank Shaw, and William White. Margaret is acquainted with most of them and the rest she knows by reputation. They come in and cluster together, speaking a little too loudly, as if they are at the meeting of some civic organization or guild, as if this is just another of the many events they regularly attend. Margaret greets them and tries to keep smiling when they make condescending jokes about wanting to see what their wives are so excited about. She also seeks out Lidian and congratulates her on the upcoming birth.

"Perhaps a girl this time," Margaret says.

Lidian shakes her head. "I shall leave that decision to God."

Margaret asks how little Waldo is and Lidian tells her that his father has taken an analytic interest in the child's development, even to keeping a detailed record of his first words. And then she raises an eyebrow which Margaret takes to mean, "You know how he turns even the most ordinary aspects of life into objects of study."

At last Margaret takes her seat at the front of the room, beside the vase of red flowers. Elizabeth directs people toward their chairs and as soon as everyone is quiet, Margaret begins. She announces that tonight they are once again returning to the Greeks and that she wants them all to cast their minds back to the time when Greek civilization was fresh and not see it through the lens of the present. She also says that it's important to acknowledge how the Greeks drew from earlier civilizations, especially the Hindu and the Egyptian.

It's odd looking out at a mixed audience. There's an uneasiness in the room that hasn't been there before. And it's such a large group. She remembers when she thought she'd be happy if six or seven showed up.

When she's done with her introductory remarks, she starts to speak of Isis, of Rhea, the mother of the gods, and of how she gave birth to Hestia, Hades, Demeter, Poseidon, Hera.

"It is from them we derive the most basic qualities of humanity—Hestia brings us domesticity, the family, the hearth; Demeter, fertility and the harvest; Poseidon, the sea and all it represents. Thus, they are not merely characters in a drama—they embody particular ideals."

She pauses then, hoping that, as in the earlier sessions, someone will fill the silence with a question or comment. And they do, first young, wealthy Frank Shaw and then William White, but instead of helping her further the discussion, they dispute her premises. Shaw argues that the Hindu system of belief is actually superior to the Greeks while the journalist White, his mustache twitching, wants to make a case for the American Indian: "Isn't there a purity and simplicity to their beliefs from which we might learn?" After that Alcott joins in and takes them on a long, circuitous detour through the Romans, the Hittites, and the Zoroastrians. Everyone knows Alcott and they are all accustomed to how, despite his intelligence and wide knowledge, he tends to perseverate, well past his audience's patience.

"And so," he concludes, "it is my fervent belief that children embody all the various forms of knowledge that have existed since the world began . . . and yet—"

"Thank you," Margaret interrupts, for she can stand no more. She's not happy with how this is unfolding. Of the women only Elizabeth Peabody has spoken, and she was cut off by Frank Shaw. The rest of them look bored, and between the heat of the evening and the size of the crowd, it's getting uncomfortably close. The fans wave and perspiration appears on every brow.

She tries to bring the group back to the Greeks but it's only partially successful. She fixes Waldo with a severe gaze, hoping he'll assist, but when he finally speaks his comments are about the recent history of France. He's trying to make some point about Napoleon representing a certain set of qualities, just as the Greek gods do, but as far as Margaret is concerned, he might as well be Bronson Alcott—except that Waldo knows when to stop.

"What do you suppose Plato would make of Boston?" William White says, obviously impressed with himself for coming up with such a clever question. "I mean if he were standing right here today?"

At last, the women arise and revolt but it's too late and too mild. They ask Margaret to return to some of the ideas she discussed in previous sessions because the men are misunderstanding the purpose of this event. She does as they request and can see some interest on Waldo's face, but just then William White passes out from the heat. He's quickly revived but after that there's no reason to continue. She makes a few concluding remarks and wishes them all a good night.

She's glad to be done, yet to her dismay, the men seem to have enjoyed themselves. They want to know what next week's topic will be. She says, "Rhea and her progeny," meaning to be sarcastic—that's what they were *supposed* to discuss tonight. But Frank Shaw says, "How interesting!" and Henry Yates, who has been mercifully silent, says he was skeptical about the value of the event, "but now I see the point."

Margaret stands at the door and offers each person her thanks as they depart—whether things went well or poorly, it remains a fact that they all paid to attend. When Waldo and Lidian approach she asks them to stay after, but he says Lidian is feeling fatigued, so they have to go. On his way out, he leans in and whispers, "I'm sorry if I misbehaved."

At last, only she and Elizabeth remain in the shop. Margaret collapses into a chair and groans.

"Was that as dreadful as I think it was?" she asks.

"They don't know how to act any differently."

"But the ladies have been so . . . I wanted to stop everything and implore them to speak out."

"Maybe you should have. But they bear some responsibility. Their lips weren't sewn shut."

Margaret shakes her head. "Why should they bother? Suppose one of them had climbed on a chair and started shouting. She'd have been heard, but to what end?"

"To the end of her marriage, perhaps," Elizabeth says, and Margaret, who wasn't expecting a joke, laughs, stops, and then laughs again, so hard her eyes fill with tears.

HENRY

A month after they open the school, they find a building in town that can accommodate them—and at a reasonable price. It's not a moment too soon. Expecting the six members of the Thoreau family, their boarders, and the school, to occupy the same house, even if it's a rather capacious, rambling house, is unreasonable. Already, one boy has put a broomstick through a window, another smuggled a muskrat in under his shirt and released it, and Henry often leads his charges in exuberant, off-key song. Furthermore, they are now up to sixteen students, including four girls.

There is still a bit of coolness between him and John but not enough to impede the functioning of the school. Talk of Ellen is simply out of the question. He does wonder if John is secretly writing her letters and sending her gifts. He keeps a sharp eye on everything that leaves the house to be mailed but so far he's seen no evidence that they're communicating. As for the letter John urged him to write, that hasn't happened either. He can't decide what to say.

In the evening, Henry sometimes goes to his father's shop and tinkers. Producing pencils as excellent as the ones made by the Germans will require finely ground plumbago indeed. He tries various methods but always ends up with something that's sufficiently powdery mixed with larger fragments and shards. He considers filtering it somehow, but then one day realizes that if he blows across a pile of ground-up plumbago, the lightest particles are wafted away by this breath. Maybe air could be used to separate the coarse from the fine.

He has continued to borrow books from Mr. Emerson, as many as he can carry. Tonight, he finds him in his garden,

143

holding baby Waldo and marveling at a yellow vegetable of extraordinary size. Henry has never been able to call Mr. Emerson "Waldo" as some Concord folk do. If he addresses him directly he uses the formal Mister, and if he speaks of him to John or Helen it's just "Emerson." Waldo is too familiar, as if they were chums at school.

"Ah, Henry, come here. Have you ever seen a squash this large?"

"I don't believe I have."

"I'm curious to see if nature will impose any limits. Every day I come out and measure its girth."

He jiggles Waldo gently and Henry is struck by seeing him thus: a portrait of the philosopher, accompanied by child and squash. Henry recently discovered Helen has her own copy of *Nature*, so he has borrowed it from her and is reading it again. This time he's going slower and is more impressed. Many individual sentences stick in his mind. Take this one for example: "Every property of matter is a school for the understanding, — its solidity or resistance, its inertia, its extension, its figure, its divisibility." That's certainly true of his experiments in pencil-making. Right now plumbago is teaching him about virtually all those things. While he tries to *divide* it into tiny particles, it does its level best to *resist*.

"My brother and I are getting ready to move our school," Henry says. "We'll be occupying the building just north of the Myer house."

"I have a wagon you can use if you'd like." Little Waldo begins to squall, and Emerson jiggles him with more vigor.

"We already have a wagon. But might I borrow more books?"

As they go toward the house, Emerson speaks about the child, random thoughts as they come to mind: "He likes water a great deal. We bathe him and he laughs. Yesterday there was a mouse in the kitchen and he seemed entirely unafraid. He has a stronger grip than you'd expect. When he grasps a spoon, there's no getting it back."

Mrs. Emerson, these days heavy with child, meets them at the door. Henry says hello, little Waldo is handed off, and he and Emerson enter the library.

This evening his selections include Tacitus, Seneca, Sibbald's *Chronicle of Scottish Poetry,* Sir William Jones's translation of ancient Indian scripture, and a volume by a man named Hawthorne that Emerson has only recently acquired. When he picks it up, Emerson says, "There's a strangeness to it I find appealing, but it made me wonder about the sort of fellow who would conjure such thoughts."

As Henry leaves he runs into Mrs. Emerson again. She no longer has the boy—he must be with Emerson's mother.

"Do you ever hire out to do odd jobs?" she asks. "Waldo has no aptitude for manual labor. He likes to look at that squash but seems not to know the gate is off its hinges. I've given up all hope of getting it repaired."

Emerson, upon hearing himself slandered, says, "You mischaracterize me," but the look he gives Henry is imploring— he'd appreciate the help.

Henry shrugs. Although he doesn't have much unused time, it would be no great inconvenience to fix a gate.

"I'll consider it payment for the loan of the books," he says.

As he walks away, he hears this exchange:

"See, and he'll do it for free."

"I suppose. I'd have gotten to it in time."

From there he goes home and begins to read. But late that night, he decides to write the letter to Ellen. Little by little he's been getting angry with himself for his failure to act. He needs to do it now.

Dear Ellen, he begins. *I have been meaning to write you for many weeks but have been busy with our new school. I expect you have heard about it from John.* He stops, rereads the sentences, and tears up the page. Calling attention to how long it's taken him is a bad idea, as is calling attention to John. He takes another sheet of paper, dips his pen in ink, and starts again:

Dear Ellen, Today I walked along the river past where we first picked berries and I thought of you. The memory of that day is one I shall cherish. The weather here is a little better— maybe the heat is gone for good. I hope plenty of snow is being saved up somewhere so it can be delivered to us in February. I like to go sledding when I can. What is the weather like in Scituate? I have little knowledge of life near the sea.

Tomorrow we move our school to a building that will accommodate more pupils. It is a bit ramshackle, but we will put it in order. By the time of your next visit all will be shipshape.

Please write and tell me what you have been doing since you left us. Your aunt Prudence is as talkative as ever, while your grandmother says little but sews with undiminished skill.

He reads it over. It's mannered and without substance, but it's the best he can do. The weather, Aunt Prudence. An odd comment about sledding. Now comes the wretched wait for her reply.

SOPHIA

Mr. Hawthorne visits again. And again and again. He contrives reasons. He has a question about her time in Cuba. A Boston publisher wants him to write a book for children—what does she think of that? He knows a man who has honey to sell. Should he put in an order for the Peabody family? It's being offered at a good price. He even invites her to come to his house. His mother has done some baking and wishes to make a gift to the Peabodys. But when she arrives, he meets her outside and tells her his eldest sister is ill and she can't come inside. He'll invite her back another time.

When Elizabeth comes to Salem again, the two of them discuss his personality and motives.

"He's quite intelligent," says Elizabeth. "That much is clear. Yet he doesn't use his intellect in an overbearing manner as some men do."

"The problem with intelligence is it can mask certain flaws," Sophia replies. "For example, I have noticed that wit can cover up a mean spirit. A man who can make you laugh isn't necessarily kind."

"In any event he keeps coming to visit. Although perhaps he does so only because this house is close to his. It could be a mistake to think he finds you appealing before he says so in his own words."

Sophia isn't sure what to make of Elizabeth's remark. What are her sister's true feelings about Hawthorne? At first, she seemed fascinated with him but now that Sophia has shown some interest, she seems to have drawn back. Or has she? With Elizabeth, it's always tempting to assume she is so busy with meetings and books and ideas that she hasn't time for anything else.

The day after Elizabeth goes back to Boston, Hawthorne comes bearing news: He has accepted a position as a measurer at the Boston Custom House and will be leaving before the week is out. Sophia looks at him and tries to contain her dismay. He doesn't seem to know what to do with his hands. They're in his pockets, then clasped, then holding his lapels.

He says, "I tried to find a position with the postal service here but then George Bancroft contacted me unexpectedly. I hardly know the man but after he described the job I couldn't turn him down."

She wasn't anticipating this. She's suddenly afraid she might begin to cry so she excuses herself and runs upstairs. When she comes back, she has the illustration she made to go with his story.

"I want to know if this looks like your Ilbrahim—in 'The Gentle Boy.'"

He takes the paper and studies it for an uncomfortably long time. At last, he looks up and their eyes meet. "From now on he will never look otherwise to me," he says.

She is touched but it doesn't solve the problem of his leaving. She needs him to tell her more. At her suggestion, they step outside and go into the graveyard next door. It's a gray afternoon, the clouds low and promising rain.

"I expect you to visit," he says. "Now that the railroad has connected Salem to Boston it's an easy trip."

"I'm something of a reluctant traveler—not unlike your sisters," she says dryly. He shouldn't be allowed to think he can simply summon her. She almost wants to punish him for going away.

"You, who went all the way to Cuba?"

"That was different. I was hardly more than a child. Now I have my work. I don't like to leave it."

He lowers his gaze and sighs. "Then perhaps you'll invite me here."

Sophia brightens a bit. "I shall. To this very place." She motions to the headstones around them. Some have scythes or hourglasses carved into them—symbols of the brevity of life. Others have winged death's heads, their mouths open in anguished screams.

Nathaniel says, "I deserved that I suppose."

They walk on to where a fence separates the graveyard from an open field. There's a sort of makeshift stile on which they sit.

"You have made the past weeks here quite enjoyable," Nathaniel says.

She blushes. It's a terrible combination of emotions and events. He is expressing himself as never before, just as he's preparing to leave. She could say she has enjoyed her time with him as well but chooses not to. Instead, she says,

"Will your new position allow you time to write?"

"Ah, spoken like an artist. Every minute is precious, and every minute taken away is a wound. Without you to visit, I'll work hard all day and then go directly to my room where I will write until sleep overtakes me. I shall have no social life whatever."

"As it should be," she says.

They are sitting side-by-side, their shoulders touching, and Sophia thinks the time may have come for a kiss, but in the next moment she feels something touching her back. She yelps, jumps up, and turns. Seeing her fear, Nathaniel jumps up as well. But it's not the hand of a spirit, it's the nose of the goat, the one who visits the graveyard at will. And now it's clear, the stile is how he does it. His owners must *want* him to visit the dead. Otherwise, why make it so convenient? They laugh together in relief but the opportunity for a kiss has passed.

As they go back toward the house, he takes her hand and leads her toward a particular stone.

"Have you ever noticed this one?" he asks.

"I seldom read them, I . . ." She peers at it. It's rather worn, the letters shallow and rounded and difficult to make out. "Here lyes . . . does that say Hawthorne? Is this—?"

"My great grandfather. The judge. The executioner of witches."

"Why didn't you show me before?"

"I assumed you already knew. You live next door. You walk here often."

"It's nearly illegible. The grass is so high it's hard to see." She looks again. "The 'w' is missing from his name."

"It's not that it's missing from his—it's that I've acquired it. I added it to obscure my lineage. Who would want to be a descendent of such a man?"

"You just awoke one day and added a 'w'?"

"Precisely. Why not?"

She can't imagine changing her name any more than she can imagine changing the color of her eyes. Your name is your name. But maybe she'd feel differently if one of her ancestors was truly evil. An executioner. Better to have an ancestor who was a witch.

"Our forefathers have no hold on us," she says, trying to be consoling.

"I'd prefer not to discuss it." He pauses. "It's beginning to rain. I think it's time we go in."

Before he leaves, he tells her he'll write as soon as he has lodgings in Boston. But he seems distracted, as if in his mind he's already en route.

When he is gone, she goes straight to her room. She sits on the bed on the verge of tears. Over the past several weeks she has gotten to know him much better but still feels there is something unknowable about him, some hidden aspect of his heart. She looks at the painting of Jessica and Lorenzo. Where before Lorenzo looked a good deal like Fernando Zayas, he has now begun to resemble Nathaniel. The city in the distance must therefore be Boston. It suddenly seems far, far away.

In the morning, she awakens with an idea. She will simply follow him there. By noon she has written one letter to Elizabeth asking if she can stay with her, and another to a sculptor of good reputation, Shobal Clevenger, asking if he is taking on any students. Lately she has been thinking she wants to learn how to work in clay. But by mid-afternoon her feelings have shifted. Nathaniel has made no formal declaration of interest. To chase after him would be a risk beyond what even Sophia, usually open to risk, is willing to take. So no, she will not go to Boston. She'll stay here and wait for him to visit, wait for him to write.

The next morning, she glances out the window and sees him walking past. He is carrying his portmanteau and so must be on his way to board the train. For an instant she considers running out to say good-bye, but instead she waves half-heartedly. He doesn't see her. His eyes are cast down.

Now she prepares to wait. Prepares to be disappointed. She goes outside and walks among the headstones and imagines herself to be a recently widowed bride. Yet before the week is out, a letter arrives:

My dear Sophia,

I had a parting glimpse of you, Monday afternoon, at your window—and that image abides with me. I have reproached myself many times for my failure to stop. Perhaps you saw me, or at least sensed I was there.

He goes on to describe his rooms in Boston and his new job at the Custom House and closes with *I wish I could see you this evening. How many times have you thought of me today? Did you ever read such a foolish letter as this? But it is my chiefest pleasure to write you and so I must.*

She reads it a second time and then goes to look down at the street where she saw him pass. How could she have questioned his faithfulness? He is not so difficult to interpret as she thought. But then another letter arrives, this one from Elizabeth, and in it are some unexpected lines:

I am pleased Nathaniel accepted the position at the Custom House here. I told George Bancroft he would be a good choice.

So Nathaniel was hired because her sister recommended him? She's confused. Why didn't Elizabeth inform her? Does Nathaniel know? Her confusion soon turns to anger. She has always been treated as an invalid or, at best, as the flighty artist. *Why tell Sophia, she wouldn't understand.* Elizabeth brought him to the house without asking her and now she's taken him away to Boston, again without asking. Of course, that's just Elizabeth's way, but what about him? Why wouldn't he tell her how he got the job? As far as Sophia knows, he didn't even make a formal application. A letter arrived calling him to Boston and without a second thought, he went.

She puts both letters in a drawer. She feels victimized. She will not respond to either of them. What sort of feelings do Elizabeth and Nathaniel have toward one another anyway? Elizabeth now actually calls him *Nathaniel.* When did that begin? She's glad she didn't decide to move back to Boston. She's afflicted with fewer headaches here in Salem anyway.

The next day she begins a new painting. Once, at the Atheneum in Boston, she saw a series of drawings of the lakes of Italy. Lake Como, Lake Garda, Lake Maggiore. The images have stayed with her and she thinks she could do a passable version of one. Lake Como, because it's so well known. She banishes Nathaniel Hawthorne from her mind. She is in Italy now.

MARGARET

Margaret has more Conversations, some with men present, some without. Because of their popularity, she is becoming renowned. Schoolgirls visit the shop on West Street simply to get a glimpse of her. They buy pencils and look covetously at expensive books and sometimes even bring tall, awkward boys with them—although upon seeing women like Margaret and Elizabeth, women who seem neither motherly nor sisterly, the boys become self-conscious and go back outside.

In celebration of what Margaret has done for the intellectual life of Boston, Lucy Cook, one of her most enthusiastic supporters, gives a party. Most of the women who subscribed attend, as well as a good number of the men—of course in many instances they are married to one another. But there are also other guests, artists and writers and politicians, so it seems, at least for that evening, as if Margaret has become the lodestone of Boston's intellectual elite. Some seem intimidated by her, which she finds upsetting. She designed her meetings to be conversational so as to diminish the distance between herself and her audience. Even when she was a child she felt as if her intelligence pushed people away. Perhaps the only solution is to make friends with kindred beings, those who put nothing before the life of the mind.

As the party continues, she begins to think about slipping out, but now here comes Elizabeth with a young man in tow. He is quite handsome, with wide-set eyes, glorious dark brown hair, and a full mouth that looks as if it could be warmly expressive, although the expression on it right now is one of dismay. It appears he'd rather not meet her, but Elizabeth is giving him no choice.

"Margaret, may I introduce to you Mr. Nathaniel Hawthorn? I showed you his book one day in the shop. He has recently moved here from Salem to begin work at the Custom House."

"Welcome to Boston. Although perhaps it's not my place to say so because I currently live in Jamaica Plain."

"You may live in Jamaica Plain, but you are most definitely a citizen of Boston," Elizabeth says.

"Is it very nice out there," Mr. Hawthorne asks, "in Jamaica Plain?"

"It is very rural out there. If you enjoy the lowing of cattle at sunrise then I suppose it's very nice."

Mr. Hawthorne looks at her as if she has said something unintelligible and Elizabeth, perhaps seeing that this meeting may not go well, scurries off.

"If memory serves, your book is a collection of tales," Margaret says. She wishes she were better at making others feel at ease, but if she puts her mind to it, she can sometimes achieve success. It's a skill one learns from teaching—from welcoming new students to the class. But already she can tell this man will resist. He looks suspicious, as if he has military secrets and she is an enemy spy.

"It is."

"A particular sort of tale? Or are they various?"

"Would you mind explaining yourself better? I'm not I sure understand."

He's beginning to annoy her. It's one thing to be shy but another to be intentionally obtuse.

"Well, are they philosophical tales or historical tales or perhaps they are tales of intrigue? Are they for sunlit afternoons, or to be read late at night?"

It's difficult to tell if he's looking at her with disdain or with confusion. She's glad he didn't attend any of her Conversations. Although if he had, it seems likely he'd have chosen a seat at the back and been speechless as a stump.

"I don't believe they can be described in such plain terms."

She doesn't think the terms she used are exactly plain but neither does she wish to argue about it. "I apologize for the implication. I'm certain they can't," she says and then tries another tack: "Tell me, Mr. Hawthorne, what sort of work do you do at the Custom House? It must be interesting to deal with ships from many lands."

"Thus far I remain unclear about my duties. I expect I will learn over time."

She almost says, "A book that defies description and a job without purpose," but she restrains herself. Instead, she simply nods.

Then just as she is about send him away—although she's not sure how—he speaks of his own accord: "I know the Peabody sisters well. We were friends when I was a child and after many years apart, we have become reacquainted. Have you seen Sophia Peabody's work? She recently showed me one of her drawings. It was very fine indeed."

Margaret's eyebrows go up. So he has at least one interest other than his writing and about this one he's willing to talk. Now, for a few minutes, they actually converse. He tells her what he admired about Sophia Peabody's drawing and Margaret says she's seen some of her paintings in Elizabeth's shop. Hawthorne even describes his lodgings, sharing a peculiar fact:

"In a rooming house, many prefer the ground floor, but I'd rather be on the top one. I dislike footsteps overhead as they make me feel I am in a grave."

When he finally excuses himself, she is relieved. At best he is an odd fellow; at worst he is conceited, self-important, and unnecessarily vague. The only excuse for being vague is a lack of intelligence and she sees no sign of that.

In the days that follow, Margaret writes a bit about the experience of the Conversations, taking care to note not just what was discussed but what it felt like to be there. Then she prepares to go to Concord. This time she will be staying a full month. Since she was there last, the Emersons' second child has been born, a girl they call Nelly. Margaret asks if that won't make the house too crowded for a visitor, but Waldo writes, "Your room is ready. If you don't come, I'll be destroyed."

When she arrives in Concord, he is at the coach stop to meet her once again. This time instead of a black suit, he is dressed like a farmer, from his bull-hide boots right up to his broad-brimmed straw hat. She has two bags, rather large ones because of the length of her stay, and he insists on carrying them both. As for Concord, the trees are just beginning to turn and the sky seems somehow bluer than in Boston or even Jamaica Plain. A fresh and unexpected breeze lifts the hat off Waldo's head and because his hands are filled with luggage, it falls to Margaret, laughing, to chase it down. He bows and she places it on his head, after which she feels somehow graceful, although grace is not a quality she associates with herself.

Lidian and Emerson's mother are both waiting by the door, each one holding a child. First Margaret coos and exclaims over the baby and then over little Waldo, who has grown a good deal since her last visit. He reaches out to grab her finger and, for the moment, Margaret keeps her focus entirely on the children. She read somewhere that if you want to be a good houseguest in a home where children are present, you must make a bit of a fuss.

Her room is the same one as last time, on the ground floor, directly across from Waldo's study. Since her previous visit it's been painted, there's a new writing table, and in the window, an Aeolian harp has been hung.

"How pleasant you've made it," she tells Waldo.

He looks about wide-eyed, as if the changes are a surprise

to him as well. "Lidian hired a fellow from up the road—you met him, Henry Thoreau—who is better than I with a hammer or paintbrush. We talk philosophy while he works."

HENRY

Ellen replies to his letter. He expected her to, but he's still surprised. Her response is polite, friendly, full of remarks about her studies, her brother Edmund, and the new horse and trap her family has recently acquired: *She is a sprightly little mare and I adore her* and *Edmund is raising a baby crow. He feeds it porridge and calls it Beelzebub, to my father's considerable dismay.*

About John, she says, *I wish your brother was here to tutor me in geography. When I look at a map I see only a muddle of lines.*

He dislikes that part. She fails to say she wishes *he* were there to tutor her in Greek. Furthermore, geography isn't that difficult. No one of normal intelligence needs a tutor to understand a map.

Undaunted, Henry sends her a book of poems by Jones Very, a fellow he knew at Harvard who has had some good success with his verse. It's a book he purchased for himself but giving it to Ellen is more important than keeping it on his shelf. Which is a surprising thought for him to have, considering his love of books.

Very's poems are strange and ethereal, so he's not sure how she will like them but it's not long before another letter from Ellen arrives, this one thanking him for the gift. She says it was enjoyed by the whole family, her father included. Well, he thinks, that went better than I thought it would, but before he can take much satisfaction from his success, he reads the next paragraph:

The book was delivered the same day as the polished stones John sent me for my curio cabinet. It was delightful, like Christmas almost.

He curses. What to do now? He needs to send her something personal, something affecting, something John can't match. What could be more personal and affecting than some of his own poems. Let John send her stones. For the next several days he writes, some new lines and some old ones, revised with Ellen in mind:

> *Up this pleasant stream let's row*
> *For the livelong summer's day*
> *Sprinkling foam where'er we go*
> *In wreaths as white as driven snow*
> *Ply the oars! away! away!*

Wreaths of snow-white foam. Quite a fine image. It's not fully accurate—the foam churned up by rowing has a beige quality to it, more the color of cream than snow, but if he were to use "cream" the image of a cow would be invoked, and he wants none of that.

He posts the letter and waits. And waits. The first two letters came quickly; this time a week passes and then two more. Did he do something to offend? Was the letter lost?

At school one morning, before the children have arrived, he asks John if he's heard from Ellen recently.

John shrugs. "A week or two ago. It's my turn to reply."

Henry nods. "Are you corresponding with her . . . regularly?"

"As regularly as you, I suppose."

What Henry would really like to know is what John and Ellen are corresponding *about,* but before he can come up with a way to ask the question, four boys burst through the door and the day begins.

Then that very afternoon, his wait finally ends. A letter from Ellen is there for him when he gets home. She says not a word about his poetry, but it doesn't matter. Nothing in the letter matters except her closing:

I have gotten permission to visit my grandmother, my

159

aunt, and the illustrious Thoreau family for a week in October.
Perhaps some exotic beast will be in the area for us to marvel
at again.
Your good friend,
Ellen Sewell

A visit! He wonders if he's the first to know. Surely, she's
told her grandmother and aunt and most likely John as well.
But wouldn't they have announced it to the family? It really
doesn't matter—what's important is she's coming. He'll have
another chance with her and won't spoil it by being sulky or
remote or too competitive.

That night at supper he mentions the letter and the news.
To his surprise, no one else has heard.

"Did she give dates?" his mother asks.

"She said the end of the month, but I'm sure she'll send
more details."

"Are her mother and Edmund coming?" asks Aunt
Prudence. There's never any question of her father visiting.
According to family gossip he considers his wife's side of the
family beneath his concern.

"She didn't mention them. But I expect she'll let us know."

Henry likes being the bearer of this news. He looks across
the table at John. Normally, his brother is remarkably even-
tempered and difficult to ruffle, but now Henry thinks he
detects some redness rising toward his ears. Henry still holds
John's trip to Scituate against him. Now John knows how it
feels.

He writes back to her that evening, telling her they're all
very much looking forward to her visit and that although it
will be too late for berrying, they might go boating on Walden
Pond.

The school continues to go well. The building they are in
now is much better for their purposes than the family home,
and, as the weather is holding, they are taking their charges

160

on frequent outings, which improves their concentration and willingness to work. Sometimes they go out to observe plants and animals and the changing of the seasons, while other times they visit places of business or industry to see the conduct of various trades. Just yesterday they went to the office of the *Yeoman's Gazette* and gathered around the typesetter to watch him place letters, one after another, in a wooden frame.

But the outings through forests and across fields are still his favorites. One afternoon they're walking along the Assabet when little Melissa Ellsworthy, small, with curly brown hair, asks if they can go fishing. She's one of the youngest in the group so some of the others take this as an opportunity to make fun of her. How can they go fishing, they tell her, when they have no lines or poles? But Henry stops and puts up a finger to silence their jibes.

"Watch carefully," he says. "Make no further sound." Then he lies down on the bank, reaches into the water, glances over his shoulder at his mystified charges, and pulls out a foot-long fish.

The children shout and clap. Perhaps they've seen it done before but he's always surprised at how little even the farm boys know about any animals they don't have to tend. More and more they seem interested in machines, especially trains. After everyone has had a chance to examine the fish, he returns it to the river, and they watch it swim away.

"Now who else wants to try?" he says, and soon all of them are lying along the bank, an arm in the water, trying to follow his instructions about how to use their fingertips to hypnotize a fish. They're as motionless as he's ever seen them and as quiet too. In the end, none of them catches anything but Henry counts it a success when two boys fall asleep.

John takes them on walks as well, yet where Henry is likely to gather them all around to look at a hill of ants, John will challenge them to a footrace or start a pinecone fight or take them swimming, even if the water is cold. Henry sometimes wishes he were more like that, more able to find fun in the moment instead of living inside his head. He resolves that when Ellen Sewall comes, he will be lively and humorous and not quite as bookish and pensive as he usually is. However, he has marked a few poems in one of the volumes he borrowed from Emerson, which he may read to her should a suitable moment arise.

SOPHIA

Despite her dismay about how Nathaniel got his new job, she forces herself to suppress her suspicions. Elizabeth was probably just doing a good deed and had no ulterior motives. She doubts Elizabeth is even capable of ulterior motives—she has no time for them. Sophia writes to Nathaniel again and he replies, telling her about an exhibit of paintings he attended. They were from Spain and his description makes them sound wonderful—ornate and exotic and shot through with gold.

Once again she considers going to Boston. She wouldn't have to relocate permanently. Yes, that's the solution—she'll make an extended visit, so she needn't explain herself to her parents or give Nathaniel ideas he ought not to have. But first she consults with Mary.

"I don't know what you see in him," Mary says. "Why not insist he visit you here in Salem. That's what Horace does for me."

Sophia won't say it aloud, but she doesn't believe Mary's approach is working very well. It's been months since she claimed her engagement to Horace Mann was imminent and it hasn't happened yet.

"I don't think Mother likes Nathaniel any more than you do. I'd rather he didn't have to come to the house."

"Do as you wish. But if something regrettable happens, don't come to me for help."

Sophia lets the matter drop. Although Mary can be quite understanding, in this instance her reservations about Nathaniel are coloring her judgment. If someone has an unconventional personality, Mary's response is to avoid them, while Sophia's is to try to figure them out.

Over the next two weeks, Sophia arranges to visit Boston. Mr. Clevenger responded positively to her request to study with him, so now she writes back to say she's ready to start. For lodgings she'll stay with her friends Louis and Cora Pyne. She'd stay with Elizabeth, but she has only one room. Although a good part of her life has been spent in Boston, this time she's especially excited about being there. This time, she will *not* stay in her room. She will attend lectures and concerts and visit the galleries. She will make herself available for social engagements. And if a headache comes to visit, she will refuse to allow it in. Most important, she will not be coy about Nathaniel or question his motives; she will simply send notice to him about where she can be found and wait for him to call. In short, she will be a fully adult woman, responsible, open to adventure (respectable adventure), and active in the world.

When she's ready to depart, Elizabeth, who is visiting Salem yet again, says she'll take the return train to Boston earlier than intended so her sister won't have to go alone. As usual, Sophia feels she's being treated as an invalid, although she must admit she appreciates the company. On the way Elizabeth tells her she thinks she has found a publisher who wants to print a special edition of "The Gentle Boy" with Sophia's illustrations.

"Oh Elizabeth, that's wonderful," she says, but once again she's a bit taken aback by Elizabeth's . . . she's not even sure what to call it . . . her *intrusive* efficiency?

"I'm sorry to have made inquiries without asking," Elizabeth says. "But I didn't want you to be disappointed if things failed to work out. You'll have to do some additional illustrations. I hope that's all right . . ."

"I would love to. And you needn't apologize. How wonderful for Nathaniel. How much work I have to do."

With that out of the way, Elizabeth tells her about a recent trip she took to Concord, where she visited Waldo Emerson.

Sophia once met him in the West Street shop and she has heard about his lectures, some of which have created a stir.

"He's quite extraordinary," Elizabeth says. "He has a devoted wife and two delightful children and no desire to do anything but write and lecture and invite kindred souls to Concord for long talks. He seems to have found a way to renounce religion without actually renouncing religion. He knows precisely which parts ought to be ignored and which ought to be embraced. But I worry he'll get in trouble. Only last month Abner Kneeland was jailed for doing nothing more than airing his views in the *Boston Investigator*. Granted, Kneeland is a full-throated atheist, but still—"

"Does Nathaniel know about the publisher?" Sophia interrupts.

"Of the edition with your illustrations? Of course. I told him as soon as I found out."

"You went to see Nathaniel?"

"Well, yes, Sophia, you don't think I'd let him move to Boston and not stop by to welcome him, do you?"

"I suppose not."

"He is not your *possession*. Nor, I dare say, does he wish to be."

"I don't know what you mean."

Elizabeth purses her lips. Sophia can see she's annoyed. They sit in silence until Elizabeth speaks: "First you want nothing to do with him and then suddenly he's all you care about. I was the one who sought him out and befriended him, but now you're going to Boston to be near him and acting as if I'm somehow in the way. You may think I'm unaware of everything that's happening, but I'm not."

It's a good thing their train is nearing Boston because neither of them speaks again for the rest of the journey.

When they are off the train and making their way along the platform, Sophia says, "I'm sorry we quarreled. It was my fault. I'm thankful for all you've done." She stops and looks up the street. "Louis Pyne is picking me up here. Would you like him to give you a ride?"

Elizabeth declines the offer—she has errands to run nearby. "Come to the shop when you have time," she adds. "I'd like to sell more supplies for artists and would appreciate your advice."

Sophia watches her walk away. When she turns, she spies Louis Pyne's carriage and raises a hand to catch his eye. Louis is a young lawyer with political aspirations and Cora was a school friend. Sophia has stayed with them before. They have a house that was clearly bought in anticipation of children but there are no children yet, so they have plenty of space. The room they put her in is small but adequate to her needs. She doesn't plan to paint much while she's here, although she did bring with her two small pieces which are almost complete— the one of Lake Como and a companion piece she's done of Lake Maggiore.

In some respects, Sophia feels sorry for Elizabeth. She's read so many books and knows so much that it's easy to overlook the things she understands less well, including how men and women relate to one another. When it comes to how the sexes interact, no amount of reading, no lectures or logic can teach you more than you can intuit. Elizabeth is expert in every sphere, it seems, except for affairs of the heart.

The next morning, Sophia sends a letter to Nathaniel telling him she's in Boston. She's careful not to be too expressive or sound as if she's overly eager to see him. She writes, *Elizabeth tells me we are to be published. Perhaps we should meet to discuss the details.* His reply comes back so quickly she thinks he must have made the postman stand and wait while he composed it: *Yes, of course. I have an idea for a frontispiece. But if you have something different in mind, I will defer.*

More importantly, he asks her to come to his rooms in the

evening two days hence. In the meantime, she meets Mr. Clevenger about her studies in clay. He turns out to be quite young, but his work is impressive. He has a studio that is what she imagines when she pictures her ideal studio, spacious, with high ceilings and large windows, one of which has a view of the sea. Seeing it makes her realize the limitations of working in her bedroom. If only she could have a place like his, even a small one, dedicated to her art.

Clevenger says he'll work with her, although only on busts and portraits in bas relief. "To do otherwise would not be correct," he says. At first, she doesn't understand but then it comes to her. He wants to eliminate any possibility he'll end up instructing a female artist about the sculpting of the human body. Only heads will be allowed.

When her first lesson is over, she calls on her friend Sarah Clarke. Sarah is also an artist, now studying with Washington Allston himself. Sophia tells her about her efforts to copy "Jessica and Lorenzo."

"I know that painting," says Sarah. "It's filled with emotion."

"Emotion held still for our observation," Sophia replies. "It's as if we are seeing the moment right before something life-altering happens."

"Right before a kiss," Sarah says.

Sarah also tells Sophia about her brother James. "Perhaps you've heard he is soon to be married. I went to Pennsylvania and met his betrothed." Yet now a peculiar look comes over Sarah's face. "May I confess something?"

"Of course."

"I didn't . . . I didn't like her very much. She seemed sweet but a bit slow-witted."

Sophia winces. Seldom has she seen Sarah be harsh. "Perhaps your opinion will improve when you get to know her better. Initial impressions can mislead."

"To be sure. But you know how I revere James. My hopes were so high."

After the visit is over and Sophia is on her way back to the Pynes', she thinks about how strange it is that those who share the same values and ideals, even a brother and sister, can make different judgments about the same person. It's especially true if love is involved.

When she reaches the Pynes' house, she finds a letter from her mother waiting on the table in the hall. She opens it and is surprised to find a second letter folded inside. "This came for you and I thought I should forward it," says the brief note in her mother's hand. The second letter? It's from Cuba, from Fernando Zayas. The instant she reads the name, she gasps.

PART THREE

Selfishness is one of the qualities apt to inspire love.

Nathaniel Hawthorne

MARGARET

Shortly after she arrives in Concord, Waldo tells her that a meeting of what he calls "The Transcendentalist Club" is set to occur at his house in less than a week. She is not unaware of this group. It consists of the Boston minister George Ripley, Bronson Alcott, Orestes Brownson from Canton, Frederic Hedge from Maine, and a few other proponents of individualism, autonomy, self-expression, and radical free thought. According to Waldo, they came together over a year ago to discuss the lethargic conservatism of Harvard and of such vaunted theologians and philosophers as Andrews Norton and Josiah Quincy, and have been meeting ever since. Naturally, she's intrigued. Envious too. The very men she'd most like to talk with have been convening and she's been left out.

"Perhaps it's not a good time for me to be here," Margaret says. Her intent is to sound slightly pitiful. She's a proud person but occasionally one needs to playact to make a point. "Won't I be in the way?"

"Quite the opposite. Lidian has been cleaning the house and preparing food for days. We expect a few of those visiting to stay the night. As for you—" She's suddenly afraid he's about to ask her to work as a serving girl on the day of the affair. But before she can form a protest, he continues. "As for you, I have been concerned that no women's voices are heard when we meet. Were I to recommend women be included, there might be some resistance, but since you're already here, as my guest, how can they object? They'll have to welcome you, whether they want to or not. I have no doubt you'll make a useful contribution. In truth, I'd rather sit here and talk with you, just the two of us, than with the lot of them."

Margaret is delighted. She knows he thinks highly of her, but this is exceptional. For the next few days, she can think of nothing else. If the weather holds, it's going to be a picnic, with a big table set up on the lawn beneath the trees. Lidian has hired some local girls to help with the preparations, but Margaret pitches in as well. Doing so voluntarily is different from being relegated to such a role. And Lidian seems to appreciate it: "It's nice to see you have some kitchen skills. I thought maybe all you knew was books."

Margaret isn't sure how to take the remark but then Lidian winks at her and laughs. She goes on to explain that since little Waldo was born, Mr. Emerson has been less chary about the use of servants. In the past he felt that doing so conflicted with his egalitarian ideals.

"And thank goodness for the change," Lidian says. "We can't afford a full-time staff but with a house this size one needs a bit of help now and then. Someone on washday or when we're expecting guests. It's a good thing people are willing to pay for the privilege of hearing Waldo talk. He says he'll never go back to preaching, but I myself don't see why he can't say what he pleases from the pulpit and simply insert God here and there. He'd make a better living that way."

Margaret is impressed by how forthright Lidian is. She doesn't criticize Waldo nor does she adulate him. Talking with her shifts Margaret's view of him a little. In his wife's eyes, high principles are of no use if he can't manage to provide.

She decides another good way to be of help is to take the children off Lidian's hands. Nelly is upstairs with Emerson's mother, so she scoops up little Waldo and carries him outside into the autumn sun. He is quite a substantial boy, not underfed. She puts his feet on the ground and he stands, gripping her thumb for support. He wants nothing more than to take hold of her spectacles; she gives him a handkerchief instead. He waves it like a flag and then begins to chew on it with such enthusiasm she has to laugh. He has a few teeth in front, but the chewing must feel good where the others are trying to come in. Waldo looks down from the house and she imagines what he's thinking: *There is my good friend Margaret.* Or, if not that, then what?

On the day of the meeting, the guests begin arriving before noon. They come by carriage, on horseback, and on foot. The ones from Boston have had only a short journey but others come from further away. The first one to show up is Orestes Brownson, who preaches in Canton. He is tall, over six feet, with broad shoulders and a full, dark beard. He strides toward the house with great purpose and, although Margaret and Lidian are outside arranging chairs, still feels it necessary to pound on the door. After him comes thin George Ripley, whose head of tight brown curls and gold-rimmed spectacles combine to make him look like a scholar-imp. Over the next hour, seven more arrive, including Bronson Alcott, Convers Francis, and Frederic Hedge.

A number of them attended her "mixed" Conversations and surely they know she and Waldo are friends, but they still seem surprised to see her. Frederic Hedge is the most direct. He walks straight over and says, "Miss Fuller, whatever brings you here?" Although she is wearing her blue silk taffeta, she expects no compliments. Those will be reserved for Waldo's recent lecture or perhaps Lidian's food.

The morning is cool but calm and promises a perfect afternoon. Margaret takes a seat under a tree near Alcott. With him, one needn't say a word—for as long as you're present he'll fill the air with talk.

"I saw you at Emerson's Phi Beta Kappa address," he says. "And wasn't it wonderful. It made me think of Fichte's ideas about self-consciousness . . ."

As he continues, Margaret listens with one ear. She's interested in Fichte's ideas about self-consciousness, but not necessarily Bronson Alcott's version of them. Nonetheless, Alcott is always amiable and optimistic, so letting him go on is no great chore. Not only that, but of all of them, he is the least likely to consider the speaking of serious thoughts to a woman a contradiction or waste of time.

She looks up toward the house. Everyone is talking, gesturing, occasionally laughing out loud. This is Waldo's dream. Why doesn't he just build a lodge and get them all to move in. But what would they do for bread? Her earlier conversation with Lidian made her think even Waldo may have difficulty earning enough to support his family. And most of these others lack his prodigious skills as a writer and speaker. Nor does she think any of them is much of a farmer or blacksmith. Maybe a community of Transcendentalists is not such a good idea. The house would fall down around them and any crops they planted would fail.

Margaret puts a stop to Alcott's stream of words, as gently as she can. Then she excuses herself and goes inside to help. Of course, none of the others do. The lunch Lidian serves is impressive. There is a great piece of beef, a leg of mutton with caper sauce, and as accompaniments, a harvest bounty of everything from cauliflower to corn to beans. Even a berry pie. They all sit together at one long table under the trees. Waldo insists Margaret and Lidian join them and leave the hired girls to serve.

George Ripley says the blessing and for that short time she can hear the birds in the trees. Then everyone starts talking again. She is between Frederic Hedge and Orestes Brownson. With one she discusses Kant and with the other, trains:

"I am concerned that a rail line is being built to Worcester," Brownson says. "Can there really be a mass of people who will make use of it? Who goes to Worcester and for what purpose?"

When the meal is over, a more substantive discussion begins. For a time they talk about their adversaries. These days whatever they write seems to draw a hostile response. Andrews Norton, who taught some of them at Harvard, has called the ideas of their group ignorant, barbaric, and "of a twisted shape." Professor George Ticknor has called them irrelevant, although not in print. Emerson shrugs it off.

"The more they are all against me, the more I feel a certain sublime assurance," he says. "Why spend time on the jealousies of Boston when we have the whole world and eternity to discuss."

For a few minutes the talk swirls out aimlessly, almost as if Alcott were its guiding spirit. Then it returns to earth and this time the topic under consideration is the need for them to have their own publication. They ought to be able to say what they want, in the form they want, and not depend on editors who may side with likes of Norton and Ticknor, or perhaps even worse, not understand them at all.

"*The North American Review* is closed to us," says Hedge. "They consider our ideas too radical to publish. As I see it, our hand's been forced."

For the first time, Margaret speaks: "If you do this, it must not be a polite little journal to decorate the parlor table and not be read. You must print what you believe, even if the consequences are dire."

On this matter she can speak with authority because she knows what it's like to have the well-being of your family depend on your reputation, whether you are a school mistress or a preacher or earning money from your words and pen. Most of what she makes goes to her mother and siblings. Like everyone around this table, if she follows the dictates of her conscience, she must acknowledge that others might be harmed.

They gaze at her for a moment and then move on. But having spoken once, she's emboldened to do so again. She suggests Elizabeth Peabody's bookshop might be a good place to sell copies of the new journal to those who don't subscribe by mail. They all know Elizabeth and nod in agreement. She also says a good name for the publication is essential. *Man the Reformer?*" says Convers Francis, tentatively. Margaret shakes her head: "I think we can do better than that."

The meeting lasts all day. They talk about Emerson's lectures (although, tellingly, not her Conversations) and about recent events, such as the Irish riots on Broad Street in Boston, Van Buren's policies, the terrible lack of jobs, and the new British queen. And also about literature, especially Carlyle's *The French Revolution* which only recently made it to America, in part through Emerson's help. Lidian reminds them that there is room in the house for any who wish to remain there overnight, but the weather is good and Boston is close so no one accepts her offer. Then, just as Alcott is preparing to depart, he says,

"I have it!"

Everyone looks at him expectantly. "Yes, Bronson?" Waldo says.

"*The Dial*. We should call the new publication *The Dial*. It's the name I use for the record I keep about my daughters, in which I write down examples of their thought and speech."

No one responds, so Alcott tries again. "Or you might think of it as a *sun*dial, in that it will transform the light which comes from the heavens into meaning for those on earth."

"That's actually quite good," says Hedge. "It has a certain weight and presence."

"And yet it doesn't reveal too much," Waldo adds.

Alcott grins. Among his better qualities is his persistence. When others have stopped trying to solve a problem, he soldiers on—and occasionally finds success.

A short time later, as the last of them ride off into the purple dusk, Waldo comes to stand beside Margaret and says, "I think that went well, don't you? Your contributions were much appreciated."

"I'm pleased you found them so," she replies.

During the afternoon, she hadn't thought about his opinion yet now she realizes that part of her was trying hard to impress him. When she's away from him she can convince herself she's his equal—in ability if not accomplishments—but when she's standing beside him she feels like a student or apprentice. As if everything depends on his regard.

That evening she encounters Waldo's mother in the hall. In all the time Margaret has spent here, she's exchanged only a few words with Mrs. Emerson. Her days are spent in her own room or the nursery, both of which are upstairs. Even when she takes a meal with the family, she rarely says a word. Occasionally Margaret overhears her talking with Lidian in the kitchen, but on the whole she takes little interest in the many visitors Waldo invites to the house. However, now she looks Margaret straight in the eye and it's clear she has something to say.

"Are they gone?" she asks.

"All except me."

"They talk a great deal, don't they?"

"Yes, I suppose they do."

"Save me from magnificent souls," she says. "I like a small common-sized one. It's easier to tend."

HENRY

Since Ellen announced her visit, Henry can think about little else. She has written two more times, once to her grandmother, as she must, and once to Mrs. Thoreau, confirming her travel plans. She may also have written to John, but he's seen no evidence of that. He doesn't like having his brother as an adversary. He'd like to wish him well but can't.

While he's awaiting Ellen's arrival, he continues his efforts to improve the manufacture of his father's pencils. He has designed a better way to grind the plumbago but remains stymied by the lack of high-quality clay. It's either too soft or too hard or of a color that shows up on the page. He tries combining the clay with different materials, from coal dust to bone meal to tree sap, and hardening the mixture in a makeshift kiln.

Then, by accident, in a conversation with a traveling tinsmith, he discovers that a maker of porcelain dishes in Boston actually imports a certain white clay from Bavaria. The book he read in the Harvard library about the manufacture of German pencils emphasized that the clay they use is white. Perhaps it's what he needs.

The next time he has a day off from school, he walks into Boston. He thinks about pencil-making for the first mile and then about Ellen for the next seventeen. Suppose they were to marry? Or, backing up a bit, suppose he were to propose marriage, suppose she were to accept, and suppose it actually happened—could he provide for her thereafter? Schoolmasters are never wealthy, even, as he is discovering, if they run their own school. Perhaps he could take over the pencil-making concern at some future date, or at least become a partner.

He's certain he could be more aggressive than his father about making sales. Why not go to Philadelphia and New York and convince shopkeepers there to place orders? For a moment then he has a vision of himself as a prosperous merchant with Ellen as his wife.

His visit to Boston is a success. He finds the porcelain factory, convinces the owner he is not a rival maker of dishes, and comes away with a bag of white Bavarian clay. When it's used up he can go back and get more, or, better yet, now that he can see what it's like, he might locate a similar product nearby.

On the way home, he comes across an encampment of Penobscots. He's always been intrigued by how they live, particularly how they manage to survive winter in their bark dwellings, so much less substantial than houses of brick or wood. They welcome him and offer him food and he buys a small woven basket for his mother because he knows she likes the ones they make. Whenever he runs across one of their villages, he feels a mixture of admiration and pity but ends up scolding himself because who is he to pity any man? For all he knows they're happier in their hearts than he has ever been.

After that his mind returns to Ellen Sewall. Maybe he could make enough to support her doing what Waldo Emerson does. He wonders how much lecturing pays. He'd have to travel, which he doesn't like, but at least he could use his reading to good effect. Although he'll never be the speaker Emerson is, he does have strong opinions about certain matters, which he'd be quite happy to share.

The idea of lecturing appeals so much that the next time he is helping out at the Emerson house he decides to ask for advice. He is in a small anteroom next to the back door, building a shelf for Mrs. Emerson's outdoor shoes, when Mr. Emerson passes by.

"I've been thinking about doing some lecturing," Henry says. "How does one get into that line of work?"

Emerson's eyes narrow. He looks at Henry in a way that reminds him of how a chicken looks at an unfamiliar type of food.

"You'd like to give a lecture?"

"Well, not just one. Several, I suppose."

"And you'd like to know how to get started?"

"Yes. Not how to write one or how to deliver it, although I'm sure you could teach me a great deal about that. I mean how do you get people to pay you?"

"Oh. Well. Sometimes they invite you and the terms are set in advance. Or you can simply rent a hall and charge admission. Of course, in that case you take the financial risk. The advertising alone—"

At that moment there are footsteps in the hall and Emerson turns.

"We're discussing lecturing. How one earns money simply by speaking. Something you've done quite well."

"Would that it were easy. Even when it goes smoothly I can't help but feel I am selling not just my words but myself. And that anyone who dislikes what I said deserves their money back."

Henry can't see who it is from where he's standing, but he has no difficulty recognizing the voice. And he knows what they're talking about. Even in Concord, Margaret Fuller's Conversations have been widely discussed. Emerson often has houseguests but why her again? Henry has a feeling that if he were to talk to her for any length of time they'd get into an argument. At times she has an annoyingly supercilious tone.

Now she comes up behind Emerson and peers in. "Mr. Thoreau," she says. He's actually a bit surprised she remembers his name. He does like her face—it's strong though not severe. Some people want everyone to appear cheerful at all times, but he respects a serious demeanor as long as it's not the kind that will curdle milk (thinking now of Nehemiah Ball).

"So," she says to Emerson, "continue with your advice."

"I was about to say just what you said. You've got to sell yourself. You can be dignified about it, but if you want anyone to attend you need to print up handbills and put them on every lamppost and tree."

Margaret Fuller raises an eyebrow. "How about telling people what they want to hear? Is that an effective method? Tell me, Waldo, how far are you willing to go?"

Henry is a little taken aback. She's teasing Emerson. Since he's been doing odd jobs for Mrs. Emerson, he's become quite comfortable around Mr. Emerson, but he can't imagine talking to him in the way she is now.

"Not that far. Nor are you. Indeed, my purpose is often quite the opposite. To tell people what they *don't* want to hear."

"He's an idealist," she says to Henry.

"Were I to deliver a lecture," Henry says, "I think my purpose would be to tell the truth. Without regard to how it falls on an audience's ears."

Emerson and Miss Fuller glance at one another. "The truth without apology," Miss Fuller says. "An admirable if not always achievable goal."

SOPHIA

Sophia goes to her room and sits down at the small desk in the corner, the envelope clutched in her hands. She recognizes this as a moment of drama in her mostly un-dramatic life. Perhaps she should wait to open it. She could go stand at the window for a time and reflect on how her life has reached this point. She could pace to and fro and even consider throwing the letter on the fire. But of course she must read it. She picks up the letter knife and slits the envelope with a single stroke. It falls open and she sees the words written in Fernando's hand. He used to send her notes to arrange their outings, to invite her to parties at the main house, to thank her for helping occupy his young cousins even though she, unlike Mary, was not being paid. He has an odd way of making his *g*s and *m*s and *t*s, having been taught the Spanish style of script. Yet his written English is flawless, as good or better than her own.

This is the first letter from him she has received. After she left, she wrote to him a few times, but he never responded. She complained to Mary, who was unsympathetic. "Well, what did you expect?" she said. "He's never going to see you again."

She reads: *My dear Sophia. It has been years since we parted but I think of you each day. I have no excuse for not writing sooner. I received your letters and read them with great pleasure but when I sat down to reply, I knew not what to say.*

She'd been holding breath and now she lets it out. She accepts his apology. At least to some extent.

The current governess is not as skilled as Mary, nor does she come with a charming sister. Indeed, my cousins want their father to bring you and Mary back. But he says by the time he made the arrangements and you returned, they would be too

182

old to need a governess. In truth they scarcely need one now.

It's not a real invitation—he's just being polite. Even if Señor Morrell did want them back, Mary wouldn't consider it. Mary is finished with Cuba. Finished with the heat, finished with the children, finished with the peculiar society of the coffee plantation, which Mary said was like being in medieval Spain. Sophia knows she'd probably have felt the same but for Fernando. As long as he was taking her riding and dancing, as long as he was making her feel she was embarking upon the first great romance of her life, all was well.

She reads on. He tells about his sister and his mother. He tells about his horses (a bit more than she cares to hear) and about the rainy season, which has been too dry. And he tells how he has had some drawings she left behind—drawings she would have thrown on the rubbish heap if he hadn't asked to keep them—properly framed.

One day I would like to travel to Boston to see you and Mary, but for now I am in Havana, occupied with certain aspects of my uncle's affairs. I know it is a great deal to ask but if you would come here for a visit, I would be so very grateful. A presumptuous request it may be, but it comes from my heart.

She looks up from the page. He must know she can't go all the way to Cuba for a visit. She and Mary never tried to hide the fact that they weren't wealthy. And one doesn't make a journey of a thousand miles without understanding the terms. *It comes from my heart.* What is she to make of that? Is this letter some kind of tentative proposal? Is it a test? Does he really expect her to take all the risk? If he thinks this letter will make her swoon, he's mistaken. She folds it up and puts it in a drawer.

She is supposed to see Nathaniel the day after tomorrow. But now Fernando's letter has thrown her into a fit of confusion. Suppose she did decide to travel to Cuba? Maybe she could borrow a little money from Elizabeth and a little more from

Mary. Having been there once, she doesn't view the journey as especially forbidding. And the cost and details of travel are really beside the point. The point is what Fernando means by *It comes from my heart.*

She goes to the shop on West Street, hoping to get some advice from Elizabeth, but it's closed. Then she remembers, Elizabeth is at some meeting—suffragists, abolitionists, proponents of some new type of education for young children, she can't remember which. So she returns to her room at the Pynes' to sit and fret.

When the day she is to visit Nathaniel arrives, she forces herself to stop dwelling on Fernando. She can't believe how much time she's spent studying his letter, especially since she has more important matters to attend to. This will be the first time she's seen Nathaniel since Salem—not so long ago, but what if things have changed?

She decides to wear her gray moiré and puts her hair in a Grecian braid. As she walks across Boston, she feels a bit scandalous. One man in Cuba is sending her passionate letters while another waits at his place of lodging for her to arrive. If six months ago anyone had suggested she'd be involved with two men, she'd have said it was impossible—how could she have time for them and still have time for her art?

The shops are closing for the day and the sidewalks fill with people on their way home. She finds the proper street and as she turns the corner, there he is, waiting for her outside. He smiles warmly. She's never seen him look quite so pleased.

"I was afraid you wouldn't know which building it was."

"You needn't have worried. Your directions were clear."

"I wanted to see you the moment you arrived."

"So now you have. I hope it was worth the wait."

For a few seconds they are speechless. He looks up and down the street as if deciding which way they should go. But then he says, "Would you like to see my room?"

She thought they were going walking—now she really does feel risqué. Her mother would be scandalized. "Do you think it's a good idea?"

"Who's to know?" he says and takes her hand.

He leads her through the front entrance and up the stairs. It seems to be a sort of boarding house, larger on the inside than it looks from the street. When they reach the third-floor landing there are five green doors. He opens one, stands aside, and motions her in. Although it's still light outside, in here it's decidedly dim. She waits while he goes to the fireplace, ignites a piece of kindling on a coal, and then touches the wick of a lamp. As her eyes adjust, she looks around, but there's not much to see. A bed, a chest, a washstand, a small table that can serve as a desk. It's very compact, very Spartan—a monk's cell. She ought to say something nice about it but doesn't know what that would be. Then it comes to her:

"You're quite close to the wharf. That's convenient."

"I am. A walk of ten minutes at most."

"And there are plenty of oyster houses where you can eat."

"As I often do. You are entirely correct." He pulls the chair out from the desk and says, "Here, sit."

"I shouldn't stay."

"Just for a moment. Let me take your cloak."

"I think I'd prefer to keep it on for now."

Again there is an uncomfortable silence. Before long her eyes adjust and she can see the room better. "You need a rug," she says. "It will help when it gets cold."

He nods. "Yes, an excellent idea."

"And something on the walls. You can't just leave them bare."

His eyes narrow and he looks around the room. "That could be distracting, don't you think? When I am here in the evening all I do is write and sleep."

"Perhaps. Or it could provide inspiration. All I know is I

should hate to wake up in the morning and look upon these walls."

"What would you recommend?"

She's somewhat surprised to have him ask her opinion. More often than not he seems terribly sure of himself and can be abrupt when dismissing ideas different from his own.

"Let me think on it," she says. "I will have a recommendation when I see you again."

Bit by bit they begin recovering the ability to converse they had back in Salem. It feels strange to be alone with him like this, but now that she's here she sees no reason to run off. She asks him about his family and gets the same circumspect response as always. He asks a similar question of her and she goes on at length about Mary and Horace Mann. She asks him about his new job and he describes it:

"Primarily I weigh and measure incoming cargoes of coal. I make note of where each is from and where, once disgorged from the hold of the ship, it is bound. I make long columns of numbers and add them up. At the end of the day I turn my numbers over to the manager who studies them and frowns."

"It doesn't sound too unpleasant."

"It's not, except when I'm sent out at night. Ships seldom arrive after dark, but if one does, I'm called to work. I row myself out and climb aboard, always fearing what I may find."

"Demons in sailors' dress?"

"Thus far, only weary sailors in sailors' dress. For which I am thankful."

"Maybe someday you will write about it."

He nods but appears dubious. "I shall call it 'The Nibblings of a Wharf Rat.' How does that sound?"

She looks outside and is surprised to see it's now fully dark. "I must go. Thank you for your hospitality," she says. "I enjoyed seeing your room."

"I promised you a walk," he says. "So I shall accompany you home."

She's worried about being seen leaving with a man at such an hour. "I would like that, but I should have left earlier," she says.

"There's a door in back. We'll exit that way."

He guides her down the stairs and through a dark hallway. Then he takes her hand as they go out into the night.

At the end of the alley, along the street, the lamps have been lit. But where they are, it's utterly dark, so dark she can't see the buildings which she knows are close on either side. If a thief were lying in wait it would be impossible to tell. Yet Nathaniel has in mind another use for the darkness. He turns and gathers her into his arms.

"Oh, Sophia," he says. "I am so happy you're here." Before she can reply, he kisses her. She looks up at him. She was expecting this to happen and welcomes it, but pretends to be surprised.

They walk out of the alley and into the yellow light. They speak very little, remarking only on how cold the breeze is for October and on whether it's better to cross the Common or go around. When they reach the door of the Pynes' house, he says, "When can I see you again?"

"Whenever you wish."

"Tomorrow?"

"The day after tomorrow."

They stand looking at one another, neither willing to be the first to part. At last Nathaniel says, "I should go. I may be called to work tonight."

Back in her room she pictures him rowing his small dinghy through the choppy waters of the harbor, alone and cold, the lantern on the prow casting a meager light into the fog.

MARGARET

The day after the gathering of the Transcendentalist Club, Margaret and Waldo are back at work. He has asked her to tell him what she thinks of an essay he's working on, one that will take ideas he presented in an address to the Phi Beta Kappa Society in an even more radical direction. As she reads the draft in her room, she hears Lidian go into his study, hears them conversing about some household matters, hears them talking to little Waldo and exclaiming about something the child has said or done.

She continues to be surprised at what a doting father he is. It can even be a bit distracting. Sometimes when the two of them are discussing something, he is so busy dandling little Waldo on his knee he has to ask her to repeat herself. But what can she say? It's more touching than annoying. He listens to the child babble and says, "His utterances are like Sanskrit. They are untranslatable but one is left with the feeling that their meaning is profound."

She hopes he will advise her about how best to direct her energies now that she is done with her translation of Goethe. She has several ideas and isn't sure which one to pursue. But later in the day, when she finds him in his library and poses the question, his reply is a complete surprise.

"The journal we spoke of at the meeting. We want you to edit it."

She must not have heard him correctly. This isn't possible.

"What do you think?" he continues. "Will you at least consider it?"

Any of them, Ripley, Brownson, even Alcott could do it. She's amazed they want her, yet even in her astonishment, she knows they made the right choice. The truth is, none of them, not even Waldo, could do a better job.

"*The Dial*," she says.

"I suppose so. Unless you can think of something better."

"No, I like it. Good old Alcott." She looks out the window and collects her thoughts. "I will want to discuss the particulars. How we'll advertise it and what the editorial policy will be. I'm not sure I can manage the day-to-day business of a publication while also soliciting and editing articles . . ."

"Most definitely not. Ripley says he'll serve as business manager. He'll handle the advertising and sales."

She thinks back on the day before. How did this happen? When the meeting broke up it seemed to her there were still a number of problems that needed to be worked out. But no matter. Her mind is now overflowing with more important thoughts.

The next morning, Waldo invites her to go with him to Watertown to hear a young minister speak. It's just the two of them, Waldo driving the gig with her beside him, so they are able to talk at length. She explains that her vision of the journal is one of complete freedom.

"I cannot be held to any set of principles. I may elect to publish things you or the others dislike. Even ideas that will place our reputations in danger."

"I would expect nothing less," Waldo says. "I have already been called an infidel by Andrews Norton. I'll be disappointed if the contents of the journal fail to enrage our adversaries. Indeed, that should be your goal."

"I must also ask about my salary," she says. "How is that to be determined?" She can think of nothing she'd rather do than edit *The Dial*, but she can't work for nothing. As successful as the Conversations were, she earned barely enough to pay her debts.

"It will depend in part on how successful the journal is.

Although I cannot give you precise terms, I promise you'll be fairly paid."

She'd like to push him on this point, get him to name an exact amount. But she understands that in a venture like this, there are no guarantees.

Even though they are talking business, she feels very close to Waldo today. She has his full attention. Her thoughts and words mean a great deal to him right now—after all, she is to be the editor of *The Dial*—and she revels in that knowledge. There is no place she'd rather be, no one she'd rather be with.

In passing, Waldo remarks that he thinks the young man they are about to hear, Horatio Phillips, is the sort of speaker Lidian likes best—"I'm told he stays close to the gospels and doesn't embellish much."

"You should have said something," Margaret exclaims. "She ought to be going instead of me." Suddenly she feels quite insensitive. It never occurred to her that Lidian might have wanted to attend. "Did you ask her if she wanted to go?"

For a moment he looks puzzled. Then he shakes his head dismissively. "I did not. Perhaps she'd have enjoyed the outing, but she takes no deep interest in these things. She'd rather stay home and write letters than travel miles to see a preacher. Remember, she lives with one and must listen to him every day."

His attempt at humor isn't welcome. Margaret would like to tell him to turn the gig around and go back to Concord. She says, "It may not be my place to say so, but it would have been better if she'd been consulted. I intend to apologize when we get back."

At the church in Watertown, she has a hard time listening to the sermon attentively, but Waldo seems engaged. Horatio Phillips is something of a prodigy. He's never been to divinity school and, although he's hardly more than a boy, his deep voice makes him sound like Moses. The meaning is in the bluster and not the words. She is surprised Waldo cared to hear him. Perhaps he was merely curious about the young man's appeal.

On the way back Waldo is silent and she's glad to have time to think. She has yet to see a marriage in which the woman is treated as well as she ought to be. From the outside, everything can seem quite congenial, quite loving, but the closer one gets, the less appealing it all seems. She admires Waldo so much, in so many different ways, that it's particularly unpleasant to find that his own marriage is no exception. Perhaps the problem is marriage itself and not the individuals involved. Two people come together out of love or some kind of necessity and commit to spending their life together. But even a short life is measured in years, and change is inevitable. And that's assuming the match was a good one at the start.

Certain remarks Waldo has made have led her to believe he still has deep feelings for his first wife, who was just eighteen when he married her and twenty when she died. People say she was beautiful and full of life. It's hard to imagine either of those things being said about Lidian. She has her own good qualities—a strong, even stately, bearing, a sharp intellect, the ability to run an orderly household. And perhaps more important than any of those, she seems unfailingly supportive of Waldo—where he goes, she will follow.

Once they are back in Concord, she has second thoughts about apologizing to Lidian. To do so would be to insert herself into their relationship and that would be a mistake. She is still nothing more than a guest and ought not to overstep.

Instead, she turns her attention to *The Dial*. She writes up a plan for the first issue and shares it with Waldo. She's confident about her ideas but wants his approval. The following afternoon she sits across from his desk and watches him as he reads. She can't wait to hear what he thinks. At last, he looks up.

"Excellent," he says. "You have taken our vague intentions and given them substance."

"So I can proceed?"

"Of course you can. You needn't ask my permission. If you are to be the editor, the decisions are yours. However, I do have one small suggestion."

"What's that?" She's suddenly worried. He may think it's a small matter, but at this stage everything is significant.

"Henry Thoreau has given me an essay on the Roman poet Persius. I think you should look at it. It is less than outstanding but more than competent. It shows evidence of genuine talent. Perhaps he could revise it for publication with your help."

So it really is a small suggestion. Mr. Thoreau a writer. She had no idea.

HENRY

At last Ellen arrives. The entire household has spoken of little else for days. "When Ellen gets here, we shall . . ." "During Ellen's visit we must . . ." "I wonder if Ellen will . . ." She used to be viewed as a pleasant but unexceptional visitor; now things have changed. Only Helen hasn't fallen under the spell. She says, "I like her very much but it's as if we're welcoming royalty. I have no idea why there's so much fuss." Then she tosses Henry a mischievous look. She knows quite well the reason for the fuss.

John and Henry meet her coach. As usual, John is calm while Henry frets. Both know they'll be competing for her attention but there's no point in discussing the matter. In fact, they'll do well to pretend they are above such pettiness. Ellen is now a grown woman, and nothing would be worse than behaving like boys.

"I was hoping the two of you would meet me," she says. "I feared it would be my aunt."

They scuffle a little over who will carry her bag, then quickly catch themselves and John lets Henry take it. With Henry on her left and John on her right, they walk up the street.

She's even prettier than when they saw her the last time. Henry glances at her profile, her long lashes, straight nose, and pink, shell-like ears. He finds how she's wearing her hair appealing.

"Do you know what you'd like to do while you're here?" Henry asks.

"I am so happy to be free of my father I don't really care. Is that a terrible thing to say?"

"Having met him, I understand your feelings," John replies. Henry has never been to Scituate, so he has nothing to add.

"He thinks I'm still a child."

"Which you are not," Henry says, stating the obvious and feeling foolish for having done so.

Upon reaching the house, Aunt Prudence and Ellen's grandmother quickly take over, insisting she sit and provide news of the family, but not before Helen and Sarah can greet her.

"We are going to have such fun," Helen says. "We shall go off together and leave all these others behind."

"What about me?" Sarah says.

"You can come, provided you consider yourself ready to hear the things grown-up ladies talk about."

"Oh, I do," Sarah exclaims.

The next day Henry can't wait for school to end. The only thing that makes it bearable is that John is similarly occupied. If he weren't, Henry would be thinking of nothing but how he's being outplayed.

After lunch, in an effort to make time fly, he abandons the regular curriculum and reads aloud. One of the books he has borrowed from Emerson is a collection of English ballads and he's discovered the children are extraordinarily intrigued by them. Death in the mines, death at sea, death in battle, death at the end of a hangman's rope and always the loved one left behind to sing the song. He selects "Mary Gray," about a girl who demands the boy who is in love with her prove himself by swimming across a raging river. Naturally, he drowns, and for the rest of her life, all she can do is weep and walk the hills. The children listen intently right through until the end.

"She made a dreadful mistake, didn't she," Henry says.

"He should have said no," says Roderick Hibbert. "I'd never do that for a girl."

"She worked her magic on him," Agatha Cartwright says, an unmistakable note of admiration in her voice. "He couldn't resist."

Neither of them is older than twelve but they consider themselves quite worldly, able to pass judgment on matters of great consequence. And Henry doesn't try to disabuse them. In fact, he encourages such behavior. Isn't that what poetry is for?

Poetry. Henry has been reading it in a white heat lately—Chaucer, Headley's *Select Beauties*, and Milton, from beginning to end. He's not sure what's come over him. He's always read the Greeks and Romans, but this is first time he's fully immersed himself in the English and Scottish traditions. He thinks he might make a collection of the best of English poetry and see if he can find a publisher for it.

Roderick turns toward Agatha and says, "You're just saying that because you like the idea of girls murdering boys."

"Bootjack," Agatha replies.

At last the school day ends. Henry quickly packs up his books and papers, pokes his head in John's room, and says, "I'll see you at home." When he gets there, he finds Ellen has gone off with his sisters.

"They went to visit Susan Sharp," his mother says, naming one of Helen's friends.

Aunt Prudence studies him. "What is it you want with her?"

"Nothing in particular. I thought we might take a walk."

"Just the two of you?"

"Whoever wants to go."

"I think perhaps *I* should like to go walking," Aunt Prudence says. "If you mean what you say."

Henry sighs, but inwardly, not so she can hear. The last time Ellen visited, Aunt Prudence took little interest in where her niece went and who she was with. Back then she treated Ellen as a child, one who was allowed to run about the forests and fields of Concord with almost complete freedom. Yet now Ellen is older and, while Aunt Prudence may not fully understand who is in love with whom, she considers it her responsibility to supervise. To send reports to Ellen's mother in Scituate. To give the girl advice. Poor Ellen, Henry thinks. Poor me.

John gets home next, then their father, and finally Ellen, Helen, and Sarah, just in time for supper. Afterward, their father gets out his flute and Henry, who also plays though not as well, joins in for a duet. Ellen seems to be enjoying herself. John plays no instrument and doesn't sing much either. And yet there he is, sitting beside her, which might be the preferable position. Their shoulders are touching, as are their knees.

When the piece ends, Ellen compliments his playing: "That was delightful. Henry, I didn't know you were so musical."

"He has many hidden talents," John says, and he doesn't elaborate. If it was anyone else, Henry would think he was being ironic, but that's not John's way.

The next day is Saturday. School lets out at noon, so Henry sets about organizing a boating party. For a moment it appears Aunt Prudence is going to follow through with her threat; then Helen intervenes:

"I'm going to town to buy some fabric for a dress," she says. "Would you come and help me pick it out? You have a good eye for color."

Prudence herself often comments on what a good eye for color she has, so Helen's request comes as no surprise.

"That rust colored one you wear so often doesn't do you any favors," Prudence says. "I say look for green."

With Prudence safely out of the way, Henry, John, and Ellen head for Walden Pond. It's a bright fall day, the kind that makes young people feel even more spirited than usual. They walk briskly, laugh at one another's jokes, and the conversation never falters. Henry knows there is some peril involved in appearing to compete with John for Ellen's attentions, but he can't help himself and begins to share his superior knowledge of nature as a way to impress her. He points out the tracks of an otter in the mud. He identifies birds by their songs.

Ellen says, "You certainly are observant. My father tells me I walk about with blinders on. He says I need to look where I'm going."

"It's not what you look at that matters, it's what you *see*," Henry says.

"I never thought of it that way. I shall share that wisdom with my father."

John shakes his head. "Henry can't pass up a good aphorism. He's got one for every occasion."

"The sun shines even on the wicked," Henry says. There's a pause and then they laugh.

Henry and John have a small boat stashed near almost every pond in the area. And if they don't, they borrow someone else's, taking the view that an unused boat is like an unused bench—no one should be upset if you employ it for its intended purpose and leave it undamaged when you're done. Today it's only a small one they built years ago, but it's good enough. John is in the bow, Henry is in the stern, and Ellen is seated between. It would be ideal if John were elsewhere. If John were elsewhere, Henry would take her in his arms and kiss her. He would tell her he has special feelings for her, feelings he's had for no other girl. He would commit himself to her and hope she'd do the same. But there in the bow sits John.

However, the way he describes it in his journal later is different: *Today I rowed in my boat a lovely young lady, and, as I plied the oars, she sat in the stern, and there was nothing but she between me and the sky.*

SOPHIA

This autumn has been uncommonly mild. In Boston, the winds that blow up and down Hanover Street and across Purchase Street next to the water are less frigid than in most years. Some days Sophia finds her cloak is almost too much.

She now sees Nathaniel several times a week. They walk, they visit coffeehouses, sometimes he comes to the Pynes' house and they sit in the parlor, and, yes, sometimes she goes up to his room, although always taking care to avoid being seen. On the days they don't meet, there is often a letter from him, filled with bits of news and small endearments. She has never been so happy. She has never had so few headaches. Not even in Cuba.

Surprisingly, Mary has returned to Boston now as well— this after suggesting to Sophia that leaving Salem was a mistake. She has taken rooms on Chauncey Place and has a job teaching young children. Sophia has a bad habit of thinking of Mary as brainless but knows that isn't true. In her own way Mary always manages to take care of herself.

"I used to think Horace's proposal was imminent," Mary says. "Now I realize that if I am in Salem and he is in Boston, it may never come to pass." Before Sophia can reply, she holds up a hand. "Don't say you expected this. He is still recovering from the death of his wife so there's good reason for his caution. But how can he begin to see me as someone who can make his life satisfying again if we're so seldom together?"

"I think it's wonderful you're here," Sophia says.

Mary shrugs. "It *is* wonderful. Now I can advise you about Mr. Hawthorne and you can console me about Mr. Mann."

Sophia finds the length of time Horace Mann is taking to get over his wife's death excessive. If he doesn't intend to remarry, he shouldn't lead Mary on.

When Sophia is not visiting Nathaniel or Mary or helping Elizabeth in the shop on West Street or taking sculpting lessons from Mr. Clevenger, she paints. Which means she's not painting very much. However, she has completed the small scenes of Lake Como and Lake Maggiore. Her plan, which came to her the night she and Nathaniel first kissed, is to give them to him to hang on the bare walls of his room. She thinks they came out rather well, although since she did them based not on the lakes themselves but on her memory of some other artist's paintings of the same lakes, she has no idea if they're true to life. So once again she is a copyist. Perhaps she is destined to be nothing more.

Yet when she takes them to Nathaniel, it's as if she's outdone Michelangelo.

"My god, you made these?" he exclaims. "How beautiful they are."

"They're yours if you want them."

"I have never owned a painting in my life."

He hangs them on the wall, and they do look quite nice, she has to admit. In his next letter, he says when he wakes up in the morning, he lies in bed and looks at her paintings and wishes she were there with him. *Wishes she were there with him.* Just reading those words makes her knees weak.

As they've been together more, Nathaniel has become increasingly forthcoming. He tells her how he came home to Salem after college in Maine and spent months and months in his room writing. He tells her how as a boy he injured his leg in the schoolyard and needed crutches to walk for a long time thereafter. And he tells her how his sea captain father sailed off one day and never returned.

"What became of him?" Sophia asks.

"He died of yellow fever in a place called Surinam. I was only three."

"So, you've never really had a father."

"My mother has told me stories about him. But no, not as a living presence."

Sophia considers her own father quite ordinary. It is her mother who educated her and her sisters, her mother who introduced them to interesting people in Boston when they were younger, her mother who insisted they have independent minds. Even so, she can't imagine her father simply being gone.

She is also beginning to understand Nathaniel's devotion to writing. It's now clear to her the long hours he spends at his desk. He won't describe the stories he is writing in any detail, but he says he has ideas for something grand, beyond the tales and sketches he's done thus far.

"The past is a deep well from which I hope to draw up something of consequence," he tells her. "I am not ready yet, but the time will come."

Although Sophia is pleased Nathaniel is being less reticent, knowing more about him only increases her curiosity. Each time he answers a question she thinks of three more to ask. One afternoon when she is visiting him in his room, he steps out to post a letter. As soon as he's out the door, she can't help herself. She looks in his wardrobe and in his chest of drawers. She pages through the letters on his desk and is alarmed to see one from Elizabeth. But when she reads it, she finds there's nothing to be alarmed about—it's simply relaying information about the publication, with Sophia's drawings, of "The Gentle Boy." She reads two more letters—one from his sister and one from an old college friend—and then makes herself stop. She shouldn't be doing this. It's a betrayal of trust and there's nothing of significance to be found.

But then she picks up a ledger book. She thinks it may be where he records his expenditures, but it turns out to be where he keeps the thoughts and ideas he collects to use in his stories—thoughts and ideas that are more revealing than any letter to a college friend:

A rich man leaves his mansion to a poor couple. They move into it and find there a shadowy servant, whom they are forbidden by the will to turn away. He becomes a torment to them.

And:

Some treasure is buried and a tree planted right over the spot, so as to embrace it with its roots.

And:

An old volume in a large library—everyone is afraid to unclasp and open it, because it's said to be a book of sorcery.

Sophia can see how the stories in his book might have started with items such as these. There are pages and pages of them, written in a quick, scrawling hand.

Some are simply striking images:

The aromatic smell of peat smoke in the sunny, autumnal air.

But others are genuinely troubling, even horrifying:

A monster to be the offspring of loveless love between two beautiful persons.

In an old house a mysterious knocking might be heard, on the wall, where had formerly been an old doorway, now bricked up.

But then she comes upon a page where the words and phrases are immediately familiar. Of course they are—they are *hers.*

A blue satin bodice laced in front over a white satin chemisette. A necklace of pearls and pearl earrings. (Ball dress, Cuba)

A bird calling "Sophia" in the woods.

She doesn't know what to think. He told her he had set down a few lines from her journal he didn't want to forget. But still there's something unsettling about it—perhaps because she's found them without asking, perhaps because they are in a notebook where much of what's written is so troubling, so fearfully strange.

She continues to read—*A man wants no natural wife but one manufactured to order. Write an essay about fire—or rather about smoke*—and is so immersed that she fails to hear him return. But something alerts her to his presence, and she glances up to see him standing there, his eyes fixed on her, the door still half open behind him.

"Oh! It's you," she says.

"So it seems."

"This—I didn't—I shouldn't have. But it's very interesting."

"I suppose I should be pleased you find it so."

"Nathaniel, I'm so sorry. Now you'll never trust me again."

The remainder of their visit is difficult. She keeps wanting him to say something about her transgression, either forgive her or erupt in rage. But he does neither. He tells her about his errand. He tells her about the progress Elizabeth has made in arranging for his story and her drawings to be published (she doesn't admit she already knows this from the letter). He tells her he'll be unable to see her for several days because his new job requires him to make a trip to New York.

As usual he accompanies her home. She tries again to apologize. "I did it because I want to know you as well as I possibly can."

"Can you understand how I might find that distressing? That I might not choose to be . . . to be *known*."

"I won't do it again," she says and then remains silent until they reach the Pynes' house. Lately they've shared kisses in the shadows beside the porch before she goes in, but tonight he only nods and walks away.

The next few days drag by. She has yet to respond to Fernando's letter and decides this is a good time to do so. As she begins to write, something occurs to her—Fernando is entirely transparent. He is romantic, expresses himself willingly, and, as far as she can tell, has no hidden parts. Nathaniel, on the other hand, hides much and discloses little. Yet unlike some men, he is mysterious by nature and not just to be evasive. Perhaps it's a mistake, but she prefers Nathaniel's hidden depths.

Therefore, she tells Fernando she was pleased to hear from him, but it is impossible for her to visit Cuba again. She writes that she hopes his work in Havana goes well. Her days in Cuba now seem like something she read about in a novel. A novel in which she wore a blue satin dress and a bird called out *Sophia* from the trees.

Once the letter is sent, she is left to worry exclusively about Nathaniel and the difficult way they parted. But when he gets back from New York, he's so preoccupied by something new it's as if she never transgressed.

"While I was traveling I was thinking about George Ripley's farm," he says with unusual enthusiasm.

She knows Ripley is a prominent reformer who is friends with her sister Elizabeth, as well as Margaret Fuller, but she's heard nothing about any farm.

"He hopes to purchase a tract of land with the intention of creating a new community—a community of like-minded people living together and sharing in the fruits of their labors. He intends it be a new model for living, one that is based on cooperation and good will."

"Where is this tract of land?" she asks.

"Near West Roxbury, on the Charles River."

"Who told you of it?" She comes and sits on his knee. She's happy to see him again, happy he seems to have gotten over her reading of his private papers.

"Why, your sister. I'm surprised you didn't know."

"She probably thought I wouldn't be interested," she says and kisses his brow.

"In any event, I consider Ripley's project worthy. So much so that I plan on purchasing a share."

She slips off his knee and steps away. Nathaniel is the last person she can imagine getting involved in such a scheme. A community of like-minded people? Who does he think has a mind like his?

"And leave me here?" she says.

"I will go and if it is successful and I am happy there, you can join me. And if not, I'll come back. Sophia, you are my future and every decision I make from now on will be with you in mind."

"Do you think being a farmer will make you happy?"

He looks at her as if the thought never occurred to him. "I shall be a writer first, a farmer second, and your husband most of all. *That* will make me happy." And then, upon realizing he just called himself her *husband*, Sophia laughs in stunned delight.

MARGARET

Margaret throws herself into editing *The Dial*, soliciting articles and poems from everyone she can think of, even, as Waldo suggested, Henry Thoreau. She finds the process intensely engaging—this may be what she was meant to do. She especially likes how the work has changed her relationship with Waldo. If they weren't equals before, they are now. She assigns him to read manuscripts and has even had occasion to overrule his judgment about a poem.

"I find the language evocative," he says.

"I find it unclear and therefore do not wish to publish it." She meets his gaze and awaits his response.

"Very well," he says and goes back to his library.

The launch of *The Dial* isn't the only project capturing the imagination of Emerson and his circle. George Ripley is now promoting a venture in communal living, which he calls Brook Farm. In only a few short weeks, it has become the chief topic of conversation among reformers in Boston and the towns and villages nearby. She and Waldo discuss it for hours, walking across fields and through orchards, while letting their manuscripts languish on their desks. Perhaps Brook Farm will be the transformation of society they've all been waiting for.

"According to Ripley, the object is to ensure a more natural union between intellectual and manual labor," Margaret says. "To combine the thinker and the worker in a new and more vital way. At Brook Farm there shall be industry without drudgery and true equality without vulgarity. Or so Ripley says."

They pause on a bridge over a stream and watch the water as it purls among stones that glisten in the sun. "Ripley is very anxious to enroll me," Waldo says. "He needs every dollar he can get to buy the farm and build cottages thereon. But can't I get the same advantages here in Concord, without abandoning my house?"

"*You* can but can anyone else? If you do not act, others may fail to act as well. Great change requires great disruption. Revolutions do not leave the old world in place." It is a measure of how things have changed between them that she feels she can take him to task for being self-protective.

"You think this portends a revolution?" he says, looking troubled.

"I don't know. I suspect when a revolution is in the offing, those closest to it may be the least aware."

He sighs. "I don't doubt that Ripley's design is noble and humane."

She waits for him to say more and finally prompts him. "However . . ."

"However, I am suitably placed already—in an agreeable neighborhood, in a town which I have many reasons to love. Here I have friends and kindred. Here I have built and planted." Again, he pauses, ponders, gazes downstream. "Furthermore, I may not be as beneficial to Ripley's community as he hopes. I am very likely to be its greatest skeptic, not because of its character but because of *my* character. I favor the idea of community in theory. But in practice? Not as much."

She's not sure if she'll join Brook Farm either, but others don't look to her for guidance. Besides, she might not have enough money to purchase a share.

"I will think on it more," he adds, perhaps sensing Margaret's feelings. "No matter what I decide to do, I want to be sure my actions don't interfere with Ripley's endeavor. I shall support it to the extent I can."

The following day Margaret finds herself at the table after breakfast with Lidian and asks how she would feel about moving to Ripley's farm.

"I'll do whatever Waldo wants of course," Lidian says.

"Of course. But you must have a preference." Margaret's not sure why she's pressing her. She knows the answer will always be "Whatever Waldo wants."

"I like our life here quite well. We lack for nothing."

"Have you told Waldo that? Has he asked you?"

Lidian busies herself clearing the table. It's almost as if she didn't hear, but Margaret is sure she did.

"I think you are . . . overly interested in this matter," Lidian says. "I understand that one's participation in this . . . this 'Brook Farm' is considered evidence of a commitment to certain ideals. That may have led you to think Waldo's decision is a matter for public debate. I assure you, it is not."

There are times when Margaret can't resist an argument, and this is one of them. Although she can sense herself treading on ground she ought to avoid, she responds: "I don't think that at all. But I must admit, my own decision depends in part on his."

Lidian turns, and the expression on her face is one Margaret hasn't seen before.

"I tolerate a great deal," Lidian says. "When I married him I understood that although I could never replace his first wife, I might compensate by making my ambitions his. Yet now it seems *your* ambitions are becoming entangled with Waldo's. If you wish to live on Ripley's farm, neither Waldo nor I will stop you. But you have no business trying to convince him to go there too."

"I haven't . . ."

"You think I'm unaware of how you feel about him, but I am not. Ripley's farm isn't the real issue. As you well know."

For once Margaret has nothing to say. She returns to her room, closing the door behind her. Her eyes fill with tears. The problem is not that Lidian has accused her unjustly. It's that she's very close to the mark. Without fully understanding what she was doing, she'd been picturing herself and Waldo together at Ripley's farm. Lidian was not in that picture. She hadn't realized Lidian has been watching and listening and drawing her own conclusions about her and Waldo. Conclusions that, if the situation was reversed, she herself might draw.

Perhaps she ought to leave. But she doesn't want to. She needs him—almost as much as Lidian does, in her own way. More tears are coming now, she is nearly sobbing, and she does her best to muffle the sound because she doesn't want either of them to hear. If only she'd met him before Lidian did. It's a thought she's had before, a pointless, destructive thought, but it is at the root of her emotions and cannot be dismissed. If that had happened, she has no doubt they'd be together—together in mind, body, and spirit, together now.

Out the window she watches the sky turn violet and the trees go black. An intense loneliness washes over her. People compliment her on her ability to talk but you can't talk to yourself. When night falls and you are alone in your room, wherever that room may be, talk is of little value. Even books are of little value if you have no one to share your thoughts about them with. She used to think intelligence was the most important of all human qualities. It's an idea her father instilled in her from a young age. Yet what good is her intelligence right now?

For the next two days, she stays in her room and works on *The Dial*. It's what she ought to be doing but it also serves as a convenient excuse.

Finally, at breakfast the third day, Waldo asks if she's all right.

"If I don't get these manuscripts read and turned back to their authors with my comments, there shall be no *Dial*," she says, a bit self-importantly.

"How may I be of help?"

"By leaving me alone." He looks at her quizzically, then excuses himself from the table and retreats.

The following afternoon she is deeply immersed in her work when there is a knock at the front door. Margaret emerges from her room to see an attractive young woman standing in the foyer with Waldo. Why, it's her young friend from Boston, Cary Sturgis, who brought so much life to the Conversations.

"Ah, you have arrived," says Waldo. "I hope you found us without difficulty. You know Miss Fuller, I believe."

She's not surprised Waldo knows Cary. They travel in similar circles and, if memory serves, when her name came up some months ago, she told him Cary was someone he ought to meet. But while she's pleased to see Cary, she's also confused. The Emersons can invite whomever they want to their home, but you'd think they'd have told her someone else was coming. Especially since she and Waldo have so much work to do.

After greetings have been exchanged, Waldo takes Cary's bags upstairs, leaving the two women to talk. Cary is wearing a pink serge dress that fits her perfectly and a bonnet with ribbons to match.

"I didn't expect to see you here," Cary says. "Are you a guest as well?"

"Yes," Margaret says, "I come to see them often. I've been here for several weeks."

"I'll relish the opportunity to talk with you," Cary says brightly. "I thought I was coming to see only Mr. and Mrs. Emerson. But with you here it will be a party of sorts."

"A party," Margaret says. "How nice."

HENRY

Ellen's visit is passing quickly, and Henry is having no luck finding opportunities to speak with her alone. If she's not with Helen, she's with Aunt Prudence. If she's not with Aunt Prudence, she's with John. Still, they have all had a fine time. The weather has been excellent, allowing them to boat and ride the neighbors' horses and visit Acton to see a traveling fair. Ellen has become almost a third sister to Helen and Sarah. Sarah in particular has developed quite a crush on Ellen, looking to her for advice about everything from how to dress to what books she ought to read.

Finally, with only a few days left, Henry invites Ellen on a walk. It takes some doing, but he manages to select a time when everyone else will be otherwise engaged. He even makes a lunch of bacon sandwiches in secret so no one will suspect his plan. However, to his great dismay, Aunt Prudence shows up at the last minute and says she's coming too.

"I know some think it's old-fashioned, but I don't like the idea of two young people going off alone," she says. "Let me get my bonnet. I'll be right there."

"I thought you had a meeting at the church," Henry says.

"They'll just have to get along without me."

They set off for Fair Haven Hill. He and Ellen walk together, Prudence only a few steps behind. Of course, she talks continuously.

"It's a fine day to be out, don't you think? But we could surely use some rain. Ellen, does your mother like that quilt I sent her? I wish I'd done it in blue instead of white. I expect it shows the dirt. I believe I have a pebble in my shoe. Wait while I sit on this stump and get it out."

He and Ellen exchange exasperated glances. What can they do? "Those who talk the most, often have the least to say," Henry whispers.

"I'm awfully sorry," says Ellen. "But I have an idea."

When they stop to eat their sandwiches, Ellen says, "Aunt Prudence, why don't you rest here and let Henry walk me up to see the view. He says it's quite a steep climb."

Ellen knows her aunt well. She may like to interfere, but she prefers not to exert herself overmuch. "I *am* a mite fatigued," she says. "Don't be long."

As soon as they are out of earshot, they laugh.

"She can be a bother," Ellen says.

"But she means well."

"I suppose she does."

The view from the top of Fair Haven Hill is striking. They can see how the rivers and streams wind down the valley, how the trees and shrubs have become every imaginable autumn color, from lemon yellow to blood red, and how the carts and carriages and drovers moving cattle raise clouds of dust as they ply the roads.

"Thank you for bringing me here. I like being with you, Henry. I hope we will always be friends."

He picks up a stone and throws it out into the blue void. "I share that hope," he says.

"You and John are so much alike and yet so different."

"I guess that's true. Though you might say that about any two humans." He wishes there was a way to disentangle himself from his brother. He doesn't like being compared.

"May I ask you a question about him?" Ellen says.

"Of course."

"How do you think he feels about me?"

Disappointment washes over him. So she cares about how John feels about her. He's confident she hasn't asked John the same question about him.

"He likes you very much."

She nods and looks into the distance. He can tell she's having complicated thoughts—which means he should *do* something—take her in his arms, accuse her of being indecisive, anything but stand mute and tug at his ear. Eventually her expression changes. "My aunt will worry about us," she says.

No sooner have they turned toward home than Aunt Prudence begins talking again. This time it's welcome. After a while, she becomes reflective and tells about her youth.

"Your mother was the one who went walking with boys," she says. "I did have some callers but when father fell ill, he needed me, so I stayed home. Yet I was not unhappy. I have always had interests and occupations. It is no great tragedy to remain unmarried."

Although Henry is only half listening, her last remark makes him uncomfortable. Is it directed at Ellen? Is it directed at him?

That night, Henry works on some poems in his room. Emerson and his colleagues have started a new magazine and he is being encouraged to submit something. He's not sure his poetry is good enough. Maybe an essay instead. He doesn't mind letting Emerson pass judgment on his work, but apparently they've named Margaret Fuller editor and he's not sure how he feels about that. The few interactions he's had with her have been rather difficult. Then again, it may not matter who the editor is. Tonight each word he writes seems false.

In frustration, he puts down his pencil. As soon as he does, thoughts of Ellen flood his mind. He considers his options. He wishes life was like *A Midsummer Night's Dream*. He and John could be Lysander and Demetrius, which would mean that at some point a second girl would show up. After some misunderstandings and humorous twists, they would pair off, two and two. But he is unaware of any such girl and so the story veers from comedy toward tragedy. Love triangles seldom end well.

Later, just before midnight, he goes out to walk. To his surprise, he finds John outside, looking up at the stars. Ellen said they were alike but different. One way they are different is that John is almost always in his bed asleep by this time of night.

"What are you—" Henry says, but before he can finish John interrupts.

"Brother, I have done it," he says. "I have proposed marriage to her."

Henry feels as if he has been struck by a fist. By a hammer. By a bolt of lightning from a towering thunderhead.

"When? When did you do it?" He can hardly get the words out. He has no breath.

John too seems breathless, although in his case it's from accomplishment and joy. "Tonight. We went for a walk."

"And what did she say? If you don't mind . . ."

"She seemed happy. Though she said she must speak to her father before she can accept."

"How good for you," Henry says. He feels as if he's speaking to a stranger—someone he met in a tavern or while walking down the road.

"You're the first one—the only one I've told. I don't think I'll tell anyone else until I know for sure."

"That would be wise," Henry says.

For the next few days, except for teaching his classes, he spends nearly all his time in the woods. He tries to keep his distress from his students, but they sense something is wrong.

"Mr. Henry, you look like my uncle when he had ship fever," says Patrick Harper. "Are you not well?"

"I'm well, Patrick. Well enough. Tend to your composition and not to me."

He avoids John as best he can. He times his walks to and from school so they won't be together and has been taking his meals on his own. He finds he can scarcely stand to be around

Ellen. He averts his eyes when she glances his way.

"If you fail to finish your work because of inattention there will be consequences," he tells the class.

"Maybe it's the grippe," says Cynthia Holmes.

SOPHIA

Unlike John Thoreau, Nathaniel Hawthorne doesn't have to wait for an answer to his proposal. He doesn't even have to ask; they both just know. Sophia buys him a small copy of William Wordsworth's poems, inscribes it lovingly, and presses it into his hand. She says, "To seal our pact." But her quick acceptance doesn't mean there aren't challenges to be faced. His family, for instance.

"What if they dislike me?" she asks.

"Any objections they have will not be about you—or your family. My mother thinks highly of your father. She let him pull three of her teeth. They are on intimate terms."

"Then why would they disapprove?"

"They think I should establish myself first. They consider a wife merely another expense."

"You have a good job," Sophia says.

"I have a job—which I intend to resign when I go to Brook Farm. I think it's best if I try things there first, before we make the announcement. As I said, if I find the location and work congenial, we might decide to make it our home."

"Then perhaps I should move to Brook Farm as well . . ."

He ponders her suggestion for a moment and then shakes his head. "You're happy here in Boston, are you not? As you know, I am a man of caution. In this as in all things, I feel the need to deliberate before I act."

She's not fully satisfied with his plan or his explanation, but she doesn't want to push too hard. At the same time, she doesn't want to become like Mary, waiting for a man to act as months turn into years. Nathaniel is passionate but his passion burns slowly. Sometimes she wishes it would burst into flame.

"Come away with me," he would say. It occurs to her that if Fernando Zayas had come to Boston instead of telling her about his business commitments in Havana, he might have had her. She seems to attract a strange breed of ardent but circumspect men.

"I expect to hear from you often," she says. "And as soon as you think it's appropriate, I expect an invitation to visit. I want to judge the place for myself."

In the days that follow, Hawthorne resigns his position. It paid well enough, but he didn't like the work and never saw it as his future. Before he can pack his things and leave, Sophia says, "I want to make a drawing of you."

"Of me? Why?"

She kisses him on the cheek. "So I won't forget what you look like while you're away."

The next night she visits his room and makes him sit for his portrait. She positions him so the lamplight illuminates his face. It would be better if it were morning, but he insisted he had things to do to get ready to move and couldn't spare the time until now.

Sophia stands back and looks at him. She moves left and looks again. She moves right and then goes to him and lifts his chin. "Stop frowning," she says.

"I'm not frowning. It's my natural expression."

"Then you're a natural malcontent."

"Please get on with it. I'm not done packing yet."

Sophia sits, her sketchpad on her knees. She works with pencil, quick strokes to begin and then slowing as she focuses on details, especially his hair and eyes.

"Be still," she says. "You keep shifting about."

"How long will this take?"

She ignores his question. She likes having him under her control. He is her subject and must follow orders. "You really are quite handsome," she says.

"You're making this very difficult."

"Breathe deeply. It will help you relax."

She wishes they could get married tomorrow. Why must he go off to join Ripley's experiment? He should be devoting all his attentions to her. Of course, if she said as much, he'd claim that's exactly what he's doing. She just wants to be in his arms.

At last she takes pity on him. "Come look," she says, and he gets up from the chair, stretches his back, and crosses the room.

He stands behind her and inspects the drawing. "This is how you perceive me?"

Sophia nods. "Are you offended?"

"No, quite the contrary. I'm flattered. It's better than what I see in the mirror."

"Of course it is. You take a rather dim view of humanity. And an even darker view of yourself."

He bends down and kisses her on the neck. "I wish I had the skill to draw you," he says. "I would make of you an angel."

Sophia shivers with pleasure. For words like those, she can put up with him going off to Brook Farm. Provided it's not for too long.

Two days later he is gone. Brook Farm isn't far, just a few miles from Boston, but now that they are truly in love, truly pledged to one another, Sophia feels as if he's boarding a ship to sail for the South Seas. As if he's going to the far side of the world.

She pays Mary a visit so she can complain. She has always used Mary for this purpose and Mary uses her the same way. "Nathaniel is gone, and I hold Elizabeth responsible."

"How do you mean?" Mary is looking pretty today, with bows in her hair and a pink blush in her cheeks that seems almost luminous, as if her skin is painted glass.

"Whenever the reformers come together to hatch a new plot, she is in the midst of it. Elizabeth and George Ripley are close friends. I promise you he wouldn't have committed to something like this without her approval."

"I think you give Elizabeth too much power. She has her enthusiasms but this time I don't believe she was the instigator. If a woman was involved, it was probably Margaret Fuller. I understand she has become quite influential. Besides, your friend Mr. Hawthorne is a free agent. He didn't have to go."

"Nathaniel rather dislikes Margaret Fuller," Sophia says. "The other night he was invited to a dinner party at George Bancroft's. When he found out she was to be present, he sent his regrets."

For a time they discuss their parents. Her father isn't having any more success with his practice in Salem than he was in Boston, so they've decided to move back. As they talk, Sophia is also thinking about whether or not she should she tell Mary that she and Nathaniel are betrothed. They agreed to keep it secret but Mary tells her everything about Horace Mann, so it doesn't seem fair.

"His moving to Brook Farm changes nothing between us," Sophia says. "It was nice when we were both here, but I intend to visit him often."

"Are the two of you . . . progressing?" Mary asks, in a tone of studied nonchalance.

"You might say that."

"Would you care to tell me more?"

Sophia doesn't like it when Mary pries, so to punish her, she discloses only this much: "I've been seeing him several times a week. In between his visits, he writes me delightful little notes. We have indeed progressed."

Mary makes a harrumphing noise. "Tell me something *new*. Something shocking."

Sophia ignores her request and says, "What about Horace? Have you seen him recently?"

"He is away on business. But the last time we were together he spoke about you and Nathaniel."

"What did he say?"

"He said he is pleased that you are happy. However, he doesn't place much value on the writing of stories. He holds that it is better to spend one's time helping the blind and indigent than scribbling for profit."

"Oh really? That's what he thinks? Well, you can tell him Nathaniel has yet to profit from his writing. Maybe that will alter his opinion. According to Nathaniel, the more he writes, the less money he has."

MARGARET

Margaret's relationship with Lidian continues to be strained. However, that doesn't prevent her from asking about Cary Sturgis. She wants to know what she's doing there and how long she'll stay. It isn't that she dislikes Cary, but couldn't she visit some other time?

"Young people of a certain character often contact Waldo," Lidian says. "And he is open to their inquiries." She is mending a shirt and keeps her eyes on her work as she speaks. "They seem to think he has something special to teach them."

Margaret knows they have lots of guests, from Elizabeth Peabody to Frederic Hedge to—it now appears—ingenues like Cary. It makes her wonder if Waldo views her as just one among many and of no special value?

"You must weary of having so many visitors," Margaret says. "Maybe this would be a good time for me to return to Boston . . ."

"Do as you please. Although in Waldo's eyes you are different from the others," Lidian replies, as if she's heard Margaret's thoughts. "He would want you to stay."

So, stay she does, but with Cary Sturgis in the house the pattern of the days changes. Margaret still works in her room in the morning but in the afternoon she no longer knows what to expect. Some days Cary goes off with Lidian, so she and Waldo talk as they always have. Other days she and Waldo meet, and Cary joins them. Cary is her usual vivacious self, although her tendency to pose impertinent questions seems less charming than before.

"Why is poetry considered superior to natural speech?" she asks one day. They are in Waldo's study, he at his desk

220

and Margaret and Cary across from him. It's an arrangement that makes Margaret feel as if he's a tutor and they are his students—as if her equal status has been rescinded.

"Well—I don't—I suppose it is—Wordsworth has argued that poetry ought to *include* more natural speech, but that's not what you're asking. What an interesting question . . ."

Margaret contemplates Cary's pretty face. The changes caused by her presence here are upsetting. One of the pleasures of visiting Waldo has been how regular and predictable the days are. And that she has him to herself. As for Cary's question, the answer is obvious. Poetry is superior because the best of it is language charged with the utmost meaning. Unlike the exchange they are having right now.

Cary is also intensely interested in Brook Farm. "I think it would be an adventure," she says. "Not like going to Brazil or Australia, but it would offer one a chance to experience a different sort of life."

"While I'm in support of Ripley's ideas, he doesn't need my presence to test them out," Waldo says, repeating his previously stated stance.

"I agree," says Margaret. "For myself, I intend to provide what financial aid I can. I expect they can make more use of that than of the labor of my hands." She holds them up for their inspection. They have callouses only from holding a pen.

That night she thinks about her remark and, acknowledging to herself that she has no money to give but also that she doesn't want to be a liar or a hypocrite, writes her mother and asks to have one of the family's cows delivered to Brook Farm. Given her circumstances, it's the best she can do.

In the days that follow, she spends more time on *The Dial* and less with Cary and Waldo. She finds it too stressful when the three of them are together. Realizing she hasn't seen the Emerson children in a while, she goes upstairs and visits the nursery. There sits the elder Mrs. Emerson holding Nelly with little Waldo playing at her feet. When Mrs. Emerson hears her, she looks up, startled, and says, "May I help you?"

"No, I just . . . I hadn't seen Nelly and Waldo lately, so I thought I'd come up."

"Did you think they'd been taken by fairies?"

Margaret finds the old lady's tartness agreeable. "I thought perhaps you might like some company."

"If you wish," she says and nods in the direction of a straight-backed chair.

They sit for a while and then Margaret, feeling the need to break the silence, speaks: "I have no experience caring for children of this age."

"Children—easy to get, but hard to be rid of," she replies.

Coming from a grandmother, the remark is slightly shocking. Yet if she can be provocative, Margaret can too.

"Do you *like* it here?"

Mrs. Emerson looks up. "I suppose I'd better," she says. "I have no other choice."

As Margaret leaves, she thinks about Waldo. He clearly got some of his frankness from his mother—which prompts her to wonder: If old Mrs. Emerson had the opportunity, what sort of lecture would *she* give.

The next day, still preferring to keep her distance from Cary, she invites Henry Thoreau to meet with her to discuss the essay he has submitted at Waldo's request. If she can tell him she met with his young friend and has given the essay serious consideration—even if she ends up rejecting it—he may not be too annoyed.

Thoreau comes to the house and they sit outside on a bench.

"How are things at your school?" she asks.

"Pretty good. We have nineteen students and have moved out of my parents' house. Whether or not the children are learning anything is another matter." He pauses as if considering the whole of his curriculum. "But I forget you are a teacher. You know the challenges we face."

"Indeed I do. But I am not sure when I'll will return to teaching, given my new responsibilities with *The Dial*."

"Given your talents, I expect you can do whatever you please."

What does he know about her talents? Perhaps Waldo said something. Or is he being sarcastic? She's not sure what to make of him. Their previous meetings have been awkward. But Waldo seems to like him so well.

"It's kind of you to say so," she replies.

She has his essay with her, but it's been face down on her lap until now. As she turns it over, she says, "Thank you for letting me read this. I found it quite interesting. Particularly the first part where you compare the satires of Persius with those of Horace. It appears you think Horace's are superior."

Henry nods. "Because Horace uses satire to lift up as well as to critique. Whereas Persius only attacks."

She nods in agreement. "That's true. You have read them both well. But in the second half, I'm not quite certain what you're getting at. It seems underdeveloped. Perhaps you'd like to work on it more."

He shakes his head. "It's quite clear. What don't you understand?"

Margaret looks up from the page. She hadn't expected him to resist. Taking a different tack, she says she finds his thoughts on religion confusing. In response, he patiently guides her through his argument, which is that religion isn't some private conversation a select few carry on inside a church but rather a conversation between the universe and every man.

"I concede your point," she says, beginning to get exasperated, "but what you say here about time . . ."

"Is quite similar to what Mr. Emerson says: 'All questions

rely on the present for their solution. Time measures nothing but itself.'"

At that moment it comes to her. It's not just Horace he has mastered, but Emerson as well. And although the essay is not without flaws, it's closer to what she hoped to publish in *The Dial* than most of the other manuscripts she has already accepted. To reject it would be wrong.

"Thank you for your clarification," she says, her tone shifting as she speaks. "It will be my pleasure to put it in our first issue. It challenges received opinion, which is our chief intent."

"Well, that's a surprise. I thought you were getting ready to turn it down." Then he grins, which catches her off-guard, and she finds herself smiling in return.

With that, their relationship has changed. They have formed a business partnership, the editor and the author. She tells him when the first edition will appear, and he asks what else she expects to include. She asks if he has any poetry she might read. He thinks for a moment and his face falls.

"I've written a poem this week but it's rather sorrowful I'm afraid."

"What is its subject? I have no prejudice against any emotion if it's plumbed with honesty and care."

"It's as honest as I could make it. The subject is love. A love I recently lost."

She understands and is touched. The poor boy. After she heard about James and the girl in Pennsylvania, she wrote poems as well. In fact, there continue to be nights when she thinks about him and tries to put her feelings into words.

Placing a hand on his arm, she feels the coarse cloth of his homespun shirt. "I'm so sorry. What became of her?"

"Another fellow got there before me. He's asked her to marry him and I expect she'll say yes."

"Are you certain?"

"Certain enough. He's good and decent. If she turns him down, she's a fool."

They sit for a time in silence. She's not used to playing this role. When she was teaching, her girls would sometimes come to her to talk about their romantic tragedies (always tragedies, never comedies). Of course, she would listen, but they were younger than Thoreau and she always assumed they could go to their mothers or aunts or older sisters if they needed serious advice.

"Writing can be a consolation," she says. "I sometimes find it so." She's afraid he's going to ask her why she has never married. If he does, she's not sure what she'll say. Instead, he asks her if she has any plans to come here to Concord to live.

"Not at present. I like my visits with the Emersons, but I think it's a bit too quiet for me."

He gets up then, thanks her for her interest in his essay, and says good-bye.

"I shall pray that your rival gets an answer of no," she says.

It's not a serious comment, just a parting quip, but he stops and turns.

"I don't believe there's any God that can answer that sort of prayer," he says and then strides off down the path. His gait is forward leaning, as if he's facing some resistance, like a farmer pushing a plow.

The next morning at breakfast Cary Sturgis asks Waldo to go walking and he says yes. This Margret considers a violation. It's not that she wasn't invited but morning is for reading and writing. While they're gone, she decides it's time for her to return to Boston. She needn't be in Concord to edit *The Dial*. Except for Thoreau and Waldo, Boston is where most of the authors live. In addition, she intends to schedule a new series of Conversations. Let Cary and Waldo do as they please. She will attend to her work.

HENRY

He leaves Margaret Fuller sitting on the bench in Emerson's garden and walks straight out of Concord. She is an odd woman—reserved, skeptical, and with a confidence in her intellect that exceeds his own. He's pleased she wants his essay for the new magazine but unsure if he'll offer her anything else. Certainly not the poem they discussed. It's too personal and not very good. He considers his writing a form of thinking on paper and not necessarily a commodity to be sold on the open market. He isn't opposed to such transactions, but they're not the reason he writes.

Emerson's suggestion that he keep a journal has turned out to be a good one. Recording what he sees and thinks and experiences throughout the day is becoming a habit—even a compulsion, albeit a satisfying one. Sometimes he writes about what he observes: *There is the distinct trail of a fox stretching a quarter mile across the frozen pond;* and other times he takes a more contemplative approach: *He enjoys true leisure who has time to improve his soul's estate.* He's tried to get his students to adopt the practice but for the most part they see it as a school exercise, more drudgery from Mr. Henry, rather than as an opportunity to open one's eyes to the world.

Since John informed him about his proposal to Ellen, he has slept little, eaten little, and walked a great deal. Ellen has gone back to Scituate—that at least is a relief—so now he watches John checking the post daily for her reply. He told Miss Fuller that Ellen would be foolish to turn John down. That is true, but he's not sure what he'll do if he has to watch his brother and Ellen marry.

He walks between two fields, one littered with the leavings

of the corn harvest and one planted with winter rye, and then enters a stand of trees. Suddenly, he sees a tanager. A red bird against green pines and blue sky! How it enhances the wildness and wealth of the woods! This bird and the emperor moth are the closest Concord comes to the tropics. Although the tanager must pay for its color with the hoarse notes of its song.

When he and John were on Mount Washington, John talked about continuing northward. At the time, Henry thought it a bad idea, but now he's not so sure. Suppose he were to keep walking, north and still further north, until he crossed into Canada—he could start a new life there. Or maybe he'd prefer the West. Ever since the journey of Lewis and Clark, the country seems unimaginably large.

But it's as if he's tethered. Any time he travels a few miles out of Concord, he feels himself being pulled back—gently at first and then more strongly, until his only choice is to turn toward home. If John and Ellen marry, they will probably live in Concord and maybe even in his parents' house, at least for a time. He couldn't stand the pain of seeing her every day. Not long ago, Emerson told him about George Ripley's new farm, where an attempt is being made to create a harmonious community of work and thought, one that isn't so bound up with money and the getting of useless goods. Perhaps he could move there. Then again, he can think of little less appealing than a group of reformers trying to create heaven-on-earth. He'd rather live alone in hell.

Darkness falls. There's no moon, and to proceed, he must use senses other than sight. His feet tell him he's going downhill, and he can hear the river off to his left. He stumbles into some dense brambles and has to back out. He tries again to find the way forward and again is thwarted. As he stands in the encompassing darkness, trying to get his bearings, he's as lonely and bereft as he's ever been. *Omnes una manet nox*, wrote Horace. One night awaits us all.

When at last he finds his way home, he goes up to his bed and falls into restless sleep. He dreams of being with John on the river, and of the camelopard, its head above the trees. And then suddenly it's morning and down below he hears the usual Sunday sounds of everyone getting ready for church. On his way downstairs he encounters Sarah. "We're having guests for dinner this afternoon," she says. "A whole family of them. They've just moved here from Boston and father invited them over." She looks up at him and claps her hands excitedly. "Henry, all the children are *girls*."

A moment later, in the kitchen, he encounters Helen, who explains that it's the Alcotts, father, mother, and four children.

"I think you've met Mr. Alcott," she says. "What's he like?"

Henry shakes his head. "Peculiar but quite friendly. A man unlike any other. I promise you he will talk."

Somehow Henry managed to miss out on the fact that the Alcotts were moving to Concord, taking up residence in the Hosmer cottage. Emerson may have mentioned it, but he's been so preoccupied with Ellen that perhaps he didn't hear. While the others are off at church, he begins making preparations for the guests, setting up a long, makeshift table of planks on wooden trestles, next to the house, under the trees.

As soon as they're back, Mrs. Thoreau puts on her apron and takes command. "Helen, the bread. It needs to go in the oven now. Sarah, peel the potatoes. Prudence, if you would be so kind as to be in charge of the gravy when the time comes, I would be very grateful. John, cover the muddy spot on the path with gravel. I can't have them soiling their shoes."

Henry she assigns to carry chairs outside and cut down the thistles so they won't snag the girls' skirts. It's a breezy fall day and already the table he set up earlier is half-covered with yellow leaves.

Soon, the Alcotts arrive. First come the girls. They appear to range from about five to ten years in age except for the youngest, a babe who is being carried by the eldest girl. They are followed by their mother and finally Bronson, whose blue eyes show relief upon seeing Henry, the only one there he knows. He wears a coat of coarse gray canvas and, betraying a certain awkwardness, keeps his hands tucked in his breeches pockets. Like many loquacious fellows, he is shy at heart.

Those who are inside making preparations come out and introductions are made. It's a good thing the weather is tolerable—the Thoreau house is spacious, but this would be quite a crowd to feed indoors.

Sarah is thrilled. Three other girls near her age and a baby for them all to tend. Mrs. Alcott goes off with Prudence, who apparently knows her from abolitionist events, while Henry, John, their father, and Bronson pull chairs together to talk.

Father welcomes Bronson to Concord and asks what brings them here.

"Many things. I shall enumerate: One, I am weary of city life. Two, I see great opportunities for business hereabouts. Three, I seem to think more clearly in the country. Four, I am a great consumer of apples and there are many apple orchards in the region. And five, Mr. Emerson often seeks my counsel, and it would be convenient to be near his home." He pauses and frowns, as if making sure he's left nothing out. Then he adds one more: "Even the name of the town bespeaks my principles. I wish my girls to grow up in a place of *concord*. A place of harmony and delight."

Father looks a bit stunned. He says, "I see you have given the matter a good deal of thought."

However, Henry knows there's more to it. Alcott's school in Boston was a scandal and the chance that he could start some new venture in the city without experiencing opposition is probably small.

Helen brings them cider and Alcott explains the salutary effects of cider, particularly on the blood. John, who is the kind of person who has little patience with Alcott's type, makes an excuse and slips away. Alcott has the high forehead of genius, yet from there the top of his pate slopes rather alarmingly toward the back. Maybe it's just the cut of his hair, but it causes Henry to wonder what the phrenology book would say.

Next, Father describes his trade and Alcott listens intently. He appears fascinated. He asks questions about the wood they use, the manufacturing process, and says he'd like to see the shop someday. This pleases father so much he says, "We can go there right now!" but Prudence overhears him and intervenes: "Don't go running off yet. Dinner is imminent. If you disappear, your wife will have your head."

That idea squelched, Alcott turns to Henry and begins asking him about his school. He also describes in some detail his own school, which was based he says, on *talk*. Henry is unsurprised. Alcott says he is deeply and constitutionally opposed to corporal punishment, which causes Henry to think about Nehemiah Ball. He'd like to get the two of them in a room together and have them debate. Or better yet, wrestle shirtless, best of three falls.

"Children must *feel* what they learn. It must be *embodied.*" He pauses for a moment and gazes out across the grassy field. "Anna," he calls. "Lizzie, Louisa, come here." The girls stop and look over. They are engaged in some kind of game and it takes a moment for them to shift their attention but now they approach, Sarah trailing behind. Their hair is down, their shoes are off, and they look a little wild.

"I'll show you how my daughters learned their letters," Alcott says. "It may be a method you could use with your own students. I found it quite effective. Place yourselves, girls."

Henry doesn't know what to expect. The girls are all about the same height with the same dark hair. Two of them smile and one looks annoyed, maybe because their father called them away from their game.

"C" Alcott says, and the one on the left turns sideways and forms a semicircle with her arms.

"O" Alcott says and the next one forms a similar shape although without an open side.

"W" Alcott says but this daughter looks exasperated. She can't make the letter because she's holding the baby. Seeing what the problem is, Alcott takes it from her, and she holds her arms toward the sky, one on either side of her head.

"Once learned in this fashion, they never forget," Alcott tells Henry. "I started them as soon as they could walk." Then he addresses the girls: "What sound does the cow make?"

"Oh father, please don't," says the one in the middle. "Not in front of our new friends."

Helen, who has come over to watch the performance, takes pity on them. "Look, the food is coming out as we speak. Let us find our seats at the table."

At dinner the conversation is lively. Alcott continues holding forth. Henry would never ask his students to make their bodies into the shape of letters, but he applauds the man for trying new things. Too many educators simply do to their students what was done to them. Alcott will be an interesting addition to Concord, of that he is sure. Before they depart, Alcott inquires about enrolling his daughters in the Thoreau brothers' school.

"Of course," says John. "We'd be delighted to have them."

"Would it be possible to pay their tuition at a later date? I expect it will take some time before my funds are transferred here."

Henry says yes, with misgivings. He realizes he might be agreeing to educate the girls for free. He can tell the family hasn't much money, and Alcott is the type who'd rather talk and hatch grand schemes than roll up his sleeves and earn an honest day's pay. For men like him, "at a later date" might mean never.

That evening, when the Alcotts have gone home, Henry finds himself alone with John outside. Nightfall has brought with it a colder breeze and somewhere not far away a solitary wood thrush is singing its eloquent song. They talk about the Alcotts and about some improvements they might make at the school, but eventually Henry can't resist asking about Ellen.

"Have you heard from her?"

"I think I may need to go to Scituate to plead my case. She says her father is considering the matter. I'd like to help him consider it faster."

"He will approve, I'm certain of it."

"I'm only a schoolmaster. I haven't much to offer."

"Go to Scituate. Take Aunt Prudence with you. That will give you an excuse to make the trip. I will manage things at the school. And we'll celebrate when you get home."

SOPHIA

Letters from Brook Farm begin arriving at once:

Dearest One,

On my first day here I was greeted by an unseasonably early snowstorm. I hope I brought enough warm clothing. I know I will miss the warmth I feel when I am in your arms.

Although I have not yet taken my first lesson in agriculture, I went to see our cows foddered yesterday afternoon. We have eight, one of the which, I am told, was contributed by Miss Margaret Fuller. Miss Fuller's heifer is a fractious beast, apt to kick over the milk pail and express reformist thoughts.

I intend to make myself useful by becoming a milk-maid and pray Mr. Ripley will assign me the kindliest cow in the herd.

My chamber is the best in the house. Though not quite so good as the apartment I left in Boston, it will do quite well. I have hung up your two pictures; they give me a glimpse of summer when outside all is snow and mud.

[Next day]

I did not milk the cows last night because Ripley was afraid to trust them to my hands. But this morning I have done wonders. Before breakfast, I went out to the barn and began to chop hay for the cattle. With such righteous vehemence did I labor that, in the space of ten minutes, I broke the tool (the name of which I've forgotten). Then I went inside and ate up a huge mound of buckwheat cakes.

And just two days later:

Most Beloved,

I have now successfully milked a cow and plan to do it again tomorrow. I am told the trick is to be gentle but firm.

This sounds reasonable but is difficult to enact when the moment comes. As a rule, cows are docile, but Miss Fuller's cow behaves in a very tyrannical manner. She hooks the others with her horns and has made herself the ruler of the herd.

I have been writing this in my room, but the fire gives little heat and the windows are not tight. Please come to visit as soon as possible. I love thee. I would thou wert with me. I would thou wert now and forever my wife.

She reads it again and again. His endearments make her heart soar. She begins to entertain fantasies of the two of them becoming farmers. And why not? He sounds as if he is learning the necessary skills. In her eyes, there's nothing Nathaniel can't do.

The next day she begins making preparations for her visit to Brook Farm. She knows Elizabeth has already been, so she goes to the shop and asks her for advice. How does one get to West Roxbury, how should she dress, what should she take with her, and are there accommodations for visitors?

"It's not the wilderness," Elizabeth says. "Dress as you do here. Take with you whatever you would take for a trip to Salem. Tell Nathaniel you'll need a room."

"Why haven't you moved to Brook Farm? You've been a supporter from the start."

Elizabeth motions toward the wall of books behind her. "Who would run this place? Besides, it's not my role. I let Ripley hold a meeting here to raise funds and I've done my best to publicize his efforts. I may consider it at some future date but for now . . ."

Sophia doesn't fully believe her explanation. "You don't really think it will be a success, do you?" she says.

"It's an awfully large undertaking. Ripley and those accompanying him have a great deal to lose." She pauses, a look of uncertainty in her eyes. "I'm not sure he can convince enough people that we are meant to live as he wants to us live. Perhaps if some great man takes up the cause . . ."

"Emerson?"

"If he would. Although why go to Brook Farm to live in someone else's ideal world when he can make one of his own devising in Concord."

"I have certain ideas about a perfect world," Sophia says, as much to herself as to Elizabeth. "And they don't involve reforming society."

A few days later, Sophia is sitting alone in a coach, rumbling up the road toward Brook Farm. The recent, early snow has melted away and the land looks well-tended and prosperous, even as it turns brown with fall. The houses in this vicinity seem quite antique, with long sloping roofs commencing a few feet from the ground and ending in lofty peaks. Some of them are overshadowed by huge old elms, and barberry hedges separate yard from yard. She feels herself to be in quite a rural state of mind. City life, town life, even village life seems cramped and artificial. One really ought to be out in the country, among the trees and birds. And the cows, about which Nathaniel has written a great deal.

She can't wait to be with him. She counsels herself to remain composed when they meet but her emotions keep shifting. Some days she thinks he is very wise to insist they wait to get married while he explores the possibilities offered by Brook Farm. Other days she wonders if he's having misgivings he isn't sharing with her. And often she's simply confused. Yet as soon as she steps off the coach in West Roxbury and sees him standing there, wearing his simple butternut-colored peasant's shirt, all is put right.

"My dove," he says, and there in front of the driver takes her in his arms and kisses her on the mouth. And then he continues to hold her until the movement of the coach forces them to step back.

"I'm so excited," she exclaims. "I want you to tell me everything."

"So I shall," he replies, and as they walk along a tree-lined lane, he describes his morning, which he spent shoveling manure.

"George Ripley calls it our gold mine. He says we'll turn ordure into riches. I must say, I find even that part of my work more fulfilling than what I did at the Custom House."

Before long they crest the top of a low hill and she finds herself looking down on Brook Farm. There are four houses, one of which is quite large, two substantial barns, a number of small outbuildings, a lovely stream (the "brook" of Brook Farm?), and fields bounded by wooden fences and stone walls.

"Look there," Nathaniel says, his arm outstretched, "beyond the barn."

"Ah," Sophia says. "The cows."

A few short minutes later they have arrived. On close inspection, the farm is less pretty than she expected—or perhaps *hoped* is the better word. There are mud holes everywhere, and the clapboards on the buildings are in need of paint and repair. Of course, this is still early days in the history of the community. Presumably things will get better and better until at some sunlit moment in the future, perfection is achieved. That's the point of a utopia, is it not?

Nathaniel takes her to the room where she'll be staying so she can leave her bags. It's just a small chamber with a bed but it will do. Then he shows her his room, in the large house called the "Hive." It's on the first floor, has its own stove, and there on the wall are the two landscapes she painted for him. "Don't they look excellent there?" he says.

She's glad she gave them to him. He seems so proud of her. They sit and talk, and she tells him about her trip down from Boston and her most recent lesson in sculpting with Mr. Clevenger. "Clay and stone may not be my medium of choice," she says, "but I am enjoying learning something new."

"At least you are working. I've not written a single story since I've been here. Scarcely even a page."

"You've written me letters . . . wonderful letters. There are things in them you've never said to me before." She's teasing him now, trying to get him to blush. Which he does.

"I write them late at night."

"Exactly how I pictured you. And doing it after a long day of shoveling—I shall use George Ripley's word—shoveling *gold.*"

They spend the afternoon touring the farm. There are fewer than thirty residents—she expected more. They stop and speak with Minot Pratt, the head farmer, who tells her Nathaniel is an excellent worker, and then they encounter George Ripley himself. Sophia has met him on several occasions in Boston, but he has been transformed. In place of the clothes of a Boston clergyman, he wears a rustic hat, tall black boots, and trousers held up with rope.

"You must come join our little settlement," he tells her. "We have ample room and I'm sure Mr. Hawthorne would be delighted. Bring your sister Elizabeth with you. Bring your father and mother. We have no dentist yet."

When he's gone, Sophia tugs at Nathaniel's shirtsleeve. "So, 'Mr. Hawthorne would be delighted . . .' What have you been saying about us?"

"Nothing. He's making assumptions. I have been quite reticent."

"As have I," she says but she wonders if Elizabeth has been talking. Maybe keeping their betrothal secret isn't possible. Maybe they shouldn't try. Yet Nathaniel keeps implying it will be a terrible mistake if his mother finds out before their financial future is secure.

Miss Fuller's cow turns out to be lovely. It's the color of caramel with an ivory face and great liquid eyes. If it has a tendency to be overbearing, Sophia doesn't see it. All it does is blink its long lashes and graze.

"This beast is not at all as you described it. You've slandered the poor thing."

"It's behaving well for your sake. The minute you've gone back to Boston it will return to its spiteful ways."

They have supper in the communal dining hall and, as one of two guests this evening, Sophia receives a good deal of attention. Everyone wants to know what's happening in the city, even though Boston is fewer than ten miles away. It's as if Brook Farm is an island cut off from the wider world.

She tries to think of what to report. "The mesmerist Griselda Upton will be doing soundings next Saturday at the Masonic Hall. The abolitionist cause seems to be gaining ground—every meeting Mr. Garrison holds draws a larger crowd. And Margaret Fuller has scheduled another series of Conversations, to be held again at my sister Elizabeth's shop."

Two of the women say they participated in the first series. They describe how fulfilling they found them but add that they probably won't be going to the new ones because Boston is too far away.

"I suppose you'll be attending," one of them says, sounding a bit envious.

"Yes, I believe I shall."

Sophia glances at Nathaniel and is unsurprised to catch him rolling his eyes.

Afterward they walk about the farm, arms linked in the failing light. He takes her to see a grapevine he has discovered which has wrapped itself tightly around an oak. She is reminded of visiting the night-blooming cereus with Fernando. That experience was so strange and exotic she could barely contain her excitement. What might they encounter in the jungle at night? These woods feel less threatening, but in his own way, Nathaniel may be more exotic than Fernando. His stories are evidence of that.

Her room is in one of the smaller houses, which they keep

ready for guests. However even though it's now fully dark, Nathaniel doesn't want her to go inside. He takes her behind the barn and kisses her, not just once but several times. She feels almost wicked. Somehow this is different from kisses stolen on the streets of Boston or even her visits to Nathaniel's room. The Pynes always expected her to return at a reasonable hour, so she could never stay out late. Here, no one is waiting up.

"Which room can we go to?" she asks. "Where we will not be seen?"

"Go to yours and close the door. Do it loudly so the others know you're there. I'll follow in a short while."

They kiss one more time and then she does as instructed, finds her room and slams the door. After which she waits in the darkness for him to arrive. Soon she hears Nathaniel enter. Or at least she thinks it's him. It takes all her willpower not to say, "Is it you?" as the floorboards begin to creak.

"Sophia," he whispers and suddenly there is light. From somewhere he has produced a candle—maybe it was under his hat.

She draws the curtain across the room's only window and goes to the door to make certain it's latched. They sit side by side on the bed. It's just a straw tick on a wood platform but it's comfortable enough.

"I'm so pleased you came to visit," he says.

"I would move here if you'd let me."

"I won't ask you to wait much longer. Please believe I'm as impatient as you. We'll reveal our secret soon."

She's nervous. She picks at a loose thread on her sleeve. He puts his hand on her hand to stop her busy fingers. She looks up and into his eyes. This is what she thought might happen, but she still feels unprepared.

He takes her in his arms and she nestles her face against his neck. Soon they are lying on the bed and she thinks perhaps this is enough. Her knowledge about these matters is limited. What will happen next? He seems confident. Maybe he's pretending. Or maybe at some time in the past he has—but that particular possibility she refuses to entertain.

He touches her and it is not unpleasant. She touches him and he removes his waistcoat. She unpins her hat. He unpins her hair and lets it fall. He has called himself her husband. This is what the word means. He arranges her skirts but isn't satisfied and so arranges them again. She's not sure what he intends and then suddenly she is. His hands are on her skin.

"How are you feeling," he asks. The candle is across room. She can see his face in the flickering light.

"I am unsure. Would you mind if I didn't speak?"

"I know of a way to do this so you won't be left with child."

She's not sure how to respond. Thoughts swirl through her mind. Each carries with it an admonishment, any one of which should be enough to bring things to a halt.

"We must be quiet," he says.

After that she closes her eyes. Now her only thoughts are about what she's feeling. Or rather her thoughts have *become* her feelings. They flow together like waves. She wonders what Nathaniel is feeling. "Heavens," he says and "My dove."

Later, they lie together in a tangle of quilts and clothes.

"I am very happy," she says, but the word happy is too simple for what she wants to express. There's wonder and a bit of melancholy—with some left-over trepidation mixed in.

"Nothing like our story was ever written or ever will be," he says.

Dear Nathaniel. Always so writerly and dramatic. He sees everything in hues of crimson and gold.

"Will they call for you in the morning?" she asks.

"Yes. I should leave soon."'

"How disappointing. I was hoping you had another plan— one that would allow you to stay all night."

He does stay for quite some time—hours it seems. But after

he's gone, she wonders if she's made a mistake. Surely Mary and Horace have done nothing like this. She tries to make herself defiant. *Nathaniel and I are different from others. Our spirits cannot be contained.* But it doesn't quite work. When it begins to get light outside she's still wide awake.

MARGARET

She's been in Boston for only ten days but she's certain returning was the right thing to do. Already she has spoken to Elizabeth Peabody about holding another series of Conversations in her shop and the first edition of *The Dial* is nearly complete. It will include an introduction by Waldo, an essay she herself has written on the nature of criticism, a review of the recent exhibition of Washington Allston's paintings, Thoreau's essay on Persius, poems by James Clarke's sister Sarah, and much more. Only one piece remains problematic. It's Bronson Alcott's rather lengthy collection of aphorisms or, in his words, "Orphic Sayings." Leave it to Alcott to style himself an Orpheus. Each "saying" names a different topic, from hope to mysticism to valor, followed by an aperçu. She reads the manuscript over and over, but her opinion doesn't change. It's still baffling. It's still nonsense. Perhaps it means something to Alcott but no one else will understand a word. Nonetheless, Waldo wants her to publish it. She may defer to him on this matter, rather than pick a fight.

One other piece Waldo asks her to include is a poem written by his deceased wife Ellen. This Margaret finds sad and touching. It begins, "Love scatters oil on life's dark sea" and goes on to tell of "living but to sigh." Margaret thinks there must be times in every woman's life when she lives "but to sigh." Perhaps every man's as well, but she's not so sure of that. While it's not an especially well-crafted poem, something about it is deeply affecting. Poor Ellen Tucker, dead at just twenty years old. She knows Waldo still mourns her deeply. Maybe he sees something of her in Cary Sturgis. She will print the poem as Waldo wishes but she wonders what Lidian thinks.

Do they discuss his first wife and his feelings toward her? Do they discuss Cary Sturgis? Do they discuss *her*?

As the magazine approaches completion, she works without rest. One day, two days, three days, her eyes red from reading by lamplight, her back sore from leaning over manuscripts, her fingers cramped from gripping a pen. There are still some parts she's not satisfied with, but she's reached a point where she's become suspicious of her own judgment. She strikes a line, adds it back, and then strikes it again. At last she decides she can do no more.

She wraps the pages in brown paper, ties them with twine, and delivers the package to Weeks, Jordan, and Company, on Washington Street, who will set the type and print it. Then she goes home and falls asleep. She dreams of her father and of wading in a river. A strange man standing on the bank stares at her disapprovingly and she doesn't know whether to get out or try to swim across. But when she wakes up, she feels better than she has in weeks.

A few days later Margaret sees Elizabeth Peabody at a concert. Elizabeth invites her to go on an outing to Brook Farm. They will leave on Saturday morning and make a picnic of it.

"I know you don't intend to move there," Elizabeth says. "Neither do I. It takes a certain type, I think, someone who is more optimistic about human nature than either of us. But it's a beautiful place and an interesting social experiment. Please say you'll come."

"I would like that. It sounds fascinating. I'll be interested to see it firsthand." She doesn't think of herself as a pessimist but maybe Elizabeth is right. She does see life as a struggle. That doesn't mean she expects failure, of Brook Farm or any other venture, but she assumes from the start that success takes more effort than most are willing to give.

When Saturday arrives, she rises early and hurries to

the West Street shop. Elizabeth said she would arrange transportation and have a picnic lunch prepared, and indeed, a pair of barouches sit ready, waiting on the street. She had been under the impression it would be just the two of them; apparently there will be others. Inside the shop she finds Jane Cartwright, who attended some of her Conversations, Thomas Hale, who once worked for her father, young Amanda Harkness who sometimes helps Elizabeth in the shop, Elizabeth's sister Sophia, and three others she hasn't met.

"I hope you don't mind," Elizabeth says. "It was rather an accident. Everyone to whom I mentioned our little trip wanted to come along. We shall have fun, don't you think?"

Margaret smiles but doesn't believe all these people just happened to want to come. Elizabeth Peabody isn't a party to "accidents." On the contrary, she is a great arranger of events.

Soon Elizabeth makes an announcement. The residents of Brook Farm are holding a harvest festival today and they are all invited. Not only that, but the wearing of fancy-dress costumes is encouraged.

At once everyone is asking where they will find costumes on such short notice, but Elizabeth cuts them off.

"I have plenty of masks and dress-up clothes," she says.

Then she disappears into the back room with her sister Sophia. When they return, they are carrying armloads of robes and scarves, headwear and masks. Everyone gathers around excitedly and selects a piece or two to try on. Margaret wants something that makes her look fashionable rather than foolish. She places a feathered tiara on her head.

"You look absolutely imperial," Amanda Harkness says. "Like a medieval queen."

"Imperious," says Margaret, in her teacher voice, but with a smile. "As in *assuming authority to which one has no right.*"

"We are waiting on one more person," Elizabeth says. "Mr. Emerson happens to be in town and I persuaded him to come."

Before Margaret can digest the news, she hears the door of the shop open and turns. It's Waldo, removing his hat, apologizing for being late, and pausing for a moment to take in the costumed throng. Margaret has time for only a quick hello and then it's time to depart. They all remove their robes and masks and file out the door.

The other passengers in Margaret's carriage are Amanda, Sophia, and a young man named Martin who is clearly interested in Amanda and no one else. Waldo is in the other carriage with Elizabeth, an arrangement Margaret is thankful for. The only subject she really wants to discuss with him is *The Dial* and this isn't the place. She's also pleased Cary Sturgis didn't come with him. That would have been difficult to bear.

While Martin attends to Miss Harkness, Margaret and Sophia talk.

"I signed up for your new Conversations," Sophia says. "I found the previous ones quite illuminating."

"Thank you for your interest. I hope they won't disappoint. Perhaps I shall include a discussion of Brook Farm. I'm curious to see if preachers and philosophers can become good farmers and vice versa—as that seems to be the principle at work."

"Oh, I believe they can. It's quite impressive what they've done."

"You've been already?"

"I have. To visit my good friend Nathaniel Hawthorne," Sophia says.

Margaret has heard a good deal about Sophia and Mr. Hawthorne from Elizabeth. In fact, once Elizabeth starts talking about them, it's hard to make her stop. Margaret sometimes senses in Elizabeth a fondness for Hawthorne that extends beyond what one sister typically feels toward the other's beau. If she's right about that, then how hard it must be for Elizabeth to watch them together, to see their affection blossom. On the other hand, if Margaret's own interactions with Hawthorne are a measure of his temperament and fitness as a spouse, Elizabeth may be the fortunate one.

"Nathaniel was among the first to buy shares in the farm," Sophia adds. She speaks his name as if it's a precious thing.

"I count myself an admirer of Mr. Hawthorne's work," replies Margaret, "disquieting though it may be."

For a time they watch the countryside pass and Margaret tells her a bit about *The Dial*. Then they switch conversational partners, with Sophia talking to Amanda and Margaret doing her best to draw young Martin out.

"I notice you have the same name as the new President," she says. "Are you pleased about that?"

"I favored Van Buren," he replies. "But I ain't yet old enough to vote."

"Nor am I," says Margaret and his eyebrows go up in surprise.

Although it's late fall, that time of year when good weather can't be counted on, today is bright and clear, perfect for an outing of this kind. When they arrive at Brook Farm, the residents have all come out to meet them, applauding as they descend from their carriages, as if this is some sort of diplomatic mission, a meeting of representatives from two city-states in ancient Greece. After they've all had a chance to mingle and say hello, George Ripley makes a speech that sounds suspiciously like a sales pitch, and Emerson, acting as spokesman for their small group, replies: "We are here to see the future. But let us not overlook the present day. The founders of Brook Farm are engaged in the noblest of endeavors: the making of an agreeable place to live."

Next, Ripley and his wife lead them on a tour, showing them the large dormitory where most of the men sleep and where the entire company dines, some smaller abodes, a shed where they make candles, soap, and hand tools, and an adjoining building where they intend to place a blacksmith shop.

As they proceed, the visitors ask questions: What do they eat and who is responsible for particular jobs and which of the comforts of city life do they most regret leaving behind? Although Margaret is mildly curious to know the answers, she's more interested in observing the behavior of certain people— Waldo, because she knows how skeptical he really is about Brook Farm, and Sophia Peabody and Nathaniel Hawthorne, because she knows they are in love.

When the formal part of their visit is over, Mrs. Ripley, a pink-faced, grandmotherly woman, asks them to don their costumes for the harvest fest. Margaret puts on the feathered tiara, a black paper mask, and a cloak of yellow silk. From somewhere Waldo has produced a cloak of his own, dark blue with a velvet hood. It makes him look royal and malevolent at the same time. Elizabeth wears a bright red wig and a ribboned stole.

Mrs. Ripley announces that more costumes can be found in the dining room, so several people follow her there. Sophia Peabody comes back in a papier-mâché rabbit mask, Hawthorne is now the Harlequin, with a cat-like face and wooden sword, and Amanda Harkness has sprouted wings. When they were told back at the shop that costumes would be required, Margaret had considered feigning an illness and going home, but seeing how everyone has been transformed, she's glad she came.

Now Mrs. Ripley leads them into the woods. They wind through stands of maples and oaks, through thickets of evergreen shrubs, and across a small stream which is bridged by a single perilous log. At last, they come upon a clearing where they find a table set with refreshments—a collation of cakes and fruit—as well as chairs in a semi-circle, facing a makeshift stage. The ground is carpeted with multicolored autumn leaves.

Soon, off to the side, a fiddler begins to play, and Margaret

is reminded of a commedia dell'arte troupe she once saw—
only this time, instead of being a spectator, she's a member of
the troupe. A pair of gypsy dancers weave in and out and she
thinks for a moment the female one might be a former student.
With the costume she's not sure.

Elizabeth comes over and says, "Now that I see what it's
like, I think I might enjoy it here. But I haven't the money to
buy a share."

Margaret looks at her, wondering if she can really be so
naïve. "You realize, Elizabeth, that it's not always like this.
Most days you'd be in the fields with a hoe."

"Oh, I know that," she says. "Still, I think it might be good
to have my routine disrupted—to be forced to live in a new
way." She pauses as if picturing herself planting a row of corn
and then adds, "I can see you disagree."

"I fear that even when the residents are not in costume they
may be playacting," Margaret muses. "If I lived here, I'd be
forever trying to expose them for what they are."

"Which is?"

"Gentle hypocrites. Good-hearted folk who don't really
believe in their own plan."

Eventually Elizabeth goes off to speak with Mrs. Ripley.
Margaret adjusts her tiara and selects a piece of cake. When
she steps away from the table and turns, Waldo is standing
right there.

"We have missed your presence in Concord," he tells her.
"You left too abruptly. When are you coming back?"

"I don't know. I felt I was in the way."

He shakes his head. "That was never the case. You should
return. You enjoy yourself when you're with us, do you not?"

"Most of the time. When I have your attention." It feels
strange to be talking as if they are on the street in Boston or in
his garden in Concord, given how they are dressed. She holds
the cake awkwardly before her and wishes she hadn't taken it.

"Well, Cary is gone. I suppose you'll approve of that. But Sam Ward and Anna Barker will be visiting soon. They are back from Europe and full of stories. Have you seen them yet?"

"They're back?" she says, pleased but also dismayed. Why didn't they tell her they were on their way? They must have written. Maybe the letter got lost. She pictures them: Sam, tall, artistic, and free-spirited, and Anna, beautiful and wise beyond her years. If James Clarke was her confidant, they were her protégés. She remembers seeing them off at the docks. She so wished she could have gone with them. Now that was an instance when her lack of money really mattered. Not being able to afford a move to Brook Farm is no great loss, but when she was unable to sail away with her young friends, her heart truly ached.

"If they're coming to Concord, I will too," she says. "I'm afraid I did find Cary a little trying, but I'll be delighted to see Anna and Sam."

"I would like that," he replies, and then, almost as an afterthought, "You look quite beautiful today."

As she thanks him in a flustered way, she wonders what caused him to make such a statement—the ridiculous tiara and cloak or something else?

Now a band of children appears on stage. When they first arrived, she wondered why there were none about and then decided they must be in school. But no, they have been off somewhere in the woods, waiting to perform. All the adults find seats and the play begins. It consists of a series of tableaux based on classic works of art, with songs in between. The children wear togas and flowing robes. They position themselves in front of painted pasteboard backgrounds and become figures from mythology and the gospels, frozen in time. As part of her work as a teacher, Margaret sat through any number of performances by school children and even the best were bad. However, this one is quite remarkable. Maybe it's only the setting, but each tableau is well presented, and the children sing like angels, their eyes looking up at the cloudless sky, their mouths in perfect Os.

When the performance ends, everyone rises. They congratulate the children and go back for more cake and break into groups to converse. Margaret thinks she might seek out Mr. Hawthorne, almost as a challenge to herself. Is he really as disagreeable as she thinks? She looks about in an effort to locate him, but the cat and rabbit have disappeared.

HENRY

John has been turned down! He went off to Scituate and came back empty handed. It never once occurred to Henry that Ellen wouldn't say yes.

This is how John tells it: "We were walking on the beach. I managed to get us away from Aunt Prudence and told her I must have my answer. Or if not, she must explain the delay."

"What did she say? It's her father, isn't it?"

"She said sweet things about me, which I won't relate because you'd laugh. But then her face turned glum and she said she made a mistake. She said she did not want to marry me and should have given me an answer sooner." He pauses and pushes his fingers through his hair. "Her father didn't figure into it. He was in New York the entire time."

"I'm very sorry . . ."

"That's not all. I think it's you she likes, Henry. Of course, she didn't say, 'Please send Henry instead,' but you are all she talked about. She said she finds you highly intelligent and that your principles are admirable. She said she wishes she had the courage to refuse to go to church."

"Are you angry with me?"

John shakes his head. "I would be angry if I thought you had gained her attention by double-dealing or pretending to be who you are not. But I believe the Henry she is fond of is the true Henry. My heart is broken but it's not your fault."

At this moment, he's not sure who he has warmer feelings toward—Ellen, because, wonder of wonders, she may prefer him after all, or his brother, whose magnanimity seems boundless.

"What should I do?" he asks.

"Please don't make me become your advisor in this matter. Ask Helen. Or better yet, determine your own course of action. But don't turn it into an object of study. You're unlikely to find the answer in a book."

In his journal that night he writes, *The night is spangled with fresh stars.* What a turn of events. He feels sorry for John but if he were to decline to pursue Ellen, John would be no better off. Should he go to Scituate himself? Should he put his feelings in a letter? Should he wait to see what action she takes? He decides that writing a letter immediately would make him seem over-eager. He needs to think on it a while.

A few days later he finds himself alone with Aunt Prudence in the parlor. Although John said to ask Helen for advice, who knows Ellen better than Aunt Prudence? Yes, she can seem old-fashioned in her views, but he suspects she's more modern than she lets on.

"Did you enjoy your visit to Scituate?" he asks, taking a seat on the bench by the window. She is in the rocker she prefers, the one she gets to sit in only when her mother is elsewhere.

"The weather was poor. It rained three days out of five. The coach we took got stuck in the mud and we had to wait until a team happened by and pulled us out. I suppose John told you all that."

"May I ask you a question about Ellen?"

She says, "Certainly," but looks suspicious. Or maybe her look says, "I've been expecting this." He can't tell for sure.

"John and I both feel we have a particular friendship with her. Especially this past year."

"You are both in love with her. Be plain, Henry. Speak facts."

He feels himself blushing, the redness spreading across his brow. He stammers: "Do you think that I . . . that she . . ."

"Do I think she loves you in return? Is that what you're asking me? I think she is quite young and doesn't fully know *who* she loves. Your brother has said nothing to me about the matter, but I have eyes. I'm aware that for him things did not go well. In the end it's her father who will make the decision. Which is as it should be. You may not be Unitarian enough for his tastes. Then again, you won't know unless you ask."

"I disagree that her father should have such power. He won't have to live with whomever he selects."

"True enough. But his daughter will. And as her father he must prevent her from making a mistake."

"But—"

"Write her a letter. If she wants you, she'll be able to convince her father to say yes. Although she is young, she's not without resources. By the time Ellen is done with him, he'll think marrying Henry Thoreau was his idea from the start."

Emboldened by Aunt Prudence, he begins to imagine what he'll say. He goes walking and as he walks, he tries out phrases: *The sun of our love . . . has risen as noiselessly . . . as the sun from the sea. And we sailors . . .* Are they sailors? Or are they fish, perhaps flying fish, the sun glinting on their wings? The trick will be to get from the metaphor to the heart of the matter. He loves metaphor and wishes he could just leave it at that. Thus, he spends his afternoon.

Then, in his room that night, he sits down to write the letter that will change his life—or so he hopes. He decides all the lush imagery he came up with on his walk will give her the wrong idea. She'll think he's trying to use beautiful words as a substitute for honest feelings. He has a few sheets of good quality paper hidden away in drawer—not the tissue-thin stuff he uses for most letters but thicker stock, the color of fresh cream. He'll do a draft in pencil and then transfer it in ink.

Dearest Ellen,

I expect your first thought upon looking at this letter will be to wonder why it is so short. The answer is in its purpose. Most letters I have sent you have been chronicles of daily life.

The doings of my family, quotations from the ever-quotable Aunt Prudence, and anecdotes about dogs and cats. (Speaking of dogs, a stray yellow hound has taken up residence on our porch. I feed him, which may explain why he refuses to leave.)

So what is the purpose of which I speak? Why, it is no less than life itself. Since you visited I have thought a great deal about the man I wish to become. At one time I expected to answer this question through my studies, but I no longer believe it can be found in a book. Rather the answer is our love.

Therefore, it is you I want for my wife. If you'll have me for your husband, then I will come to Scituate whenever you ask and fall upon my knees. I understand you will need your father's blessing. For that I can only hope.

Yours most affectionately,

Henry Thoreau

He makes only a few changes and is surprised it came out so well. Of course, maybe he's deceiving himself. In the end, only Ellen's opinion will count.

He copies the letter onto the good paper, taking care not to smudge. Just before he seals it, he opens it up again and adds a postscript:

I have chosen not to bring John into this but leaving him out entirely seems false. So I will simply say John is the best brother a man could have.

SOPHIA

The children's choir is nice but rather dull. The entire affair should have been held at night. Then they could have had bonfires and dancing. Sophia has never attended an event with bonfires and dancing, but she's sure she'd like it if she did.

On the whole, she has little interest in the activities being played out before them and doesn't think Brook Farm is where she and Nathaniel will end up. But she's happy to be with him, happy to walk and whisper as the clouds move rapidly across the sky. The costumes they found here at Brook Farm are much better than the makeshift ones Elizabeth provided. The first time she saw Nathaniel in his, she shivered. The Harlequin's jacket and evil-looking cat mask fit his personality better than his own clothes.

"Oh my," she said when he put them on. "I find that very appealing."

"My dove has a dark side," he replied. "Fancy that."

As the children's program concludes, she says, "Let's go," and begins to pull him into the woods. Nathaniel balks.

"Your sister . . ."

"She's busy talking. And who's to say we can't go for a walk."

"For a walk?"

"To your room."

"Then quickly," he says, "before anyone sees."

He leads her back by a different route than the one they used before. Her heart is pounding. She laughs and then covers her mouth. Even though they're surrounded by thick undergrowth, she's afraid they'll be spotted, afraid they'll stumble on some Brook Farm residents who didn't attend the masquerade.

As they walk, Sophia says, "Miss Fuller and I talked about you on our way here."

"For what reason? What did you discuss?"

"She said she's surprised you moved here. She doesn't think you're the type of man for a place like this."

"What does she know of me or this place? I wish you wouldn't speak to her. She seems to consider passing judgment on others her absolute right."

Just then the houses and barns come into view. For a moment, they remain in the shadows beneath the trees and look to see if they'll be observed. Fortunately, there's not a soul in sight. They hurry to the door and she waits for Nathaniel to let them inside.

"Imagine someone coming upon us like this," Sophia whispers. "If questioned I'll be as mute as a rabbit. And you, my dear, can only meow."

After standing there for a moment Nathaniel turns. "It's locked," he says. "We can't get in. It's never been locked before." While she waits, he goes to the side of the building and tries the window, only to come back and tell her it's closed up tight as well.

Sophia says, "Do you think someone is suspicious—they didn't want us to get in?"

He takes off his mask and shakes his head. "I have no reason to believe so. Maybe there's somewhere else we can go."

But the spell has been broken. It's too great a risk and they have too little time. It won't be long before the others return. "Nathaniel," she says, "are we terribly sinful?"

She intends the question to be at least partly in jest, yet he looks at her as if she has asked something of enormous import. After a moment he says, "There are many sinful things in the world but neither you nor anything you touch are among them." His words are accompanied by a look of such grave intensity she has to lower her eyes. Then, with nowhere to go, they sit outside on a bench, his arms around her, until it's time for her to return to Boston.

For the next several days the warmth of his words is enough to sustain her. Eventually, she begins wondering how to move forward from what seems like a kind of romantic limbo, where love can be felt but not acted upon. It would be so much easier if he didn't insist on keeping it a secret. Part of the pleasure of being engaged is telling people you're engaged. In fact, isn't that almost the point?

She distracts herself from these thoughts by returning to her work. Through her association with Mr. Clevenger she has been offered a commission to do a bust of Laura Bridgman, a blind and deaf girl at Samuel Howe's Perkins School. Although only ten years old, the Bridgman child is becoming well-known for her ability to communicate and learn.

When Sophia visits the school, she takes nothing with her, not even a sketch pad. Mr. Howe greets her at the door and, as they go down the hall, he says,

"She will know you are present simply by your footsteps."

"Can she speak," Sophia asks.

"She speaks with her fingers," he says. "You won't be able to understand because you do not speak the language, so I will interpret for you."

They reach the door to her room and enter. There she sits, by the window. In her lap is some needlework. In every respect she looks like an ordinary ten-year-old girl except that she has a strip of blue felt tied across her eyes. Her hair is straight and brown, her neck is slender, and her complexion is fair.

Mr. Howe moves a chair from across the room and places it within reach of the girl. "Please," he says, and Sophia sits. She's never been face-to-face with a blind person and doesn't know what to do. Yet soon Howe's fingers are marking Laura Bridgman's palm and then her fingers are marking his. Sophia watches, fascinated, as Howe speaks: "She says she would like to read your face."

257

Sophia instinctively leans forward as Laura Bridgman puts one small hand on either cheek and proceeds to touch her nose, her lips, her eyelids, her forehead, and her hair. She is reminded of the various headache treatments she has received over the years, from leeches to massages to magnetism, and thinks this might work equally well.

"Can you tell her I think she is pretty? And can you ask her if she would mind if I were to make a likeness of her—a sculpture out of clay."

Mr. Howe sets to work with his fingers again. After a moment, Sophia's eyes move to the girl's face. For the most part it's motionless but occasionally her jaw quivers, as if, behind her closed lips, she's forming words with her tongue.

"She says she would be delighted to have you sculpt her image. And that if she is truly pretty, a likeness of her should be pretty too."

Sophia laughs. What a delightful child. She wasn't sure what to expect, wasn't even certain she'd follow through with the commission, but now she can't wait to get to work.

Back in her room she sketches the girl from memory and realizes to her surprise that she hasn't thought about Nathaniel Hawthorne or Brook Farm for hours. It wasn't long ago that she believed her headaches and her art would make marriage impossible. But then she met Nathaniel and her headaches diminished. That leaves only her art. Just to be safe, she should be forthright with him: "After we are married, my days shall be spent with a paintbrush in hand and my nights with you in my arms." As the sentence forms in her mind, she smiles. Let us see what he says to that.

She goes back to see Laura Bridgman several times. She sketches her, measures the distance between her eyes with calipers, and asks Mr. Howe to encourage her to make different expressions—of happiness, of anger, of remorse. Then she goes to Clevenger's studio, takes a lump of clay, and begins.

Being with the girl and seeing how intelligent and alive she is makes Sophia feel guilty. Her headaches, her quarrels with her sisters, the challenges she faces in art and love are nothing compared to what Laura Bridgman must deal with every hour. As a result, she decides she must make of her life what she wants it to be and not allow illness to slow her progress or expect Nathaniel to lead the way. It shall be the life of an artist married to Nathaniel Hawthorne in a house surrounded by trees.

MARGARET

After the Brook Farm outing, Margaret made some inquiries to find out more about Sam and Anna's return. Apparently, they landed in New York—that's why she has yet to see them. It still doesn't explain why they didn't write to say they were en route, but sometimes when you travel letters are misdirected or you lose track of time. In any event, she has made contact with them. They will meet at Waldo's at the end of the month.

But right now she has work to do. She reads a chapter of a new biography of Voltaire thinking she may write a review of it. She composes a letter to her mother about family finances. And she makes some notes about the next issue of *The Dial*. Then a messenger from the printer arrives. The first copies have just come off the press and he's there to deliver one. As she opens the package, her hands tremble. She approved the final proofs so she knows quite well what it will look like but that's not the same as holding the finished item in her hands.

There it is: *The Dial: A Magazine of Literature, Philosophy, and Religion. Volume I.* She's not one to be self-congratulatory, far from it, but it does look quite nice. A glance at the table of contents suggests high standards and substance, as well as variety. Something for every discerning reader. A literary feast. And the cover is a perfect lilac, the color of actual lilacs in bloom, a pale purple with a hint of blue.

For the remainder of the afternoon, she reads through it for what must be the hundredth time. There are a few pieces she might exclude if she were to start all over again. The poems by Christopher Cranch, for instance, including one about the aurora borealis:

Who can name thy wondrous essence,
Thou electric phosphorescence?

What was she thinking? By all accounts he's a good minister but he's no poet. Yet, on the whole, she's proud of how it turned out. One advantage of a magazine over a book is that this is the first of what should be many volumes.

"The next one will be better," she says aloud.

That night she sleeps with her copy on the night table and is pleased to see it still there in the morning when she wakes up.

Over the next couple of weeks, reviews start to appear. They are not kind. One paper calls the contents "moonshine" and another "a sort of fungus." A Providence journal terms it "mostly unintelligible" and a newspaper from Philadelphia, "duck tracks in the mud." She knew this might happen. Indeed, she may even have invited it by putting so many controversial voices in a single place. She knows what Waldo will say—"I welcome them" and "If I haven't made trouble, I haven't done my job." But her armor isn't quite as strong. She worked so diligently on it, for so many hours.

Her biggest mistake was agreeing to publish Alcott's "Orphic Sayings." The furor surrounding his now-defunct school means that many commentators are pre-disposed to pounce on any venture with which he's associated. She still doesn't know why Waldo was so insistent. She's inclined to agree with the reviewer who called Alcott's piece "a train of fifteen railroad cars with one passenger." Which is to say, a large vehicle with very little inside.

Although she is seldom mentioned by name, the attacks feel personal. Even worse, she's afraid Waldo and Hedge and Brownson and the others will think the bet they placed on her was a mistake. The one bit of good news comes from Horace Greeley at the *New York Weekly Tribune*. He calls *The Dial* "the most original and thoughtful periodical ever published in this country." It's an overstatement but far better than an attack.

When it's finally time for her to leave for Concord, she feels an enormous sense of relief. She wants to escape Boston, get away from the reviews, away from society. Sam and Anna are already there, and Waldo says she should plan to stay as long as she wants.

It's late November, so although she leaves Boston before noon, it's almost dark when she arrives. She steps off the coach and looks up and down the street. A frigid November wind makes her draw her cloak in tight. She was expecting someone to meet her and now begins to wonder if there's been some confusion about the date. Fortunately, she knows the way and it's not a long walk—she'll send someone back for her bags. As she turns onto Lexington Road, she is pleased to see Waldo's house entirely lit up.

She raps on the door, it opens, and suddenly there they are, her friends and light and warmth and laughter, and she's so relieved—relieved to see Sam and Anna again, relieved to be staying with Waldo again, relieved to be out of the wind—that she begins to weep.

"Margaret!" Anna exclaims. "Sam, you forgot."

Sam's hands go to his head. "Oh my god, I'm so sorry."

"He was supposed to meet you," Anna says.

"We were talking," says Waldo, who is standing behind them with little Waldo in his arms. "It was my fault entirely. Feel free to beat me black and blue."

They usher her into the parlor and want her to sit down, but first Margaret asks where Lidian is. After last time, she wants to approach her in a positive way. Waldo tells her she's in the kitchen, so Margaret goes and finds her. She's seated near the fireplace, reading by lamplight—the Bible it appears.

"Good evening, Lidian. I just arrived. How's Nelly? Doing well, I hope."

"She's upstairs with Waldo's mother. I would take you up and show you, but I fear she might wake up."

"Of course, I'll see her tomorrow. I only wanted to come and say hello."

Lidian looks surprised, even taken aback. Maybe it's too obvious a gesture. Maybe it seems insincere. Which, Margaret must admit, would be a fair charge.

"Thank you," she says. "Waldo is pleased you're here."

Back in the parlor, Sam is showing Waldo some engravings of masterworks he purchased while in Italy.

"I think it's time I learned more about art," Waldo tells him. "I want you to be my guide."

"I'm so glad to see you," Margaret says to Anna, taking her hand. "I didn't realize how much I missed you until now."

"Mr. Emerson—Waldo—told us about your editorship. They made the wisest possible choice."

She shakes her head. "I'm not so sure. But I'd rather not discuss that now. I want to hear about your travels. Don't leave anything out."

All that evening and through the next day, they talk and talk. Anna and Sam tell about their journey, painting remarkably vivid pictures with their words. Sometimes Lidian comes in with one or both of the children. They all exclaim over baby Nelly, blonde, with an impish smile, and every meal seems like a party, even if all they're having is bread and cheese. Occasionally Waldo disappears into his library or goes off for a time with his son. More often though he's in the middle of the room, the most talkative one of all.

"I must go back to England," he says. "I should like to see Carlyle again."

"The trains have begun to make getting about so easy," Anna says, and Sam adds,

"There's no place like Geneva. The most beautiful lake you've ever seen."

It's so good to be with Sam. He likes the same sort of books she likes and has come back from Europe with a satchel full of poetry and philosophy, all of which he's happy to loan. If he weren't quite so young, she could see herself becoming infatuated with him. She thinks there might be something developing between him and Anna, although she rather hopes not—if that happens they'll go off and be one another's best friends, leaving her behind.

Maybe the best thing about this gathering is that for once Margaret doesn't feel the need to be the best conversationalist in the room. She's happy simply to listen and sit with Anna by the fire. It's such a joy to be with the three of them. If *this* could be her community, she'd move here tomorrow and never leave.

Even when the question of *The Dial* comes up, they manage to make everything better. "Waldo let me read some of it before you got here," Sam says. "What you have done is brilliant. To assemble such a group of contributors and persuade them to give you their best work . . ."

Waldo, when they discuss the reviews, is as defiant as she expects him to be: "When the next one comes out, I hope the attacks are even worse. By their fury we shall measure our success." His voice sounds positively martial, as if he's readying himself for war.

As the end of the week approaches, the intensity of their first days together subsides. Waldo goes back to work on a more regular schedule and Margaret does so as well. She and Anna also find time to stroll into town and visit the millinery shop, and Sam sits down to tell her about what he's been reading. Currently he is in love with Balzac and George Sand. "The French are the future," he says. "I know you will never renounce the Germans but let me give you *Eugenie Grandet*. The characters will make you swoon."

Even with Anna and Sam there to occupy her, she tries to visit with Lidian daily. And by doing so, she makes a discovery. She'd always wondered how Waldo, with his light, self-deprecating sense of humor, had chosen a woman so outwardly dour. Now Lidian reveals her own sense of humor, sometimes even directing it at her husband and his friends. She can impersonate the pompous Orestes Brownson, has much to say about Alcott's peculiar notions regarding which foods to eat and which to avoid (those being the vegetables he calls "downward-growing" such as radishes and beets), and, when Margaret says something about the Transcendentalist Club being rather too fixedly male, Lidian goes to a drawer in the kitchen and pulls out something she wrote. Its title is "A Transcendental Bible." At first Margaret doesn't understand, but as she reads, it becomes clear—Lidian has penned a satire of transcendental thought:

Never confess a fault. You should not have committed it and who cares whether you are sorry.

Never speak of the hope of Immortality. What do you know about it? It is egotistical to cling to it.

Loathe and shun the sick. They are in bad taste, and may untune us for writing the poem floating through our mind.

She looks up from the page. Lidian is working to keep her face flat and unexpressive, but there's a twinkle in her eye. Margaret shakes her head. Like most good satires, this one aims to produce laughter and outrage at once:

Despise the unintellectual, and make them feel that you do by ignoring their remarks.

Never wish to be loved. Who are you to expect that? Besides, the great never value being loved.

And finally, *Let us all aspire after this Perfection!*

Margaret can't remember when she's read anything so delightful and so fierce. It ought to appear in the next issue of *The Dial*. "This is wonderful," she says. "I had no idea you were such a wit."

"I have always found it difficult to take seriously many

of the things others worry themselves over," she says. "But not everyone understands. I expect Orestes Brownson"—she shifts now into his voice, both self-important and ponderous—"would profoundly object."

Margaret laughs but then covers her mouth. Here in this house it just doesn't seem right.

"Does Waldo know," she asks.

"He most certainly does," Lidian replies. "He found it quite amusing. Although there were times he had to force himself to smile."

HENRY

While Henry awaits Ellen's reply he decides to pay a visit to Brook Farm. Emerson went there and when he got back, told Henry it was worth seeing, whether one agrees with their philosophy or not.

"It's a commendable experiment," he said. "I can't see it working for me but it's a better use of time and money than the great majority of efforts to improve society. You ought to take a look yourself."

Even for Henry it's a bit far to walk, so in exchange for a week's tuition, the father of one of his students allows him the use of his horse. From the moment he starts out, there's a bitterly cold wind and he almost turns back. But he's stubborn about such things and before long he's more than halfway there. He pulls his hat down tight so it won't blow off, fastens the top button of his coat, and forges on. The skin on his cheeks begins to feel brittle and then numb. Despite the weather, there are farmers out casting manure and pulling turnips and gleaning a few ears of corn, the ones the crows have missed.

When at last he sees a sign for West Roxbury, he catches up with a man leading an ox and asks him to stop.

"Greetings," Henry says, shouting to make himself heard over the wind. "Do you by chance know where I might find Brook Farm?"

The farmer looks up and nods. "Keep on as you are to Newton and turn at the pond." After a short pause, he adds, "Can you tell me what they're doin' at that place? Some say it's not moral but since I live close by, I think I ought to be told."

"I'm afraid I know less than you. But if I witness any depravity, I'll lodge a complaint on your behalf." Then Henry makes a clicking sound to get the old farm horse moving and trots on up the road.

He follows the farmer's directions and before long reaches the top of a low hill. From there he can see a cluster of houses and barns, all gray and weathered with wisps of smoke curling up from the chimneys into the colorless sky. He doesn't want to announce himself, so he tethers the horse in some trees and approaches on foot. He knows several of those who are living here, founder George Ripley included, and if they see him, they'll make a fuss. They'll try to feed him supper and want him to stay the night. Worst of all, they'll try to sell him a share.

But with the wind as it is, and the day cold and getting colder, there's not a single resident in sight. It looks like an ordinary farm although a little less well kept-up than most. Emerson told him the unmarried men live in one house and the women and children and families in the others. He can tell which is for the bachelors by the boots out front.

A man comes out of one of the houses and walks toward a barn. A woman comes out of the same house and follows the man. He thinks it might be Ripley and his wife but he's too far away to know. The man turns and in the open space between the house and barns they stand and shout at one another. They wag their heads and shake their fists and for a moment it appears they're about to come to blows. Just as he's considering going down to intervene, they turn and walk in opposite directions. Soon both are out of sight.

After a while it begins to snow, and he decides he's seen enough. As he returns to the horse, he has a sudden vision of the whole place as a deserted ruin, the windows broken out, the paint weathered off, the chimneys collapsing, and the doors banging in the breeze. He's not even sure why he came. If this is utopia, he rather not partake.

On the ride back it snows hard all the way, icy flakes driven by the wind. By the time he reaches the outskirts of Concord he can barely see the road. He leaves the horse with its owner, sorry to have put the beast through such an ordeal, and trudges across the fields toward home.

When he enters the house, Helen takes one look at his rime-encrusted clothes and laughs. "My goodness, Henry, where have you been?"

"I went to see Brook Farm."

"You did not."

"I did. I wanted to see why everyone is talking about it and what those who live there find appealing. But if I had to pick one word to describe it, I think it would be *bleak*."

"Was it really that bad? Take off your coat and tell me what you saw."

As he sits with Helen by the fire and describes his trip, he realizes there is but a small number of people he genuinely enjoys being with. Mostly the members of his family, especially John and Helen. That doesn't mean he dislikes his students or the people he meets around town. But he has high standards for those with whom he'll actually sit and converse. Emerson of course is another, and surprisingly, Alcott as well. He can picture himself on some future spring evening settling down with Bronson to chat. Some call Alcott eccentric, yet that word in its original form simply means not sharing the same *center* as others. To Henry that sounds like a condition to which one should aspire.

"The fact that some fellow and his wife were arguing doesn't make it a bad place to live," Helen says when he's done telling her about Brook Farm.

"It wasn't the arguing. It was that I could imagine the rest of them watching through the windows and gossiping about it that night."

The next day he's back at school and Alcott's daughter, who's only been enrolled for a short time and has up until now been quiet, makes herself known. It happens when he's teaching his students about the Hindu gods. It's not a part of the regular curriculum but that's one advantage of operating your own school—other than John, who's to know?

"Mr. Henry, how far away is India," asks Miles Prosser.

"Across the ocean and beyond Africa. On the other side of the world."

"Why don't the people of India have the same god as us?" asks Jacob Smith.

"That's just the way it is. It's not unlike the Greeks. Remember when we talked about Hermes and Ares . . ."

"And Artemis and Athena," says Louisa Alcott, from the corner of the room. "Who were all children of Zeus."

Henry hears her voice, but it takes him a moment to locate her. There she is, a small girl in a large desk near the back. Until now, the only thing he's noticed about her is that she often reads a book surreptitiously, keeping it out of his view. When they studied the Greeks she was not yet a member of the class, but given who her father is, he's not surprised she's well-informed.

"Exactly. Although as I understand it, the Hindus have many more gods than the Greeks. Some of them even have assistants—minor gods to help out."

"Something like angels then?" Louisa asks.

"Yes, I suppose so. Although I've never thought of it that way before."

She furrows her brow. "I think I would enjoy meeting them. I'd like learning about the games they play and the foods they eat," she says.

"The gods of India?"

"No, Mr. Henry, the *people* of India. If the gods are like angels, then they're invisible, don't you think?"

Everyone, Henry included, laughs.

Then it happens. When he gets home from school, the letter he has been waiting for, the one on which he has placed all his hopes, arrives. As soon as he spots it, he and Helen glance at one another, but before she can say anything, he snatches it and runs up to his room.

He should have gone to see Ellen instead of trying to do this by mail. That way if she had arguments to make against his proposal, he could have countered them on the spot. But it's too late now. He opens it and the first line breaks his heart:

"Dear Henry, I never felt so bad sending a letter in my life."

He might as well stop there. Why did he even think he had a chance? If she didn't want John, she surely wouldn't want him. The next line continues in the same apologetic vein: "My great fear is that after this we won't remain friends and that the freedom of expression we feel when we are together will be lost."

The rest of the words seem empty, meant only to fill the page. In the end, she blames it on her father: "He knows about Mr. Emerson and his circle and has heard you are part of it. He thinks it best for me to wait until I am older and can marry someone who has a more Unitarian frame of mind."

When he looks up from the letter, John is standing at the door.

"Bad news?" he says.

"As bad as can be. Her father objects to my beliefs."

"I'm sorry, Henry. I was sure she'd tell you yes. She'll regret it one day."

"You'd think she'd have found one of us adequate."

"Well, there you have it. The problem with that girl is she's got good judgment," John says. They attempt unsuccessfully to smile.

Thereafter, he feels only despair. He thinks about going on a trip somewhere, but he can't leave the school. Nor is he the kind to run away. Rather, he turns inward, keeping to himself, reading poetry, writing in his journal, and as always, walking in the woods.

One day, shortly after receiving the fateful letter, he passes the house the Alcotts have rented. Outside, Bronson Alcott is building something out of branches, a sort of bower over a log bench, although since it's almost winter the branches have no leaves. Henry wonders what he has in mind. The structure looks as if it's made of wrought iron rather than wood. It doesn't seem like it will be very inviting unless the intention is to create a place to sit and brood.

"Greetings, friend Thoreau. Where are you off to?" Alcott says.

"I have no destination."

Alcott looks up the road, back at the stark structure he's building, and then at Henry. "Might I come along?"

He'd rather not have company, but it would be unneighborly to turn him down. "Be my guest," he says, and Alcott drops the branch he's holding and falls in by his side.

"Louisa finds your school most agreeable," he says.

"I find her agreeable as well. She is a passionate reader but pays attention in class only to that which interests her. Not unlike myself."

They walk on in silence, Henry slowing his gait when he notices Alcott is having difficulty keeping up.

"Tell me," Alcott says, "do you attempt to develop a common conscience among the children?"

He knows a bit about Alcott's theories of schooling and wonders if this is one that got him in trouble. "I don't believe so," he says. "Please explain what you mean."

"Suppose a child misbehaves. Do you engage the group in determining his punishment? As we do in society at large?"

The idea strikes him as ridiculous. What if their recommendation is that their classmate be stoned? Then again what does he know? Alcott has given much more thought to education than he has. And the truth is, Ellen's letter has turned his mind into a muddle. Still, he'll answer as best he can.

"Well, when a child misbehaves, the first thing I do is . . ." But at that moment he realizes Alcott is no longer beside him. He turns and sees him a few steps back, gasping, trying to catch his breath.

"Are you all right?" Henry asks.

Alcott nods and waves him on, but as he does so, he says, "A revolution in human affairs is now in progress. The world shall be what we make of it. I enjoyed our conversation. Please stop by again."

That night in his journal, Henry writes, *I want to go soon and live away by Walden Pond where I shall hear only the wind whispering among the reeds.*

PART FOUR

We are ever dying to one world and being born into another.

Henry David Thoreau

SOPHIA

Sophia works on the bust of Laura Bridgman, but while she's doing so, she comes to a conclusion about herself and Nathaniel: It's time to stop talking and act.

The first step is to get him to leave Brook Farm. In her letters, she begins to say things like *I don't know how you're finding time to write* and *Do you really think milking cows is your calling?* and more boldly, *Isn't it time to give up on Ripley's ideas and come be with your dove?*

Yet he ignores her messages or fails to hear them. Instead of writing about Brook Farm, he writes about her: *You have taught me that I have a heart. You have thrown a light deep downward and upward into my soul. You have revealed me to myself.* She's touched, thrilled even, so much so that she feels feverish when she reads them, but they don't help solve the problem—he is there, she is here, and they're not going to be married as long as that remains unchanged.

She decides she could use some advice about how to proceed, so she invites Mary for tea. But the formality of such an invitation from her own sister makes Mary suspicious. As soon as she's taken her seat she says, "Sophia, why am I here? I hope you've not done something horrible. If you have, I'd rather not know."

"No, nothing horrible. Unless that's how you'd describe being engaged to Nathaniel because that's what I've done."

"Oh. Well. I guess I knew it would happen. You've been keeping it a secret, haven't you? You're not very good at secrets. You shouldn't even try."

"At least I'm telling you first. I'd never tell mother such a thing without testing it out on you. And Elizabeth and I seem

277

to quarrel when we discuss him, although I'm not quite sure why."

"Elizabeth is Elizabeth. She hoped Hawthorne would be hers, although for different purposes than those you have in mind."

Sophia pours the tea and then gets to the real reason she invited Mary today.

"He's out there at Brook Farm and I'm afraid months will turn into years. What can I do to get him to leave?"

Mary begins to laugh, first a titter she tries to contain and then gales of laughter, unlike anything Sophia has ever heard from her before.

"What has come over you?" Sophia asks.

When at last Mary catches her breath, she says, "Really, sister, you are asking *me* how to make a man stop his procrastinating? How long have I been waiting for Horace to take action? I have built my life around *his delays*. Everything I do is because of *his delays* and I see no end in sight."

Sophia sees what she's done and can't believe she was so blind. And now she realizes why Mary's laughter was so extravagant—it was fueled in part by pain. "I'm so sorry," she says. "I wasn't thinking. I shouldn't have . . ."

But Mary interrupts. "You needn't apologize. I certainly don't mind your asking me for help. Although I may not be able to solve my own problems, I can still give advice to you."

Sophia then explains why they've been keeping their engagement a secret—Nathaniel's family and their expectations that he not marry until he's well set up.

"I doubt that it has much to do with money," Mary says. "They live in that house with the shades pulled down and rarely leave, and when they do, they dress all in black. They think he should still be there with them. The moment he tells them about you, they'll realize he'll never return."

"But what I can do?" she asks. "He seems under their sway."

"Indeed he is. So you must make him confront them. And when he does, you must go with him. Though you are small and often suffer from poor health, you are also brave. You will face them down."

When Mary is gone, Sophia thinks about what she said. She scarcely knows Nathaniel's family. Yet her sister is right, they must be told she and Nathaniel are in love. How can she persuade him to do so? She will find a way.

In her next letter she tells him she needs to see him: *I don't wish to go to Brook Farm again. Couldn't you come here?*

I'll come for the day on Thursday, he writes back. *Anything for my dove.*

When he arrives in Boston there are kisses and embraces and more kisses, although once again they have no place to be alone. They try sitting by the waterfront to talk but an icy north wind drives them away, so they go to Elizabeth's shop to warm up.

"Oh my," says Elizabeth to Nathaniel. "I didn't expect to see you here today."

"As you might imagine, a farm in winter is rather dismal," he says. "In fact, Brook Farm as a venture is becoming dismal. At least in my eyes."

"I'm so sorry to hear that," Elizabeth says, but Sophia is delighted. Part of her work may be done.

"Can we stay here and visit?" Sophia asks.

"Why not go upstairs?" These days, as a cost saving measure, Elizabeth and their parents are living in rooms above the shop.

"We were hoping for some privacy."

"Of course," says Elizabeth. "Use the back room. I'll see that you are left alone."

The back room is occupied by Elizabeth's lending library.

Books and magazines are everywhere, tumbling out of shelves, cascading across tables, and in stacks on the floor. When she first opened, it was all quite orderly but as the months have passed, it's become more a nest of books than a library. They clear off two chairs and pull them side by side.

Once they are settled, he takes her hand. "I think I know why you asked me here."

"You do?"

"You are with child."

It's such an unexpected remark, she laughs aloud. "No, I am not."

Nathaniel is so self-possessed that it's usually difficult to make him blush, yet now his whole face turns red.

"I thought—"

"I understand, I'm sure you did. You're very sweet, Nathaniel." It pleases her to see him so disarmed. "What I want to talk about is marriage. I want to know what the impediments are."

"Impediments? I'm afraid I don't understand."

"You went to Brook Farm to find us a place to live. But it seems that's not working out. So what will happen next?"

He nods slowly, in gathering recognition. "You think I'm avoiding it."

"I don't know why it has to be secret. How does that help?"

For a moment he's silent but she can tell he's preparing to say something. "I promised my mother that I would not marry without her approval, which she will not give until I have money and a house to live in."

"It is a relief to hear you say it. I feared you had changed your mind."

"Oh, my Sophia," he says, putting his arms around her. "How we torture ourselves with misunderstandings. The only change is that my love has grown."

She thinks about what Mary said—that it's about more

than money—so she decides to take a risk: "She has a hold over you. You want to please her. They expect you to come back."

He nods. A look of something like resignation appears on his face. "My father died so unexpectedly and so far away that in the months afterward, I thought my mother might die as well. Yet, she took care of us by herself and never complained. So, yes, she will find it difficult to let me go. If we had a house to live in, she would feel less pain."

Outside, the winter sun is a white disk and the wind that chased them away from the water has followed them to the shop. It rattles the windows and makes a moaning sound as it rushes up the street.

"I would marry you tomorrow if I could," Nathaniel says.

She likes hearing it but feels defeated. In a way it would be easier if his mother was opposed to him marrying under any circumstances, at any time. Then Sophia could dismiss her as nothing more than a bitter old woman dressed in black. This problem is more concrete, composed of a roof and walls and a door.

"I can wait," she says bravely. "Others have waited longer and been happy brides."

If he's going to make it back to Brook Farm tonight, he needs to leave now. They go into the front room and he says good-bye to Elizabeth, gives her a kiss, and goes out into the cold.

Sophia watches through the window as he disappears up the street. "My kingdom for a house," she says, her shoulders sagging. Then she turns to Elizabeth and proceeds to tell her the whole thing. Mary knows, she might as well know too. As she speaks, she studies Elizabeth's expression, worried about how she'll respond. In truth she's never fully understood how Elizabeth feels about Nathaniel. Did she start out caring for him but then give up when she saw him looking at Sophia? Or does she continue to have feelings but now holds them inside? And will there be a moment when it all comes out?

However, when Sophia is done telling the story, Elizabeth says, "That may not be as great a problem as you think. There's an empty house in Concord that belongs to Mr. Emerson. If I tell him it's for my sister, I expect he'll rent it cheap."

MARGARET

While Sam and Waldo engage in their studies of Italian art, Margaret and Anna bundle up against the cold and go for a long walk. Anna has come back from Europe with an elegant fur-collared coat. Margaret thinks it makes her look like a countess and wishes she had one too.

She remembers how it was before Anna left. They would stroll along the Charles in Cambridge and dream aloud. Anna grew up in New York society, but despite her background of privilege, she began to idolize Margaret almost as soon as they met. Margaret could feel it, the intensity and passion of her regard and gaze. She's used to the adulation of adolescent girls, but Anna is older than her students as well as more world-wise, so her esteem has always meant more.

"What will you do now that you're back?" Margaret asks.

"Oh, there are many possibilities. I may teach. And having experienced the pleasures of travel, I want to travel more. I would like to see the Far West. I would love to find a job that's truly meaningful—like the one you're doing with *The Dial*."

They walk hand-in-hand, following a narrow country road with a line of pines on one side and open fields on the other. High in the trees a great black raven looks down and scolds them with a harsh caw.

"I may not be able to continue doing it for long," Margaret says. This is something she hasn't told anyone yet, not even Waldo. But Anna has always been easy to share secrets with. That's part of the reason she missed her so much.

"Why not? When you talk about it, it sounds ever so interesting and fulfilling. Am I wrong?"

"No, you're not wrong. It makes me feel that I am of value.

I can ask for nothing more. Except that I be paid."

Anna stops in her tracks. "They haven't paid you? Are you serious?"

"I'm afraid I am. It took everything we had to get it printed. I told George Ripley—he's managing the funds—that I would wait until money began coming in from sales to collect my part. Unfortunately, sales have been slow."

"Oh, Margaret. What are you living on? I can loan you some money. You need only ask."

"I have enough for now. But thank you for the offer. You're always so kind."

A little further on, they stop to rest on a rock wall. The wind has diminished and the afternoon sun is producing a little warmth, making it tolerable to sit and talk. Anna puts her arms around Margaret and pulls her close.

"I'm sorry I didn't write more letters while I was away," she says. "I have no excuse."

"No one values the written word more than I, but it's no substitute for times like this. When true friends are apart, each new letter seems to carry with it a little less of the person who wrote it. It's not unlike when someone dies. Despite our best efforts, their memory fades."

"Well, I am quite alive," Anna says. "And, as for your simile, I do not approve of it at all."

After that they sit for a time, gazing across an open field. Margaret feels more at peace than she has in some time. She loves Anna. She loves Waldo and Sam, and might even come to love Lidian, as strange as that may seem. She has a great capacity for love but there are always obstacles, often of Margaret's own making. She presses too hard, she's too insistent that her feelings be returned, she's too easily hurt. Perhaps it would be better to accept her life as it is and carry on.

On their way back to the house, she encourages Anna to talk about Europe again. Margaret appreciates how she weaves in tales of mishaps and misunderstandings so it's not merely a bland travelogue:

"And then we found ourselves being led down a path to a farmyard. My Italian was so wretched the man thought I wanted to buy a donkey and we didn't realize our mistake until we were half a mile from town."

Margaret laughs and says, "I still intend to go to Europe someday. I've been saving a little money. I'll go without books and paper before I'll break into my travel fund."

The next day yet another visitor arrives. It's Cary Sturgis, stopping in for a few days while on her way to Peterborough to visit her aunt. Margaret is dismayed—as far as she knows, Cary wasn't invited. Fortunately, Waldo seems a good deal less enthralled by her than before. He's not outwardly cold, but after Cary has been there a day, she corners Margaret and says, "What's come over Waldo. I think he may have eyes for Anna. If I were Lidian I'd be furious."

"Don't be foolish. He talks to Sam more than Anna—more than any of us in fact. He has eyes for whoever can tell him something interesting and new."

"Perhaps *I* have something interesting to tell him," Cary says, a note of petulance edging into her voice.

Margaret raises an eyebrow. "Is this Cary Sturgis, of whom everyone is envious, being envious herself? I do believe it is."

"People are envious of me?"

"Of course they are, Cary. Look in a mirror and you'll see why."

As Cary flounces off, Margaret decides she's almost beginning to like her again. She's back to behaving as she did when she was attending the Conversations—full of her own youth and unafraid to say what she thinks. Acting her age instead of pretending to be fully adult.

Eventually, they all tire of being cooped up indoors and organize a ride in a hay wagon out toward Fitchburg, up hill and down dale, through a brisk but sunny afternoon. Margaret intends to enjoy the event but soon starts to feel she's watching the scene from a distance rather than being fully immersed. Even when she is chatting with someone, a certain aspect of her mind is observing from off to the side. The only person she's ever known who lives within his own thoughts as much as she does is Waldo. But he seems able to put on a public face, one of amiable good fellowship, without difficulty. For her it's not so easy. In her experience, there's no similar public face a woman is allowed to don.

In an effort to break out of her mood, she moves across the wagon to sit by Anna. "Which young men are in love with you these days?" she asks with a playful smile.

"I'll tell you when we're alone. I don't want the others to overhear."

"So there *is* someone. Or maybe several. Let me see if I can guess." She tries name after name, but Anna only shakes her head. That is, until she says, "Sam Ward." Then Anna's eyes shift and, under her breath, she whispers, "*Stop.*"

Back at the house they roast chestnuts in the fire and then drowse—on the divan, in a chair with legs sprawled out, or curled up on a rug near the hearth. It's as if they've been given a sleeping potion. By the time the last of them stumbles off to bed, the sky outside is getting light.

The following afternoon there's a knock at the front door. Some of them have yet to emerge from their rooms, but Margaret is already up working. Upon answering it she finds Henry Thoreau standing outside. The two of them are not exactly old friends, but since he's now one of *The Dial*'s authors and might well contribute to the magazine in the future, she feels considerably more cordial toward him. Greeting him warmly, she invites him in.

"I'm here to see my room," he says.

She has no idea what he's talking but before she can ask

him to explain, Waldo emerges from his study.

"Henry—oh yes, I did ask you to come today, didn't I. However, I'm afraid someone is staying in your room. What about next week, will that be all right?"

Before Thoreau can reply, Lidian appears, and between the three of them, it comes out that the Emersons have offered him a job. What with their growing family and Waldo's inability to do much more than speak and write, they need some help. Thoreau is going to move in and serve as a hired hand.

When the room arrangements have been clarified, Margaret says, "Have you seen it? The first issue?"

Thoreau nods. "Waldo brought me a copy. I like it very well."

"Henry will have some new things for the next one," Waldo says.

It's doesn't seem like the right time to talk about editorial matters, but Waldo is looking to her for a response. "Of what nature?" she asks.

"I'm not sure yet. Maybe something about walking," Thoreau replies.

"Walking?"

"In the winter."

"I see."

Is he incredibly plain spoken or is it a disguise? She's unsure. Before she can ask for clarification, Thoreau disappears with Waldo into his study leaving her standing with Lidian in the hall. Lidian looks at Margaret and remarks, "Waldo's interest in young poets usually diminishes over time. But with Henry it grows and grows."

The revels at the Emerson house continue for a few more days. Margaret, after considered observations, believes Cary and Anna are both in love with Sam. They compete for his attentions, Cary, by being outrageous—she is reading Bulwer-Lytton's *The Last Days of Pompeii* and uses the word "concubine" at every opportunity—and Anna, by waiting on Sam as though she's already his wife. Margaret would like to admonish them both. And Sam too, for rewarding such behavior with sweet words and approving looks.

As for Waldo, he stands back and watches. It's almost as if he's orchestrated all this for his own entertainment. Then, without warning, something angers Lidian and the anger is directed at Margaret—just as she'd begun to think the two of them were becoming friends. It begins when she says to Lidian, "I don't know how you put up with it all. Waldo seems to thrive on having bookish young people about, but they do fill up a house."

"I find it interesting that you set yourself apart from them," Lidian says. "Yet, in your own way you are as coy and provocative as Cary. How do you think that makes me feel?"

For once words fail her: "I'm not . . . I never meant . . . You misread me . . ."

"I don't think I do," Lidian says and strides away.

HENRY

When Lidian Emerson first invited Henry to move in, he didn't understand what she was asking.

"You're going away?" he said, thinking they wanted him to watch the house while they were gone.

"No, I simply need the help. Waldo is busier speaking and writing than ever, and with a second child I can scarcely keep up. I have a girl who comes to work in the kitchen, but Waldo invites so many people to visit I have to remind him we don't run a hotel. I need someone who's handy with tools and knows how to garden. So I thought of you."

A month ago, he might have turned her down. His room up under the eaves in his parents' house is fine. But being rejected by Ellen has changed him. He feels different—sad and confused about his place in the world. He had everything planned if she'd said yes. They'd have a found a little house with some land to farm. He'd have continued teaching for the time being but eventually, he might have turned the school over to John. He'd have . . . . Well, he'd have done lots of things. But now that she's said no, he hasn't any plans, save for what he's going to do tomorrow and perhaps the day after that.

So he accepted Mrs. Emerson's offer. In his present state of mind, any change will be good. If he doesn't like it, he can go back home. He thinks he'll enjoy being around Emerson. Especially his library. Henry sometimes thinks his idea of paradise is a library in the woods. This will almost fill the bill.

When he gets word that the Emersons' house party is over and their guests are gone, he puts some clothes, his journal, and some books (most of which belong to Emerson anyway) in a satchel and walks the short distance to the house on Lexington

Street. The explanation he provides to his family is restrained. He doesn't want them to be concerned:

"I'm going to help Mrs. Emerson for a few weeks. If you need me just let me know."

"That's nice of you, Henry," his mother says, hardly seeming to notice. She and Aunt Prudence have become more and more involved in the abolitionist cause, so they are always going off to one meeting or another. She won't mind having less wash to do and a plate she won't have to fill.

"I hope it makes you feel better," says Helen. Since learning about what happened with Ellen, she has been very solicitous about his welfare, more than anyone else.

His room in the Emerson house is at the top of the stairs. There's a good view out the window, a sturdy writing table, and plenty of space to store his things. His trip to school will be about the same distance as it was before but he'll be making the walk alone instead of with John. Maybe it's good that the two of them will spend more time apart.

He's surprised to discover Margaret Fuller is still there. She keeps to her room. When she does appear, something about the way she and Lidian glance at one another makes him think they're not getting along.

Lidian said she wanted a handyman, but Emerson seems to have different ideas about how he's to spend his time. Waiting on the table in his room is stack of books about the natural history of Massachusetts. When he asks what they're doing there, Emerson suggests he review them for *The Dial*. Henry examines them one-by-one: *Insects* by T. W. Harris, *Flowering Plants* by Chester Dewey, *Fishes, Reptiles, and Birds* by D. H. Storer, and *Quadrupeds* by Ebenezer Emmons. He likes the plain-spokenness of their titles.

Before he's there for many days, he discovers the pleasure of being around young children, little Waldo in particular. Sometimes, in the evening, Henry will be at his desk preparing lessons for the next day or making a new entry in his journal, when he hears some miniscule noise behind him, tiny footsteps or quiet breathing, as of a mouse. When he turns, there stands little Waldo, observing him with great blue eyes. The boy has only recently been allowed to climb the stairs by himself, so he does it as often as possible—especially now that this strange fellow with a rather large nose is living in the house. After Henry figures out what the boy is up to, he makes sure to leave his door ajar.

"Do you like music?" Henry asks one day. Waldo nods, so he gets out his flute and begins to play a tune. The boy takes a seat on the floor and listens with great concentration. As Henry finishes, Waldo waves a finger in the air. "Again," he shouts, "again."

After that, Henry carves little Waldo a flute of his own, using cedar, the wood most Indian flutes are made from. The instant the boy has it in his hands, he begins marching about the house while blowing it so loudly Henry feels the need to go to Lidian and apologize.

"I shouldn't have," he says. "I didn't know this would be the result."

"That's quite all right, Henry. Now you'll just have to teach him the proper way to play it. Please don't take too long."

In addition to reading Emerson's books and playing with little Waldo, he does a bit of carpentry, but it's difficult to accomplish much. As soon as he starts working, Emerson appears and wants to talk. He'll say he's been pondering this subject or that one, sometimes politics, sometimes theology, and what does Henry think? Before long the tools are set aside and they're in his study, pulling books off the shelves.

Henry recalls the cold afternoon when he looked down at Brook Farm and decided it wasn't for him. In his opinion, you don't need a charter or a contract and you don't have to move somewhere special to have a community of the like-minded. All that's required are two people who wish to share their thoughts. Of course, Emerson is an unusual man, whose thoughts are far more interesting than most, but Henry has conversed with the commonest of laborers and found that worthwhile as well.

He also discovers, to his satisfaction, that the great lecturer Waldo Emerson doesn't always need to talk. One evening Henry asks him if he wants to walk to Fair Haven Hill in the morning to the see the sunrise. "I believe I would enjoy that," he replies.

They leave in full darkness and are standing on a shelf of rock at the highest point when the first rays of the morning sun hit the ice-covered river below. Soon a little farmhouse in a hollow comes into the light, then an old bridge, and finally the snow-mantled mountain called Wachesett in the distance, like a great cloud that has fallen to earth. The entire way there, walking through the darkness single file, neither of them said a word.

Henry remembers when he came here with Ellen. Much has changed since then and the view from Fair Haven Hill seems to reflect those changes. Where once it was warmly autumnal, now it is frigid and white. Yet it remains inspiring. There is a spare and inhuman beauty to winter unmatched by other seasons.

At last Emerson speaks: "Who owns the landscape?"

"Which part?" Henry is teasing. He's aware that's not what Emerson is asking. Instead of replying, the great man merely shakes his head. He knows Henry too well to take the bait.

When the sun is fully above the horizon and shining on their faces, Henry says, "If I'm to be at school on time, I need to leave soon." So they return as they came, again in silence. To Henry, the two hours they spent going up the hill and then back down on that cold morning are as rich in meaning as any two hours they've been together. While they are both men of words, it seems they can get along without them, satisfied with the other's presence and with knowing they are each seeing the same sights and hearing the same sounds.

That night in his journal he records an idea that came to him during the walk: *I think I could write a poem to be called "Concord." For argument I should have the River, the Woods, the Ponds, the Hills, the Fields, the Swamps and Meadows, the Streets and Buildings, and the Villagers. Then Morning, Noon, and Evening, Spring, Summer, Autumn, and Winter, Night, Indian Summer, and the Mountains on the Horizon.*

SOPHIA

On a snowy December morning, Sophia and her sister Elizabeth are in a coach bound for Concord to see a house. Elizabeth arranged the trip with Sophia's blessing. There is still no date set for the wedding and Nathaniel's family still doesn't know about their engagement, but she is determined to move forward. He will just have to keep up.

Snow fell overnight, and their journey is as silent as any she can remember making. The horses' hooves and coach wheels on the road make no sound. The air is cold and still and the few birds that haven't gone south must be sleeping in.

"I'm afraid we won't be able to afford it," Sophia says.

"Mr. Emerson will be reasonable. He wants you living there."

"I hope it has a nice garden. I hope it has a stove and not merely a hearth. I hope there are lots of windows—I despise a house that's dark."

They give the driver a little extra to drop them right at the house and watch him pull away. Sophia looks up the snow-covered path leading to the front door, her imagination alive with what the future might hold. Somewhere inside is a study for Nathaniel and a studio for her and, yes, a nursery, painted yellow and white. There appears to be a sufficient number of windows and for a moment she pictures them lit, as if for a party, with guests on the way.

So deep is Sophia in her vision she doesn't notice that someone has come round from behind the house.

"Mr. Thoreau," Elizabeth says, and Sophia turns.

It's a young man in boots and canvas jacket, squinting into the low winter sun. "Greetings," he says. "Mr. Emerson asked me to come over and let you in. He's going to Boston today and regrets he can't be here himself."

"This is my sister, Sophia," Elizabeth says.

Sophia reaches for his cold hand. "Thank you for showing us the house."

They stand for a moment looking up at its austere front as he explains that it was built by Mr. Emerson's grandfather and that Emerson himself lived there until he moved across town. "It ought not to stand empty," Thoreau adds. "I feel sorry for the old place when I pass."

"I enjoyed what you wrote for *The Dial*," Elizabeth says.

"You read it?"

"I did."

He furrows his brow. "I would change a few things if I had it to do over again. But on the whole I am satisfied."

They proceed toward the door, Sophia and Elizabeth following in Thoreau's tracks. He unlocks the house and then enters the room at the left, throwing open the heavy curtains to bring in the light.

"It's a little musty," Thoreau says. "You can tell it's been closed up. Then again, the place is soundly built"—he raps on the wall to prove it—"and Mr. Emerson said to assure you the roof doesn't leak."

Sophia knows very little about houses, but she does her best to inspect each room. The banister on the stairs needs repairing, the carpet is so threadbare it might as well be rolled up and disposed of, and two of the second-floor rooms have no furnishings so they'll need to find the money for that. Although the air is frigid throughout, she can imagine it warm.

"Elizabeth, what do you think?" she whispers. She's wishes this Thoreau fellow wasn't listening.

"I believe it will do nicely."

"Will there be just the two of you?" Thoreau asks.

Sophia looks to Elizabeth. "Us? No," she says but before

she can continue, Elizabeth interrupts.

"I explained the situation to Waldo. He can tell you if he wants."

Thoreau looks a little embarrassed. Either Emerson already told him or he's figured it out for himself.

"How much is it?" Sophia asks.

"He said to tell you a hundred dollars for the year."

Sophia glances at Elizabeth. Nathaniel was paying four times that for a single room in Boston. She wonders if Emerson knows how much he's underpriced it—even if he wants them here and even if Elizabeth is a friend.

The tour over, they go outside and wait as Thoreau secures the door.

"*A hundred dollars for the year*," Sophia whispers into Elizabeth's ear.

Now Elizabeth adopts a business-like tone. "It's all quite satisfactory," she says to Thoreau. "Please inform Mr. Emerson my sister will write him about the details. And do give him my best wishes and tell him I hope to see him soon."

"Good day then," Thoreau replies, and without another word, strides off into the trees.

Elizabeth waits to make sure he's gone and then says, "You might not believe it, but Waldo Emerson speaks very highly of him."

"Someone has broken his heart," Sophia says. "I can hear it in his voice."

Back in Boston Sophia ponders her next task: getting Nathaniel to tell his mother they are engaged. She calls him back from Brook Farm and says, "I will come to Salem with you. She will see how in love we are and understand." She also intends to tell him about the house but before she can continue, he interrupts.

"I don't think you recognize the difficulty of what you are proposing," he says, shaking his head.

For the first time, she feels herself becoming genuinely angry with him. "Is it really so difficult? Well, it will only become more difficult with time. Or are you suggesting we should marry and let your mother find out after the fact?" She sets her small mouth in a hard line and shakes her head.

"No, you are right," he says, yielding. "I must. I truly must. You will help me find the words."

"The irony of that," she says.

"I know, I know. Since last we talked I've been examining my reluctance. I think I can now explain it to you better than I could before."

"Please," she says. "Do."

They go for a walk with no destination in mind, up one street and down another, some busy and some deserted, paying attention only to one another's words. Nathaniel speaks of his unexceptional childhood in Salem, a childhood of which Sophia had a glimpse. He then went off to college in Maine, where he made a few good friends and nurtured his love of books. But after that, instead of going out into the world, he returned to live with his mother and sisters, retreating to his room. There he stayed, not just for weeks or months but for years.

"My life was dark, but it was the life I chose. My sisters and I passed in the hallway like ghosts. Downstairs, my mother mourned my father's death, although it had happened twenty years before. And then I met my Sophia, who saved me. But you see, they only know me as the young man up in that room. That is who I am to them and who I shall remain. And yet, for us to be together, that young man must perish."

She understands and doesn't understand. Who would want that sort of life? What mother would want to condemn her son to such an existence? She studies his face. Has he told her everything? This time he said nothing about the main obstacle being their lack of a suitable place to live. She decides to keep her recent transaction with Mr. Emerson to herself for the time being. But she's done waiting. If he demurs any longer, it will be the end of them. She insists they go to Salem before the week is out.

Two days later they are on the train. Sophia says, "You should speak to them as if this is the most ordinary thing in the world. Men and women marry. They leave the families they were born into and make their own." She remembers Mary saying that his mother and sisters remind her of a coven of witches. Of course, that's Mary's way of talking, her silly dramatics, but at the moment she's having a hard time not thinking of them as such. And she is on her way to release Nathaniel from their spell.

MARGARET

She left Concord shortly after the others. The unpleasant exchange with Lidian was too much. Before she departed, she apologized, even though she didn't think she was to blame.

"Please forget all about it," Lidian said. "There were simply too many people in the house. It upsets my nerves."

"Are you certain that's all it is?" She expected her to say yes, so as to put the matter to rest. Instead, Lidian took the opportunity to elaborate.

"I sometimes think he still cares for his first wife more than he cares for me. She was like Anna and Cary."

"How do you mean?"

"Fresh. Spirited. While I am neither."

"But his first wife is no longer alive . . ."

She looked at Margaret as if she'd made an obvious error in logic: "That only makes it worse."

After that exchange, Margaret had the feeling there will always be an uneasiness between herself and Lidian. As Waldo's wife, she sees everything in relation to Waldo and therefore is unable to see Margaret for herself.

Later that same day, she spoke with Waldo about the next issue of *The Dial*. Once again, he encouraged her to be bold. He wants the traditionalists in Boston to get red-faced when they read it. In his view, the more upset they are, the more credibility *The Dial* has. She also mentioned her unpaid salary. "I know," he said, almost sheepishly. "I will talk to Ripley." But that didn't give her much hope.

All in all, it was a disappointing visit. Yet now, quite unexpectedly, she is feeling revived. The reason? She has begun a new piece of writing. The idea came to her while in the coach from Concord to Boston. It will be about women and men, in history and in the present day, especially about how women are surrounded by arbitrary barriers that constrain their lives. It is a topic about which she has thought a great deal, but she has never before attempted to directly address the problem, as an unambiguous fact.

As soon as she's unpacked, she clears her writing table of all but pen and paper and begins: *Many women are considering within themselves what they need that they have not, and what they can have, if they find they need it. Many men are considering whether women are capable of being and having more than they are and have . . . Without enrolling ourselves at once on either side, let us look upon the subject from that point of view which to-day offers.*

Something tells her that this will engage her more deeply than anything she's written in a long while. She writes swiftly, easily, and doesn't stop until well past midnight.

The next day she rises and goes directly to her desk: *What woman needs is not as a woman to act or rule, but as a nature to grow, as an intellect to discern, as a soul to live freely.*

She continues on through the day, into the evening, and through the morning of the next day. Then she stacks the pages in a neat pile and re-reads them. Satisfied she is off to a good start, she eats lunch, dresses warmly, and goes out.

It's cold and gray but the streets are full of commerce, of businessmen and ladies shopping and horses pulling drays. Two peddlers shout at one another, barrels of something sweet smelling, perhaps molasses, are being rolled up a ramp, and she stops to watch a man taking a photograph of a fire wagon before she continues on. Her destination is Elizabeth Peabody's shop.

When she arrives, Elizabeth is serving a customer, so Margaret looks around. There on a table is *The Dial,* not just one or two, but a dozen well-displayed copies in the form of a lilac-colored pyramid, and she feels a tremendous sense of pride. From the beginning Elizabeth has been a great supporter. However many copies have been sold, Elizabeth must be responsible for at least half.

When the customer is gone, they chat about what they've each been doing since they last met.

"I'm just back from Concord," Margaret says. "Sam Ward and Anna Barker were there. They've returned from their trip, perhaps you've seen them. Cary Sturgis was visiting too, being her usual flirtatious self."

"It sounds quite lively," Elizabeth says.

"Oh, it was," replies Margaret. "A little too lively. I'm glad to be back."

Elizabeth then tells her about going with Sophia to look at the house.

"So she and Hawthorne are to be married?" Margaret says. "I had my suspicions, but I must say, I didn't think he'd commit."

"No one is supposed to know. Not until he tells his mother. They're on their way to do that now."

"But a house in Concord," Margaret says. "I guess this means he won't be staying at Brook Farm."

"It turns out he dislikes Brook Farm intensely. I never understood why he went there in the first place. He and my sister are similar in that neither of them has much interest in politics or philosophy or the society around them. They'd both prefer to stay in a room behind a door they can lock and create their works of art."

"Then they should be a good match."

"We shall see," Elizabeth says. "They certainly seem convinced they are in love."

Margaret then explains that she is beginning work on the next edition of *The Dial* and wants Elizabeth's advice. From whom should she solicit articles and what overall tone should the magazine take? As usual Elizabeth is full of sound ideas. She has read the first one carefully and even made some notes.

Before Margaret leaves, Elizabeth says, "The men who created *The Dial* are not wealthy, but neither are they poor. It's unfair of them to expect you to go without pay."

"But I consider it the most important work I've ever done."

"In this world, important work is *paid for*," Elizabeth says emphatically. "Do not let them take advantage of you."

She carries Elizabeth's words back to her desk, where she begins at once to write: *Not only is man vain and fond of power, but the same want of development, which thus affects him morally in the intellect, prevents his discerning the destiny of woman. The boy wants no woman, but only a girl to play ball with him, and mark his pocket handkerchief.*

Late that afternoon, she rereads what she's written. On the whole, it seems strong but abstract, lacking in the reality of daily life. If there is something of meaning to be said about the condition in which women currently find themselves, it must be rooted in how they spend their hours and not only in history and philosophy. It must have the vitality of the best of her Conversations, the ones where everyone spoke with honesty and from their hearts. She tries a sentence, crosses it out, tries another, crosses it out and refuses to be discouraged.

HENRY

He's asleep in bed when there's a knock at the front door. He hears Lidian answer it and then hears her climbing the stairs. Before she can reach the top, he's pulled on his trousers and stepped into the hall.

"It's your sister Helen," she says. "Your brother has taken ill, and you're wanted at home."

"Taken ill? How?" he asks, but Lidian doesn't know. He quickly finishes dressing and follows her down. At the bottom of the stairs stands Helen, looking more sleepy than upset.

"Something's wrong with John?"

"Yes, come along," she says and leads him out the door. Outside it's shortly before sunrise, with a scattering of stars and the moon like a cup hook still visible overhead.

As they walk, she explains. A few days ago, John cut his finger while sharpening his razor. Then the finger became infected and now he has begun to feel ill.

"I don't think you're needed," Helen says, "but Mother insisted. Father's gone for the doctor and should be back soon."

When they get home, Henry goes straight to John's room. He's in bed but looks like himself, neither flushed nor pale.

"What are you doing here?" John says.

Henry shrugs. "I've stropped my razor every day since I was fifteen and never once cut myself. Maybe you ought to grow a beard."

John smiles and in his smile Henry discerns some pain.

"How are things at the Emersons'?" John asks. "Are they giving you lots of work?"

"Actually, I'm spending most of my time being a nanny.

It's not what I expected but I don't object. I have a feeling once spring is here I'll become their gardener. Waldo Emerson knows many things, but if he had to grow his own food he'd starve."

John smiles again, grimaces, and speaks: "If I'm not feeling up to going to school tomorrow . . ."

". . . I'll get Helen to fill in."

Now Helen brings a damp cloth and places it on John's forehead. Although the room is chilly he says he's getting hot.

"How's that?" she asks.

"Just what I needed," he replies.

For a time they sit in silence. Then Sarah comes in, carrying a book. She perches on the end of the bed and begins to read.

"Tell me about your book," John says.

Sarah looks up. "It's about a girl who falls in love with a man who has a secret past."

"Is it interesting?" Helen asks.

"It is to me. They live in a castle," she says.

"I wouldn't like to live in a castle," says Helen. "Too many rooms to clean."

Their mother is in another room resting. John didn't sleep well and she was up with him through the night. Out the window long icicles hang from the eaves.

Now they hear a noise downstairs and all of them turn toward the door. Doctor Bartlett has arrived. Up he comes, step by weary step. When he appears, their parents are right behind him. No introductions are necessary—he has treated the family for years. Henry takes the doctor's hat and ulster and puts them on a chair. Bartlett says, "My wheels were frozen to the ground when I got up this morning. But now the sun is out so maybe we'll get a thaw."

As the doctor prepares to examine John, everyone except their mother leaves. She'll play the role of nurse should that be required.

CONCORD

Henry goes up to his attic room. He's only been living at the Emersons' for a few days but it's like he's returning from a long trip. The bed is neatly made, the desk lacks its customary clutter, and all the books are shelved. He opens the desk drawer and takes out two of his father's pencils, not yet sharpened. They go into his pocket for when he's back at the Emerson house. Although he's been too busy to help out much with pencil-making, his father has taken his ideas and put them into practice. He even found a nearby source of good clay. As a result, Thoreau pencils are now of superior quality, as good as any that can be purchased.

Out the window Henry sees Prudence and old Mrs. Sewell leaving. They must be on their way to church. He'd forgotten it was Sunday. They'll be the only ones from this house attending services today.

After a while, he hears the doctor and his mother talking and goes back down. They are on the landing outside John's room. The door is closed behind them.

"You can go in," his mother says.

"What is it?" he asks.

The doctor looks to his mother for permission and she nods. "Lockjaw," the doctor says bluntly.

"What can we do?"

"Very little I'm afraid. Go be with him as your mother said."

He collects himself and opens the door. Does John know? He can't tell. His eyes are closed and his hands are in fists at his side. Henry watches as he opens them, spreads his fingers wide, and then clenches them into fists again.

Soon Helen comes in and her eyes meet Henry's. She knows too.

"Is there anything we can get you, John?" she asks.

"The doctor says it will not take long," he replies.

Henry grasps the bottom of the chair to keep from bolting

from the room. He hears a rushing in his ears. Helen's eyes fill with tears and she turns away.

As the day goes on, the disease begins to make itself known. Late in the morning John begins from time to time to grind his teeth. By mid-afternoon he's having painful muscle spasms in his back. After that Sarah is no longer allowed in. His jaw clenches and saliva runs from the corners of his mouth. His fever worsens and he begins to sweat. Then for a while the symptoms diminish and he is calm.

"I don't know whether I should want to get on with this or hope for more time," John says.

"Are you in pain now?" Helen asks.

"Not at present. Maybe I'll get some sleep."

But only seconds later, another spasm begins. Henry sits and holds his brother's hand but doesn't know what to say.

Their parents come in every so often, but Henry and Helen insist they are the ones who should be with him, so after a few minutes they leave again. Their mother can be heard sobbing in the hall.

With nightfall it worsens. Spasms cause John's back to arch, nearly breaking him in two. In the lamplight his eyes look wild. He barely catches his breath between spells before another starts again. They try giving him some whiskey to dull the pain, but he vomits it back up. After that Helen begins to cry and leaves the room. Henry thinks they're alone but then feels a hand on his shoulder and realizes his father is behind him. When another spasm comes, his father holds on for dear life, as if he's in a boat on a stormy sea.

"I'm going for Doctor Bartlett again," his father says. Then he hurries down the stairs and out the door.

At lengh John falls asleep. Henry sits in the dark and watches. He tells himself if John can make it to morning he'll be all right. He remembers one afternoon when they were boys, sitting on the fence and trading stories, their sides aching with laughter, their eyes flooded with tears. When the sun comes up the spasms start again. A little later, Helen reappears. She says she went to their school and sent the children home.

John's eyes are closed and he's motionless, but upon hearing Helen, he says, "It's Monday. I'd forgotten. Thank you for doing that."

"Eldon Brown told me to give you a dose of cider vinegar," Helen says.

"Eldon is full of advice," adds Henry, and John offers a weak smile.

They hear their father return but for a long time he doesn't come up. When at last he does, he calls Henry into the hall. He looks at the floor and speaks: "Doctor Barlett wouldn't come back. He says there's nothing he can do."

Shortly thereafter, the convulsions recommence, more intense than ever, wave after harrowing wave. Henry knows they can't continue but they do, for hours it seems. Then he feels something change. He sends Helen to get their parents and Sarah and bring them to the bedside. He puts his arms around John and holds him as best he can. At two o'clock in the afternoon his brother dies.

SOPHIA

They walk from the Salem train station to the house on Herbert Street, arm in arm. She'd forgotten what a great dingy hulk it is. And to think Nathaniel spent most of his life there before they met.

"Any advice before we go in?" Sophia asks.

"No matter how much she dislikes the news we are delivering, I can promise she'll treat you with respect."

Sophia considers that a small comfort. Does it matter if the lioness who devours you treats you with respect?

They knock and his sister Ebe answers the door. Nathaniel says she's the one most likely to be their ally. Upon seeing them, she doesn't smile but neither does she frown.

"I trust your journey was pleasant. People say the train is now the best way to get to Boston, but I have yet to try it out."

"It's quite comfortable," Nathaniel says. A cat appears from somewhere and rubs itself against his ankles, no doubt remembering him.

Ebe guides them into the parlor where they find his mother and sister Louisa, side-by-side on a settee.

The room is even darker and more forbidding than Sophia expected. Dark red curtains cover the windows and there are no adornments—no vases or ceramic statuettes and not a single picture on the walls. It can't be a matter of money—she's been in meaner houses and people always seem to make do. They cut illustrations from mail order journals or frame a piece of handwork or display a few dried flowers. No, this is an intentional expression of their abstemious view of life. Poor Nathaniel—forced to live this way. Another cat comes out from behind the curtains, then spies Sophia and dashes away.

They've all met before so there's no need for formal introductions. "You remember Sophia Peabody," Nathaniel says. She takes a seat as directed by Ebe while Nathaniel takes another. They have been placed, perhaps intentionally, half a room apart.

"I'm sorry it's been so long since I've visited," Nathaniel begins. "I hope all of you are well."

"Well enough," his mother says. "Although I have had some stiffness in my joints and Louisa is experiencing her usual winter catarrh."

"I am eager to hear about Brook Farm," Ebe says. "Your letters make it sound idyllic."

"I'm afraid I exaggerated to prevent you from worrying about me," he says. "The location is idyllic, but for me the plan on which it was founded is too constraining. I won't stay out the year."

He continues telling about Brook Farm, answering Ebe's questions about what life there is like and why he wants to leave. They seem almost to forget Sophia's in the room. If it were some other setting, she'd consider them rude, but for now she's relieved. She uses the opportunity to study them. They are all dressed in their customary black, the same as when she met them the first time. It must be all they wear. His mother has a strong face, but it's narrower than Nathaniel's, so his broad forehead must come from his father. She wonders if there's a picture of him she could see.

When at last he's done telling them about Brook Farm, Louisa goes to get coffee. Yet another cat follows her out, yellow instead of black like the two she's already seen.

"Sophia has been commissioned to sculpt a bust of Laura Bridgman at Samuel Howe's school," Nathaniel says. "You may have heard of Laura Bridgman—the blind and deaf child with the remarkable mind."

"I have read of her," his mother says. "Is she very beautiful?"

"Why, yes," Sophia says, a little surprised to find herself included. "Indeed she is."

"How does she communicate?" asks Ebe.

"She makes signs with her fingers; then her teacher tells me what they say."

"How interesting," Ebe replies. "I would hate to be blind, but I don't think I'd find it a great inconvenience not to hear."

Now Louisa returns with cups and saucers on a tray. Although Sophia doesn't particularly like coffee, she's not about to turn it down. Her gaze wanders. Beneath the china hutch she sees cat number four.

Nathaniel asks about old Mrs. Marshall who lives up the street. Sophia has never heard of her but apparently she's a family friend. Once again Sophia is left out of the conversation, although this time it seems more natural and less like an intentional slight. Now that she's had a chance to observe them, she thinks Ebe, under the right circumstances, might be quite affable. But Louisa is painfully shy and his mother still seems fierce.

At last the moment comes. Nathaniel glances at her and begins:

"Sophia and I are here for a particular reason. We have, over these several months, come to the conclusion that we share a certain—that we wish to—that we have *developed* toward one another a feeling of mutual regard. And that, therefore, we wish to form a lasting union. Thus, we present ourselves to ask your approval, which we hope you will unreservedly provide."

There, it's out. She's proud of him. She knew he'd do it but it's a relief nonetheless to have heard him speak the words.

His mother's eyes narrow. Louisa looks into her cup. "I knew it," Ebe says.

"And when shall this event occur?" his mother asks.

"As soon as I am able to leave Brook Farm," he says. "Not later than this summer, perhaps in the month of June."

"And how long, may I ask, have you known?"

This Sophia recognizes as a trap. Too long and she's been kept in the dark; too short and they're being rash. Right now his mother is directing her gaze at Nathaniel but occasionally she glances at Sophia, as if to pin her to her chair.

"For myself, since the day we met," he says. "For Sophia, since I was able to persuade her that I have a heart."

Sophia wants to go and kiss him, but his mother is still looking at her and she couldn't move if she tried.

There follows a terrible silence. Sophia wonders who will speak first.

It's Nathaniel's mother. She says, "Well, I can see it is done."

"We have your approval then?" he asks.

Once again she is silent. Finally, in a low voice, a voice tinged with anguish or perhaps doubt, she says, "It seems I have no recourse."

When, a few minutes later, they take their leave, all of them act as if the visit has been entirely congenial, as if nothing unpleasant transpired. But as soon as they cross the street, Sophia bursts into tears.

"What's wrong?" Nathaniel says. "We were successful."

"I'm sorry. I've been holding everything inside."

"When they know you better, they will love you."

"Do you think so? I can't be so optimistic. Not after today."

Interestingly, the question of whether they could afford a place to live never even arose. Was that only Nathaniel's invention? She doesn't care and doesn't intend to ask him to explain. He's still unaware that she's let a house in Concord and for some reason feels this isn't the right time to tell him. It seems a small matter now.

Later that week, when Nathaniel has returned to Brook Farm, Sophia receives a letter from Ebe. She opens it hoping it will be conciliatory, but it's hardly that. Even after a second reading, she's not sure how to describe it: *I hope nothing will ever occur to render your future intercourse with us other than agreeable, particularly as it need not be so frequent or so close as to require more than reciprocal good will.* In other words, mutual toleration is the best she should expect.

Well, so be it. She and Nathaniel will be living in Concord, in Mr. Emerson's house and not in Salem. Interaction with the Hawthorne women should be minimal. If Nathaniel wants to visit them, he can go alone.

MARGARET

There was a time when Margaret wanted very much to be part of Waldo's circle, even a time when she was intrigued by the idea of moving to Concord to live, but her feelings about that are changing. Five or ten years from now she doesn't want to be struggling to earn a living by writing and editing for and amongst a coterie of eccentrics. Because, as harsh as it may sound, that's what they really are. Yes, sometimes a small group can spawn a revolution in culture and thought, but more often they whither and disperse. She remembers seeing Sam and Anna off at the docks. What if she'd gone with them and never come back? What if she'd started a new life far away?

She goes to see Elizabeth again to discuss some matters related to *The Dial*, but this time Elizabeth has sad news to share. Henry Thoreau's brother has died. Margaret knows Henry only through their occasional meetings at Emerson's house and interactions related to *The Dial*. She never met his brother. But she's certain Waldo is distraught and feels pain on his behalf.

"Henry and John were very close," Elizabeth says. "I too once lost a brother. However, I understand this was quite sudden. When our dear George passed we could see it coming for a long time."

Margaret thinks about her father's death, which was sudden as well, but she doesn't bring it up. While some react to tragedies experienced by others by telling all the ways in which their own life has been similarly touched, she prefers to keep such matters to herself. Back at her room, she writes Henry Thoreau a letter of condolence and then returns to work.

In the essay she is presently composing, she has come upon

the idea of using her own life as an example for the reader to consider. But to avoid being self-aggrandizing, she gives herself a different name, Miranda, borrowed from her favorite of Shakespeare's plays.

I was talking on this subject with Miranda. Her father was a man who cherished no sentimental reverence for woman, but a firm belief in the equality of the sexes. She was his eldest child and came to him at an age when he needed a companion. From the time she could speak and go alone, he addressed her not as a plaything, but as a living mind.

This is the particularity she has been searching for. It allows her to write about a single life, which is hers or very much like hers, while also writing about all men and women, as the philosopher does.

As she continues, memories of her childhood wash over her. She remembers how her father taught her with great sternness, almost too much sternness, but also with respect. And she remembers walking in the woods after his lessons, her mind ablaze with the questions she would one day bring to her Conversations, about the purpose of life and how one can become who one is meant to be. She remembers going with her mother to visit a poor woman with a sick husband and, upon seeing how the entirety of that woman's life was lived within yards of a soot-begrimed hearth, in a house that was little more than a hovel, she felt overwhelmed by a combination of pity and revulsion. Which choices and forces, she wondered, might lead her toward such a life and which could lead her away?

She writes: *Thus Miranda was early led to feel herself a child of the spirit. She took her place easily, not only in the world of organized being, but in the world of mind.* There's the rub. For all Miranda's independence and intelligence, she remained an outsider. The higher forms of education and literature and politics were closed to her. And she noticed that while she longed to have access to the world of men, men never wanted access to the world of women. Men do not feel themselves outsiders because the most prestigious of clubs is the one they all enter at birth.

She stops there. If she completes the essay and publishes it, how will it be received? Will it be attacked or simply ignored? Better the former than the latter. She is reminded of a line from an essay-in-progress Waldo sent her to read: *Trust thyself: every heart vibrates to that iron string.*

The next day she turns her attention back to *The Dial*, writing letters to potential contributors and reading the articles and poems that are already trickling in. She also receives a letter from an editor in New York who wants her to go work for him. It's flattering to find that she's becoming well known, but she can't seem to tear her thoughts away from the essay; that evening she continues to add to it and give it shape. A nor'easter rattles the window glass, and the room is colder by the hour. She wraps herself in quilts and carries on.

Then one afternoon a letter arrives from Waldo. Nothing strange about that, but something makes her think it is not editorial correspondence of the usual kind. She opens it and reads:

Dear Margaret,

My little boy Waldo has died. All his wonderful beauty could not save him. He gave up his innocent breath on Monday night and now my world is ruined. He had what is called Scarlet Fever. Shall I ever dare to love anything again? Farewell, O my Boy!

A gasp of anguish, of choked horror and despair, issues from her throat. First John Thoreau and now this, all within a matter of days. The poor man. She knows what it is to lose a parent, but it must be far worse to lose a child. She pictures him with little Waldo and in so doing realizes that the Emerson she knows is really two men—the public one, who is earnest, reserved, sometimes humorless and often lost in thought; and the *father*, who is warm, laughs easily, and would rather spend an afternoon with his children than with the greatest minds of the day. She'd like to go to him at once but cannot, not without an invitation. Lidian might not want her there and she has no desire to bring anything but comfort to their household. She composes a letter, the only time she's ever written to them as a pair. It takes her several drafts to arrive at something that seems right:

Dear Waldo and Lidian,

I am deeply saddened by your loss. There has never been a child for whom I had higher hopes. I cannot be reconciled to the fact that I shall see him no more.

Five years he was an angel, and I cannot understand why one with such a golden future was torn away. If the few times I saw him have left me with such feelings, how much worse must yours be, who saw him every day.

I have no doubt that together you shall bear up under this burden, as terrible as it is. If I can be of service to you, at any time or in any way, you need only ask. Give a kiss for me to sweet Nelly. It is a blessing that she is too young to fully comprehend what has been taken from her.

She writes a second letter to Emerson's mother, who has spent so much time caring for little Waldo. This tragedy may hurt her most of all.

After she posts them, she tries to go back to work but finds herself unable to. All she can think of is Waldo and Lidian in their house, which is now filled with sadness. The sadness will be like smoke, stealing into every crack and impossible to get out.

HENRY

In the hours and days after John's death, he feels hollow, without purpose, blank. Everyone in the house is overcome by grief but he is unable to share his in the communal way the others do. His mother and Helen sob in the kitchen. His father holds Sarah in his arms. Prudence and Grandmother Sewell take over the cooking and cleaning. While Henry aches to disappear.

At John's funeral, Bart Frost, minister of the First Parish Church, chooses for his texts "For what is your life? It is even a vapor, that appeareth for a little time and then vanisheth away" and "Man cometh forth like a flower and is cut down." Henry approves. He couldn't have chosen better himself.

It's the coldest winter in ten years, so when the grave is halfway dug they have to fill it with wood and set a fire before they can go as deep as they must. After the coffin has been lowered in, Helen covers it with straw because she doesn't want to hear the ugly sound of stones and frozen clods striking the lid.

The day after the funeral, Henry begins feeling a stiffness in his own jaw. He gets feverish and thinks, *This is impossible* but also *This is as it should be.* He goes to sleep thinking he won't wake up again but the next morning the stiffness and fever are gone.

He dresses, pulling on wool leggings and his warmest sweater. Then he finds his skates and walks to the river, which is frozen two feet down. He's not a graceful skater but his short, choppy stride carries him forward at a good rate. There's not another soul about and it's not long before Concord is far behind. He's never known the river to be frozen so hard

317

and the ice to be so smooth. His mother once asked him if he ever feels lonely when he goes out by himself. He laughed, the question was so absurd. But feeling lonely is different from feeling abandoned, and today he feels more abandoned than ever before.

Soon it begins to get dark. He's lost track of how far he's gone, although surely it must be miles. The moon rises and still he skates on. At last, he turns back. When he gets home it's the middle of the night, but Helen is waiting up for him.

"Henry, please don't go away like that," she says. "Not right now. I was worried sick."

"I'm sorry," he says. "I forgot myself."

"I expect we'd all like to do that," she replies.

He takes off his coat and gloves and tries to warm his hands at the fire, but it's been allowed to burn down for the night, so there's little warmth to be had.

"I think I may close the school," he tells her.

"Just like that? I could help teach if you wanted."

"I don't think I care to do it without him." He finds something about this embarrassing and has difficulty meeting her eyes.

"But how will you make a living?"

"I haven't thought that far ahead."

He goes up to his room and takes Plutarch's *Morals* off the shelf. Finding his favorite passage, he reads aloud: *The soul, being eternal, after death is like a caged bird that has been released.* It's the first thing he's read or thought that offers him any true consolation. He has always loved birds and now John is among them. He sets the book aside and falls asleep.

But the evening of the next day, Louisa Alcott comes to the house. She's been to the Emersons' and something terrible has happened. Their little boy has died. Henry, Helen, and their mother all heard the knock and converged to answer it. Now they stand in horrified silence, watching Louisa walk away from the house across a field of snow.

CONCORD

"How is this possible?" his mother says. "We only just buried John and now another son lost?"

"I'm going to see them," Henry says, and coatless, goes out the door.

He runs all the way. When he arrives, a neighbor woman lets him in. "Such a pity," she says. "Such a terrible pity."

"May I see Mr. Emerson?" Henry asks.

She motions to his study. "In there," she says. "But perhaps you ought to knock."

He does as she says and hears a muffled invitation to enter. Inside, he finds Emerson bent over his desk, pen in hand. The desktop is covered with paper, more even than when he is in the midst of composing one of his celebrated lectures. When he looks up, his face is a tear-stained mask.

"You heard. My poor Waldo."

"I'm so sorry."

He runs his hand through his already disheveled hair. "I thought nothing could befall me which nature could not repair. I was wrong. So very wrong." Then, noticing that Henry is surveying his desk, he adds, "I am writing letters. I want people to know."

"What can I do to help?"

He shakes his head. "You have your own tragedy. Simply coming here is enough."

"May I stay a while? You can continue writing. I would just like to sit."

"Of course," he says, so for the next hour Henry does exactly that. He watches Emerson write and he looks out the window at the snow and the gray sky and then fixes his gaze on the carpet where the pattern looks like a map.

Eventually, Emerson says, "I'm done for now. I will write more tomorrow but these are ready to send."

Henry nods. "I think I'll go home. But I'll come back tomorrow if you don't mind."

319

"Let me give you a coat. It's too cold to be without one."

"Thank you but it's not far. I'm fine the way I am."

He gets up and goes out into the hall. There he encounters Lidian, who is coming down the stairs. Her face is ashen, and her eyes are red and raw. As he looks at her, she reaches out and takes his hands. "Oh, Henry," she says, and they embrace, both of them in tears. He cried when he was alone after John's death, but this is less restrained. If souls are like birds as Plutarch says, then he feels his own rising inside him. It wants to escape but is trapped in the cage of this life.

SOPHIA

She intends to get married and move to Concord, but this winter the very word "Concord" sounds like death. Maybe they should choose another place. After the stories of tragedy make their way to Boston, it is all anyone talks about. Elizabeth is so distraught she stops filling her calendar with the usual variety of social, literary, and political events and seldom leaves her shop.

Since their visit to Salem, Sophia and Nathaniel have carried on their courtship mostly by way of letters between Boston and Brook Farm. They have selected a date and location for their wedding and any time Sophia senses in Nathaniel a return to his former tentativeness, she responds with force: "We have dealt with your mother. The only other obstacles are minor. Our future together is set." Finally, in early March, she receives the letter she's wanted most—the one telling her the day he'll be returning to Boston. He has given up on farming and will be coming home.

While Sophia has been waiting, she has completed the bust of Laura Bridgman and is pleased with the response. Mr. Clevenger seems almost jealous and Washington Allston, upon seeing it, said that in clay she has found her true medium. But then for the first time in months she has a headache. She had almost convinced herself they were a thing of the past. She puts herself to bed and enters the strange but all too familiar land of pain. Her mouth tastes of metal and there's a ringing in her ears. She tries to eat a little toast but can keep nothing down. She takes a pill and sleeps for a long time, a whole night and half the following day.

When she wakes, there sits Mary beside her bed. Sophia can't remember letting her in, but she's pleased to see her.

"Are you feeling better?" Mary asks. She has always been the most sympathetic member of the family when Sophia's ill. There's a small amount of playacting in it—Mary enjoys the role of nurse—but that doesn't keep Sophia from valuing her care.

"I think so." She sits up in bed. "Yes, I believe I am."

"Well, tell me," Mary says, "what date have you selected?"

"For the wedding? June. The twelfth or the nineteenth."

"And the location?"

"You'll laugh."

"I'm sure I will."

"Elizabeth's shop. It's going to be small."

Mary does laugh. "Among the books and skeletons?"

"The skeletons can be my bridesmaids." She reaches for a hairbrush on the table beside the bed. "It appears Nathaniel's family won't be attending. So it will be just Mother and Father, you and Elizabeth, and a small number of friends. Not more than ten I expect."

A year or two ago, Mary would have had a fit. She'd have told her such a plan was ridiculous. Too small, too odd, and thoroughly lacking in romance. But they're getting older and their imaginations have been tempered by experience and time. Where once Sophia envied her for Horace Mann, she's begun feeling sorry for Mary and can now think of little that would make her happier than hearing her sister and Horace were to be married—and preferably very soon.

While Sophia brushes her hair, Mary stands and begins to move about the room. She picks up a shawl and some stockings Sophia has left hanging over the back of a chair, neatly folding them all. She looks out the window at the morning traffic and then at herself in the mirror, her judgment rendered in the form of a frown.

"Have you told him about the Emerson house yet?" she asks.

Sophia shakes her head. "I intended to, but the time never seemed right. I'm afraid he'll say no. I think I'll just take him there and make it a surprise."

"You like to court disaster," Mary says.

The recent tragedies in Concord now enter Sophia's mind. "I think often of Mr. Emerson and his wife. Can you imagine losing a child of that age?"

"I cannot. I would murder myself in the aftermath. But I'm told they have another child so I suppose they must live on."

The next morning, Sophia feels much better—although not as well as she does later that week when Nathaniel finally returns.

He leaps from the coach and she laughs with delight as he pulls her to him so hard her feet leave the ground.

"Were they sorry to see you go?" she asks.

"I have no idea. The whole place is in a bad way. Ripley is selling off his personal library to cover expenses. I bought a few of his books myself."

"You didn't feel mercenary in doing so?"

"I don't expect to get back a single dollar of what I invested in the place. So no, I did not."

Then Sophia says, "I have a surprise for you," and takes him directly to Elizabeth's shop. In his absence the first copies of *The Gentle Boy* have been delivered. Already some are on display. She and Nathaniel sit side by side and open it. It's a small book and if Sophia were to be truthful, she would have to admit she's a little disappointed in the printer's work. But what really matters is that they are joined between the covers, she and her beloved, and even if not a single copy is sold, it will sit forever on their shelf. When she looks up, she notices Elizabeth watching from across the room. Sophia fears that her sister's feelings about Nathaniel and herself will never be entirely unmixed.

Later that evening, after they have left the shop, Nathaniel says he knows somewhere private they can go: "I have a friend who's away." She doesn't question him. Being with him is all she wants. As soon as the door is closed behind them, they embrace. He kisses her mouth, her eyes, her neck. This time the process of disrobing is less awkward. This time they are both less shy. This time she knows what to anticipate so she's more in control of her thoughts. But there are noises in the street and when it's over, Nathaniel is in a hurry to leave. So as pleasant as it is to be with him, the experience isn't fully satisfactory. *When we are married*, she thinks. Only then will everything be right.

Despite Mary's words of caution, Sophia has already scheduled a trip to Concord for Nathaniel and herself. She'll let him settle in Boston for a few days and then take him to see the house. She tells him it's a place Elizabeth knows of, which is true, and that if they don't like it, they can look elsewhere, which is *not* true—she's already sent Emerson an initial payment along with a note telling him she'll be bringing Nathaniel to see it. He says he'll leave the key above the door.

On the way there, Nathaniel is so affectionate she's relieved there are others in the coach to impose restraint. She has some reservations about the intimacies they've engaged in. Of course, such things happen before marriage—consider, for instance, the lewd but oft recited joke about the first child arriving in six months and the remaining ones in nine—but not in her circle, not to any of her friends. Then again her friends may be doing just as she's doing—engaging in the activity while keeping it to themselves. She ought to have a more direct talk with Mary about these matters—Horace has been married, after all.

"I'm happy to look at the place," Nathaniel says as they near Concord, "but I've tried the rural life and didn't like it much. Please tell me you're not going to make me live on another farm."

"Not a farm. But I would like a nice garden."

"Nor should you expect me to be too neighborly. I've heard stories about Waldo Emerson and his acolytes. Margaret Fuller, for instance." He shakes his head. "I'd be happy to be far away from her."

"Have you met him?" she asks, lowering her voice. The old couple sitting across from them is having their own conversation, but still . . .

"Emerson? In fact I have."

"And you don't like him?"

"I neither like him nor dislike him. I am indifferent."

Sometimes he can be so critical, beyond what's fair. She's on the verge of chiding him, but before she can do so, they arrive. She peers out the window. Concord looks different from the last time. Instead of gray and wintery, it's brown and muddy—with a tinge of green on a few shrubs and trees as their leaves struggle to emerge.

They are let off in the middle of town, in front of the Middlesex Hotel.

"According to Elizabeth it's in this direction," Sophia says, and they walk up the road. The day is unexpectedly mild and at last Nathaniel seems to be getting in the proper mood. He begins teasing her, saying, "Is it this one?" about every house they pass. "According to Elizabeth it has two gateposts made of stone," she replies.

Suddenly there they are, looking up the path at what, to Sophia, is its welcoming façade.

But Nathaniel frowns. "It's rather large. It could be more than we can afford."

"Don't be so quick to judge," she says, then takes his hand and pulls him toward the door.

The key is where she was told it would be; yet before she can fit it in the lock, the door swings open to reveal a tall man dressed in black. Sophia jumps and says, "Oh! Sir!" and Nathaniel says, "Excuse me," while stepping back. It's none other than Emerson himself.

"I didn't know you'd get here so early" he says, nearly as befuddled as them. "I was checking to see that things were in order."

Sophia looks at Nathaniel. "I wanted to surprise you," she says and then the whole story comes tumbling out. By the time she's done, Nathaniel is annoyed and Mr. Emerson dismayed, so she feels like a fool. Mary was right, not telling Nathaniel in advance was a bad idea. But then she remembers what happened in January.

"Mr. Emerson, we heard about your son," she says. "We're very sorry for your loss."

His face changes. He shuts his eyes for a moment, and she can see his mind going somewhere else. Finally, he speaks: "Thank you for your concern. We are finding ourselves again after our dreadful nightmare. One expects the world to end but no, the sun rises and the winds continue to blow. Nature seems to forget that she has crushed her sweetest creation. Yet I cannot forget."

"Of course not," Nathaniel says. "Nor would you want to."

Emerson nods. "Indeed. Please come inside."

PART FIVE

Build, therefore, your own world.

Ralph Waldo Emerson

MARGARET

When the daffodils are beginning to appear on hillsides and along stone walls, Margaret visits Concord again. She occupies the same room as always and, in no time, the old pattern of work and talk she shares with Waldo has resumed. Thoreau is there too, just as before, in the room at the top of the stairs. Waldo says he stayed away for a while after his brother's death. Then one day, without a word, moved back in. However, he has closed his school. As for Lidian, she now spends most of her time upstairs with Nelly and Waldo's mother. They've even hired a cook to reduce the strain. When Margaret and Lidian cross paths, which isn't often, Lidian is congenial but Margaret can see in her eyes the deep damage done by her son's death.

As soon as she arrives, she informs Waldo that she will no longer edit *The Dial*. She wasn't sure how he'd respond, yet in the event, he is magnanimous. He will take over the job. "Let there be a rotation in martyrdom," he says. But she will continue writing for the magazine and is looking forward to seeing her now-completed essay in print. She's calling it "The Great Lawsuit." Near the end she wrote, *Let us be wise and not impede the soul. Let her work as she will. Let us have one creative energy, one incessant revelation. Let it take what form it will, and let us not bind it by the past to man or woman, black or white. Jove sprang from Rhea, Pallas from Jove. So let it be.* When the last word was written and she set down her pen, she felt transformed. As if her old insecurities and hidden feelings of irrelevance had been exorcised. As if these words, in this essay, were ones she was always meant to write.

She thinks this may be her last visit to Concord for a long while. Month-by-month, her restlessness and feelings of dissatisfaction have increased. She can't put her finger on a specific cause, but she wants something new. Now that she's worked on *The Dial*, she wonders about other ways of earning money as a writer. It wouldn't have to be in Boston. Although many of its citizens would disagree, Boston is not the center of the world.

This time of year Concord is perfect for long, leisurely strolls. She sometimes runs into Bronson Alcott, who seems to thrive no matter where he is. "Margaret Fuller!" he bellows when he sees her and comes striding across a field to spend a little time by her side. He's always writing something, building something, growing something, and his enthusiasm makes his projects sound interesting, whether or not they actually are. Lately, he has returned to the subject of education. Apparently, his ideas about schooling and the teaching of children are catching on in England.

"I've been invited there to lecture," he says. "A woman in London wants to start a school based on my principles."

"Really?" Margaret says, trying to contain her surprise. "You must be delighted."

"Oh, I am. Though I'm nervous about the crossing. I expect I'll become seasick. Do you think there's any way to avoid it? I probably shouldn't tell you this, but Waldo Emerson is giving me some money to make the trip."

"Will you take your family?"

"No, I'm afraid we are too many. My brother will stay with them while I'm abroad."

When they've gone their separate ways, she thinks, "If Bronson Alcott can pack up and sail across the ocean, why can't I?"

Then one day news arrives that *the lovers* are on their way. That's what they've all taken to calling Sophia Peabody and Nathaniel Hawthorne, who are moving into the house known as the Old Manse. Waldo still hasn't abandoned his plan to build an intellectual utopia in little Concord, so of course he's pleased.

Margaret chides him. "Why is it you want to bring everyone here, but Brook Farm has no appeal?"

"I believe in neighborhoods, not communities," he says.

She raises an eyebrow. "You believe in making distinctions where none exist."

Even those who don't share his dream of a New Athens find the Peabody-Hawthorne romance intriguing. Sophia is lovely, although a bit fragile, while Hawthorne is brilliant but given to dark moods. It should be entertaining to have them around.

Henry, who is the last person Margaret would expect to take an interest in them, has been going over to the Old Manse almost every day for the past two weeks, getting the garden ready. "If it's all dug and planted when they arrive, it will serve as a nice welcome," he says. As with Lidian, she can see how Henry has been wounded by his loss. There's a tentativeness about him that wasn't there before. "I'm not doing much writing," he tells her. "I find it hard to sit still."

Margaret doesn't plan to visit the newlyweds right away. She'll wait until they've settled in. But Waldo and Lidian go immediately, the day they arrive, even though rain is pouring down. When they get back, she asks for a complete report.

"The first thing I did was call her *Mrs. Hawthorne*," Waldo says. "You should have seen her blush. I don't believe I've ever seen such a joyful bride."

It's good to see the two of them taking an interest in something joyful. It's good to see Waldo smile.

"And what of Mr. Hawthorne? How did he appear?"

"Well, Margaret," he says with mischief in his voice, "I've heard it said that you and Nathaniel Hawthorne are sworn enemies. I don't know if that's true or not, but I hope you will not hold it against me if I say I found him both hospitable and candid. I saw little of the coldness about which others speak."

"Newcomers have every incentive to put their best foot forward," she says. "Besides, you're their landlord. Do they seem pleased with the house?"

"Pleased? They ran up and down the stairs, they counted the rooms, they looked out each window and praised the view."

But Lidian is less sanguine, which comes as no surprise. "I think perhaps they are both a little impressed with themselves. Everyone says that about Mr. Hawthorne—he couldn't conceal it if he tried. But I think Sophia sees being married to him as some sort of personal victory. She won't hesitate to show him off."

Later that night, after Lidian has gone to her room, Margaret visits Waldo's study and soon finds herself conversing with him about the nature of love. It's a topic they've discussed before but this time they go deeper. He insists that love is simply a phenomenon, a natural occurrence. And marriage is nothing more than a contract.

"The individual soul should be considered primary," he insists. "The union of two souls will always be provisional, made up of a pair of distinct parts. Perhaps it would help if we simply recognized it as such."

"Don't you think," she responds, "that there are different sorts of love and also different sorts of marriage? Of course, there are marriages that exist only for convenience or that are entered into under fraudulent conditions. But surely some of them must reach a higher plane . . ."

She assumes the case they've been referring to is that of the Hawthornes, but now she begins thinking of Waldo's marriage. To what extent are the ideas he espouses about love a commentary on his own life? She doesn't ask. As comfortable as they are having this kind of debate, there are certain lines she should not cross. Therefore, she takes another tack.

"I know that some women, especially married women, see me as privileged. They are jealous of my accomplishments and of how men are inclined to treat me as an equal. But they have so much that I have not."

As soon as she says it, she wants to take it back. It's too revealing and, furthermore, if Waldo chose to, he could say, "Are you really envious of Lidian, who has so recently lost a child?"

But whether he is flummoxed or merciful or just too tired to continue, they leave it at that. She goes to her room and listens to the rain, which has continued throughout the day. She and Waldo come close to one another, but in the end they always draw back. She thinks, "His light will never understand my fire." It occurs to her that the essay, which she thought was finished, may need another draft.

The next day, apropos of their late night discussion, news comes that Sam Ward and Anna Barker are to be married. She's not at all surprised. The day she went to the wharf to send them off on their journey she could already see the signs.

HENRY

Before the Hawthornes arrived, he planted peas, beets, beans, turnips, parsnips, cabbages, and corn. One thing Henry has learned about the writing trade is that there's not much money in it. If Nathaniel Hawthorne intends to live by his pen, he'd better have a good garden. There may be times when what they grow will be all they've got.

Henry is surprisingly busy these days. The Emersons keep giving him new tasks around the house, he's been doing some work for a few farmers in the area (seventy-five cents for an afternoon of moving stones), and he's walking and writing more than ever. He's even been teaching Emerson how to graft fruit trees. Henry is sometimes astonished at how little Emerson knows about certain domains.

"This branch, cut from a different tree, will now grow and bear its original variety? How is that possible?" Waldo exclaims.

It's like talking to the children at school.

The school. He tries not to think about it. Sometimes he has to walk by it on his way somewhere. Then he keeps his eyes forward and passes as quickly as he can. But his former students can't be avoided. "It's Mr. Henry!" they shout and come running up to him. They know what happened to John, but when you're eight years old, you don't carry it so heavily. You remember the good times and move on.

He should never have opened the school. Without the school, John would have remained in Taunton (where he was quite happy), he wouldn't have been rejected by Ellen, he wouldn't have cut his finger with the razor, and he wouldn't have died. Henry knows such reasoning is flawed, yet it's also inarguably true. True or not, it changes nothing. He can't reason John back to life.

One day he hears that the Hollowell Place, over on the Sudbury River, is up for sale. He knows exactly where it is, and in a flash it comes to him that his true destiny is to be a farmer. He goes and finds the owner, a man named Baker, and before he realizes what he's saying, offers him four hundred dollars—which Baker immediately accepts. It's a rundown place with fields that have been poorly managed and a barely habitable house. But it will be a way for him to make a new beginning. He can model himself on Theodorus, the farmer-philosopher in Virgil, who philosophizes as he labors and has no ambitions except to feed his body and his mind.

Back at Emerson's place he fetches a broken wheelbarrow from behind the shed and starts repairing it. As soon as it's fixed, he'll fill it with his belongings and push it to his new home. As he toils, Margaret Fuller comes outside to watch.

"Mr. Thoreau, good evening," she says.

He looks up at her. "I think you ought to call me Henry—since we're back to living in the same house."

She smiles in a way that might be condescending—he can't tell—and says, "Whatever you prefer."

After that, he continues to work on the wheelbarrow, and she continues to watch. While he refits the wheel on the axle, he says, "I'm writing that essay—the one I told you about."

"The review of the books Waldo gave you?"

"I've finished that one already. I'm referring to the one about walking."

"Ah, yes, I remember. Walking in winter. I'm afraid I find the idea unconvincing. An entire essay on a subject as plain as that?"

He prepares to contest her idea of "plain" but before he can begin, he sees two people veer off the road and proceed toward the house. It's a woman he's not seen before, with

Baker, the man he bought the property from, following a few steps behind.

"Are you Thoreau?" the woman asks.

Henry nods and puts down his tools while Margaret takes a step back.

"My husband made a mistake. Our place is not for sale."

"We had an agreement," Henry replies, yet even as he speaks, he knows it won't stand. No money has changed hands, and Baker's wife looks more committed to winning the argument than he is to owning a farm.

"I'll give you ten dollars for your trouble," Baker says, removing his hat and looking profoundly ashamed.

Henry shakes his head. "No need. You can have it back. Or better yet I simply won't take possession. It will have been yours all along."

The woman looks surprised. She says, "I heard you were obstinate. I guess I heard wrong." Then they turn and go back the way they came.

"You bought a farm?" Margaret says, sounding a little stunned.

"This afternoon. But now it's been repossessed."

"I didn't know you wished to be a farmer. Is this something you've been considering for a while?"

He picks up the wheelbarrow, which still isn't fit to roll, intending to throw it back behind the shed. "I don't know what I wish," he says. "There was no considering involved. What shall I do with myself? My thoughts are all tangled and inverted. Except for the grieving thoughts I have about my brother John." And then he turns away.

The next night, as a full moon rises, he goes out walking. The sky in the west is purple and the only star is the evening star, above the treetops straight ahead. A nighthawk, made visible by the white bars on its wings, makes a graceful loop before it dives. The first lightning bugs of the year are out, greenish points of fire in the tall grass.

All at once he feels as if he's a homesick man coming home. He disposes of the superfluous and sees things as they are: rocks, small white flowers, a patch of moonlight between two elms. The darker it is the better he sees.

A mile or two from town, away into the stillness and solitude, the problem of existence is simplified. It is as if he has come upon an open window. He sees out and around himself. He listens to his thoughts and to the world. At last, his nerves are steadied. This walking, this uncomplicated movement through space and time while his mind travels widely and where it will, is the one thing he cares to do.

SOPHIA

The wedding was, more than anything else, a relief. After she learned that Nathaniel's mother and sisters were going to stay at home with their cats, she decided to invite only her immediate family and a few close friends. She didn't want Nathaniel to feel overwhelmed.

It was held not in the shop, but in the rooms above it where her parents live. Mary helped her design a dress, cream silk and linen with satin trim. Sarah Clarke braided flowers into her hair. Her father gave a charming speech and her mother cried. Sarah's brother, James, recently back from Pennsylvania, performed the ceremony. When it was all over and everyone was laughing and talking and eating cake, she looked around and saw Nathaniel standing all alone. She'd have been alarmed if she hadn't known he preferred to be that way.

By mid-afternoon, they were en route to Concord. Soon it began to rain but through the stagecoach windows she could see flashes of sun between the clouds.

"A shower of diamonds," she said.

"You ought to write poetry. You have the gift."

She elbowed him. "You're teasing. How would *you* describe it?"

"I'm perfectly serious. Everything you say is poetry. Tell me what you think of your husband. In rhyming couplets, please."

When they reached Concord and were let off at the Old Manse, the rain still hadn't stopped. They held hands and ran up the tree-lined path toward the door, splashing through puddles as they went. Once inside she removed her bonnet and stepped out of her soaking shoes. Someone had started a fire for their arrival, and she was thankful for the warmth. Then, as they ventured further into the house and Sophia's eyes began to adjust, she gasped. The entire place had been painted, new wallpaper had been hung, furniture had been moved in, and there were flowers in every room.

"Mary?" Sophia said. "Or maybe the Emersons? I love it—a mystery for us to solve."

They went through the rooms like children looking for hidden toys. The pantry was stocked with food and upstairs was the bedroom furniture she herself had painted with Romanesque frescoes while waiting for Nathaniel to give up on Brook Farm. On the walls, her paintings of the Italian lakes had been hung.

They'd been there less than an hour when the Emersons arrived to welcome them.

"Who did all this?" Sophia asked, motioning to the flowers and freshly papered walls.

"It was a communal effort," Mr. Emerson replied. "Various friends and neighbors pitched in. The Alcott girls helped. Henry Thoreau planted the vegetable garden out front."

"It's very kind of you all," Nathaniel said.

Sophia considered saying something to Emerson's wife about the death of her child but decided against it. She would mention it some other time.

As they left, Mrs. Emerson said, "You are to call on me for anything you need." Though her look and voice were forbidding, her words were kind.

A week passes and Sophia and Nathaniel walk down to the river which runs behind the house. They sit on the bank and watch the water. It's smooth and reflects the sky. Yesterday Nathaniel went fishing and brought back six fat, bronze-colored bream for supper. She cooked them up, surprised by how good they tasted and especially by what an excellent cook she was. Who needs Boston or Salem or Brook Farm when you can have all this?

"We are as happy as two people can be," Sophia says.

"We are as happy as two people can be without becoming ridiculous," Nathaniel replies.

Since that first day of rain, the weather has been ideal. Even though it's July the full heat of summer has yet to arrive. They've already set up their respective studies, precisely as Sophia planned. However, they have yet to spend much time working—they are always in each other's arms.

As a wedding present, they received a music box, so after they're done sitting by the riverbank they go back and play it. It runs down and they wind it again. Suddenly, they decide to dance. It's the first time since Cuba Sophia has waltzed. The rooms in their new house are large enough for waltzing. What a wonderful fact!

The next morning they set off for Walden Pond. Mr. Emerson says it's the best place for a picnic, especially this time of year. On the way, they come upon a tiny blue-green pool in the midst of some hemlock trees.

"I wonder if anyone else knows it's here," Sophia says.

"I'm certain someone—" he begins, but Sophia cuts him off.

"I believe we *discovered* it. No one has ever seen it until this moment. Only the forest creatures."

"Ah, yes, I agree," says Nathaniel, playing along. "I hereby claim this body of water for Queen Sophia. It shall be hers until the end of time."

While he's speaking, she removes her shoes and stockings, lifts her skirts, and wades in.

"Sophia, what are you doing?" he asks.

"Come join me."

"Yes, well. I really don't—"

"Nathaniel, *come join me*. No one will see us, if that's what you fear."

They never make it to Walden Pond. They wade and splash

and then sit in the sunlight and dry off. They kiss and lie back and once again she has to persuade him that they won't be discovered. It's all quite thrilling and feels scandalous, but of course it's not, because now they are husband and wife.

On the way back, they are walking along the river when who should they encounter but Henry Thoreau. He has on a straw hat, stout shoes, and gray trousers. Nathaniel steps in front of her protectively, as if they're being approached by some wild man of the woods. Before any awkwardness can occur, Sophia speaks up:

"Mr. Thoreau. What a fortunate accident. I hope you received my note of thanks for the gardening you did for us. Of all the wedding gifts we received, yours was the best."

She introduces him to Nathaniel, who tells Thoreau he knows him by reputation. Then Thoreau proceeds to praise *Twice-Told Tales* at length and in considerable detail. When he's done, Nathaniel looks pleased but perplexed. And with good reason—it's not often a man appears in the forest to tell you he's read your book and then proves it by making comments as perceptive as any you've heard.

As they walk on with Thoreau at their side, he provides information about the river. He seems to know everything, from its depth, to the names of fish inhabiting it, to where, come January, they'll find the best ice for skating. Then suddenly he begins to get excited:

"Oh, I have to show you," he says. "Right along here is where the Wampanoag used to camp." He scans the bank for a moment, takes several steps forward, drops to his knees, and begins to dig. A few seconds later he extracts something from the dirt. It's an arrowhead, which he proceeds to clean and polish on his sleeve. He hands it to Sophia, who is thrilled.

"Look Nathaniel, look what he found! Not a hundred paces from our door."

"Remarkable," Nathaniel says.

Thoreau clambers to his feet and brushes off his hands. "I find it useful to remember that people occupied this place before me. We are not the first, nor will we be the last. I wish you a happy life here in Concord," he says and continues on his way. They stand and watch as he disappears into the trees.

"What a lovely day," says Sophia as they return to the Old Manse. "And isn't Mr. Thoreau interesting?"

"Indeed he is. Also rather unattractive. Such a nose."

"Nathaniel. You're terrible . . ."

"No, you mistake me. I prefer a man like that to a handsome one. I place more trust in him."

She recalls something her sister Mary once said about Nathaniel: "He's so handsome women stop in the street and stare." But she keeps the thought to herself.

They decide to have a party on the weekend. They invite the Emersons and the Alcotts and Margaret Fuller and even Elizabeth who makes the trip from Boston and plans to stay the night. Mary can't come because she's busy with Horace, and Henry Thoreau says he'll definitely attend but then doesn't, to no one's great surprise.

They talk and laugh and eat and then talk more, until quite late. Bronson Alcott tells about his upcoming trip to England and Elizabeth, who has never been out of Massachusetts, seems to know exactly which sights he should see. Outside, the Alcott children frolic in the moonlight and quarrel over who gets to care for Nelly Emerson. They'll pretend she's their baby sister until it's time to go home.

Even Nathaniel seems to enjoy himself. He tells stories about Brook Farm, most of them comical, although since Margaret Fuller is present, he avoids mentioning her cow. Later, Emerson and Alcott take him out to the garden to show him how the sow bugs damaging his tomatoes can be thwarted. When he comes back inside, he's visibly pleased. He says, "Damn the sow bugs and damn their way of life."

At last, the guests begin to depart. First the Alcotts and then the Emersons, but Margaret Fuller stays behind. She wants to visit a little longer since Elizabeth is there. They sit in the parlor and Sophia glows with the pleasure of her new home. She tells Margaret how the sculpture she did of Laura Bridgman appears to be leading to other commissions and listens as Elizabeth and Margaret gossip about certain intellectuals in Boston, which she finds entertaining, even if she doesn't know them well.

When the time comes for Margaret to leave, Sophia says, "You can't go alone. Not at this time of night. Nathaniel will escort you." Although she knows they don't get along, it has to be done.

He disappeared a while ago so she goes upstairs, thinking he might have gone to bed. But there he is at his desk, pen in hand. When she says his name, he looks up and turns. In the candlelight he looks half-mad, as if he's emerging from a dream. He blinks and shakes his head. "Nathaniel," she says again and finally he begins to seem like himself. So this is what she has to look forward to.

She tells him about Margaret and, to her surprise, he stands up, shrugs into his coat, and doesn't complain. Before they go back down the stairs, she says, "Thank you. You are a sweet man."

He kisses her forehead. "Anything for you," he replies. "Even this."

MARGARET

As they walk through the village there's not a soul about. In a few windows she can see a candle burning, but it's after midnight and most of the houses are dark. So far, Hawthorne hasn't said a word. When she can tolerate the silence no longer, she speaks:

"Do you think you'll like it here?"

"I expect I shall. However, my surroundings mean little to me."

"I might say the same of myself. But Sophia seems extremely happy. Surely, you must value that."

He glances over at her. Perhaps she's being too personal.

"Very much," he says.

The moon is low and the sky is a river of stars. At the end of the street, the trees stand like a gateway into some mysterious land. She has never had the affinity for nature Emerson has but at times like these its grandeur can't be ignored.

"I have a question for you," Hawthorne says.

She can't imagine what it could be. Maybe he wants to publish something in *The Dial*. But he'll have to go to Waldo for that now.

"I want to gain a deeper understanding of Goethe. At present I know very little. I've heard about your book and have been told you have mastered his work. Where would you suggest I begin?"

She's stunned. No one, not even Waldo, has ever made such a direct appeal to her expertise. "Let me think," she says. "There are so many—the scientific Goethe, the poetic Goethe, the philosophic. And, of course, the Goethe of *Faust*."

Hawthorne points to a stone wall along the road and says,

"Do you mind if we sit?" She agrees and follows him as he continues speaking. "I was thinking of starting with your translation of Eckermann's *Conversations*. And then move onto the novels and *Faust*."

If he's trying to flatter her, he's done a good job of it. Does he have a motive other than self-improvement? How unexpected this is!

"I would be honored to have you read my book. And delighted to talk with you about Goethe at any time."

"What is it you find so admirable about him," he asks.

"A question I can answer with ease: His great learning and overwhelming intelligence. He is what I measure myself against—which means I always fail."

They sit in silence for a time and Margaret wonders how she so misjudged him. It appears they have more in common than she thought.

He says, "Do you ever think about traveling to Germany and visiting the places he lived and worked?"

"Oh, constantly. There's nothing I'd rather do."

"But I suppose your work with Emerson's magazine keeps you here."

"I'm done with that," she says, rushing to reply. "I'll still write some things for it but I'm no longer the editor. It took too much of my time." She's surprised to discover how important it is to her to make her separation from *The Dial* clear. Yet she says nothing about the lack of pay because revealing that would be embarrassing. It would make her sound foolish and inconsequential.

"If not *The Dial* then what?"

"I've been corresponding with an editor in New York. He wants me to work for his newspaper. I'm quite close to accepting his offer." This is first the time she's told anyone. Saying it aloud makes it seem almost definite. She could be gone by the end of summer, possibly even before.

"We'd better be going," he says. "My wife will wonder where I am."

He leaves her on Emerson's doorstep and strides off into the night. She opens the door as quietly as she can but once inside discovers Waldo and Lidian are both in the kitchen and wide awake. Not only that but they're having a bit of a spat.

"I thought it was appalling," Lidian says.

"The fact that they did it or the fact that she showed you?" Waldo replies.

"Both, now that you mention it. It was as if she actually expected me to be impressed."

Noticing her standing there, they stop and explain:

"We're talking about the Hawthornes," Emerson says. "Apparently they've inscribed something on the bedroom windows upstairs. Right on the glass, using Sophia's diamond ring."

"During the party she took me up and showed me," Lidian tells her. "It was a sort of poem with their names underneath. As I said, she seemed quite proud of what they did."

"And so Lidian wants me to . . . I don't know what—put them out of the house?"

"That's not what I said. But I do believe you should mention it. They move in and immediately deface the property. Panes of glass are not cheap. Do you think whoever lives there after them will appreciate what they left behind?" Then Lidian turns to her and asks what she thinks.

Although Margaret would like to tell them she finds their bickering rather amusing, she says, "I refuse to take sides. Waldo, I expect you wouldn't grant such latitude if you were renting the house to an old bachelor and he did the same thing. But should they receive some sort of dispensation because they are in love? Yes, perhaps they should."

Waldo sighs. Lidian grumbles under her breath. And Margaret goes off to bed.

CONCORD

In her room, she thinks about Hawthorne and wishes she'd met him earlier—and then reminds herself that she did but failed to see him clearly until now. It's after midnight but she's not at all sleepy. A line from Goethe comes to her: thinking is easy, acting is difficult. She goes to the desk and gets out paper, pen, and ink. She will write to the editor in New York tonight. It's time to stop thinking and act.

HENRY

He visits the Hawthornes often. This surprises him. He wasn't nearly as excited about their arrival as most and even after he met them, he wasn't sure they were his sort. But they're always so cheerful, at least when he's around. And they seem genuinely interested in learning about gardening and the river and Concord and birds, which he takes as a sign of good character and intelligence. How strange that some people can live in a place and care nothing about its history, its flora and fauna, or the geographical features that lie only steps from their door. Best of all, Hawthorne is something of a walker. Already they've been on several hikes.

However, there are limits to how much of nature Hawthorne is willing to absorb. One morning he says to Henry, "Take me somewhere secret, where you go to be alone." Henry doesn't even have to think—he knows just the place. Before Hawthorne can utter another word, they are headed east out of Concord, through a sunlit wood, across a farmer's field, over a ridge, and down into Gowing's Swamp. There's no other location quite like it. It has pools and boggy areas and bubbling springs and rivulets and an incredible variety of plants, from tall black spruce to tamarack to sundew to sheep laurel, with lichen of many varieties forming a carpet underfoot. Deep inside this globe of greenery and moisture they stand for a moment and listen to the moving water, the buzzing insects, and the birds. Henry says, "Isn't it sublime?" Hawthorne slaps a mosquito, looks down at his soaking shoes, and says, "Get me out of this dreadful hole."

A more successful outing is the one they take in Henry's boat. It's the *Musketaquid*, the one he and John built together and used for their trip north. This time, Hawthorne is outspokenly appreciative. He says, "I don't know how you manage to steer it so perfectly. Your paddling seems effortless and takes you exactly where you wish to go."

Henry explains that when some Indians visited Concord a few years ago, he found that he had acquired, without being taught, their precise method of guiding a canoe. He says, "If you do it often enough and pay close attention, the water shows you how."

When they are done, he notices Hawthorne admiring the boat and it comes to him that he wants to be rid of it. The memories associated with John are too painful and he will never be able to use it with real pleasure again. Considering the matter no further, he says, "I'll sell it to you. The house you live in backs right up to the river. It makes no sense to be without a boat."

Hawthorne agrees at once, paying him seven dollars, the full price he asks. Henry has only one regret: Later in the week he learns from Sophia that they have changed the boat's name from *Musketaquid* to *Pond Lily*. From a name that came from the Indian past, a name that means grass-grown river, a name that was as mellifluous as it was muscular, to *Pond Lily*. It causes him to pause and consider the power of names. It's almost as if changing the name changes the thing itself. But now they own the boat and may call it whatever they wish.

When Henry looks upon the Hawthornes' marriage, he's both envious and amused. They've gotten themselves a large black dog and a small white cat, which they talk to as if the animals are children. Sophia sometimes dresses not like one of the humble wives of Concord but as if she's on her way to a ball—this in the middle of the day. And they have started to keep a joint journal—he writes on one page and she on the next. Henry can't imagine participating in such an endeavor. His journal belongs to him alone.

As a rule, Hawthorne is more interested in talking about writing than Henry. But one day Henry decides to show him a draft of his essay on walking—the one Margaret Fuller had so little enthusiasm for. When Hawthorne is done reading it, he says,

"I like it very much. It's true, unpretentious, and literal in observation. You show the reader every leaf while also giving the wild beauty of the entire scene."

"You don't think it lacks—" he searches for the exact term—"metaphysical depth?"

Hawthorne throws up his hands. "I know the sort of thing you have in mind. I read *The Dial* from cover to cover and most of it was too ethereal for me. You should go your own way. My only suggestion is that you reconsider your optimism about nature. Hasn't it ever occurred to you that there are things in these woods of which you ought to be afraid?"

He'll say this much for Nathaniel Hawthorne: He has a passion for words and sentences and books that exceeds even his own. They are his stars and planets. They fill his heaven. When the two of them talk of literature Hawthorne's eyes get bright and his voice fairly trembles with intensity. He knows the poets of the present day as well as those of the past. He knows his Shakespeare and his Milton. In the end books are the universal currency among people of their kind.

The day after he and Hawthorne discuss his essay, Henry goes walking alone. As he passes Hubbard's Grove, he spies a woodchuck three or four rods from the fence. The woodchuck begins to run and Henry runs alongside. The woodchuck stops and Henry stops. They run again and stop again, and at the end of it, find themselves observing one another from a distance of less than three feet. The woodchuck's eyes are black with chestnut-colored irises. Its hair is a coarse gray-brown and its feet are black. In shape and size it might be described as a very small bear. Or maybe a large burrowing squirrel with hardly any tail.

Henry makes a chittering sound and the animal chitters back. Henry offers it the end of a twig and it takes it in its teeth. It has long incisors, two above and two below. Henry offers it some checkerberry leaves, but the woodchuck turns them down. For a long time, they study one another through the fence. Thus, he spends this summer afternoon, under a cloudless sky.

SOPHIA

Nathaniel is off with Henry Thoreau leaving Sophia at home alone. Nathaniel and Henry are a peculiar pair, both fundamentally unsocial, but yesterday she heard them laugh so loud and long she went out to the garden to see if something was amiss. She loves being married even more than she expected and can't get enough of Nathaniel's company; but that doesn't prevent her from enjoying the experience of having the place to herself. Although she's never been one to sing, she does so now as she glides from room to room. The house has a long central hallway, and she opens the doors at both ends and lets the breeze blow through. She rearranges the paintings and goes out to pick fresh flowers. Once the flowers are in jars and vases, she goes out to gather whortleberries, enough for tonight's dessert. Their dog Leo follows her about, as does their cat, who has yet to be given a name—it's Nathaniel's job to come up with one and he likes to deliberate.

As idyllic as it all is, Sophia is a little worried about money. Their rent is more than reasonable but they have no income whatsoever. Yet her faith in Nathaniel is infinite. He will write something remarkable or get another job. She doesn't know if he's worried. He tells her almost everything but sometimes almost isn't enough.

She especially likes having a house large enough for guests. The week after the party, Mary came down from Boston and stayed overnight and then Cary Sturgis did the same. As Cary was leaving, she whispered that she much preferred their company to that of the Emersons. In two weeks Nathaniel's mother will be with them for five days. Five days. She's girding herself for that.

CONCORD

She goes upstairs to Nathaniel's study and looks out the
window. How fortunate they are to be surrounded by flowers
and trees. With the river beyond. Already, in this room, she
and her husband have left their mark. Taking turns with her
diamond ring they inscribed a few lines on the window glass.
Most of the time it's invisible but when the sun shines at a
certain angle, especially late in the day, it can be read:

Nath'l Hawthorne. This is his study.
The smallest twig leans clear against the sky.
Composed by my wife and written with her diamond.
Inscribed by my husband at sunset,
in the gold light.

Author's Note

Concord is a novel. Like most writers of historical fiction, I've drawn on history while making certain changes in an attempt to create a story that is involving and coherent. These changes include altering the rate at which time passes, occasionally shifting the sequence of events, slightly adjusting some aspects of geography, and leaving people out of the picture if they don't contribute to the overall effect. I have also changed the names of some secondary characters to prevent confusion: Henry's sister Sophia is called Sarah, and Emerson's daughter Ellen is called Nelly.

To write this novel, I found the journals and letters of the principal characters enormously useful. They are available in academic libraries and, increasingly, online. In a number of instances I've placed phrases or sentences from primary sources in characters' mouths as dialogue, or in their minds as thoughts. I also drew on the many fine works of biography, literary history, and criticism that exist. Hundreds of books and articles have been written about these individuals. Some of my favorites include *The Flowering of New England, 1815-1865* by Van Wyck Brooks; *The Days of Henry Thoreau: A Biography* by Walter Harding; *Margaret Fuller: A New American Life* by Megan Marshall; *The Peabody Sisters: Three Women Who Ignited American Romanticism*, also by Megan Marshall; *The Lives of Margaret Fuller* by John Matteson; *American Bloomsbury* by Susan Cheever; *Emerson Among the Eccentrics: A Group Portrait* by Carlos Baker; *Hawthorne: A Life* by Brenda Wineapple; and *Henry David Thoreau: A Life* by Laura Dassow Walls (which appeared after my novel was substantially complete). I wish to give special credit to *Henry*

Don Zancanella

David Thoreau: A Life of the Mind and *Emerson: The Mind on Fire*, both by Robert D. Richardson. It was my good fortune to take classes on nineteenth century American literature from the late Dr. Richardson at the University of Denver, and suspect the seed for this novel may have been planted there.

Acknowledgments

Thanks to those who read drafts of this novel and provided valuable comments and encouragement: Courtney Angermeier, Mary Buckelew, Jack Johnson, Dorene Kahl, Tom Keyes, Laura Langlie, Michael Moore, Betsy Noll, Mark Vogel, and Jean-Louise Zancanella. Thanks also to Mark Vogel and Jack Vogel for tramping around Salem with me on a cold November day.

Thanks to Walter Cummins and Serving House Books for bringing this book into the world.

I also wish to acknowledge a few special teachers who helped me get here: Barbara Totherow, Ben Nelms, John Edgar Wideman, and the late John Williams and Burton Raffel.

Finally, thanks to Tony and Jean-Louise for tolerating my writing obsession, and to Dorene for her keen editorial eye and readerly intuition, and for her love and support. She makes it all worthwhile.

About the Author

Don Zancanella is the author of *Western Electric*, which won the John Simmons/Iowa Short Fiction Award. He's the recipient of an O. Henry Prize and has published widely in literary magazines. After many years in New Mexico he now lives in Boise, Idaho, with his wife and their assortment of rescue dogs.

CPSIA information can be obtained
at www.ICGtesting.com
Printed in the USA
LVHW031810280323
742830LV00008B/462